Alexander Death

(The Paranormals, Book Three)

by J.L. Bryan

Published September 2011

www.jlbryanbooks.com

ISBN-10: 1466339101
ISBN-13: 978-1466339101

Cover art by Phatpuppy Art (www.phatpuppyart.com)

Acknowledgments

Writing the *Jenny Pox* books has been an amazing journey. I want to thank all of the people who have helped along the way, starting with my wife Christina, who has always been a great and sympathetic supporter as well as a valuable "first reader" who helps improve the story as I'm writing it.

My main editor for these books has been North Carolina author Scott Nicholson, who does a fantastic job of straightening out the story and finding things to improve. Author Vicki Keire also did a thorough proofing of *Alexander Death*.

The beautiful covers for all three books are from Claudia at Phatpuppy Art, who is a delight to work with.

These books have enjoyed great support from too many book bloggers to name. A few who have worked especially hard to promote include the Bewitched Bookworms, Jenny from Supernatural Snark, The Slowest Bookworm, Kim from Caffeinated Diva, and Ashley from the Bookish Brunette. Book bloggers do everything to let people know that my books are out there!

Additionally, I would like to thank Amanda Hocking, whose enthusiastic support and generous help has done everything to help me reach new readers.

And that's who I want to thank most of all: the readers who have come with me on this journey. I am always amazed at the intense response Jenny's story gets from readers, and I love to hear from you! You can reach me at my website (www.jlbryanbooks.com) on Twitter (@jlbryanbooks) or on my Facebook page (linked on my website).

Thanks to all of you!

J.L. Bryan
September 18, 2011

More books by J.L. Bryan

The Paranormals Trilogy
Jenny Pox
Tommy Nightmare
Alexander Death

The Songs of Magic Series
Fairy Metal Thunder

Other Books
Helix
The Haunted E-book
Dominion
Dark Tomorrows (short stories)

For Christina

CHAPTER ONE

Seth found the little bird in the manicured grass under one of the old, moss-heavy oaks in the front yard. It cocked its head as he approached, then spread its wings and attempted to fly away, but it couldn't get airborne because one wing was bent and crooked. It flailed and rolled through the grass, trying to escape him.

"It's okay, Bird," Seth said. He dropped to his knees and crawled to the bird, thinking this would scare the little creature less than if he walked towards it at his full height. Seth paid no mind to the grass stains on the knees of his white Easter pants.

Seth studied the bird. It was blue, so, by Seth's logic, it must have been a bluebird. He wondered what had happened to the bird's wing, if an animal had attacked it or if it had just fallen and forgotten how to fly. Or maybe it never could fly. It looked very small, like a baby.

"What are you doing, Seth?" Carter ran out of the house and across the front yard toward Seth. "You have to hurry!" His approach startled the bird, which screeched and rolled around again, flapping its useless wing.

"Shh!" Seth said. "You're scaring him."

"Don't shoosh me!" Carter said. He was ten years old, while Seth was only six, and Carter thought being older made him boss of everything. "Mom wants you to come in now, 'cause it's time for church."

"I'm coming," Seth said, but he didn't move from his hands and knees.

"What's that?" Carter stood beside Seth and looked at the bird with the flailing wing.

"He's hurt," Seth said. "We have to help him."

"We can't," Carter told him. "If the mom bird smells a person on the baby, she won't take care of it anymore."

"Doesn't look like she's taking care of him, anyway," Seth said. "He's stranded."

"We have to go."

Seth heard his mother in the back yard, calling for him.

"We can't leave him here," Seth said. "Something will eat him."

"What do you want to do?"

"I can keep him in my room until he's better." Seth reached for the bird, but it hopped back from him, opening its beak.

"Mom won't let you do that."

"Are you gonna tell on me?" Seth asked.

"I don't have to. She's going to notice a bird, Seth."

"Seth! Carter!" their mom called in the back yard. "Come here right this instant!"

"Let's go," Carter said. "We're gonna get in trouble."

"Wait." Seth crawled toward the bird and slowly reached out with both hands.

"Leave it alone, Seth," Carter said. "It's probably got germs."

"He doesn't have germs!" Seth said.

"How would you know?"

"You don't know everything, Carter."

"Seth!" their mom called again.

"I know you're gonna get grounded if you don't come on," Carter said.

"Wait..." Seth crawled closer to the little bird, which seemed to be losing its energy. "Almost..." He scooped up the bird in both hands, taking care to avoid the broken wing, since it probably hurt. The bird bit him anyway, drawing drops of blood from Seth's thumb with its sharp beak.

"Told you it would bite, dummy," Carter said.

"No, you didn't. And I don't care." Seth stood up, holding the bird in both hands. Carter gaped at the grass smears on his pants.

"Oh, you're gonna get in trouble..." Carter said.

"Am not." Seth looked at the tiny bird quivering in his hands. "I'll help you," he whispered. "You can live on my dresser. That's like a tree."

"Seth, you can't bring that bird..." Carter began, but Seth tuned him out.

Something was happening. Seth felt his hands grow hotter and hotter. The bird chirped and squirmed in his fingers, and now Seth could feel heat flowing out from his palms. He didn't understand what was happening.

Then the bird hopped to the edge of his left hand, extended both wings, and jumped. It fell for a moment, but it flapped furiously and straightened out its course, skimming over the grass. Then it climbed up through the air in a wide, slow spiral, to perch on a dark, thick limb overhead. It tweeted a few times, and Seth thought it sounded happy.

"Okay, we can go now," Seth said. He turned to walk toward the car, but Carter caught him by one shoulder. Carter was staring up at the bird.

"Seth, what did you do?" Carter whispered.

"Nothing," Seth said. "He's okay now. I'll tell Mom about it."

"No!" Carter said. "You can't tell anyone."

"How come?"

"Seth, that bird had a broken wing. When you touched it, the wing straightened out and healed up. I watched it happen."

"So?"

"So that's...weird. Really weird, Seth. Nobody can do that."

"I can!" Seth said.

"You have to keep it secret."

"You're just jealous 'cause you can't do it," Seth said.

"No, Seth." Carter turned Seth to face him. Carter had light brown hair and green eyes—he looked more like a Mayfield, from their mom's family, than a Barrett. "I'm serious now. People will treat you like a freakazoid if they find out you can do that. It's not normal to heal things with your touch."

"Jesus could do it," Seth said.

"And look what happened to him."

Seth thought about it. "Oh..."

"Just keep a secret for now," Carter said.

"Even from Mom and Dad?"

"Even from them."

"For how long?" Seth whined.

"Until I tell you it's safe," Carter said.

"When will that be?"

"I don't know. I'll tell you."

"Seth! Carter!" their mom yelled. She wasn't in the back yard anymore. She'd circled the house and now stood on the driveway in her high heels and purple dress, her arms folded, eyes glowing with anger.

"We better go," Carter whispered. "Don't tell anyone."

"Jonathan Seth Barrett!" their mother shouted as they approached. "Look at your pants! What have you been doing?"

"I was just..." Seth pointed toward the treetops, but Carter shook his head. "Just playing."

"In your *Easter* clothes?" their mom asked. "Get inside right now. You can't go to church looking like that."

"Okay. Sorry." Seth hurried toward the front door. Before he went inside, he looked at the high limb again, meaning to wave good-bye to the bird, but it had already disappeared.

CHAPTER TWO

Seth was in his room watching *Star Wars: Attack of the Clones* when the house phone rang. He was expecting to hear from Wooly—Chris Woolerton—about Seth's plans to visit Charleston and stay with Wooly's family. Seth was looking forward to hanging out at the beach with Wooly and his friends. Wooly had been the most popular fifth-grader at Grayson Academy, known for his pranks, his encyclopedic memory for dirty jokes, and the *Playboy* magazines he had snuck into the dormitory.

In the fall, they would both be in sixth grade, the last grade before you moved on to Grayson's secondary school, Grayson Preparatory. Until then, they were the oldest kids, the rulers of Grayson Primary.

Seth hurried to answer the phone.

"This is Sheriff Frank Young," the man's voice said on the phone. "Opawasee County, Florida. Can I speak with Mr. or Mrs. Jonathan Barrett?"

Seth's name was Jonathan Seth Barrett, and he considered making a joke of it and saying "I'm Jonathan Barrett." But the police officer clearly wanted to talk to his father, and his tone was dead serious. Seth immediately thought of Carter, his fourteen-year-old brother who had gone on vacation to Florida with a friend's family.

Seth opened the door and yelled "Dad! Phone!" Nobody answered, so he sighed and hurried down the stairs.

He found his father in his office, surrounded by the heads of dead animals—not just deer like everyone had, but wolf and bear heads, too, animals killed by Seth's great-grandfather. The office intimidated Seth, as if the whole place exuded death and despair. The desk, liquor cabinet and other furniture were hand-hewn from dark, heavy wood sometime in the nineteenth century.

Seth's dad, Jonathan Seth Barrett III, sat at the gray IBM PC on the desk, surrounded by heaps of open file folders. He wasn't quite forty years old, but traces of gray had already appeared in his hair, along with deep worry lines on his face. The years of managing the family's diverse, worldwide investments had aged him prematurely. Like the office itself, his father was intimidating to Seth—he seemed to make the air around himself dark and heavy.

"Hey, Dad?" Seth asked, hesitantly. His dad didn't like being interrupted when he was working, and he was liable to bite Seth's head off.

"I'm busy, Seth," he replied without looking up.

"But there's a phone call."

Seth's dad glanced at the two phones on his desk—one was the regular house line, one of them was for business. A red light blinked on the display panel of the house phone, indicating a call on hold.

"Take a message," he told Seth.

"But it's the police," Seth said. "From Florida."

"Florida? What's Carter gotten into this time?" He shook his head as he picked up the phone. "This is Jonathan Barrett," he said. Then he listened, and his face drew into a deep frown. "I'm sorry, could you...repeat that?"

Seth wondered what his older brother had done. Carter had a pretty good nose for mischief. At Grayson, he'd once gotten in trouble for dying the pool in the aquatic center pink the night before a swim meet, which had gotten him probationary status and ultimately cost Seth's dad a bit of money. Carter said his main regret was not using enough red food dye—he and his friends had wanted the water blood-red. Another time, Carter had been in trouble for sneaking over to the Kingsroad School, a girls' prep school a couple miles from all-male Grayson Academy.

"I understand," Seth's dad said, furiously scribbling information on a legal pad. "We'll be there as soon as we can." He hung up the phone. Then he stared at Seth. His face was going pale, and he had a look like he'd been punched in the stomach.

"What's happening, Dad?" Seth asked.

"It's Carter." His dad stood up.

"What did he do?"

"I have to talk to your mother." Seth's dad walked past him, and Seth followed him to the stairs. "Wait," his dad told him.

"You want me to wait right here in your office?" Seth asked.

"Just wait somewhere."

Seth followed his father to the old, wide staircase, built of dark oak, but he stayed at the foot of it while his father ascended.

"Dad, what's going on with Carter?"

His father glanced back at Seth, briefly, but said nothing. Seth watched him disappear into the dark upstairs hall.

After a minute, Seth tiptoed up the stairs after him.

Seth made his way down the wide upstairs hall, past the door to the third floor, which Seth never opened. The third floor was scary, full of his great-grandfather's stuff, and Seth's grandfather had remodeled it into some kind of crazy maze. Carter said it was to confuse Great-Grandfather's ghost, in case it came back to haunt the family. Seth's parents would not confirm or deny the story, and usually changed the subject when Seth asked.

At the end of the hall, the door to the master bedroom stood ajar. Seth leaned an ear against the open crack, wanting to hear the news about his older brother.

He didn't need to eavesdrop, though, because the first thing he heard was his mother's scream.

"No!" Iris Mayfield Barrett's voice echoed through the house. "No, no, no!"

Seth nudged the door open another inch. He could see a mirror on his parents' wall. In the reflection, his mother sat at the foot of her bed in her bath robe, her hair disheveled, her face in her hands. She was shaking her head.

Seth's father stood over her, his arms crossed, looking down at the floor.

"We have to go," he said.

"I can't," she said.

"Then stay here with Seth," he told her. "I'll go by myself."

Seth's dad took a coat from the closet. He looked at Seth's mom, weeping on the bed, and his jaw worked as if he were trying to come up with something to say. Then he walked toward the door without saying anything.

"Don't go," Seth's mom said.

"I have to go."

"I need to see him." She stood up and went to the closet. "Let me get ready."

Seth's dad opened the door and looked at Seth. "I told you to wait."

"What happened to Carter?" Seth asked.

His dad looked at him, then back into the room as if he expected Seth's mom to answer that one, but she was out of sight in the walk-in closet.

"Seth," his dad finally said, "There's been an accident. A car accident."

"Is Carter okay?"

Seth's dad sighed. He was quiet for a moment, then he said, "Carter didn't survive, Seth. We have to...." His voice choked up, but he swallowed forcefully and held it back. "We have to identify the body."

Seth stared at him, unable to process this. Carter had been here only yesterday, chasing Seth through the house and threatening him with noogies.

"But he can't be," Seth said. "He can't be...dead, can he?"

"I'm sorry, Seth." His father gripped his shoulder awkwardly for a second, and quickly let go. "I don't know what to say."

"No, that's not right." Seth backed away from his dad. He could feel the sting of tears in his eyes as he shook his head. "That can't be true!"

Seth ran down the hall and into Carter's room. He looked around at the baseball trophies, the posters of girls in bikinis, the electric guitar Carter had begged to get last Christmas, but never learned how to play. It didn't seem possible that he wasn't coming home. Carter had gone to the beach for a week, and then he'd be back. That was supposed to be the plan. He wasn't supposed to be gone forever.

Seth felt something cold and hard strike him right in the stomach. He collapsed at the corner of Carter's bed, crying and screaming and overwhelmed and confused.

It was twenty minutes before his parents came to collect him.

***

Seth's dad drove a Cadillac STS, black on the outside and the inside, with satellite GPS, a built-in telephone, and a radar detector mounted on the dashboard. Seth usually enjoyed riding in it, because he could imagine it was the Batmobile.

Tonight, he wasn't enjoying anything. He sat in the back seat and watched the interstate mile markers whip past. His parents sat in the front, not talking. He felt like he was very small in the back, and that a huge chasm of empty space separated him from his parents. Their silence, added to the fact that nobody had turned on the stereo, left him feeling completely alone. The ride was long and miserable. Rain spattered the car as they passed through south Georgia on the way to Florida.

Though his dad drove around ninety miles an hour, slowing only when the radar detector began to beep, it was hours before they reached the Opawassee County Sheriff's Department. The glowing blue numbers on the dashboard read 3:48 AM. Barely a dozen words had been spoken the entire way, and then only when Seth's dad announced he was stopping for gas, and asked if anybody was hungry. Nobody was.

The sheriff's department was a low cinderblock building, with a couple of annexes built onto the back. One of them had barred windows, and Seth guessed that was the county jail.

Seth followed his parents into the grungy police station, which had a dirty linoleum floor and harsh, flickering fluorescent lights that made everybody look like walking corpses. Seth's dad spoke in a low voice to the uniformed cop at the front desk, while Seth and his mother sat on one of the hard wooden benches in the waiting area. A few feet away from Seth sat an old man with long, tangled gray hair and a matted beard. His bloodshot eyes stared into empty space, and he stank like urine.

After a few minutes, Seth's father returned. "Iris, come with me," he said in a low voice.

"What about me?" Seth asked.

"Just wait here," his dad told him.

"But I want to see Carter!"

"I said wait." Seth led his mother away, and an officer escorted them through a door, away from the front area and out of sight.

Seth glanced at the strange old man beside him, but the old man didn't seem aware of Seth, or of anything much that was happening around him.

Seth trembled, wondering what his parents were doing, and what Carter looked like after the accident. He thought about the bird he'd healed, about four years ago, and how Carter had told him to keep it secret.

Seth felt his hands growing hot. He could do it again, he realized. Maybe he could heal up Carter and bring him back. Then everyone would know about Seth's secret, but who cared? He had to bring Carter back, or it would be his own fault that his brother was dead.

Seth jumped to his feet. Nobody told him to sit back down, so he walked toward the door through which his parents had left the room.

"Hey, kid," the cop at the front desk said. "You can't go back there."

"But my brother's back there. I have to help him," Seth said.

"Sit down and wait for your parents. Now."

Seth hesitated a moment—you were supposed to do whatever the police told you, but this cop wouldn't understand what Seth could do. Seth charged through the door.

"Hey!" the cop shouted after him.

Seth ran down a corridor, ignoring the desk cop's shouts. He hurried past a group of cops who were talking in low voices, and one scowled at him.

He reached an intersection with another corridor and hesitated. Fortunately, signs were posted here. One of them said "MORGUE" with an arrow pointing to Seth's left. He gulped. The morgue sounded like a scary place, full of dead people and maybe zombies and other monsters that might grab at him. But that was where he would find his parents and his brother.

Seth moved down the hall, which was dark from so many overhead lights being burned out. Those that remained were flickering, creating an unsettling strobe effect as he ran towards the big double doors labeled MORGUE.

Seth pushed a door open and ran inside, holding his breath—he expected to be surrounded by dead bodies immediately, corpses piled up to the ceiling and staring at him with cold, sightless eyes. And maybe their heads would turn toward him, and their hands would reach for him, like the undead in those horror movies on cable that Seth wasn't allowed to watch, but sometimes did anyway.

The first room was just an office, though, with filing cabinets and two desks. A heavyset black woman dressed like a nurse sat at one desk.

"Excuse me?" she asked. "What are you doing here, kid?"

"I gotta find my parents." Seth looked around the room. Only one door led out of the room, besides the one he'd just stepped through. That had to be where everybody was.

"You don't want to go in there," the lady said. "Why don't you sit right down—" She gestured toward the empty chair at the other desk, but Seth blew right past her and shoved the next door open.

"Damn it, kid!" the lady shouted after him.

The next room was large and freezing cold, like a big cave, with a stainless steel autopsy table right in front of him. Rows of metal cabinets stood against the back wall. One of these cabinets was open, the drawer inside fully extended, and it held a body covered in a white sheet.

A morgue attendant in scrubs stood on one side of it, holding up a corner of the sheet. A suntanned man with a mustache and tie was beside the morgue attendant, gauging Seth's parents, who stood on the other side of the drawer, looking down at what the attendant had unveiled from under the sheet.

Both of Seth's parents were as pale as ghosts, and Seth's father seemed to slump, as if life and strength were draining from him. Seth's mother stared without moving.

"That's him." Seth's dad nodded.

The morgue attendant tried to cover the body again, but Seth's mom stopped him with her hand. She didn't say anything, just kept staring.

Seth ran toward them, and as he passed the mustached man in the coat and tie, he finally saw his brother laid out on the cold drawer. His eyes were shut, and a crust of blood had dried in his nostrils and at the corner of his mouth. His left side seemed shrunken, as if it had collapsed.

"Carter!" Seth said, making his parents jump. He grabbed Carter's cold, stiff hand in both of his, squeezed his eyes closed, and concentrated. He felt the strange heat build in his palms.

"Seth, what are you doing here?" his mother gasped. Seth's father just gave him an odd look, as if deeply worried about something. It would be years before Seth knew enough about his great-grandfather to

18

understand what might have passed through his father's mind at that moment.

"Come on, Carter..." Seth whispered. He imagined the bird with the healed wing springing from his hand. He felt the heat grow more and more intense in his hands—but it didn't flow anywhere.

"Seth, you shouldn't be here," his mother whispered. His father put his hand on Seth's shoulder to nudge him away from Carter's body, but Seth gripped Carter's hand even tighter.

"I can fix him," Seth said. "You don't understand. If I just try...if I just..." Seth opened his eyes and looked at Carter's face. One of Carter's eyelids slowly pulled open, revealing a slice of green iris. Seth felt some hope and pushed harder, trying to imagine the healing heat rolling out of him, deep into Carter, repairing everything that was broken...

But nothing happened. The heat didn't move into Carter's frigid body. Seth's hands felt like they were on fire, but Carter was beyond his ability to heal.

"Seth!" his father snapped. "That's enough." And he pulled Seth away from Carter.

"No!" Seth screamed. "Just give me another chance, I know I can fix him, I know it..."

Seth's father led him away while he screamed and struggled. Seth's mother followed, tears streaming down her face, rubbing her forehead as if the situation were just too much to process.

"Please," Seth whispered to his dad. "I can bring him back to life."

His dad cut him a sharp look. "Why do you say that, Seth?"

"Because I can..." Seth's voice trailed off. His father's dark blue eyes scrutinized him, looking at Seth like he was some strange alien who had replaced his son.

"Have you ever brought the dead back to life before?" Seth's dad asked.

"No, but..." Seth wasn't sure how to begin to explain about the bird with the broken wing. All his thoughts were jumbled, and he felt pain at Carter's death and a sense of failure that he couldn't save his brother. How could he put all of that into words?"

"Jonathan," Seth's mother whispered. "Why on Earth would you ask him such a thing?"

Seth's father's jaw worked, tensing and relaxing under his cheek as if his teeth were grinding together.

"We have to take care of this paperwork," Seth's dad finally said as they left the morgue. "Then find a place to sleep."

"I don't think I'll ever sleep again," Seth's mother said.

Seth looked back as the door to the morgue swung closed behind them. Carter hadn't moved, and he would never move again.

The funeral in Fallen Oak drew a huge crowd, made up of locals as well as far-flung relatives and business associates of the Barrett family. Dr. Goodling led the service at Fallen Oak Baptist Church, though Carter would naturally be buried in the family cemetery on the Barrett's land outside town.

"It is always difficult when the Lord takes one so young," Dr. Goodling said. "It is a struggle to find the words to express the profound grief, the loss of promise and hope...a struggle to remember that God has a greater plan, and no man knows the place nor the hour..."

Seth sat in the front pew, staring at his polished black shoes. He knew he bore some of the responsibility for his brother's death, because if he'd only gotten to Carter faster, he could have healed him. His fists clenched and unclenched all the way through "The Old Rugged Cross" and "Amazing Grace."

As they left the church, a strikingly pretty blond girl in a prim black dress rushed up to Seth. It took him a moment to recognize the preacher's daughter, Ashleigh, since Seth's family rarely attended church. Her eyes were huge and gray and wet with tears.

"Oh, Seth, I feel so bad for you," Ashleigh said. Though they'd rarely spoken, she threw her arms around his neck and hugged him tight. "I can't imagine what it must be like," she whispered in his ear.

Seth felt a weird, warm glow fill him, as if the girl's touch had filled him with a deep sense of love. He broke down and began to cry, and he hugged her back.

"Ashleigh, don't pester that boy," said Mrs. Goodling, the preacher's wife, who had caught up with her daughter. She took Ashleigh's hand and reeled her back from Seth.

Seth and Ashleigh continued looking at each other while Ashleigh's mother pulled her back into the church, and Seth's dad hurried him out to the car. Seth's heart was thumping. He would think of that moment, the painful mix of misery and love, the compassionate look in Ashleigh Goodling's eyes, many times over the following few years.

20

At the family graveyard, where rows of monuments were enclosed by a high brick wall, Seth watched them bury Carter under the monument with his name inscribed on it. Seth's own grave marker stood beside it, a dark obelisk, with Seth's name and birth year already carved in place, waiting for his turn to die.

At their house, people ate and drank and spoke in low voices. Seth was introduced to more distant relatives, including his great uncle on his mother's side, Senator Junius Mayfield of Tennessee, a man with a balding scalp and a face like a basset hound.

As Seth walked away, he heard Junius whisper to his pretty young assistant: "I told Iris it was bad juju to get mixed up with Barrett family. You'd listen if I told you that, wouldn't you?"

"Of course, sir," the assistant answered, and she gave him a dazzling smile. "I always take your advice."

Seth made his way to the back yard, away from everyone. Beyond the peach orchard, on the far hilltop, he could see the brick walls and wrought-iron gates of the family's private graveyard. Carter was there now, and Seth's parents would follow him there, and Seth himself. And that would be the end of the story.

CHAPTER THREE

Years later, on the night of the Charleston riot, Seth searched for Jenny until the National Guard cleared the streets.

The riot had erupted during the Southeastern Funk Fest, an outdoor music event by the water. Seth didn't know why the riot had started, but it had been huge, sudden, and violent.

He'd completely lost Jenny in the chaos. It didn't help that she'd been running away from him, understandably angry at what she'd seen —Seth, with a strange naked blond girl on top of him. Seth didn't know what had come over him to make him hook up with that girl. It almost reminded him of Ashleigh's enchantment, the power to make people feel love, or at least intense attraction. But Ashleigh was dead, so she couldn't have been behind it.

He narrowly avoided getting swept up into a paddy wagon with a group of teenage rioters, and finally made his way back to The Mandrake House hotel. Jenny would know to find him there, if she wanted to see him—although, considering what Jenny had last seen him doing, he doubted that she would be looking for him anyway.

That girl was gone, thankfully, by the time Seth returned to the hotel. In his suite, he checked the sitting room, the bathroom, and both bedrooms. Nobody was there.

He walked out onto the balcony to think. Below him, pulsing blue light filled the streets—local and state police, Homeland Security. An armored transport cruised very slowly down Battery, with National Guardsmen perched on the sides, looking for signs of trouble. The authorities had arrived and dispersed the rioters in an incredibly short amount of time, almost as if they'd been expecting something big and chaotic to happen.

Seth wanted to call Jenny, but of course she didn't own a cell phone. He needed to call Darcy and find out why she hadn't made it back to their hotel room, but he couldn't find his Blackberry. He wondered where he'd left it. He'd been fairly drunk earlier, before the sight of Jenny's angry face sobered him up.

He tried to retrace the steps that had led to him bringing the other girl—what was her name? Allegra?—back to his hotel room. He certainly hadn't intended to cheat on Jenny, despite the encouragement of Wooly and friends. His memories around the girl were fuzzy, as if suffused with a weird golden light, the way it had felt whenever Ashleigh touched him.

It wasn't possible that Ashleigh was involved, though. Ashleigh was dead, and Seth was responsible for what he'd done, drunk or not.

Seth felt completely drained—the crowd had crushed in around him, leeching his energy, which had gone to heal any number of kids who were bleeding or injured from the riot. He staggered to his bed, leaving the bedroom door open so he could hear if Darcy returned. He turned up the volume on the phone on his bedside table, in case either Jenny or Darcy decided to call.

He closed his eyes, trying not to imagine Jenny caught in the middle of the riot, with people pushing in around her. He didn't want to think about what the mob might have done to Jenny—or what she might have done to them, and how it would upset her if she infected anyone with the Jenny pox.

The phone never rang.

***

Seth awoke sticky-eyed and sick in the morning. He checked the other bedroom, where there was still no sign of Darcy, who was supposed to be there. The odd girl had made friends with Jenny after

Ashleigh's death, and Seth had brought her to Charleston for college orientation this weekend, since they were both starting at College of Charleston in the fall. Darcy, like Jenny, had disappeared the previous night.

He looked at the room phone. He didn't know Darcy's cell number by heart. He did know Jenny's home phone, but he didn't want to get her in trouble with her dad if she hadn't returned home yet. She already had enough reasons to be angry with Seth.

He wandered downstairs to the hotel's dining room. Maintenance men were fixing broken windows from the riot, and the hotel's promised "Southern-style" hot breakfast was not being served. There was only some cold cereal and coffee available in the lobby.

Seth helped himself to a huge bowl of Frosted Flakes and a Styrofoam cup of coffee. He ate quickly and sloppily, drawing disapproving stares from more elderly hotel guests. Using his healing touch sucked out his energy, even burning away at his body mass if he didn't eat a gigantic pile of calories. It worked the same for Jenny.

When he was satiated, he approached the front desk, where the hotel manager was on duty, a slender man with a pencil-thin mustache and a seersucker suit. He raised an eyebrow at Seth's disheveled appearance and the clumps of strawberry blond that stuck up from his head.

"May I help you, sir?"

"Hi," Seth said. "Things got pretty crazy last night, huh?"

"I believe we shall endure. We are fully insured." The manager gestured at his computer. "If there is nothing further, I'm afraid we have a great deal of work to do this morning, cataloging the damage to our exterior."

"There was a girl who checked in with me, but she disappeared last night."

"How unfortunate." The manager resumed tapping at his computer keyboard.

"I was wondering if anybody's seen her.

The man sighed. "May we assume she was blond, scantily clad and quite drunk? We did have to ask such a person to leave the premises."

"Um...no, that's a different girl," Seth said. "The one I'm looking for has glasses and she's really, you know, pregnant." Seth held a hand out in front of his stomach, not sure why he was demonstrating what the word meant. "So somebody might remember her. Her name's Darcy

Metcalf?"

The hotel manager raised his eyebrows—both of them this time, not just the one.

"Metcalf," the manager said. "Am I to understand you were sharing her room on the fifth floor?"

"Fifth? No, we're on the third. Seth Barrett?"

The manager tapped at the keyboard. "Ah, yes, Mr. Barrett. This is a bit confusing, sir. We had to call the police for someone matching that name and description. She had a room on the fifth floor, which she reserved, we eventually discovered, using a stolen credit card."

"What? No, that's not right. We were on three, with my credit card, which isn't stolen."

"Hence the aforementioned confusion, sir. If she was staying with you, at your expense, why would she then rent a room on the fifth floor using a stolen credit card?"

"Well, I don't fucking know, man," Seth said, and the manager flinched a bit. "You must be confusing two different people."

"You propose that there were two women answering to the name Darcy Metcalf?" the manager asked. "Both of them pregnant?"

"That doesn't make any sense, either," Seth said.

"I refer you once again to the aforementioned confusion, sir," the manager said.

"To be clear," Seth said. "While Darcy was staying with me, she also rented a room on the fifth floor? With a *stolen* credit card? That doesn't sound like her at all."

"Perhaps I should not disclose this," the manager said, "But it might be the case that the card in question was stolen from the lady's father."

"Then it wasn't all that stolen, was it?" Seth asked.

"The father reported the card stolen, sir."

"Okay...then where's Darcy now?"

"We handed her over to the police," the manager said. "I presume you will find her in the city jail, in need of someone to post a bond."

"Well, shit," Seth said, and the manager flinched once again. "Okay. Where's the jail?"

"I will have to research that, as few guests of this hotel face problems with the police, as one can imagine."

"Just tell me where to go."

"I would be more than happy to do so," the manager said. He

printed off a Google map with directions to the jail and slid it across the desk. "Do let me know if there's anything further that will make your stay at the Mandrake House more comfortable. Perhaps we might direct you to a bail bondsman, or a criminal defense attorney."

"Yeah, very funny," Seth said. "Thanks for the map."

He tipped the man a dollar—normally he would tip more, but he suspected the hotel manager was subtly being a douche to him throughout the conversation. Then he walked out to his car.

The jail was a zoo, full of parents bailing out kids who'd been swept up from the previous night's riot. Seth had to wait in line.

"Weeell, look what the dog dragged in," a voice said beside him. Seth turned to see Darcy Metcalf's father approaching in his wheelchair —Mr. Metcalf was a very obese man who'd lost a foot to diabetes. His face was blood-red, and he sneered at Seth. Darcy's pale, cringing mother trailed behind him.

"Mr. Metcalf," Seth said, surprised.

"Don't you 'Mr. Metcalf' me, you dumb fancy-pants ball of shit," Mr. Metcalf said. "Run off with my daughter on a Friday night, then I come to find out I got to bail her big ass out of jail on Sunday morning? In goddamn *Charleston*. What do you got to say for yourself?"

"We were just coming here for orientation," Seth said.

"Oh, I bet you orientationed the shit out of her, didn't you?" Mr. Metcalf said. "Who's gonna pay for this baby, that's what I want to know."

"Morris—" his wife began.

"Shut up. I got a few things to say to Little Lord Fancy-Pants here. I had to pay Darcy's bond, and how am I gonna afford that when I'm on disability?"

"I'll pay her bail—" Seth said.

"Naw, here's what you're gonna do. You're gonna call up your daddy and tell him the Metcalf don't have to make no mortgage payments for the next three months. That's what you're gonna do."

"I'm sure something can be worked out—" Seth began.

"You bet your ass something can be!" Mr. Metcalf interrupted. "Matter of fact, make it four months. I got a pregnant slut daughter to feed."

"Morris!" his wife gasped.

"I'm sure this is a misunderstanding, sir," Seth said. "Darcy and I are both going to College of Charleston, and she asked for a ride to

26

orientation."

"College of Charleston!" Mr. Metcalf roared. "Darcy ain't going to college, richy-pants. She got a baby. She's gone take that job at the Taco Bell in Vernon Hill, she knows what's good for her."

"She's not going to college?" Seth asked. "That doesn't make sense. Why did she want to come with me?"

"I guess so you could stick your pecker in her babyhole," Mr. Metcalf said.

"Morris!" Mrs. Metcalf gasped again.

"Darcy and I aren't together like that," Seth said. "I didn't even want to bring her. It was just a favor to my girlfriend, Jenny."

"Jenny got-damn Morton!" Mr. Metcalf said. "It's a bad crowd she's fallen in with. No wonder she got knocked up."

"Daddy?" Darcy's voice whispered. A woman in a guard uniform had escorted her out, and now removed the handcuffs from Darcy's wrists. Darcy look dirty, confused and terrified.

"Darcy, what happened?" Seth asked. "Where's Jenny?"

"Jenny?" Darcy looked him and up down. "Seth Barrett. Are you talking about Jenny Mittens?"

"Don't you talk to that boy!" Mr. Metcalf interrupted. "You come right over and wheel me out of this goddamned place."

"Darcy, I don't understand what's going on," Seth said. "Have you seen Jenny?"

"No!" Darcy cried. "Why would I have seen her? Is she in jail, too?"

"Why did you get a room on the fifth floor of the hotel?" Seth asked. "Was Jenny staying with you? To spy on me, maybe?"

"I don't know!" Darcy wailed. Tears were already running down her face. "I don't even know why I'm in Charleston! I can't remember a dang-blasted thing! Honest Abe I don't!"

"Darcy, language!" her mother said.

"You tell Mr. Fancy-feathers I expect to get paid back for them charges on my credit card, too," Darcy's dad said. "What was you thinking, Darcy? We don't stay nowhere nicer than the Motel 6, since I lost my foot. We don't own a bank like some folks."

Seth just looked at Darcy, hoping for some kind of explanation from her, but the girl looked like she was tottering toward a nervous breakdown.

"Darcy!" her dad said. "Wheel me on out of here. I'm gonna whup you good when you get home."

"Okay, Daddy." Darcy was blubbering as she turned his wheelchair and rolled him through the crowd toward the door.

Seth watched them leave, more puzzled than ever. Why had Darcy swiped her dad's credit card and rented a separate room, when Seth had rented a two-room suite for them to share? And why had Darcy come to orientation at all, if she wasn't going to college?

Altogether, it had been a terrible and senseless weekend.

Seth returned to the hotel, gathered up his overnight bag and the little suitcase in which Darcy had packed her things for the weekend, and then he checked out.

He climbed into his blue convertible, lowered the roof, and drove home through the stifling heat and humidity. The packet of orientation papers sat on his passenger seat, weighed down by his overnight bag. He wasn't looking forward to college. He wasn't looking forward to much of anything these days. Jenny had grown increasingly distant from him, and angry at him, over the last several weeks—even before last night's events—and he didn't understand why.

He drove home to Fallen Oak, feeling very cold inside, and very alone in the world, just the way he'd felt after his brother died. He still missed Carter a lot—without him, there had been nobody he could talk to, until he met Jenny.

28

CHAPTER FOUR

The Cessna soared through the night over the Gulf of Mexico, which lay like a black chasm below. Though Jenny was tired and sore, she found the night sky around her dazzling, and she was feeling giddy at her impulsive choice to run off with Alexander. The narcotic pain medicine he'd given her was helping, too, putting a nice warm and fuzzy halo around everything.

She gazed at Alexander, the boy who'd stepped out of her dreams and into her life, just in time to rescue her from the mob whipped up by Ashleigh's opposite—whose name was Tommy, according to Alexander.

Alexander stared straight ahead as he piloted the small aircraft.

The mystery of where he'd come from and where he was taking her thrilled Jenny. She felt like she knew him very well—in her dreams of one of their past lives, he'd been an ancient king of Sparta, someone who had protected her and cared for her. He had found a purpose for her deadly touch. Life must have been easier, Jenny thought, in those past incarnations when she could attribute her deadly touch to some god or demon, some easy myth where she could fit. The modern world had no such comfort to offer.

"Alexander," she said. "Tell me more about the past."

"Which past?" He grinned at her. He had a nice smile, and his dark eyes glittered, framed by his shaggy brown hair. His clothes were simple—a white shirt, tailored jeans—yet seemed terribly expensive. His shirt had felt soft and smooth to her touch, like it was made of cashmere. Maybe it was. Jenny wondered what a cashmere T-shirt must cost.

"Any of them," Jenny said. "Greece, maybe."

"You know about Greece already," he said. "I should tell you about Egypt."

"I had a glimpse of Egypt," she said. "But it was all mud huts then. No pyramids or anything, not yet. They thought I was some kind of goddess. My job was to decide if people were guilty of crimes, and then punish them." Jenny paused, trying to recall the scrap of past-life memory. "I think I believed them, when they said I was a goddess. What else was I supposed to think?"

"Oh, that's primitive," Alexander said. "There's a more interesting one a couple thousand years later. I was a pharaoh called Netjenkhet. And your name was Hetephernebti. It was an age when people had time for really long names like that."

Jenny laughed.

"We conquered north into the Sinai, south into Nubia, expanding Egypt in both directions," he said.

"Was it always about war?" Jenny asked. "All of our lives?"

"The humans make war constantly. As long as we live among them, we must be like them. When they discover the things we can do, they either kill us or worship us. It's difficult to live in peace among them. They don't love peace enough for that."

Jenny thought about the mob Ashleigh had raised against her in Fallen Oak. It had been a slow build, really—from the time Seth healed her dad in front of too many witnesses. He'd saved her dad's life, but it had really fired up the town on the subject of witchcraft. With plenty of help from Ashleigh, of course.

"And what are we, exactly?" Jenny asked him.

"We're old."

"I know that."

"I mean 'old' measured in eons," he said. "We're outcasts, leftovers from the chaos before the universe. We've been human, off and on, for maybe a hundred thousand years—maybe longer, it's hard to judge, there are just a lot of lifetimes of lurking around in caves with hunters and gatherers." He tapped the side of his head. "All those early lives kind of run together. Like we were all sleepwalking."

"But before that?"

"As formless beings wandering in the abyss?" he asked. "Billions of years, I would say."

"Then where do normal human souls come from?"

Alexander laughed. "I wouldn't know. They seem like snowflakes to me, winking in and out of existence."

"Do they reincarnate like us?"

"Anything's possible."

Jenny frowned. "I thought you would know more, if you remember so many lives."

"I know plenty. Just not that."

"I still don't understand this whole 'before the universe' thing." Jenny was eager to learn. She'd yearned for someone to explain this to her, to make sense of the memory fragments she had brought back from her glimpse beyond death.

"When you're ready, you can see it all for yourself," Alexander said.

"How?"

"I'm going to show you."

"When?"

He laughed. "Any of us can wake up and remember what we are. But it's a process. I'm going to help you through that process, Jenny. So you can remember me. So we can be fully together, with both of us knowing who and what we are."

Jenny chewed on that, not entirely sure she liked the sound of it. The only thing she knew for certain about her past lives was that she'd done plenty of horrible things, which she regretted remembering. She looked around the cockpit and switched to a less-scary subject. "What do you do, Alexander?"

He studied her for a moment. "I live. I look for opportunities. I try not to miss out on the wonders of being human."

"Okay...but I mean more like, what do you do for work? I'm guessing you're not a waiter."

"I don't think we should define ourselves by our work."

"You didn't mind mentioning that you were a pharaoh."

He smiled at her. "And you were my queen."

Jenny rolled her eyes.

32

"I have friends in Mexico," he said. "They have some special uses for my ability."

"What do you mean? They need zombies?"

"They do."

"For what?"

"Agriculture."

"What, like a zombie ranch?"

"That's the plague-bringer I remember," Alexander said. "A mind full of curiosity."

"That's how you think of me? The plague-bringer?"

"Plagues have been a powerful shaping force in human history," he said. "You were behind some of them."

"Ugh. And what are you? The dead-raiser?"

"Exactly. You're remembering already."

"Nope, just thinking. So your opposite...?"

"She can listen to the dead. Pick apart their memories. She listens to the dead, I command them."

"But she hates you."

"We've never gotten along very well."

"Why not?"

"War." Alexander shrugged. "We've ended up on opposite sides too many times."

Jenny felt like he was being evasive, but the painkillers made her brain feel like thick oatmeal. It was hard to think straight, or make too much sense out of his words. Then she had a memory-flash of Seth, with the strange girl on top of him, the girl who looked so much like Ashleigh...

She opened the brown pill bottle again.

"Careful," Alexander said. "Those are strong."

"I like them," Jenny said. She popped a pill and settled back in her chair to watch the stars.

Later, they banked into a long, low curve, the plane angling down into the darkness below. The plane's control panel beeped and a red warning light appeared.

"What's that?" Jenny asked.

"Nothing," he told her. "We're just out of gas."

"What?"

"Don't worry. We don't need much more."

"Are we there already?" Jenny peered down. "I don't see any

airport."

"There isn't one." Alexander turned on the radio and spoke in rapid Spanish. "Jenny, help me watch for the fires."

Jenny squinted. Below a pair of bright red spots flared in the dark. Then two more, and two more, in straight, parallel rows. She pointed. "Is that what you're looking for?"

"It is. Fasten your seatbelt, Jenny."

The plane spiraled down toward the rows of firelight. Alexander dropped to the ground between them, and the plane rattled and shook, jarring Jenny back and forth and up and down as it bounced across the rough, uneven earth. The weedy dirt landing strip was illuminated by a row of old oil drums on either side of it, with raw flames pouring out the top. Each barrel was immediately extinguished as the plane rolled past.

"This is such an impressive airport," Jenny said. "Do they have a Starbucks?"

"Welcome to Chiapas International, specializing in people and cargo looking to avoid, ah, excessive government regulations." Alexander braked the plane, and it dragged to a halt between the last pair of flaming oil drums. These, too, were extinguished. In the plane's own lights, Jenny could see the rocky track extending forward several more yards, before it the view turned to rocks and thick forest.

"You're a smuggler," Jenny said.

"Nope. I have friends who are smugglers. The only thing I'm smuggling is you." Alexander flipped off the landing lights, leaving them in darkness.

"And you're sure we're safe here?" Jenny looked at the solid black outside the window.

"Safety is something no honest person can guarantee," Alexander said. "But if anybody tries to mess with you, just kill them."

Jenny laughed. "Great advice. Do you handle all your problems that way?"

"I try to avoid problems before they ever happen." Alexander opened his door, and Jenny heard men speaking in Spanish outside. "But sometimes, people just have to die. Welcome home."

He hopped out of the plane. Jenny opened her door but couldn't see where she was going, so she waited for him to help her down.

CHAPTER FIVE

Dr. Heather Reynard of the Center for Disease Control stood in the morgue of the Medical University of South Carolina and looked at the bodies that had been collected from the residential street in downtown Charleston. There were just over two dozen of them, every age, every condition.

Also in the room were the dean of the medical school as well as the county medical examiner Cordell Nolan, who had returned the bodies with the help of local police, and two morgue assistants who had witnessed the bodies' departure from the morgue. She wasn't sure what to make of their story.

"So," Heather said, "He comes through this door. He opens the drawers. And then...could you review the next part again?" She looked at the two morgue assistants, one an older black man named Corinthius, the other a twenty-four-year-old kid with dark green hair, whose name was Steve.

"And then that's where it gets fucked up," Steve said. "He starts bringing them back to life. Bam, bam, bam, one after the other they sit up, and he sicks them on us like a pack of wild dogs—"

"Not like a pack of dogs," Corinthius interrupted. "More like a pack of turtles. They were slow, dragging their feet, but they were coming for us. He could make them attack."

"And how exactly did he bring them back?"

"Hell if I know," Steve said.

"I meant, what exactly did you see him do?" Heather asked.

"He touched 'em," Corinthius said. "That's all. He touched each of them one time. Then he did kind of a funny wave with his hand—" Corinthius raised his own hand, "And then they got up and walked toward us. That's when we ran the hell out of here."

"It's not my job to deal with zombies," the green-haired kid whined. "They're supposed to be fully dead when they get here, and then stay that way. I ought to get hazard pay or overtime or something."

"Kid's got a point," Corinthius said, with a glance at the dean. "Ought to at least get some extra vacation time."

"We'll see," the dean said.

"Every one of 'em was dead last time I saw 'em," the county medical examiner said. "Got more injuries now than they did before. All post-mortem, of course. Mostly cuts and scrapes."

"That's all he did?" Heather asked. "He just laid his hands on them, and then he could animate them?"

"You gotta believe us," Steve said.

"I do believe you," Heather said. "I've reviewed the hospital's security footage. I saw them walk. I just can't begin to figure out how."

"Sure would be easy if we could write it off as some kind of frat prank," the medical examiner said. "College kids horsing around."

"Easy, but not true," Heather said.

"Hell, I've worked in government for years," the medical examiner said. "Nobody gives a possum's ass hair about the truth. Everybody wants what's easy."

"Not me," Heather said. "I want to know who this guy is, how he got these corpses walking, and why. What did he accomplish? Did he give any clue about his motivation?"

"Only the Devil knows the Devil's true intentions," Corinthius said. The county medical examiner nodded along with him, but the dean gave a small, derisive snort.

"He did say something about destroying the world, didn't he?" Steve asked.

"That's not what he said," Corinthius replied.

"He did! I remember! 'Death and destruction to the world.'

Something like that."

"He said, 'I am Death, destroyer of worlds,'" Corinthius said.

"What does that mean?" Steve asked.

"It's from Hindu mythology," Heather said. "But the quote comes from Robert Oppenheimer. He said that when he detonated the first atomic bomb. He was talking about himself. 'I am become Death.'"

"Sounds like the Devil to me," Corinthius said.

"Hell yeah it does," Steve said. "I don't believe in God, but I'm starting to believe in Satan."

"If we could step back from the theology a moment," the dean said. "It's clear that, at bottom, this will turn out to be some sort of hoax. The bodies must have been manipulated in some way. Like puppets. They must have been rigged."

"If he rigged them, it was too fast to see," Corinthius said. "All he did was brush his hand over each one."

"Then perhaps they were rigged before he arrived," the dean said.

"Nobody was in or out of here last night," Cornelius said. "We keep a visitor's log."

"Then perhaps they had inside help for their prank. From someone young and immature, with access to the morgue." The dean gave Steve a hard look, and the green-haired boy scowled back at him.

"I didn't do nothing, man!" Steve said.

"I would say it bears further investigating," the dean said.

"They didn't show any sign of rigging when we found 'em," the medical examiner said. "No cables, no ropes, nothing. If you're saying somebody slipped in here, rigged up them corpses with some kind of high-tech remote control, ran 'em through the streets, and stripped all signs of the rigging before any police showed up—well, damn, that's pretty thorough."

"It's also the only logical explanation," the dean said.

"For which there is absolutely no evidence," Heather said.

"What do you expect me to say?" the dean snapped at Heather. "You want me to believe their crazy story about zombies and...and necromancy?"

"We should take their observations for what they are," Heather said. "These men saw what they saw. We may not have an explanation yet, but any explanation needs to be based on evidence. Not on conjecture."

"Conjecture? Have you never heard of a working hypothesis?" the dean asked.

"That would need to be based on some kind of evidence, too," Heather said. "This looks supernatural on the surface, but don't be so eager to dismiss the supernatural that you rush into the first plausible idea. If we're going to be scientific, we must be comfortable letting the unknown remain unknown until we learn something concrete."

The dean sighed. "At least this happened in the middle of a riot. I won't even need to put out a press release explaining things."

"But we have to figure out what really happened," Heather said. She looked above the autopsy table, where the overhead lighting fixtures had been ripped away. "We found them with the metal bars from the lighting mounts. And brooms, mops and other blunt objects. Each one also carried a full-size cadaver pouch. What do you suppose those were for?"

"Maybe they were like to-go bags," Steve said. "So someone could pack them up and ship them."

"That's stupid," the dean said.

"At least it's a thought," Heather said. "But the bodies were abandoned, with no sign of the..." Heather wanted to say *zombie master*, but stopped herself. "The perpetrator. Either they served his purpose, or he changed his plans."

"It was one hell of a riot in the streets last night," Corinthius said. "Seems to me he wanted to push his way through the crowd. Beat his way, if he had to."

Heather nodded, thinking this over. "And what about the body bags?"

Nobody had any ideas to offer.

"Can we arrive at any consensus?" the dean asked. "At least for the public? There may be inquiries."

"Spin isn't my department," Heather said. "I find facts. It's up to other people distort them for political reasons."

"Very funny," the dean said.

"Man, are you gonna cover this up?" Steve asked. "You can't cover this up!"

"Calm down, Steve," Corinthius said.

"I think we've heard enough from the morgue assistants," the dean said. "Let's leave them to tidy up down here. Shall we go to my office?" He looked at Heather and the medical examiner.

"Oh, damn, it's a conspiracy!" Steve said. "Corinthius, can you believe—"

"I can believe you better head over to maintenance and get us some new brooms and mops," Corinthius said.

"But, they can't, I mean—"

"Kid, we don't get paid enough to worry about this shit." Corinthius said. "So don't."

The dean glared at Steve. "Do you want to keep your job or not?"

Steve looked between them, outraged. Then he stalked out of the room.

"We were going to your office?" Heather asked.

The dean looked at Corinthius and pointed to the door where Steve had left. "Keep an eye on him. Keep his mouth shut."

"I'll keep an eye on him," Corinthius said. "But if I knew how to make him shut his mouth, I'd have done that months ago."

The dean frowned and led Heather and the medical examiner out of the morgue.

As they rode the elevator towards the dean's office, the cell phone at Heather's belt crackled. She had it in "walkie-talkie" mode to stay in touch with other investigators.

"Dr. Reynard?" the voice on her phone said. It was Schwartzman, director of Public Health Surveillance. Her boss.

She grabbed the phone. "I'm here."

"You'll want to come by the emergency room," Schwartzman said. "There are patients with symptoms of Fallen Oak syndrome."

Heather's heart beat faster. "Are you sure?"

"You're the expert."

"There aren't any experts. Are the bodies being quarantined?"

"No bodies. These are live cases."

Heather nearly dropped the phone. The mysterious Fallen Oak syndrome had killed over two hundred people in the town of Fallen Oak, South Carolina. Intensive study of the bodies had revealed no vector of any kind—no virus, bacterium or fungus—despite the horrific symptoms, including boils, tumors, pustules, rapid necrosis of the soft tissue.

Only one person was known to have symptoms of the disease without dying. That was Jenny Morton, an eighteen-year-old girl from Fallen Oak. Heather had identified Jenny as a possible immune carrier of the disease, with the help of Fallen Oak residents, particularly another teenager named Darcy Metcalf who had provided some anecdotal as well as photographic evidence of Jenny exhibiting the symptoms.

Heather had tested Jenny's blood and hair but found nothing at all. She'd never had a chance to examine patients who were both alive and showing symptoms.

"I'll be down there right away." Heather punched the button for the next floor, and the elevator stopped.

"What's Fallen Oak syndrome?" the county medical examiner asked.

"It's a federal issue," Heather said.

"If there's some new disease running around my city, I'd say that's pretty damn local," he said.

"I can't say anything." The doors opened and Heather stepped off the elevator. The medical examiner followed her.

"I want to speak to your superior," he said.

"Convenient," Heather told him. She pressed the "down" button, since they'd already passed the floor where the emergency room was located. "He's waiting for me."

"Does the CDC usually fly in to investigate riots?" he asked.

"No."

"So why are so many of y'all around today?"

"Just lucky, I guess," Heather told him.

He squinted at her and rubbed his chin. "You got to tell me if there's some kind of epidemic coming."

"I don't believe there is." Another elevator arrived and opened, and Heather stepped inside. He followed her.

"Then why are you here?" he asked.

"I was sent here," Heather said. "That's really all I can say. You'll have to speak to Dr. Schwartzman if you want any information."

"That doesn't sound like a good arrangement to me."

Heather shrugged. The White House, worried about the upcoming election, had gone to great lengths to cover up the outbreak in Fallen Oak. She didn't want to risk getting in trouble.

They met Schwartzman at the emergency room. He introduced Heather to the administrator in charge of the ER, a very tall black woman with a stern look on her face—likely she didn't appreciate the CDC camping out in her hospital.

"You have to share some information," the medical examiner said to Schwartzman. "If there's an issue the local health authorities need to know about—"

"I'll be happy to answer your questions in a moment," Schwartzman said. "Let me just get Dr. Reynard started."

"I want to see this syndrome you're talking about," the medical examiner said.

Schwartzman sighed. "I don't believe your authority extends to the living. Wait here."

The medical examiner scowled, but he didn't follow as Schwartzman led Heather to a room sliced into small sections by green curtains.

"I had them moved together," Schwartzman said. "You get to work. I'll try to pacify our country doctor before he forces me to make a big federal case out of this mess."

Heather took a deep breath and stepped through the first curtain.

A girl with thick, dirty blond dreadlocks occupied the bed. Her hands were swathed in bandaging.

"Hi there..." Heather looked at the chart. "Allison. I'm Dr. Reynard. How are you feeling?"

"Radiance," the girl said.

"Excuse me?"

"I told them, I go by Radiance. That's my true name."

"Okay...Radiance." Heather strapped on a pair of latex gloves. "I just need to look at your hands."

"Why's everybody so interested in my hands?" Radiance asked. "Do I have some freaky disease or what?"

"Let me have a look, and then we might know something." Heather gently unwrapped the bandaging and removed the padding underneath.

The girl's fingers were covered in thick, leaking blisters, swollen pustules, and dark, knotted tumors at her knuckles. The combination of symptoms did indicate Fallen Oak syndrome.

"Do you have any other infected areas?" Heather asked.

"Just my hands."

"Did you touch anything unusual? Come into contact with any strange people or animals?"

"I was at the big show last night," Radiance said. "You know, the festival? I must have touched a lot of people. Made out with one dude. And then the riot, that was a lot of people running into each other."

"Does anything in particular stand out?"

Radiance looked at the floor. "I don't remember much, man. I was pretty much wasted last night. Like everybody else, you know what I mean?"

"Were you drinking?"

"Yeah...stuff like that."

"We're trying to track the spread of a certain pathogen," Heather said. "So any information you can give me would be a big help."

"Is it serious?" Radiance looked at her hands. "Am I gonna die from this? Seriously, you have to tell me."

"It looks like you'll be fine," Heather said. "But I need some samples." She opened her field kit and took out a cotton swab. "Can you hold still for me?"

"Whatever," Radiance said.

Heather took swabs from the running infections on each of the girl's hands, dropping the Q-tips into test tubes for later study.

"I have to ask whether you encountered a particular person," Heather said. "An eighteen-year-old girl. Very skinny. Long black hair. Blue eyes. Named Jenny. Does that bring up any memories for you."

"Oh. Her."

"You remember her?"

"Yeah..." Radiance looked around nervously, fidgeting in the hospital bed. "I do."

"How did you come into contact with her?"

"She's the one with the disease?"

"Possibly."

"Well, it was crazy," Radiance said. She looked Heather in the eyes. "You know, I'm totally nonviolent. I really am. I don't even eat meat."

"Okay. But...?"

"But this girl—it's like we all went crazy."

"Could you be more specific?"

"This girl was at the middle of everything. That's how the riot really started, you know? Everybody attacking her."

"Why did everybody attack her?"

"Because...." Radiance was looking at the floor again. "Because somebody told us to."

"Who? And why?"

"I don't know *why*, man. It was just like a voice from above. A voice from the heavens. Saying this girl, you know, you have to stop this girl."

"Jenny?"

"If that's her name, yeah."

"Stop her from what?"

"Stop her from, like, evil. It's hard to explain."

"And then what happened?"

"Then everybody went after her."

"Just like that?" Heather asked. "A voice from somewhere told you to attack her, and everybody listened?"

"You don't understand. Everybody was scared shitless, man, and it all like focused on this one girl."

"You're right, I don't understand that."

"It's like she was the *problem*, man. And stopping her was the *solution*."

"The solution to what?"

Radiance shook her head, setting several dreadlocks swinging. "It doesn't make sense now. But it did then."

"Did you attack her?"

"Everyone did."

"With your hands?"

Radiance looked down at her infected, swollen hands, and she said nothing.

"Then what happened?" Heather asked.

"It was just craziness. Everybody attacking everybody. One big, violent clusterfuck. For no reason at all."

"But you say the riot started with everybody attacking her?"

"Yeah. Then it spread into just total insanity. Does any of that make sense to you?"

"I can't say it does," Heather said.

"It's so not like me," Radiance said. "Really. I don't believe in violence, ever. You have to use visualization and stuff if you want to make the world better."

"Were you trying to make the world better by attacking her?"

"In a weird way that totally doesn't make sense when I try to explain it," Radiance said. "Yeah. It seemed like she was the evil, and everything would be so much better if we just got rid of her."

"What happened to the girl after you hit her?"

"I don't know. Lost her in the crowd, everybody trying to attack her. Then people were attacking me and I fought back. That's all I really remember. Then I woke up with this shit this morning—" Radiance held up her hands. "So I came to the hospital."

"You didn't have these symptoms last night?"

"Maybe I did. I was pretty out there, you know? I'm just saying, I really noticed them this morning."

"Okay. We're going to keep monitoring you, Radiance. The doctors here will keep treating your hands, and we'll see how it goes."

"The doctors here? What do you mean? Where are you from?"

"The Centers for Disease Control."

"Oh, fuck." Radiance touched her hand to her forehead, then looked at her hand, shuddered, and pulled it away from her face. "I'm totally fucked, aren't I?" she whispered.

"There's no reason to think that at this point," Heather said. "I think if the infection had been fatal, you would have died by now. You look to be in good health, based on your chart here. Hopefully these will heal up soon." Heather closed her kit and picked it up.

"And what if they don't?" Radiance asked.

"Then we'll treat it more aggressively," Heather said. "We're monitoring this closely, Radiance. You're in good hands." Heather wanted to bite back those words the moment she said them.

"Oh, very funny." The hippie girl looked down at her diseased hands.

"We'll talk again soon," Heather said. "I'll keep you updated as we learn more information."

"Thanks, I guess," Radiance said. She continued staring at her hands while Heather left.

The other patients who'd been isolated in this room fit similar patterns. They were mostly students who'd been caught up in the riot. They had symptoms of Fallen Oak syndrome, almost exclusively on their hands and arms. When pressed, a few of them admitted to attacking a girl meeting Jenny's description. The rest of them fell silent and refused to give Heather solid answers about it, clearly ashamed of themselves.

Heather left with plenty of test tubes of infection samples. She would send them to the lab in Atlanta. If this was truly Fallen Oak syndrome, the lab would find no pathogen at all.

A deadly disease with no identifiable vector. The walking dead. A riot that seemed to have begun with people attacking Jenny Morton, under orders from an unknown person.

Heather was beginning to miss the days she'd spent tracing the cholera epidemic in Haiti. Though politics had forced them to obscure the results of that study, too, at least the basic facts had made sense to Heather and the other researchers.

These events in South Carolina were starting to look more and more like the supernatural, and Heather didn't like that at all.

CHAPTER SIX

Ashleigh and Tommy rode fast through the night, stopping only to refuel the bike and to eat at a Waffle House outside Greensboro, Georgia, since nothing else was open that late at night. They devoured plates of omelets, hash browns and biscuits with gravy, to the amazement of their waitress. Both of them were drained from the massive energy it had taken to incite the riot. They needed sleep, but Ashleigh insisted on putting hours between them and Charleston before they rested.

She clung to his bike as the interstate rolled away beneath them. The road was nearly deserted, except for occasional clusters of eighteen-wheeler trucks ferrying cargo through the early hours of the morning.

Ashleigh tried to imagine what must have happened to Jenny. The mob had closed in around Jenny, attacking her from every direction. Naturally, Jenny would do her thing and unleash a plague on the crowd in order to survive. This time, the CDC and Homeland Security and the National Guard would all be waiting, thanks to that epidemiologist Dr. Reynard, who Ashleigh had played like a mark at a carnival.

Maybe they would just kill Jenny, but maybe they would capture her and keep her locked up for testing. Ashleigh didn't mind if Jenny was dead, but she really preferred her alive, imprisoned and suffering for a long, long time. If Jenny died, then she might reincarnate somewhere, and Ashleigh would have no idea where to find her.

Ashleigh felt the glow of victory even in her deep exhaustion. Now she was free to proceed with her own life.

They finally stopped riding at sunrise, and they checked into a "Heartache Motel" in Tupelo, Mississippi. Ashleigh supposed the motel's name was as close as the owners could come to ripping off an Elvis song without getting sued.

Tommy led the way into the small motel room, which smelled like a hamster cage. The air conditioning unit chugged in the window, and a streak of putrid green color stained the wall and carpet underneath it. A couple of faded Elvis posters were framed on the wall.

"Nice place." Ashleigh tossed Darcy Metcalf's huge purse into one chair. "Reminds me of the Ritz-Carlton in Manhattan."

"I'm running low on cash," Tommy said. "I'll have to rob somebody soon. Unless you have any?"

Ashleigh had a PayPal debit card worth just over two hundred thousand dollars, but she wasn't going to tell him that. "I'm sure you'll come up with some money," she told him. She took his hand and gave him her best smile. Her touch didn't have as much effect on him as it did on most people, which made him harder to control, but he was still useful to her.

"Just have to find a place without security cameras." Tommy flopped back on the bed, and it let out a painful rusty squeak. "Maybe some ratbag gas station."

"Or destroy the security tape before you leave," Ashleigh said.

"Huh. Good idea." He rubbed his head, watching her.

Ashleigh looked at herself in the mirror. She possessed Esmeralda's body, which was a huge step up from inhabiting Darcy Metcalf's pregnant, farting form. Esmeralda had long, attractive legs, a decent body, a very pretty face. With some makeup and new clothes, Ashleigh could really make this work.

"Hey, Ashleigh?" Tommy said.

"Yes?" She gave him another cheerful smile.

"I was wondering if…?"

"What? Spit it out, boy."

"I was thinking maybe I could hang out with Esmeralda for a

while?"

Ashleigh wanted to scowl at him, but she kept the smile frozen on her face. "Oh, you want to talk to her?"

"Yeah. Just check on her, you know?"

"Of course." Ashleigh lay on the bed beside him. "Do we have to do it tonight?"

"Yeah, I want to."

Ashleigh sighed. She could feel Esmeralda at the back of her mind, bound up by the golden threads of Ashleigh's love. She had no intention of letting the girl out again, which could give Esmeralda a chance to change her mind about letting Ashleigh's spirit ride around inside her.

Still, she needed to pacify Tommy. She might as well do it now, while he had deep purple patches under his eyes and would probably pass out anytime.

"Okay, Tommy. Just give me a minute." Ashleigh closed her eyes and laid her head on the pillow. She needed to sleep, too.

After a few seconds, she opened her eyes and smiled. "Tommy!"

"Is that you?" Tommy cupped her chin in his hand.

"Yeah, Ashleigh's asleep," Ashleigh said.

"Are you okay with all of this?" Tommy asked. "Having her inside you?"

"Oh, yeah. I love Ashleigh." She moved closer to him, so that their bellies and hips were pressed together. Then she slid her hand around the back of his neck. "And I love you, too. I missed you."

"Me, too." He kissed her, and she let herself enjoy it for a while. He cupped her breasts in his hands, and Ashleigh slid one hand under his shirt to feel his hard, warm stomach. Tommy was definitely hot, and she needed a little fun.

Ashleigh sat up and stripped off her shirt while he watched with low, drowsy eyelids. Then she hiked up his shirt to his armpits, meaning to undress him, but he didn't raise his arms.

"Come on, Tommy," she said. "Help me out here."

He didn't move. She looked at his face again, and his eyes were closed. She kissed his mouth again to see if that would wake him, but he didn't stir.

"Tommy? Are you asleep?"

He didn't answer.

"Loser," she snorted. Then she climbed out of bed to grab a hot shower before sleep.

*** .

Esmeralda Medina Rios lived with her mother Guadalupe in an apartment in Los Angeles. Tommy and Ashleigh rode into the graffiti-covered cinderblock complex, and Ashleigh's lip curled at the scene.

"I told you it was ugly," Tommy said. "Should we just keep going?"

"No." Ashleigh took off her helmet. "We have nowhere else to go right now. We have to use Esmeralda's identity."

"What do you mean, use her identity?" Tommy asked as Ashleigh got off the bike.

"Well, of the three of us, you're an escaped felon and I'm dead." Ashleigh kicked the locked saddlebag where her bones were stored in her high school backpack. "So, if we're going to put together any kind of life, we start with Esmeralda's life and go from there." Ashleigh looked at the stripped corpse of an automobile that occupied the parking spot next to them. "Though it doesn't seem like she has much to build on. What does she do for a job, again?"

"She's a mortuary cosmetician," Tommy said. "Actually, she's an intern, but she's working toward her degree—"

"Oh, gross. I am not doing that." Ashleigh crossed her arms.

"You don't have to," Tommy said. "Just let Esmeralda out to do it."

"Right. Duh," Ashleigh said. "But I think it's time for a career change."

"To what?" Tommy asked. He was leading them down the broken, spray-painted sidewalk towards Esmeralda's mother's door.

"I have a few ideas," Ashleigh said. "But I have to look around. There's a big mid-term coming up in the fall, you know. The President's going to lose control of Congress."

"Who cares?" Tommy stopped in front of an apartment door. "You're not like some political junkie, are you? Politics are boring."

"Power isn't boring," Ashleigh said. "Don't you ever think about using your gift for something bigger than, you know, just robbing stupid liquor stores? Something on a much bigger scale?"

"Like robbing a bank?" Tommy asked.

Ashleigh rolled her eyes.

"So, should we knock?" he asked. "See if she's home?"

"No, we shouldn't *knock*," Ashleigh said. "I'm playing Esmeralda, and this is her home, so..." Ashleigh fished Esmeralda's keychain out of Esmeralda's purse. "Hopefully, she's got some decent clothes for me."

They walked inside. The apartment was tiny, with a living/kitchen area divided by a bar. Spanish-language magazines were neatly arranged on the coffee table. Ashleigh looked at the framed posters on the wall: Jesus, Mary, and one saint after another stared back at her.

"Okay, we get it, you're Catholic," Ashleigh whispered.

"What did you say?" Tommy asked.

"Esmeralda!" One of the doors leading off the living room opened, and a large Mexican woman in a bright dress burst out. She looked at Ashleigh, burst into tears, and hugged her tight. Ashleigh was guessing this was Esmeralda's mother.

The woman spoke a rapid stream of Spanish, catching Ashleigh off-guard. Ashleigh had taken three years of Spanish, under the tutelage of Señora McDonald at Fallen Oak High School, but nobody had never spoken so rapidly in her class.

Then the woman slapped her and began barking words in a booming, angry voice. Ashleigh picked out individual words, like *afraid* and *worried*, and then the lady started pointing at Tommy: "*Quién es? Quién es?*" Who is he?

"Mama," Ashleigh said, in halting Spanish. "This is Tommy. He is my boyfriend now."

"No!" the woman snapped. She spoke very rapidly again, repeated the word *Pedro* several times.

"Who is Pedro?" Ashleigh whispered to Tommy.

"Esmeralda's old boyfriend," Tommy whispered back.

"Mama," Ashleigh said. "He and I are not together anymore. Tommy is my boyfriend now."

The woman got up into Ashleigh's face, screaming and jabbing her finger into Ashleigh's chest.

"Okay, this sucks," Ashleigh said. "Tommy, scare her."

"Are you sure?" Tommy asked.

"Never ask me if I'm sure!" Ashleigh snapped.

Tommy sighed and took one of the woman's thick arms. She gasped and stared at Tommy with widening eyes.

"El Diablo," she whispered.

"What did she say?" Tommy asked.

"She called you the devil," Ashleigh told him.

"Yeah," he said. "I get a lot of that."

"Sit down and be quiet!" Ashleigh snapped at Esmeralda's mother. The woman sank to the couch, shaking in fear while Tommy held onto her wrist.

"Tommy will be staying with me for a while," Ashleigh said, in careful Spanish.

"Here? In my home?" Esmeralda's mother asked in Spanish. She was staring in terror at Tommy's face. "No, no, no..."

"Yes, yes, yes," Ashleigh said. "He is mine and he is staying with me." Ashleigh smiled at the woman's fear and anguish. Ashleigh could have used her own touch to make the woman feel love instead of fear. That would also have made her more compliant...but this was so much more fun.

Esmeralda's mother shuddered on the couch and covered her eyes with one hand.

"I think she gets the point," Ashleigh said. "Come on, Tommy, let's check out the rest of this dump."

Tommy released the woman's arm, but she made no move to stand up. She leaned forward, cupping her face in her hands, weeping in fear.

Ashleigh followed the short hall out of the living room. There was a bathroom on one side of the hall. She opened the door across from it and walked into Esmeralda's room, which was decorated with posters of Latin soccer stars, many of them shirtless, along with a collection of Day of the Dead masks in one corner. Another corner held a desk stacked with textbooks on mortuary science.

Tommy closed the door behind them. "How long do you think she'll put up with us?"

"Longer than we'll put up with her," Ashleigh said. She opened the closet door. "Oh, my God," she whispered. "This is horrible. Can you see this, Tommy?"

"What is it?"

"I hate all her clothes." Ashleigh pulled a long skirt off a hanger. "Look at this beaded hippie Mexicany crap."

"I think you'd look cute in that."

"Shut the fuck up, Tommy." Ashleigh ripped clothes from the hangars, throwing them in a big heap on the closet floor. She left only a few jeans and blouses hanging. "This sucks. We have to get some money and go shopping."

"Esmeralda probably won't like you wrecking her closet like that." Tommy opened an embalming textbook, flipped through some pictures, and winced. "Hey, look, they're reattaching this guy's jaw to his face." He turned a gory picture toward her.

"Gross," Ashleigh said. She folded her arms. "Esmeralda is so gross."

"She is not!" Tommy snapped. "And you're just going to make her mad, the way you're acting. Why don't you let her out so she can deal with her mom for us?"

"Don't tell me how to do shit," Ashleigh said. "Esmeralda's perfectly happy to curl up inside and let me handle things. That's a lot of responsibility she's putting on me, but somebody has to do it."

Tommy didn't seem convinced, so Ashleigh kept talking.

"Look." Ashleigh sighed. "She knew her mother was going to be hostile about us bringing you to live here. She didn't want to deal with it. I'm doing Esmeralda a favor."

"If you say so." Tommy sat on the bed and continued looking through the pictures of dead bodies. "Will Esmeralda come and talk to me now?"

"Fine." Ashleigh closed her eyes. This game of make-believe was going to get old fast. She could already tell. She opened her eyes. "Tommy!"

"Esmeralda." Tommy smiled at her.

"Don't talk," Ashleigh said. She took the book from his hands and tossed it aside, then she straddled his lap. She started kissing him. "I need you," she whispered.

"I need you, too," Tommy whispered in her ear. She pushed his shoulders until he lay on his back on the bed. She pinned his hands down while she kissed him.

"What about your mom?" he whispered.

"I am not worried about her." Ashleigh took off her shirt. He watched as she unhooked her bra and tossed it aside. "Are you ready for me?"

"I'm ready, Esmeralda," he whispered, and then he pulled her down on top of him.

Sucker, Ashleigh thought.

CHAPTER SEVEN

Jenny took Alexander's hand and hopped down from the plane. The night was hot and steamy, and she was immediately covered in sweat. With the fiery landing-light barrels extinguished, the only illumination came from flashlight beams that slashed thin yellow lines across the deep darkness. Overhead, she could see a swatch of night sky brimming with stars, but most of the sky was blotted out by the high, dense treetops. Their landing strip appeared to be hacked out of raw jungle.

A couple of men hurried to refuel the plane from rusty, extremely unsafe-looking metal drums. Alexander spoke in rapid-fire Spanish to the handful of men around him, and they laughed.

"This way," Alexander said. His hand found hers in the dark. "Hold on so you don't get lost. The rainforest is full of predators."

"Sounds great," Jenny said. She let him lead the way by the thin glow of his flashlight. His hand felt warm and strong around hers, and again she felt the dark electricity of their powers mingling wherever their skin touched. He made something wicked and reckless stir inside her. She should have been terrified at the strange surroundings thousands of miles from home, but his touch extinguished her fears.

"This way." Alexander helped her up into the back of a stripped-down Jeep, then sat down beside her. Ahead of them, the driver lit a cigar and cranked up the engine. Jenny could see nothing of the driver except for the glowing tip of the cigar.

"Wait." Jenny felt the seat underneath her. "We're just on a flat metal thing. Where are the seatbelts?"

"Seatbelts?" Alexander asked. The driver stomped on the gas, and the Jeep surged forward into darkness, fishtailing its way through low-lying limbs that snatched at Jenny's hair. Jenny screamed and grabbed Alexander's arm.

The headlights flared to life, casting dim light on the green mass of trees, limbs and vines surrounding them. They followed a narrow, overgrown trail, bashing through undergrowth along the way. She caught a glimpse of the driver's battered green cap, his heavy black mustache, his grin around the cigar locked between his teeth.

Then the lights went out again, but the Jeep seemed to be accelerating, even as it made sharp turns along the winding trail. It skidded sideways at a tight bend, then straightened out.

"Why did he turn the lights off?" Jenny asked.

"Lights can make us visible from the sky," Alexander said. "Not safe to leave them on."

"Okay, but—" Jenny let out another gasp as the Jeep charged uphill, pushing her backwards. She flailed out her other arm and caught hold of the roll bar overhead. "Is this safe?"

"Manuel knows what he's doing," Alexander said. He wrapped an arm around Jenny's waist, though, as if to stop her from flying out.

"I wish he'd turn the lights on again," Jenny whispered. Her teeth chattered together as the Jeep bounced and slid its way through the jungle.

A minute later, the lights did come on again, to reveal that they were tilted at a sharp angle, following a narrow, crumbling dirt trail hacked into a mountainside. Jenny looked down along the steep, rocky slope beside her. If the Jeep toppled over on its side, as it seemed ready to do, it would roll and crash along more than a thousand feet of sheer moonlit rock.

Jenny closed her eyes again.

The Jeep plummeted forward like a roller coaster shooting down the first big hill. It slung her back and forth as it descended the steep trail, and then started climbing again. Jenny was starting to feel sick to her stomach, and she was pretty sure their driver was laughing.

They turned—sharply—onto a wider dirt road, which brought them to a high, uneven rock wall. The Jeep braked to a halt, and the headlights shone on a closed gate in the wall, which consisted of two large doors that appeared to be made of sheet metal. The driver, Manuel, hopped out of the Jeep, leaving the engine running as he approached the gate.

The wall was about ten feet high, a jumble of different stones cemented together. All over the wall, little glints reflected the headlights. Jenny realized that these were jagged pieces of glass embedded in the concrete. It looked the builders of the wall had stuck broken bottles everywhere, especially along the top, to slice up the hands and feet of anyone who tried to climb over.

Manuel unlocked the sheet-metal gate and pushed both doors open on rusty, screeching hinges. He drove the Jeep through, then hopped out again to lock the gate behind them.

They were on a paved path now, though many of the paving stones were missing, leaving empty sockets of water and mud. Ahead, Jenny saw a few buildings made of adobe, and a sprawling two-story main house made of stone, with balconies, staircases and chimneys jutting out here and there. The place looked almost medieval to Jenny. Candles burned all over the exterior of the house, outlining balconies, windows and doorways like strings of Christmas lights.

A low one-story cottage sat beside the main house, and a barn, and then the remains of another adobe building with a collapsed roof and hollow doorways.

"Welcome to *Casa del Fuego*," Alexander said. He jumped out of the Jeep and offered his hand, but she didn't take it as she climbed down. She was feeling numb from the long, fast, jarring drive, and maybe from the painkillers, too.

"Is this where we're staying?" Jenny asked.

"This is my place," Alexander said. "Nice, secluded, with strong ocean air to invigorate the mind. Can you smell the salt in the air?" He closed his eyes, and she studied his face in the moonlight. He looked so much younger when his eyes were closed.

"I think I can hear the ocean," Jenny said. Waves crashed somewhere beyond the house.

"You can hear it all night," Alexander said. "There's no sound more peaceful. Let me show you around." He led her toward the house, across an unkempt yard full of tropical wildflowers. Behind them, Manuel drove the Jeep into the barn.

They walked up three steps to the front door, which was made of heavy hardwood and reinforced with thick metal bands. Jenny noticed that the windows on the first floor were all barred.

"This is really your house?" Jenny asked. "Do you always keep candles burning everywhere?"

"We might have dressed it up a little for you." He grinned.

The front door opened for them. A short, dark man in fatigues and a T-shirt stood inside. An AK-47 assault rifle was strapped to his back. He gave a huge smile and stood aside for them to enter.

"Iztali," Alexander said to the man, "This is Jenny."

"Jenny." Iztali smiled again and nodded his head slightly. "*La bruja*?" he asked Alexander.

"*Si,*" Alexander replied.

Jenny smiled back at him as she passed. He closed the door behind them, then crossed his arms and remained beside it.

Three more people, a young man who resembled Iztali, a gray-haired woman, and a young woman who might have been Jenny's age, stood in the front hall. The arched space was illuminated by more candlelight and glass lanterns set into wall niches. The house did have electric lights, but they were all turned off.

"Yochi, Noonsa, Kisa," Alexander said to them. He spoke a few words in a language Jenny didn't recognize—it didn't even sound like Spanish to her. Or French, which Jenny had taken in high school to avoid the risk of Spanish class with Ashleigh Goodling.

"Jenny," Alexander said, putting his arm around her. They nodded to her, and the young, darkhaired woman smiled.

"Jenny, this is Yochi." Alexander indicated the young man, and Jenny noticed the machine pistol holstered at his belt. "He helps with a few things around here. Like security."

"Nice to meet you," Jenny said, but the man didn't respond.

"And this is Yochi's aunt, Noonsa, and his sister Kisa," Alexander said, introducing the two women. "They keep us from falling into barbarism. Kisa has your room prepared for you. And some clothes she bought for you."

"Wow, thanks!" Jenny said.

"Hungry?" Kisa said to Jenny, and she pointed at Jenny's stomach.

"No, I'm fine, but thanks," Jenny said.

"You sleep?" Kisa asked. "You bath?"

"She's offering to run a bath for you," Alexander said. "Kisa's in charge of keeping you comfortable. She knows a little English, too."

Kisa nodded quickly.

"Oh, that sounds really good, thanks," Jenny said to Kisa. "But I can do it. Just show me where."

"Let her do things for you," Alexander said. "I hired her to help me."

"With what?" Jenny asked.

"Just to take care of your needs. Food, cleaning, laundry—"

"That's crazy," Jenny said. "I'm not a baby."

"You want me to fire her?"

"Oh, no!" Jenny said. "Don't fire her. Yes, I would like a bath please, Kisa. In fact, if you could show me the bathroom like right now, that would be pretty ideal. Thank you!"

Alexander spoke a couple words in that strange language again, and Kisa led Jenny down the curved hallway. With the earthen building material and the candlelight, it seemed more like a cave than a house.

Kisa led her upstairs and to a spacious tiled bathroom at the back of the house. Jenny excused herself and closed the door, then let out all the pee she'd barely held in throughout the Jeep ride.

The bathtub was in the corner, made of rock and inset with bright pebbles. It was right up against a large window, which was open to catch the salty breeze from the ocean.

When she was done, she opened the door and let Kisa inside.

"Bath now?" Kisa asked with a smile. She began filling the rocky tub with hot water.

"Um," Jenny said. She pointed to the glass window by the tub. "How private is this?"

Kisa looked where she was pointing and shook her head. "All ocean. Okay."

"Really?" Jenny leaned out the open window, but she could see nothing in the darkness except for the stars overhead, stretching to the horizon.

Kisa picked a handful of tropical flowers from a bowl by the sink and tossed them onto the bath. "I wash hair?" she asked, reaching for Jenny's long black hair, which was quite dirty and tangled at the moment. "I braid?"

"No!" Jenny snapped, backing quickly away from her. "Don't touch me. Um, no touch. Please. Okay?"

"No touch?" Kisa frowned. She looked down at her hands, studying them, as if searching for a reason why Jenny didn't want to be touched by her.

"Right. No touch. Thanks."

"Okay, no touch." Kisa looked hurt, and Jenny felt bad, but she didn't know what else to say. She didn't want to infect this nice girl with Jenny pox.

Kisa left the room and closed the door. Jenny hesitated, but the bath looked extremely inviting. The whole house was kept very clean and neat, probably by the two women.

Jenny removed her dirty tennis shoes, her jeans, her gloves. It always felt nice at the end of the day when she could finally take her gloves off and let her fingers breathe a little.

She looked at herself in the mirror. Big purple and yellow bruises were splattered all over her face, her ribs, her legs, where the mob had hit her and kicked her. They were already fading, though—Jenny healed faster than most people, and she never got sick.

She sat down in the hot bath and laid back, letting her hair float out all around her head. She looked up at the tiled ceiling. This was all crazy, she knew. Hitching a ride to Mexico with Alexander, whom she only knew from dreams of a distant past life. He'd saved her, though, from the mob, and apparently from Homeland Security, the CDC, and the National Guard, too.

She thought about her father, alone in the hospital. Only he wouldn't be alone anymore. June would have gotten there hours ago, and June was much more calm and sane than Jenny. June could even hug him, try to comfort him with human contact, things Jenny herself could never do.

The door to the bathroom opened, and Jenny sat up and gasped, covering herself with her arms.

"No fear," Kisa said. She lay a thick towel, clothes, and a pair of sandals on the bathroom counter. "No touch, no fear." She left again quickly.

"Thank you," Jenny said, but Kisa had already closed the door. She was already making a bad start with that girl. And if Jenny was going to hide out here and wait for the United States government's interest in her to fade, she really did appreciate having a girl her own age to talk to, especially one who spoke some English. Jenny could help Kisa learn more English words, and maybe Kisa could help Jenny learn Spanish, or whatever language everybody was speaking.

Alexander had gone to a lot of trouble to bring Jenny here, and she still wasn't entirely sure why. Her previous elation and recklessness was slowly sinking, and doubt and worry started creeping in. She could understand well enough why Alexander would want to reconnect with others of their own kind—so far, Jenny herself knew only Alexander, Seth, Ashleigh, and Ashleigh's opposite, Tommy. And the last two were just monsters. Seth wasn't looking so sweet himself these days, either.

She imagined him embracing the slutty blond girl, but the image made her sick and she blinked it away.

She thought instead of Alexander—his bizarre power, animating the dead with his touch. He could control them, but he said his power was greatly enhanced by Jenny's touch. She wondered how that worked. He would probably show her, since that had to be the real reason he'd gone to all this trouble for Jenny.

And she thought of Alexander some more—his dark, intelligent eyes that looked at her and knew far more about Jenny than she knew about herself. The muscular feel of his arms and chest when he carried her. Because that was the other thing about Alexander. He could touch her. His touch did something to her, too. It charged her up, made her feel powerful. And a little bit high.

Jenny felt herself growing warmer, and found her hand creeping down between her legs as she thought about him. She stopped herself, remembering how Kisa had just walked in the door unannounced. She didn't really have any privacy here.

Jenny hurried through the bath, and quickly dried and dressed herself. Kisa had left her a lightweight, brightly colored dress.

She gathered up her dirty clothes and wet towel and walked out into the hall.

"What do you think you're doing?" Alexander asked. He leaned against the wall next to an open bedroom door.

"Where's the laundry room?" Jenny asked.

"Are you kidding? Just leave stuff like that in the bathroom. Kisa will clean it up."

"I can do it," Jenny said.

"Look, this is your room," Alexander said, pointing to the open door beside him. "Kisa is staying in the room next to yours." He walked a few steps to the next door and knocked on it. "You need anything—like somebody to pick up the bathroom—you just tell her."

"I don't want to bother her," Jenny said.

"I think you kind of miss the point of having servants."

"You're right, I kind of do," Jenny said.

Kisa opened her bedroom door.

"Hi, Kisa," Jenny said. "Can you just show me the way to the laundry room?"

Alexander spoke to her in that strange language that didn't really sound like Spanish.

Kisa took the dirty clothes from Jenny and carried them toward the stairs.

"No, wait!" Jenny said. "I didn't tell you to take them, I was just asking..."

Kisa turned back with an impatient look on her face.

"Never mind, sorry." Jenny waved and shrugged, feeling completely awkward and lost in this situation. Kisa turned away and carried the clothes downstairs.

"I feel like I'm being such a bitch to her," Jenny said. "I'm really not trying to do that."

"You'll be fine," Alexander said. "She's just an employee."

"But I don't like making her do petty stuff like my clothes."

"You're a woman of the people now." Alexander grinned. He took both of her hands in his.

"I am." She didn't mind him holding her hands. She could feel herself starting to blush.

"You must have spent a lifetime Marxing it up somewhere along the way," he said. "Wild times."

"Wild times," she repeated, barely aware that she was echoing him. She was looking into his eyes. His gaze burned holes through her—he was seeing through her, into the deep inner part of herself that was many lifetimes old. Jenny wanted to know everything he knew about her. And she was already fighting an aching urge to see where else he might want to touch her.

"What are you thinking about?" he asked.

"Oh...nothing." Jenny pulled her hands back and crossed her

arms. "Good night, Alexander."

"It's almost sunrise. Want to get some breakfast?"

"I don't think so." Jenny stepped inside her room. "Alexander, I need to call the hospital back home and check on my dad."

"We can't," Alexander said. "The feds could be monitoring the hospital, hoping you'll call."

"But I have to know how he's doing."

"I can send somebody to check on him. Someone who won't be traced back here."

"And I need to let him know I'm okay, too."

"We'll take care of it," he said. "Just get some rest."

Jenny closed the door. There was a lock on the knob, so she turned it into place.

The bedroom was decorated with some very old handmade furniture, vases with fresh flowers, and a couple of landscape paintings. Jenny lay back on the bed and kicked off the leather sandals. She could feel the vast distance separating her from her home and her father—it was like a terrible ache in her stomach.

Everyone was safer this way, she told herself. Jenny needed to be thousands of miles from anyone she loved. She brought too much danger to the people around her.

Though she was troubled, she was also exhausted, and it only took a minute for her to fall into a deep sleep.

CHAPTER EIGHT

Jenny woke to a flood of daylight and the sound of rusty hinges.

"Huh?" Jenny sat up. The door to her room stood open, but she was pretty sure she'd locked it the night before.

"Good morning, Jenny," a girl's voice said. Jenny turned to see Kisa pushing open the glass shutters of one of Jenny's two windows. The other was already open, and a soft, salty breeze tousled its curtains.

"What time is it?" Jenny asked. Kisa looked back at her and frowned. Jenny remembered the girl spoke little English, so she pointed to her own wrist, as if she wore a watch. "Time?"

"Oh!" Kisa held up three fingers. "Three."

"Three?" Jenny got up from the bed. She stretched, and her whole body ached from the beating she'd taken in Charleston. She managed to avoid shrieking in pain. "Guess I slept all day."

Kisa smiled, but this might have meant she didn't understand Jenny at all. "Clothes. For you." Kisa indicated a folded outfit on a small table at the foot of the bed. "Mine," Kisa added.

Jenny picked up the clothes—there was a traditional blouse, with many narrow vertical lines of bright color, and a pair of jeans. There were also sandals, which would probably be nice in this tropical heat, but Jenny didn't like leaving so much of her skin bare.

"Thank you." Jenny held up the shirt, smiling. "This is very pretty."

Kisa smiled. "Very pretty? You like it?"

"I love it."

"I make breakfast." Kisa hurried to the door.

"Oh, you don't have to..." Jenny began, but the other girl was already gone.

Jenny dressed in the clothes—they were a little loose on her, but light and comfortable. She put on her own shoes, but left off the socks because they were filthy. Then she pulled on her gloves.

She looked out the window and had to catch her breath. Below her, the back yard sloped down to a cliff. The rock wall framed the entire yard, but chunks of the wall along the cliff were deeply cracked or broken away, leaving the impression of a row of bizarre rock sculptures.

Beyond the cliff, the ocean sprawled out to the horizon, glittering with millions of golden flecks of reflected sunlight.

"That's beautiful," Jenny whispered. She hurried downstairs and through the kitchen, where Kisa was slicing up a mango while a tortilla fried on the stove.

"Eat breakfast soon, Jenny!" Kisa said.

"I want to go out and look at the ocean," Jenny said.

"Coffee?"

"Yes, please! Thanks! Want to go outside with me?"

"I make breakfast."

"Okay. I'll be right back." Jenny pointed towards the back door, which stood wide open to catch the open air.

Kisa smiled and nodded, possibly understanding Jenny's meaning.

Jenny walked outside. There was a huge patio paved with clay tiles, shaded by a roof. The patio had furniture arranged in clusters, like outdoor rooms—a dining table with chairs in one area, a pool table in another.

For one weird moment, the entire place reminded her of Seth's house in Fallen Oak, as if there were some deep similarity under the surface of the two places, though she couldn't quite put her finger on it. Then she shook those thoughts away. She didn't want to think about Seth, or anything back home. She might be in deep over her head here, but this was where she needed to be. All of this felt increasingly like a dream, where she got to be somebody else in a completely different world. She definitely enjoyed that feeling.

Jenny continued beyond the patio and into the huge sunlit yard, which was mostly wildflowers mowed short like a lawn. She crossed the yard, past Iztali and Yochi, who were working at some sort of brick-lined firepit. They didn't look up at her.

Jenny leaned out between two broken pieces of wall.

Below her, the rocky cliff was a sheer, straight drop to a silvery beach more than a hundred feet below. Jenny watched a large wave roll in and crash, the water spreading across the beach and slowly flowing back into the ocean.

"Watch your step," a voice said, and Jenny jumped. Alexander had walked up behind her without making a sound. His dark, longish hair blew in stripes across his face. His laughing eyes looked down at her. "What do you think?" he asked.

"It's amazing here," Jenny said. "Why is the beach gray like that?"

"Volcanic sand."

"I've never seen that before. So...how did you get a place like this?"

"Not so hard." Alexander swept his arm around to indicate the buildings. "This used to be a private retreat of Senator Hector Ramirez, a big gun in the Institutional Revolutionary Party. After the Zapatista uprising in '94, he was too scared to vacation here. The place was abandoned for a decade. Real mess when I moved in."

"The what uprising?"

"Some of the local revolutionaries took over a big chunk of the state in 1994," Alexander said. "And in a lot of places, the federal authority still hasn't returned."

"So this is kind of a dangerous place," Jenny said, thinking of the broken glass embedded in the walls.

"Only if you go looking for trouble," he said.

"Why do you live here?"

"Papa Calderòn needed me close to the Sierra Madre,"

Alexander said. "The mountains, where we do a lot of work. So he gave me this place."

"He's your boss?"

"Yep. Everything you see belongs to him."

"And his name is really Papa...something?"

"That's what everyone calls him."

Jenny looked down at the ocean again. "Why did you bring me here?"

"You need a place to hide for a while." He took her hand. "And I need you. I always need you." He stepped closer, his face overshadowing hers, and Jenny's heart beat faster.

She pulled her hand back. "I don't have all the memories you do," she said. "I only know you from my dreams. You're still new to me."

"You'll remember." Alexander smiled and started back toward the house, where Kisa was setting out Jenny's breakfast on the outdoor dining table.

"When?" Jenny asked.

"I'm already working on it." Alexander walked away into the house.

Jenny walked back up the gentle slope to the dining table, where Kisa had set out coffee, eggs, and a corn tortilla topped with beans and green chiles. There was also a big sliced mango, probably plucked from one of the trees in the front yard. Kisa smiled and stepped back, pulling out the chair in front of the food.

"That's so much," Jenny said as she sat down. "You should have some."

Kisa just smiled. Jenny gestured to the empty chair across from her, but Kisa waved both hands and backed away. Apparently, she intended to just stand and watch while Jenny ate.

Jenny bit into a slice of mango, and sweet juice dribbled down her chin. It tasted like candy.

"Oh, this is so good!" Jenny said to Kisa, who smiled and nodded quickly. Jenny could never be sure how well the girl understood her.

While Jenny ate, Alexander returned and tossed a thick roll of bright Mexican pesos onto the table. Kisa's eyes bulged at the spool of money.

"I have to run out for work," Alexander told Jenny. "Kisa and one of her brothers will take you into the city."

"Why?" Jenny asked. She never liked the idea of going into cities. Too many crowds, too many people to avoid touching.

"Shopping, so you can get clothes that fit," Alexander said. "I don't mind watching Kisa's jeans sliding off you, but you might have a different opinion." He sat across from her and dropped a pouch made of bright woven fibers onto the table between them. Jenny frowned at him.

"I don't want to go into any city," Jenny said. "I hate shopping. I can just wear what I have."

"But you'll want something for the party tonight," Alexander said.

"What?"

"That's why Iztali and Yochi are getting the grill ready." Alexander gestured to where the two short, muscular brothers were preparing the large brick-lined pit. "We're having a party to welcome you here."

"You don't have to," Jenny said. "I don't like parties."

"What's not to like? Musicians, wine, pig roast—you can meet some of my friends—"

"I really don't want to," Jenny said. "I'm serious. I can't be around people."

"Why not?" Alexander asked.

She scowled at him. "You know why. Nobody can touch me."

"No touch!" Kisa said, shaking her finger.

"What she said," Jenny said.

"So you throw on a pair of gloves and something with sleeves," Alexander said. "Don't get drunk and try to make out with anybody, and you'll be fine."

"But I have to be so careful with a crowd like that," Jenny said. "It's really hard to avoid contact, you know? It's the most stressful thing in the world. Can't we just keep things quiet?"

"Wow," Alexander said. "No cities. No shopping. No parties.

Who are you?"

"I'm just me," Jenny said.

"But you're not." He studied her eyes. "You're still asleep in there."

"I'll have more coffee, then." Jenny held her empty coffee mug toward Alexander. Kisa immediately lifted it from her fingers, and Jenny hurried to pull her arm back to avoid any contact with the girl.

"No touch, no touch," Kisa repeated, rolling her eyes just a little. She carried the coffee mug inside for a refill.

"She doesn't have to do every little thing for me," Jenny said. "It's kind of weird."

"I hoped she would make things easy for you. And you do need clothes. You'll be staying here a while."

"Unless I change my mind," Jenny said.

"Well, obviously," Alexander said. "But the feds are searching for you. They know you killed hundreds of people—"

"Ugh." Jenny buried her face in her hands. The reminder of her own evil nature was like a punch to the gut.

"—and they want to know how," he continued. "They'll probably be watching your father. How much does he know?"

"Basically everything," Jenny said. "He knows what I did. He kind of hates me now, I think."

"How could anyone hate you?" Alexander said.

"Maybe if I killed your wife and a bunch of people you'd known your whole life, you'd hate me, too," Jenny said. "I deserve it. He was always too nice to me."

"Are you feeling any pain?" Alexander asked. "From your injuries?"

"It'll be okay," Jenny said. "I heal fast."

"I know you do."

Kisa placed Jenny's coffee in front of her, and Jenny smiled and thanked her. Alexander opened the woven pouch and took out a few oval-shaped, yellow-green leaves.

"Chew some of these." He put the leaves in his mouth and smiled as he crunched into them. "Spit them out when you're done. They'll help with the pain."

"Yeah?" Jenny placed a few of the leaves in her mouth. Her tongue began to turn numb.

"Chew it," he said.

Jenny chewed, and a pleasant numbness filled her mouth. She felt it spreading slowly through her head.

"What is it?" she asked.

"A little local coca leaf," Alexander told her, putting another in his mouth.

"You mean chocolate?"

"Nope," Alexander said. "Kills pain, clears the head, gets you moving. Just the thing for running through mountains. Coca."

Jenny stopped chewing. "Coca, like cocaine?"

"Don't worry, it's totally organic," Alexander said.

"Isn't it addictive?"

"There's only a little tiny bit in the leaf. Kisa likes it, too, don't you?" Alexander held the bright little bag out to her. Kisa smiled and took a big handful of the leaves.

"Whoa, leave some for the rest of the class," Alexander said. He dropped the bag on the table in front of Jenny. Jenny hesitated, then took just a couple more. They really were helping with her pain. She felt energized, too, suddenly in a mood for adventure.

"So," Jenny said, "My first day here, and you were really going to just send me off shopping somewhere?"

"I don't want to, but I have to meet with some people. I've been away for a while, searching for you. Now I have to catch up."

"Are they running low on zombies?" Jenny asked.

"Very funny."

"I thought it was a serious question. What are you really going to do?"

"Pick up money from a few people and pay it to a few other people."

"Sounds pretty easy."

"It does sound that way," Alexander said.

"When do I get to see the zombie farm?"

"Zombie farm?"

"You said you use them for agriculture." Jenny made an exaggerated show of looking around the back yard. "I don't see any zombies working around here. So where are they?"

"Up in the Sierra Madre," he said. "In the jungle."

"Cool. Let's go there." Jenny stood up, feeling a little dazzled. "I'm done eating. My appetite's just, zip, totally gone. Come on, let's do another crazy Jeep ride. That was fun."

"I wish we could, but I have more boring things to do."

"Fine. When's the party starting? Soon?"

"Later." Alexander stood up. "You could go shopping if you want something to do."

"You're right, I could." Jenny snagged the roll of money from the table and stuffed it in her pocket. "Okay, have fun working. I'm going down to the beach. You want to go to the beach, Kisa?" Jenny pointed at the girl, who nodded.

"Whatever you want to do," Alexander said.

"I know," Jenny said. She grabbed the bag of coca leaves from the table. "And we're taking these with us. Kisa, how do we get to the beach?" Jenny pointed over the edge of the cliff.

"Beach?" Kisa smiled. She motioned for Jenny to follow.

"We're going to the beach," Jenny said, stuffing a few more leaves in her mouth as she walked. "See you at my party."

Kisa led her into the old adobe barn, where the Jeep and a couple of banged-up old trucks were parked.

"We're driving?" Jenny asked.

Kisa opened a doorway at the back of the garage, into a small, dark room.

"Um, this is the way to the beach?" Jenny asked.

Kisa nodded.

Jenny stepped into the doorway. Kisa raised a large trapdoor in the floor of the room, revealing a rocky hole beneath the floor. Jenny peered down into the opening. It was a sloping cave chimney, with steep steps carved into the rock. A spot of sunlight glowed far below.

"Hey, nice shortcut," Jenny said.

Kisa took a kerosene lamp from a hook on the wall and ignited it. She started down the steps, holding the lamp high. Jenny followed her down.

The cavern took them most of the way down, and then they stepped out of a small nook in the rocky cliff. There were more steps here, but they were harder to find among the thick weeds, and sometimes at strange angles to each other, as if someone had wanted them to blend with the cliff side.

Kisa removed her sandals before stepping onto the sand, so Jenny stopped and took hers off, too. The gray volcanic sand was soft under her feet.

They walked out to the edge of the ocean, letting the clear water flow around their ankles. Jenny gaped out at the endless blue ahead of her. She'd never seen so much emptiness.

"What ocean is this?" Jenny asked Kisa. "The Atlantic? Pacific?"

Kisa gave her an amused smile. "Pacific."

"Okay." That gave Jenny a slightly better idea of where she was. Somewhere in the southwest of Mexico. She opened the woven bag and took out a few more leaves. "And this is what they do? Alexander, and his boss, Papa Calzone or whatever? They grow cocaine. And they use zombies to do the work."

Kisa took the leaves from Jenny's hand, placed them in her mouth, and smiled. "Thank you."

"Oh...I guess you missed my point." The leaves inside Jenny's mouth were turning dry and bitter, so she spat them out.

Kisa pointed to Jenny's gloved hand. "Why no touching?"

"Oh...that's hard to explain," Jenny said. Thinking fast, she removed one of her gloves. Then she pressed her fingertip to the inside of her forearm. She concentrated on sending the pox to that spot in her arm, until a diseased blister opened. Then she removed her fingertip and showed Kisa the damage. The girl's eyebrows raised and her mouth dropped.

"My skin is very sensitive," Jenny said. She pointed to the damage. "Weak. My skin is very weak."

Kisa nodded slowly. She looked Jenny in the eyes. "You are

74

witch?"

"No. What? I'm telling you, I have this disease where my skin breaks and bleeds very easily." Jenny didn't like hearing the word *witch*. People who called her that usually ended up trying to lynch her in front of a courthouse.

"*La Bruja*," Kisa said. "The witch. For Alexander, for Papa Calderòn. For the dead."

Jenny knelt and rinsed her arm in the salt water. "No, not a witch."

"It's good," Kisa said. "Papa Calderòn...has many...*cómo se dice?* Witches? *Los astrólogos? Las psíquicas?*" She grew visibly frustrated, then spoke rapidly in the unfamiliar tongue Alexander used with Kisa and her family.

"I'm sorry, I don't know Spanish," Jenny said. "*Je parle...je parle un peu...français,*" Jenny attempted.

Kisa laughed. "I know..." She held her fingers a pinch apart. "English." She widened them as much as she could. "*Español.*" Then she pointed to herself. "Maya."

"Maya? That's what you speak?"

Kisa tapped her chest and smiled wide. "Maya."

"Mayan? Like the people who built the pyramids?" Jenny tried to make a pyramid shape with her hands."

Kisa nodded and copied the gesture, seeming to understand Jenny. "Maya."

"I read about Mayans in ninth grade Social Studies, but I though they were ancient. I didn't know there were still Mayans in the modern day," Jenny said.

Kisa just smiled—Jenny might have exceeded her English.

"Well, that's cool," Jenny said. She looked up and down the deserted beach. "Can we go swimming?" She pointed to the ocean and mimed swimming.

Kisa shrugged, looked up and down the beach, then smiled and nodded.

Jenny set her shoes, jeans and shirt on a boulder and waded out into the ocean in her underwear. The water was like a hot, salty bath.

Kisa glanced around again, then removed her dress and followed Jenny into the water.

"*La bruja*," Kisa said, pointing at Jenny's forearm.

Jenny looked at her inner forearm, where she'd created the bloody blister, supposedly evidence that she had some skin disorder. The blister had already healed itself, leaving no trace.

"You caught me." Jenny pointed to herself. "I am a witch."

Kisa laughed and dove into the water, swimming out and away from her. Jenny floated on her back, looking up at the expansive blue sky, the puffy white mountains of the clouds radiant with golden afternoon sunlight. Kisa seemed to understand that Jenny had strange powers, and to be perfectly okay with that.

"I'm really starting to like it here, Kisa," Jenny said. "I think I could really like it here."

CHAPTER NINE

The party began at nightfall, while the sun sank into the Pacific, filling the house and grounds of the walled compound with rich red and orange light. The burning hues of sunset lingered for an hour, and Jenny was beginning to understand why this place was called *La Casa del Fuego*—the house of fire.

Men had spent the whole day decorating the back yard with rows of potted bushes full of bright flowers, interspersed with large sculptures of skulls painted with cheerful floral designs. Candles burned everywhere, planted in neat lines along all the flower beds, or tied to the plants themselves, to light the lawn.

"What are those skulls?" Jenny asked.

"Day of the Dead decorations," Alexander said.

"Oh, I've seen that on TV," Jenny said. "It's like Halloween, right?"

"The day after," Alexander said. "The first of November. But I brought them out tonight because I knew you would like them."

"I really do," Jenny said. "They're so...scary and pretty at the same time."

Alexander sat at the head of the outdoor dining table, facing the setting sun. Jenny sat at his right hand. Kisa stood near Jenny's elbow to wait on her, and she refused Jenny's invitations to sit down and relax. Kisa also helped the elderly Noonsa, as well a couple of Mayan girls hired for the occasion, bring out wine and food from the kitchen.

Yochi and some of his cousins roasted piles of fish and shrimp over the firepit. Women brought out corn tortillas and a dark chopped-vegetable sauce that roasted the roof of Jenny's mouth, though it was delicious. Jenny sipped dark wine to cool the burning, then tried the hearts of palm in a cooler, vinegar-tasting sauce. The food was all unusual but very, very good.

"Have your dessert first. Life is short," Alexander said, sliding her a glass tray full of tiny, delicate sugar skulls decorated with shells of bright candy and circles of dark, strong chocolate, richer and thicker than any Jenny had ever tasted before. She could have eaten a hundred of the chocolates.

Alexander introduced Jenny to the headman of the nearest Mayan community, a fishing village a few miles away, and his entourage, who took some of the empty seats at the table and conversed with Alexander in their local language, which Alexander seemed to speak fluently. They all laughed, and Jenny felt a little awkward. They went on speaking in Mayan for a few minutes, occasionally looking at Jenny, occasionally laughing.

Jenny elbowed Alexander. "What are you talking about?"

"I apologize for talking business at dinner," Alexander said. "We're in the middle of building a network of clinics to serve the local villages. Some are in desperate need of basic care. They will be free to the poor, cheap to those who can afford it, donations welcome." He smiled.

"What's your part in that?" Jenny asked.

"I'm paying for it."

"Oh. That's really nice of you."

"Wait until you hear about the new village schools,"

Alexander said. "The plan is to bring in the best of Western education, specifically science and math, languages and history, and I have some ideas about how to do this cheaply. The curriculum will also integrate detailed study of Mayan history and culture. I believe in helping to strengthen the local people in their struggle against the rule of Mexico City."

Jenny had a million questions now, but he was pulled into a deep conversation with the men from the village.

Mayan musicians in bright woven costumes ornamented with tropical feathers played drums, flutes and a horn made from a conch shell, filling the party with fast-thumping music that attracted a number of party guests to dance. So far, most of the attendees were Mayan, and they wore a mixture of traditional and modern clothing.

The sun vanished into the ocean, the entire yard was lit only by candles. Costumed fire dancers performed to the music, swinging burning flames around themselves to create elaborate trace patterns in the air.

"What do you think?" Alexander asked, pouring Jenny a second glass of the spicy wine.

"This is amazing," Jenny said, watching the musicians. Dancers in tall headdresses had joined them. One had two huge white wings made of real feathers, which fanned out from his back each time he raised an arm. "Is this some kind of holiday?"

"This is your welcome party," Alexander said. "I brought everyone here to celebrate you. Still hate parties?"

"This one's pretty nice so far," Jenny admitted. Not knowing any of the guests, or their language, actually put her at ease. All she could was smile and say, *"Taal teelo,"* a greeting she'd picked up.

"I have something for you." Alexander placed a dark wooden box on the table in front of her, small enough that she could pick it up in one hand if she wanted. Its lid was engraved with a stylized image of a spotted jaguar with a squarish head and large teeth.

Jenny traced her finger over the carving. She tapped her

fingers nervously on the little box. She was a little scared to see what he was offering.

"Go ahead," Alexander said.

She slowly lifted the lid and set it aside. Inside, arranged on a bed of black velvet, was a silver bracelet wrought to look like a ring of Mayan skulls. Intricate little floral and geometrical glyphs were carved into each skull. The eyes were black opals with faint traces of blue and violet.

"Oh..." Jenny breathed. It was scary and beautiful all at once, overwhelming her. She felt her heart beating faster.

"You love it," Alexander said.

Jenny couldn't take her eyes off the bracelet. "This is really mine?"

"That's how presents work. You love it, don't you?"

"Of course." Jenny slid the bracelet onto her left wrist. It was sized to fit her perfectly. "Oh, thanks, Alexander." She looked up at him and hesitated. Her first instinct was to kiss him. But Jenny had spent a lifetime learning not to touch people, especially out of affection. She reached out an arm toward him, thinking she might give him a hug. Alexander embraced her and kissed her cheek.

Jenny laughed and pulled away. The spot where his lips had touched her face felt like it was on fire.

"Thanks," Jenny said. She studied the bracelet again, unable to look at him for fear of blushing or just losing control of herself. She struggled to ignore the deep, dangerous feelings he conjured up inside her.

"How did you know I would like this?" Jenny asked him, without daring to look at him. "A lot of girls wouldn't."

"I told you," he said. "I know you."

"I'm into skulls and death, apparently." Jenny thought of her first date with Seth, on Halloween, how much fun they'd had dressing as members of the undead and hitting the haunted houses. It had somehow been the most romantic night of her life. She tried not to think about it.

Fortunately, more guests arrived to distract her. Manuel escorted a group of four Hispanic men in dark suits and ties toward the table, and Alexander rose to greet them in Spanish. Alexander paid particular attention to one of them, a middle-aged man wearing several gold rings. The other three men were much younger than him.

"Jenny," Alexander said, "This is Ernesto Calderon, Papa Calderon's nephew."

Jenny smiled at the man and spoke one of her new Mayan greetings, which brought a bemused expression to his face. Alexander laughed.

"Maybe we should try English," Ernesto said. "I have brought someone to meet you." He nodded at his men, and they stood aside. An old Latina woman in a plain dress and some kind of black head scarf approached. She was very short, and leaned on a cane with one gnarled, trembling hand. Her mouth was wrinkled and collapsed into itself, and her sparse hair was white. She stared at Jenny with small, black eyes.

"Señora Emygdia is one of my uncle's advisors," Ernesto said, while old woman hobbled closer to Jenny. There was a horrific smell, like the rot of a dead animal, emanating from the woman, and Jenny was feeling a little scared of her. The woman raised one small, misshapen claw of a hand and pawed at the air while she stared unblinking at Jenny. This strange gesture did not put Jenny at ease.

"My uncle wishes that she study you," Ernesto said. Everyone around the dining table had fallen silent, watching the old woman and Jenny.

"Why?" Jenny asked.

"To assess you," Alexander said. "She's a holy woman. Or a very unholy woman. Whatever. A very old *bruja*. She's been sent to look you over for Papa Calderon."

The old woman reached her clawed hand towards Jenny's face.

"Um, can we warn her about the not-touching-me thing?" Jenny asked.

Alexander spoke in Spanish, and the woman drew her hand back and asked him a question. Her voice was low and hissing.

Alexander replied, and the woman's eyes opened a little wider.

She closed her eyes and waved her hand around Jenny's head and body, walking in a slow circle around Jenny. Jenny didn't know what to do, so she crossed her arms and tried to look calm.

Finally, the old woman opened her eyes. She spoke in a low, croaking voice to Ernesto. Then one of Ernesto's younger companions escorted her back inside.

Ernesto and Alexander conversed in Spanish. Ernesto frowned, with a few wary glances at Jenny, while Alexander seemed to smile wider as he spoke.

"What's happening?" Jenny asked Alexander.

"One second," Alexander said. "Kisa." The girl straightened up at the sound of her name. Alexander made a gesture with his hand, and she nodded and hurried inside.

"What did the old woman say?" Jenny asked.

"She said you had a deadly power, and you cannot be trusted," Alexander said. "Which is just how I remember you."

"Thanks," Jenny said.

Kisa returned with a large glass bottle of tequila and several shot glasses.

Ernesto took one glass and spoke to Jenny in English

"Papa Calderon welcomes you into our house," Ernesto said. "May God grant us a full harvest and a shitload of money."

Alexander raised a glass to that and motioned for Jenny to take one, too. Jenny, Alexander, Ernesto and Ernesto's two remaining companions drank together.

The tequila scalded Jenny's throat and chest, and she went into an unstoppable coughing fit. The two younger men laughed and pointed at her, which made her angry enough to glare at them. She was amazed that they actually fell silent under her look and decided to walk off for a look at the roasting deer.

Kisa pressed a glass of water into Jenny's hand. Jenny drank it down, then gave her a grateful smile. "Thanks."

Kisa returned with a different drink for Jenny, something called *taxcalate* that tasted like milk sweetened with cinnamon. This was also delicious.

More food arrived, first shrimp with tortillas and tomatoes and spicy peppered salsa, and then tender fish in a tangy tomato sauce seasoned with bright herbs, fried plantains and freshly cut mangoes. Jenny ate and drank and watched the dancers in their incredibly elaborate costumes and makeup. This whole event seemed terribly expensive to her.

She looked up and down the crowded table, where everyone was talking in either Spanish or Mayan. She felt a warm glow towards all these people, though she barely knew them. Maybe because they seemed to value the exact thing that made Jenny such a freak, and they had a place for someone like her.

After she ate, the party broke into smaller groups, and many people went to dance.

"Jenny, I have to go up to my office with Ernesto for a minute," Alexander said. "Boring stuff. Back in a minute."

"Oh, yeah." Jenny drunkenly waved him away. She invited Kisa to finally sit down and stop hovering over her. The girl hesitated.

"Come on." Jenny pointed at the chair beside her. "You're off duty. Have a drink." She held up her wineglass to Kisa.

Kisa smiled, looked around, then sat beside Jenny and poured herself some wine. Jenny clinked her glass against Kisa's, and they drank.

The wine made Jenny chatty, and so she talked to Kisa and to anyone else who came and went at the table. Though nobody really understood her, they seemed friendly enough. At one point, Kisa and Jenny managed to discuss how Jenny's gloves didn't match the beaded scarlet red dress Kisa had provided Jenny for the party. Kisa offered to make new gloves for Jenny, but Jenny insisted it would be too much trouble.

Later, Jenny staggered inside and found her way to the back stairs, which led up to the bathroom near Jenny's room. She tugged at the door handle, but it was locked, so she slumped against the wall.

She felt a little dizzy and a little panicky, too. She was in a place where everything and everyone was unfamiliar, and she had no idea how to get home from here. She wondered about her dad, whether he'd recovered from Tommy's fear-inducing touch, whether he was worried about her. And what about Seth? Did he miss Jenny...or was he relieved she was gone?

Two Latina girls in skimpy dresses stumbled out of the bathroom, laughing, and wandered away down the hall. Jenny hurried inside to use it. When she was done, she washed her hands and splashed handfuls of cool water on her face. She wanted to forget about her problems back home. Things were like a dream world here, and that was just what she needed.

When she stepped back into the hall, she smelled something burning. She followed the smell to a cloud of blue smoke hanging in front of a closed door. Somebody was smoking weed in there, and Jenny felt like joining them.

The old Jenny would have stood there for a minute, then turned away, too shy to approach strangers. But now she was filled with drunken resolve. She wasn't poor little Jenny Mittens anymore, suffering abusive songs on the playground, disdained and dismissed by everyone. She was a killer. A monster. And Alexander understood that and embraced it. Here, she could be herself, whoever that turned out to be.

Jenny pushed open the door. It wasn't a bedroom, but a large office, and Alexander himself sat with his legs crossed on top of a hand-carved wooden desk. Some of the party guests were here, seated on long leather couches, including Ernesto Calderon and two of the men who'd come with him, and a few young women in tight, low-cut dresses, including the two who'd stumbled out of the bathroom earlier. One of the girls was making out with one of Ernesto's men. The Clash pulsed out of a sleek black stereo, a very different sound from the Mayan band performing outside.

"Jenny." Alexander smiled, and smoke curled up from his mouth. He held a long wooden pipe decorated with feathers. "How do you like your party?"

"I'd like it more if you'd share." Jenny closed the door behind her and crossed the room toward Alexander, holding out one hand. Alexander grinned and passed her the pipe, and Jenny puffed on it. She coughed out a hot cloud of smoke, her eyes watering.

"Don't be so greedy," Alexander said, still smiling.

"Very funny. I needed this." Jenny took a couple more puffs and held the pipe toward Alexander, but he motioned for her to pass it to one of Ernesto's men who sat nearby. "Good stuff," Jenny commented as she handed it off. "Kind of minty."

"Only the best for my parties," Alexander said.

"Alexander, this is all great, and I'm glad you're hiding me here." Jenny's words came out slurred. "I just keep waiting for the other shoe to drop."

"It's not all parties down here. We have a lot of work to do."

"What kind of work?"

"No need to talk about it tonight," Alexander said, with a glance and a smile at Ernesto. "Tonight, we eat, drink and get fucked up."

Ernesto slapped the ass of the girl on his lap, and she giggled and stood. Ernesto pushed to his feet and approached Alexander, speaking in Spanish and grinning.

"A little more?" Alexander asked. He looked at Jenny and shrugged. "Why not?"

"A little more what?" Jenny asked.

Alexander pushed off the table and landed on his feet. Behind where he'd been sitting, an antique mirror in an ornate ebony frame lay flat on the table, though it looked like it was intended to be hung on a wall. Rows of white powder as thick as Jenny's middle finger had been laid out across it, and a razor blade and a glass straw sat at one edge of the mirror.

Jenny watched Ernesto pick up the straw and snort some powder into each nostril, consuming about half of one of the thick lines. Ernesto pinched his nose and looked up while his female companion sniffed up the rest of the line.

"Is that cocaine?" Jenny asked. She'd never done cocaine, but she knew that if you were sniffing a powder, it was probably coke or crystal meth. She'd seen cocaine once, when Ashleigh framed Jenny for using drugs at Seth's family Christmas party. Seth's parents happened to love Ashleigh and hate Jenny, so they hadn't believed the truth.

"It's our stock in trade," Alexander said. He watched one of Ernesto's men and another of the young women sniff white powder from the mirror. "The great provider of all things."

"What's it like?" she asked.

"As high-grade as anything on the market. Took a little jiggering to get it to grow this far north, but we had a top botanist on the case. We're going to make a fortune on this crop, cutting out the middleman." He laughed. "Well, we're the middleman. We're cutting out the supplier. Jenny, I can't wait to take you up and show what we have going. Things are going to pick up big with you around, though." He took her hand, and Jenny felt that dangerous electricity between them, crackling almost palpably between his palm and hers.

"But what about the law? Won't we go to jail?"

"The law is what men make of it," Alexander said. "The key is to buy the men who make the laws. Or the men who enforce them. Ideally, both. You'd be amazed how little money it takes."

"You're crazy." Jenny shook her head. There was a lot of danger lurking right under the surface here. Over on the couches, Ernesto's men had shed their suit coats, revealing large firearms holstered under their armpits. Most of the men she'd seen were armed. Part of her felt afraid to be among such people...but part of her was excited, too.

"I have to get out of here," Jenny told Alexander. "I'm going back outside."

"Wait," Alexander said, but Jenny didn't. She hurried down the hall and the steps, out past the patio full of eating and drinking and dancing and drums, past the candlelit region of the yard and into the darkness beyond. She was moving in the general direction of the barn and the dark, partially collapsed building.

She stopped when she heard snarls ahead, like wild animals ready to attack. It came from the direction of the partially collapsed building. With a thought, she summoned up the pox as strongly as she could. Blisters tore open from her fingertips to her shoulder blades. If some fierce creature meant to jump on her, she was ready.

Jenny moved closer to the sound. She couldn't see anything inside the old building. Its window and door holes showed only complete darkness, from which the snarls were rolling out.

The snarls from the building grew louder. Jenny raised her arms, ready to fight back.

Someone grabbed her shoulder, and Jenny grabbed the person's arm and pumped it full of Jenny pox. It was a purely defensive response—this was a human, not a beast, and she wouldn't have done it if she'd had time to think.

"Watch out," Alexander said. "You could kill a man that way."

"I thought something was attacking me."

"Are you sure I'm not?" he asked. The strange throaty snarls and growls sounded again from the abandoned building, louder and angrier this time.

"What's in there?" Jenny asked.

"Just some unspeakable, inhuman horrors words cannot describe. Did you have dessert?"

"I'm serious."

"I am, too. Flan with cacao sauce? You don't want to miss that."

"I'm not hungry." Jenny looked down the dark, sloping stretch of yard toward the moonlit sea. "I feel like running. Want to race me to the cliff?"

"Half the cliff's crumbled away. It's not safe."

"That's what makes it fun." Jenny let go of his arm and raced toward the cliff.

"Look out!" He chased after her. "You can't see where the wall's broken."

Jenny headed directly for the largest gap in the wall, where there was nothing but stars beyond, but she pretended not to notice at all. She was going to make him catch her. She put on speed.

"Jenny!" he called after her, running faster. "You have to

slow down!"

"You're just slow!" she yelled back over her shoulder. Jenny ran frequently in the woods on her dad's land. It was a great way to beat back stress and anxiety, to feel like you were putting the world behind you.

She lowered her head and pressed forward. The toothy, broken gap in the wall yawned in front of her. The ground there was broken and craggy. A misstep could send her tumbling down the cliff to the beach.

She heard his footsteps behind her, but realized she didn't really care whether he caught her or not. If she went over the cliff, so what? She would die and reincarnate again, bringing all her evil back with her. Even death wasn't an escape.

She reached the crumbling edge of the cliff and saw the endless dark of the ocean below, glimmering with reflected starlight. It might not be a permanent escape, but it was something.

Then his strong arm wrapped around her waist and hauled her back, just as a piece of ground broke away beneath her foot. She heard it roll and crash down the cliff.

He pulled her backward, and they collapsed on the ground, his arms around her. Alexander was panting.

"Why did you do that?" he asked.

"Why were you so slow?" Jenny touched her fingers to his chin and traced his jawline. "I could have died."

"Don't do that again. I don't want to wait another lifetime for you."

"Then you'll have to be faster." Jenny's hand found its way around to the back of his neck. She pulled herself closer to him, and then finally gave in to what her body was urging her to do—had been urging, if she was honest with herself, ever since she first saw him. She kissed him, pressing her lips hard against his lips. The tingling, electric feeling she felt whenever they touched was amplified a thousand times over.

He pulled her close against him, kissing her and grunting as they rolled in the dirt like animals in heat. His hand slipped under her dress, his fingers wrapping around her thigh. Jenny tugged at the waistband of his pants.

"Where can we go?" she whispered.

Alexander's face drew back from hers. "We shouldn't. How much wine have you had?"

"I know what I want." Jenny's voice was slurred. She rolled onto her back, pulling him on top of her. She could hear the waves crash below them.

"You know what you want right now. Tomorrow you could change your mind." Alexander stood up, brushing away dirt. "It shouldn't happen like this. I want you to respect me in the morning."

Jenny sat up on her elbows. "You're kidding, right?"

He smiled in the moonlight and offered his hand to help her up. Jenny ignored it as she stood.

"Come on, Alexander," she said. "Don't you like me?"

"That's what I'm trying to show you." He took her hand and led her back to the party.

CHAPTER TEN

Seth sat in his room on Monday morning, looking at pictures
of Jenny on his laptop. He'd taken them with his Blackberry,
which had somehow gone missing during the weekend in
Charleston. One of them showed her in a long, old-fashioned
white dress, laid out in a patch of golden sun on one of the huge
boulders in the woods behind her house. Her eyes were closed
and she was smiling. Tiny, flowering weeds grew from cracks in
the rock.

He had called Jenny's house Sunday evening, but nobody
answered. He left a message on the raspy old answering machine.

Seth worried that Jenny had been swept up by the police in
the riot, like a lot of other people, but surely they would have let
her use the phone by now to call her dad. Seth called the jail
anyway to check, but they didn't have a Jenny Morton.

Seth wondered where she might have gone. She obviously
wasn't with her new BFF Darcy, since he'd last seen Darcy getting
picked up by her parents at jail, and Darcy didn't seem to have

92

any idea where to find Jenny. Darcy had even called her "Jenny Mittens," as if they'd never been friends. Seth couldn't imagine where Jenny might have gone, unless she'd just gotten in her car and started driving, maybe angry at Seth and wanting to escape everything. She was somewhere on her own now, and Seth worried about her.

There was nothing left for him to do, though, so he was reduced to just looking at pictures of her and feeling anguish over what he'd done with that random girl in Charleston.

Then he heard the thunderous pounding on the front door, and the sound of boots. Seth ran to a front window and looked out.

On the driveway below, several Homeland Security vehicles had arrived, including a couple of small trucks. Men in black body armor and gas masks were rushing inside the front doors of his house. He wondered how they'd even opened the front gate—maybe they had some kind of device that could mimic the remote control signal for gates like theirs.

Seth panicked, wondering if he should run or hide. His mom was home, though, so he couldn't just disappear.

"Uh, Mom?" Seth called down the back stairs. He'd last seen his mom in the family room, drinking wine and watching some movie with Drew Barrymore. His dad was away at the bank. "Somebody's here!"

Two men in gas masks arrived at the foot of the stairs and began racing up toward Seth. "Don't move!" one of them shouted. His voice was full of electric crackles, transmitted by radio from inside his mask to a speaker mounted on the exterior.

Seth's natural reaction to armed masked men charging up his stairs was to turn and run, so he did that, but another pair of Homeland Security guys were already waiting in the upstairs hall. They were closing in on him from both sides, and he had nowhere to escape. He stopped and held up his hands.

The men who'd pursued him up the stairs seized him and slammed him hard against the wall, so that Seth saw sparks behind his eyes. They wrenched his hands behind him and bound them with some kind of hard plastic zip ties. Then they slammed his face into the wall again.

"What did I say to you?" one of them asked over his radio. "I said don't move. That means you don't fucking move." They pulled Seth back, then slammed him into the wall a third time. Seth felt his nose pop, and tasted a hot stream of blood that spilled over his lips.

They hauled him downstairs to the library, where his mother was already seated in one of the old wingback chairs, her hands bound in front of her with one of the industrial-strength plastic zip ties. She gasped when she saw Seth's face.

"What did you do to him?" she demanded.

"He resisted." They threw Seth onto the rug in front of the fireplace, and then pointed the snout of a machine gun at his head.

"I want to call my attorney," Seth's mother said.

"Afraid not," one of the masked Homeland Security guys replied. "We're not here under a search warrant. We're here under a national security letter. That means you can't call anybody, and you can't tell anybody we were here."

"That's crazy!" she replied.

"It's the law."

Three of the masked men stayed with them, their guns pointed at Seth and his mother, while the others joined the mob searching through the house. Seth heard glass breaking and the loud thuds of furniture being overturned.

"What do you want?" Seth asked.

"I think you know who we're looking for," the federal cop said. "Tell us where she is."

"I don't know!" Seth said.

"Seth, what in the world is he talking about?" Seth's mom asked.

"I don't know," Seth repeated, more quietly this time.

They spent an hour searching the house and grounds while the three men watched Seth and his mother in the library. Finally, a small group of the Homeland Security officers returned to the library, and one of them peeled off his gas mask, revealing a middle-aged man with graying hair.

"Okay, we're getting tired of this," he said to Seth. "Tell me where she is."

"I don't know where she is," Seth said.

"Who?" Seth's mom asked.

"Jennifer Morton," the older man replied. "Where is she?"

"The Morton kid?" Seth's mom asked. "That's what all this is about?"

"Tell us where to find her."

"If you let me look in my husband's office, I can probably find her address. Her father does some repair work for us now and then—"

"We've already been to the Mortons' hovel out in the woods," the man said. "Nobody home. We believe she is attempting to evade custody."

"What did she do?" Seth's mom asked.

"That's not relevant," he replied.

"You broke into my house and assaulted my son," she said. "I think I deserve to know why."

The gray-haired Homeland Security man sighed. "I want to interrogate them separately. Move the kid out of here."

Two of the masked men grabbed Seth up and stood him on his feet, then marched him from the room.

"Where are you taking him? Bring him back!" Seth's mom shouted.

"Ma'am, you're going to have to shut the hell up," the older Homeland Security man said.

"We're going to bury you in the biggest lawsuit you've ever seen before this is through," she told him. "We'll get you fired."

"Good luck with that." The Homeland Security man followed Seth and his armed escorts down the hall. They opened the double doors to the dining room and dragged Seth inside.

A woman was already sitting at the center of the long table, dressed in a yellow hazmat suit with the CDC logo printed on it. She'd removed her hood and gloves, as if they'd determined there was no threat here, and she was typing at a laptop. She looked up when they entered the room.

Seth recognized her—she was the CDC doctor who'd come to Jenny's house during the quarantine, and left with samples of Seth and Jenny's hair and blood. Seth wondered what she'd found.

"What's up, Doc?" Seth asked her.

"Sit down," the gray-haired Homeland Security man said, and the two masked men pushed Seth into the chair across from Heather.

"You remember me, Seth?" the doctor asked.

"Dr. Reynard," he said. "You're an epidemicist."

"Epidemiologist," she corrected. "I apologize for the wreck they made of your house. I wanted a much more subtle approach, but who listens to me? How are you feeling? It looks like they got you pretty bad. I should check you for trauma—"

"We're searching for a fugitive," the Homeland Security man interrupted. "We don't want to give anyone advance warning."

"Well, you're not doing a great job," Seth said. "She hasn't been here in days."

"Seth, just tell us where to find Jenny," Dr. Reynard said. "That's all we want from you. Then these guys will leave your family alone."

"I really don't know where she is right now. I already told them that."

"When did you last see her?" the Homeland Security man asked.

"Thursday, I think," Seth replied.

"Where?"

"We went swimming at the reservoir. We had a fight. I haven't seen her since. What is all this about, anyway?" Seth asked, though he was pretty sure he knew—two hundred dead bodies discovered on the town square of Fallen Oak, all of them festering with Jenny pox.

"We're asking the questions," the Homeland Security man said. "Did she mention any plans? Where she might be going?"

"No. I'm surprised she wasn't at home. Hey, I don't know why you're here, but you must be looking for the wrong person. Jenny hasn't done anything illegal."

Dr. Reynard's eyes narrowed. "I want to talk to him alone."

"Not until he answers a few questions," the Homeland Security man said.

She glared at him. "I'll get your answers."

The man looked from her to Seth, then shrugged. "You got twenty minutes." He stepped towards the double doors.

"These guys, too." Dr. Reynard pointed to the two masked guards with their guns trained on Seth.

"I'm supposed to provide you security," he said.

"Seth's not the threat," Dr. Reynard. "Besides, you've got him restrained. Just leave the guards outside the door."

He sighed. "It's your ass, doctor." He waved, and the two masked men followed him out and closed the doors.

"This is pretty strange work for a doctor." Seth smiled at her. He'd learned that a little flirting went a long way when he was dealing with older women.

"Where is she, Seth?"

"I really don't know."

"Which is what you would say even if you did know," Dr. Reynard said.

"True," Seth replied. "But, lucky me, I don't even have to lie. I've been looking for her, too. Is she in some legal trouble?"

Dr. Reynard stared at him for a minute, then scowled. "Don't even give me that."

"Give you what?"

"I know Jenny is an immune carrier of a fatal pathogen," she said. "I know she killed two hundred people right here in your town, right in front of the courthouse. Don't bother putting on some show for me. Don't you care anything about those dead people? Their families?"

"I thought those people died from some kind of chemical leak," Seth replied. "The news said so."

"Don't be cute."

"I can't help it."

"Asshole!" Dr. Reynard stood up and paced along the dark

paneled wall of the dining room. "I have more than two hundred corpses we're holding in deep freeze. I have some minor cases of the same disease—we picked those up in Charleston, so I know she was there Saturday night. So were you. We found the hotel on your credit card history."

"I was just there for college orientation. You can probably find that out, too, since apparently nothing's private anymore."

"And I have a couple dozen walking corpses. Want to explain that to me?"

"Walking corpses?" Seth asked.

"I'm getting tired of the stupid act, Seth." Dr. Reynard tapped at her laptop, then turned it to face him.

On the screen, Seth watched a security camera video—black and white, date-stamped, the movements jerky because the camera clearly only took a couple of frames per second.

It was a wide corridor, probably in a hospital, judging by the beds stored against one wall. A longhaired young man in black sunglasses, a white T-shirt and jeans led a group of assorted other people. Something was wrong with how the rest of the group moved—sluggish, dragging their feet. Some of them had huge and obvious wounds in their heads or torsos, which looked like they should have been fatal. They each dragged a black body bag in one hand and held some kind of blunt object—broom handles, broken lighting fixtures—in the other.

"Here's something else you need to explain," Dr. Reynard said. "Some guy walks into a morgue. He somehow animates a group of dead bodies, and they march out into the street. Later we find the bodies in a heap in an upper-class neighborhood in downtown Charleston. They didn't even bother climbing into their body bags for us."

"That's pretty crazy," Seth said. As he watched the looped footage of the dead bodies shuffling through the corridor, his blood turned icy and a knot formed in his guts.

He'd heard once before of somebody who could animate the dead—Seth's own great-grandfather, who had used zombie labor to work his more remote fields. Seth had only recently learned this from his father.

"You know something," Dr. Reynard said.

Seth just gaped and shook his head.

"Say something," Dr. Reynard said. "Who is this guy, Seth?"

He used to be one of my ancestors, Seth thought. *Now he's back in a new body, with a new name.*

"I've never seen him before," Seth told her.

"Bullshit."

"Who is he?" Seth asked.

"I want you to tell me everything," she said.

"About what?"

"Here's what I think, Seth. I think Jenny was planning to see how much damage she could really do, how many people she could wipe out at once. And when the heavy Homeland Security presence showed up, you people somehow started this riot as a smokescreen to help her escape. And she slipped away—if not with you, then with him." She tapped the young man on the screen.

"With him?" Seth asked, feeling alarmed. If this guy really was the reincarnation of the first Jonathan Seth Barrett, then he might be very dangerous. Seth's great-grandfather had been a tyrannical man, feared by his own children and grandchildren.

"Do I have things right so far?" Dr. Reynard asked.

"Definitely not. Jenny would never want to hurt anybody."

"Except your neighbors here in town. The mayor, the police...a lot of kids from your school. Guys you used to play sports with." Her eyes narrowed. "She's a mass murderer, Seth. You seem like a decent kid. I can't believe you'd protect someone with so much innocent blood on their hands."

"Innocent?" Seth snapped. "How would you know? What if it was a lynch mob screaming about witchcraft? What if they tried to kill her, and she was just defending herself?"

"Is that what happened? A lynch mob?" Dr. Reynard drummed her fingers on the table for a minute. "So that's why nobody in town wanted to talk. They didn't want to tell us about their relatives trying to kill a teenage girl. Is that it?"

"It was just an example." Seth tried to make himself calm down, but the things she'd said about Jenny were getting under his skin.

"A pretty specific example. So your view is that Jenny acted in self-defense?"

Seth took a deep breath to calm himself. He needed to be smart about this. "Jenny didn't do anything."

"Aren't we a little past that now, Seth?" she asked. "I know Jenny has something deadly. I watched her blood cells destroy healthy cells under a microscope. Honestly, I'm getting sick of all this horror-movie crap. Diseases with no vector. Zombies marching through the streets of Charleston. I want a straight story from you."

"You wouldn't believe a straight story from me."

"I'm all ears." She stared at him, waiting.

After a minute, Seth shrugged. "There's nothing to tell."

"Fine. You can get charged with two hundred counts of murder along with your girlfriend. I'm pretty sure they have the death penalty in this state."

"She's not even my girlfriend. She broke up with me last week."

"Did she?" Dr. Reynard rolled her eyes.

"Seriously. She was mad at me because I'm leaving for college. And that was it."

"Why doesn't she infect you, Seth? Are you immune? Or can she decide when she's contagious and when she isn't?"

"Infect me with what?"

"The Jenny pox."

Seth flinched a little at that. How did Heather know those words?

"Talk to me, Seth."

"You want me to talk?" Seth asked. "I'll talk. You people just ripped through our house for no reason. You come in here and talk to me about zombies? Zombies? And accusing my ex-girlfriend of murder, when everybody knows it was some crazy chemical leak?"

"Come on, Seth—"

"Maybe you didn't check into my family," Seth said. He leaned forward, pressing his counterattack. "My great-uncle Junius Mayfield is a sitting United States senator. He's not going to like hearing how his niece and her son were attacked in their own home for no reason. If I were you, I'd stop harassing people with your crazy ideas. We can bring the hammer down on you. We can destroy you. Who are you to go to war with my family? You're a nobody."

Dr. Reynard was deep red and shaking with rage. "You're not going to get away with anything. And neither is Jenny." She stood, slammed her laptop closed, and tucked it under her arm. "My job is to find and eliminate threats to public health, and that's what I'm going to do. I don't care who you are or who you know. The President has declared this a national security issue. Now go whine about that to your uncle."

She pushed open one of the double doors and stormed out. "He's all yours," she told the two guards, who had removed their gas masks. The two of them stepped into the dining room, weapons raised toward Seth. For a moment, he wondered if they were actually going to shoot him.

"Women are crazy, huh?" Seth asked. They didn't respond. "Hey, nice guns. What kind are they?"

The Homeland Security men just stared at him coldly.

***

Later, Seth and his mom watched from the wreckage of their foyer as the federal police vehicles pulled out of their driveway.

"Did they hurt you any more?" his mom asked.

"No."

"They kept asking me questions about that Morton girl," she said. "'Where is she? Where did she go? Where do we find her?' Just the same thing over and over."

"Mine went pretty much the same way," Seth said.

"I knew that girl was bad news, but I had no idea how terrible she was. What do you think she did, Seth?"

"I think they have the wrong person."

"Your father and I keep telling you to stay away from her. You'd better listen now. God only knows what crazy things she must be doing to have Homeland Security after her like that."

"They make mistakes, too," Seth said. "Jenny's never done anything bad."

"You're too trusting of people, Seth." She looked around at the mess of toppled furniture, and she glowered. Then she took her cell phone from her purse.

"Who are you calling?" he asked.

"Silas," she told him. Silas Deever was the family's personal attorney. "And then your father. And then, maybe Uncle Junius."

"The guy said it was a national security letter," Seth said. He didn't want his father—or his great uncle Senator Mayfield—digging into this and finding out exactly why the feds were after Jenny. "That means you can't tell anybody they were here."

"Like hell I can't," his mom said, and she started making phone calls.

Seth had a sinking feeling. He wished he could get in touch with Jenny to warn her about how seriously they were searching for her, and how they might kill her the moment they found her. But he still had no idea where she could be. He just hoped she was safe.

CHAPTER ELEVEN

When Seth's dad came home, Seth just played dumb—he had no idea why Homeland Security would be searching for Jenny. He kept up the act on the conference call they had with Silas Deever, who advised them that there was little they could do to get compensation for the extensive damages to their house, but he would look into it.

Then Seth's mother took Seth to the hospital to get his nose checked out, though Seth assured her he wasn't hurt badly. By the time they reached the emergency room, his nose wasn't even swollen. Seth's healing powers had fixed him up quickly.

The next morning, Seth decided to call Darcy Metcalf again, since she was the only person who might have any information about Jenny. The girl had claimed to remember nothing, but that was in front of her parents. Maybe she could give Seth some idea of where Jenny had gone.

He'd lost Darcy's cell number along with his Blackberry, though, so he had to look up the Metcalfs' home number in the local phonebook. He dialed, and Darcy's dad answered.

"Can I speak to Darcy, please?" Seth asked.

"Who is this?" her dad barked over the phone.

"This is..." Seth almost gave his own name, then remembered how much Darcy's dad seemed to hate him. "This is...Hank."

"Hank? Who the hell is Hank? Why are you calling my daughter?"

Seth remembered something Darcy's dad had said at the jail: *She's gonna take that job at the Taco Bell in Vernon Hill, she knows what's good for her.* "This is Hank from Taco Bell," Seth said.

"Oh, the Taco Bell! Finally." Then Seth heard him scream: "Darcy! Pick up the damned phone! It's the Taco Bell!"

Darcy picked up another extension. "Hello?"

"Don't screw this up, Darcy," her dad said. "You need to get your ass a job."

"*Daddy!*" Darcy said. "He can hear you!"

"Well, it's true, Hank from Taco Bell," Darcy's dad said. "You hire her, she'll work hard, pregnant or not. She works hard around the house, worked hard in school, up til she got knocked up by that no-good boy —"

"Dad, please!" Darcy said. Her dad finally hung up.

"Darcy, it's Seth Barrett," Seth said.

"Oh, jeepers," Darcy said. "What do you want?"

"I need to talk to you." Seth wondered if Homeland Security was listening to his phone calls. "Can you meet me somewhere?"

"I don't want any part of your witchcraft, Seth Barrett," Darcy said.

"My what?"

"I know you and Jenny are in league with Satan."

Seth was confused—Jenny and Darcy had become friends, even had sleepovers together. Now it was like someone had pushed rewind and loaded up an older version of Darcy.

"I want to talk about what happened in Charleston," Seth said.

"Do you know how I even got there?" Darcy asked. "I can't remember a gosh-blamed thing. And my dad's all angry about it. He says I ran off with you, but I don't remember doing that."

"We can talk about all that," Seth said. "So can you meet me?"

"I guess," Darcy said. "But it has to be somewhere public. And somewhere my dad won't see us together." Her voice dropped to a whisper. "For some reason, he thinks I've been having sex with you."

"Oh," Seth said. "Well, just name a place."

Thirty minutes later, Seth sat in a plastic booth at the Taco Bell in Vernon Hill. He watched Darcy fill out a Taco Bell employment application.

"'Work experience,'" Darcy read. "My dad gives me a lot of work at home, and I've done tons of volunteering for church and things. You suppose that counts?"

"The church stuff might help," Seth said. "So, what do you remember about this weekend, Darcy?"

"Nothing!" She looked up from the form. "You're supposed to tell me what happened. That's why I'm here. Well, and the job application."

"I was going to Charleston for college orientation," Seth said. "You told me you were going to the same college and you needed a ride to orientation."

"I wish I were going to *any* college," Darcy said. "Stupid Taco Bell."

"Why did you tell me that?" Seth asked.

"I don't *know*! How many times can I say I don't know what happened? It's all a fuzzy haze and nothing makes sense."

"Then what's the last thing you remember?"

Darcy looked at him for a long time, tucking her lower lip under her teeth and gnawing on it. "I don't know if I should tell you."

"Who else can you tell?" Seth asked. She looked pretty upset, he thought, so she must have something to share.

"Well...okay." Darcy looked around the Taco Bell, then lowered her head and spoke in a whisper. "They said they were angels."

"Who?"

"Both of them." Darcy looked around again, though the dining area was empty except for a very elderly couple arguing over the small Nachos Supreme they were sharing. "One said he was Tommy Goodling."

"Goodling?"

"I believed him 'cause he had beautiful gray eyes, just like Ashleigh's. And he reminded me of her a little bit."

"Who is Tommy Goodling?"

"Ashleigh's cousin. Well, he said he was Ashleigh's cousin. But later he said that he and the girl were both angels."

"Who was the girl?"

"Some Mexican girl that was with him. And anywho, he told me that Ashleigh Goodling had a special task to do on Earth, but since she was dead, she had to..."

"She had to do what?"

"This is going to sound weird."

"Everything's weird these days. Believe me."

"They said I had to let her use my body for a little while," Darcy said.

"And you agreed to that?"

"They were angels! Or they said they were."

"You believed them?"

"You don't understand, Seth. When he touched me, I felt..." Darcy shivered and crossed her arms.

"Horny?"

"No, Dumbo! I was afraid. Not just afraid, but *really* afraid, like trembling in awe. Just like in the Bible, when God or an angel has a message for somebody. I've never felt so afraid in my life. When he touched me, I knew he was *something*." Darcy frowned. "But now I think maybe he wasn't an angel. Maybe he was a demon sent from Satan."

"Maybe," Seth said. "So you're saying they wanted to put Ashleigh's soul in your body? Like *The Exorcist*? A possession?"

"But it couldn't really have been Ashleigh's soul," Darcy said. "She was rude and used a lot of swear words at my parents. And stole my dad's credit card. That doesn't sound like the Ashleigh I know. It was probably some demon. Some girl-demon, I think."

Girl-demon, Seth thought. *Sounds like Ashleigh to me.* "So all this time, you've had Ashleigh controlling you?"

"Somebody claiming to be Ashleigh," Darcy said. "But really an evil spirit, maybe."

Seth thought about how Darcy had become friendly with Jenny and gotten close to her. It was Ashleigh, pretending to be poor, awkward, friendless Darcy so Jenny wouldn't be too suspicious of her. Thoughts whirled in his mind—Ashleigh and her opposite Tommy must have set some kind of trap for Jenny. The zombie-maker, the guy who was possibly the reincarnation of Seth's great-grandfather, had been involved, too, but he couldn't be sure how.

"And then what happened?" Seth asked.

"I said okay, I would help out Ashleigh and the angels," Darcy said. "Then the Mexican girl angel took my hand."

"And then?"

"Next thing I remember, I was at the hotel in Charleston, getting picked up by the cops. Everything in between is just like little bits and pieces of dreams that don't make any sense." She looked down at the job application again. "Shootsy. Who can I put as a reference? All the main people at church are gone."

"Did they tell you where they came from?" Seth asked. "Tommy and the other girl? Or where they were going?"

Darcy shook her head. "Heaven, I guess. Or Hell, if they were really demons and not angels."

"Did they say what Ashleigh was going to accomplish while she had your body?"

"No, just that it was very important."

"What else can you tell me about them?"

"That's all I know, Seth." She looked up at him. "So I asked you to take me to Charleston with you?"

"Yes."

"And you said yes?"

"I did."

"Um...we stayed in a hotel together?" she asked.

He nodded.

"So did we, you know...?" she blushed.

"Oh, no, we had separate rooms. It was a suite."

"Oh." Darcy looked down. "'Cause it's okay if we did, you know. I mean, I wouldn't feel too bad about it."

"We didn't, I promise."

"Yeah. Why would you want to...do *that*...with a big fat ugly girl, anyway?" Darcy shoved to her feet. She was sweaty from the humidity and the weight of her advanced pregnancy. "I have to go turn this in. Thanks for telling me what a total jacktard I've been."

"Darcy, you're not ugly," Seth said.

"Just leave me alone, Seth," Darcy told him. "I'm tired of everybody treating me like crap." Then she lumbered to the front counter and smiled as she turned in her application to work at Taco Bell.

Seth looked down at the chili cheese burrito on his tray, still untouched in its paper wrapper. He was still confused, but Darcy had given him a lot to chew on. Somehow, Ashleigh's opposite had brought Ashleigh back and put her in Darcy's body. The unnamed Mexican girl seemed to be part of that. Darcy had mentioned taking that girl's hand, so the girl's power seemed to depend on touch, too, just like Seth and Jenny, and like Ashleigh and Tommy.

He didn't know how everything fit together, but he was starting to make some guesses. Ashleigh had taken over Darcy's body and somehow lured Jenny down to Charleston. Ashleigh's opposite, Tommy, might have used his power to induce fear in order to start the riot, creating a smokescreen against the government agencies that were also looking for Jenny. It would also be easier to kidnap someone in the middle of a riot, when craziness and violence were happening everywhere.

Then, maybe, the zombie-maker had moved in to capture Jenny. Maybe people who were already dead were immune to Jenny pox, in which case the zombies would have done the actual seizing of Jenny.

He didn't like the picture that was emerging at all. He'd been thinking Jenny was just avoiding him because he'd hooked up with that girl in Charleston. Now it looked like Ashleigh and her opposite had teamed up with two others of their kind in order to capture Jenny. He wondered where they all were now, and what they were doing to Jenny, and how he could possibly hope to track them down.

Seth was sure of one thing: if Ashleigh Goodling was back in the world, then Jenny was in a lot of danger.

CHAPTER TWELVE

Ashleigh studied herself in the mirror as she applied lip gloss. She could see the reflection of Tommy behind her, sprawled on Esmeralda's bed in his underwear, smoking a cigarette and flicking the ashes in the sill of the open window.

"You look slutty," he said.

"Too slutty?" Ashleigh asked. She checked herself out—low-cut blouse, short skirt, a band of brown skin visible between them. High heels.

"Depends what you're planning to do," Tommy said.

"I plan to volunteer and then get hired."

"Guess it depends whether it's a dude or a chick making the decision."

"It's a dude," Ashleigh said. "I do my research."

"Why can't I come with you? We don't have to show up together, they don't have to know we're together. I can help you out."

Ashleigh applied mascara. "Tommy, I think you're still pretty rough around the edges for this work. You're going to need some training."

"I'm not a dog."

"Polishing, then."

"I'm not a piece of furniture, either." Tommy shoved off the bed and came up behind her, grabbing her around the waist. She could feel him getting hard, poking his way up under her skirt. "I'm a man."

"Stop it. You're sleeping with Esmeralda, not with me." Ashleigh smiled at him anyway. She enjoyed the time they spent in bed together, when she pretended to let Esmeralda's personality out to play. Tommy never seemed to mind that "Esmeralda" was more interested in sex than in conversation.

"I can only see her when I look at you," he said. "Let her out for a minute before you go." He kissed her neck. "Esmeralda, are you in there?"

Ashleigh pulled away from him. "If you're such a man, why don't you get a job?"

"I don't do jobs." Tommy flopped back on the bed. "Don't like people ordering me around. I get enough of that from you."

"Then get a hobby," Ashleigh said. "Do something with yourself. We've been here a week and all you've done is smoke and drink and fuck."

"That's the life," Tommy said. He pulled a thick wad of cash from his pocket, from a couple of muggings he'd committed on the way across the country, plus a gas station he'd robbed in New Mexico. "If this is because you need money—"

"It isn't," Ashleigh said, though she took several bills from him anyway. "If I'm going to do what I plan to do, and you're going to be Esmeralda's boyfriend, you have to do something respectable. It doesn't have to be great. Just legal."

"I'd rather talk to Esmeralda about this."

"Plus, you're an escaped convict," Ashleigh said. "You need to keep a low profile. You can't just be robbing people every time you need cash."

"That's what I do," Tommy said. "How do you expect me to get a job? I can't use my Social Security number, the cops'll find me."

"We're in a city full of illegal immigrants with jobs," Ashleigh said. "Figure it out. It's not like you're busy all day." She turned to face him. "How do I look?"

"You better not sleep with anyone else," Tommy said. "That's Esmeralda's body. Get laid when you've got your own."

"I'll take that as a *You look great, Ashleigh, and good luck today!*"

Ashleigh said. She kissed him on the cheek. "I have to go. We can let Esmeralda out to play when I get home. Okay?"

"Hurry the fuck back, then."

Ashleigh walked out through the tiny living room/kitchen and into the parking lot. A short but very muscular Latino man leaning against a low-riding black Acura stood up when she emerged from the apartment, and he folded his arms and scowled at her.

Ashleigh tried to ignore him and hurry to the bus stop, but he stepped onto the sidewalk and blocked her way.

"What are you doing?" he asked. "Just going to pretend you don't see me?"

"Sorry?" Ashleigh looked closer and realized that this must be Pedro, Esmeralda's boyfriend. Ashleigh recognized him from the pictures in the living room and in Esmeralda's mother's bedroom, though oddly Esmeralda didn't have any pictures of him displayed in her own room. "Oh, hi, Pedro."

"'Oh, hi, Pedro?' That's it?"

"What do you want?"

"What do *I* want? What do *I* want? The same thing as your mother wants. I want you to tell us where the hell you've been all this time, and get rid of that filthy gringo you brought back with you. He scares your mother, do you know that?"

"Everything scares my mother." Ashleigh shrugged.

His eyes narrowed. "You've changed. There's something different about you. Your eyes. Did you get contacts?"

"So what?" Ashleigh said. "Get out of my way, Pedro. I'm busy."

"Too busy for me. But not too busy for him." He pointed his chin at her apartment. "What good is he? Your mother says he's got no job, *nada.*"

"I like him. So, go away." Ashleigh tried to pass around him, but Pedro seized her arm and squeezed it hard enough to bruise the bone, and she cried out in pain.

"I love you, Esmeralda," he said, his eyes burning into her. Clenching both her arms now, Pedro sank to his knees in front of her. "I want to marry you. Say you'll marry me, right now."

"Let me go, jerk!" Ashleigh said.

"Not until you say yes. I know it's the right thing. I can feel it. You and me, together—"

"Take your hands off her." Tommy must have been watching

through the window, because he came out of the apartment and walked quickly toward Pedro.

"You!" Pedro snarled. He stood up, let go of Ashleigh and raised his fists. "You get out of here. Esmeralda is mine."

"Not anymore," Tommy said.

Pedro charged. Tommy dodged his first punch, then hit him in the face. Pedro ducked low and jabbed two quick punches into Tommy's stomach. Tommy staggered back, clutching his guts, and Pedro decked him in the face.

"Had enough?" Pedro asked.

Tommy shoved Pedro back into his car, and Pedro's head thumped on the Acura's windshield. Pedro swung at Tommy, but Tommy turned his head and let it glance off his cheek. Then he seized Pedro's throat in one hand, pressing his head back on the windshield.

Ashleigh watched Pedro's eyes swell wide with fear.

"You're never going to bother her again," Tommy snarled. "Understand?"

"Fuck...you..." Pedro managed to say, though he was trembling badly.

Tommy flung him to the concrete and dealt a series of sharp kicks to Pedro's abdomen and head. Pedro curled up, bleeding from his mouth and nose.

"Are we clear now?" Tommy asked. Pedro just shivered on the ground, staring up at him.

Ashleigh leaned over Pedro. "Sorry, guy. I just don't like you. You're too annoying. And short." Then she turned her back on him and kissed Tommy. "Thanks for protecting me. I have to catch the bus."

As she walked away, she heard Pedro mutter the word "bitch" under his breath. Tommy kicked him again.

Ashleigh rode one of the city buses, checking her face a few times in a compact mirror. She wanted to look her best. Fortunately, Esmeralda was decently cute, so that gave her something to work with.

Ashleigh was getting worried about the lack of news from Charleston. They'd set up the riot successfully, and the last time she'd seen Jenny Mittens, the crowd was closing in all around her. Ashleigh had been in a hurry to get out of town, because Jenny had killed Ashleigh on her last rampage.

According to the news, there had been a riot, but not any fatalities. There was no talk, even on the Internet, about tons of people dying or suffering horrific disease. Either the government had decided to cover this one up, too—which would be extremely difficult, with all those thousands of witnesses—or, even more ridiculous, maybe Jenny just hadn't fought back, and had allowed the mob to beat her to death. But again, there weren't any reported deaths.

Ashleigh's plan must have had a flaw somewhere, but she couldn't tell where it was. She'd set up the same conditions that made Jenny flip out in Fallen Oak, but it looked like she hadn't gotten the same results. What had changed? Had Jenny herself changed, so that she wouldn't even defend herself?

As she stepped off the bus, Ashleigh try to clear those worries from her mind. She had work to do.

Her destination was obvious—a large space in a strip mall, the windows papered with posters that read "Brazer for Senate." Eddie Brazer was a current U.S. Representative, looking to take an open Senate seat in the upcoming election. The President only had a 35% approval rating nationally, and 19% in California. Brazer was part of the opposition party expected to gain more seats in the House and take over the Senate. He looked like a good horse to ride.

The inside of the office buzzed like a beehive. People sat at long tables, folding and stuffing mailers or talking on telephone headsets. Ashleigh smiled at everyone she saw, but made a direct path to the office at the back.

A man in his thirties sat behind the desk, typing as he looked among three computer monitors. She knew his name was Freddy Sanchez, and he managed this campaign office for the Congressman.

"Hi there," Ashleigh said, knocking on the open door as she entered. He looked up at her and squinted his eyes.

"Do I know you?" he asked.

"I'm Esmeralda," Ashleigh said. "I'm here to volunteer."

"Donna handles volunteers." He pointed over her shoulder to the crowded main room.

"Oh, I'm so lost." Ashleigh moved closer, bumping her hip against the side of the desk, and she lay her hand on top of his. Love poured out from her into him, and his pupils dilated and a drunken grin spread over his face. "Can't you help me at all?"

"I suppose I could do something." His eyes flicked down her body to her short skirt. "What kind of volunteer work would you like to do?"

"Just anything to help Congressman Brazer." Ashleigh squeezed the man's hand. "He's so involved in issues that I'm passionate about. Like the environment, and inner-city education...Homeland Security, that's important, too..."

"You've studied his record a little." Sanchez smiled.

"I've studied it *a lot*," Ashleigh told him. "I think he'd be such a good senator. We need people like him to take care of the country. Don't you think?"

"Of course." Sanchez took her hand. "We'd be happy to have you. Let me just get some information for our database."

Ashleigh sat across from him and leaned back in the chair, letting him get a good look at Esmeralda's thighs.

"Name?" he asked.

"Esmeralda Medina Rios."

"Phone number?"

"You want my phone number?" Ashleigh giggled.

"It's strictly professional," he said, but he was starting to blush.

"Well, we'll try to keep it that way." Ashleigh winked.

He took her phone number and address. She held his arm as he led her out to one of the long tables, where people separated by flimsy dividers talked on telephone headsets and tapped at computers. A few heads turned and eyebrows raised at the young woman clinging to the office manager.

"Just have a seat at this station." He kept his hand on Ashleigh's shoulder as she took the cheap, hard office chair. With his other hand, he opened an application on the computer. "The system calls potential donors for you. All you have to do is follow the script."

"I can do that."

"Here's your headset. I can put that on for you," he said. Ashleigh smiled as he slid the headset into place and adjusted the microphone in front of her mouth. She pressed his hand against her cheek.

"Will I ever have a chance to actually meet him?" she asked, looking up at him.

"Sure. The congressman stops by occasionally for meet-and-greets with the volunteers."

"I just want to tell him how important he is to people in my community."

"And I'm sure he'd like to hear that." He beamed down at Ashleigh. "I'll make sure to introduce you."

"Thanks," Ashleigh said, and winked. He watched her as the

autodialer system connected her to a past donor. Ashleigh read from the screen: "Hi, Mr. Wilson? I'm calling on behalf of Brazer for Senate. Representative Brazer appreciates your past generosity, and hopes you will support his bid to bring his vision for a brighter, greener America to the U.S. Senate..."

CHAPTER THIRTEEN

At breakfast, Alexander gave Jenny a blank postcard featuring the Space Needle.

"To send your father," he explained. "You said you didn't want to worry him."

"What do I tell him?" Jenny was feeling sickly from the wine and liquor, and embarrassed at how she'd thrown herself at him during the party. She hoped he didn't bring it up.

"Anything," Alexander said. "Tell him the open road beckoned. Tell him you're alive and fine. Just don't tell him where you really are. It'll be postmarked Seattle when he gets it."

Jenny took the pen he offered and wrote a quick note to her dad, assuring him he was fine. Alexander passed it off to Manuel, who carried it out of sight.

Jenny poked at her eggs, then sipped coffee. "I don't feel like eating. My stomach's all, you know."

"I bet. You were wild last night. Do you always hit it that hard?"

"Only when I'm in Mexico, on the run from the law. What are we doing today?"

118

"Visiting the zombie farm."

"Sounds creepy," Jenny said.

They left the breakfast for the staff to clean up. In the front drive, Manuel had parked a pick-up truck with a tarp covering the payload. As they approached it, Jenny heard snarling and growling from under the tarp.

"What's under there?" she asked Alexander as he opened the passenger door for her.

"Just walking the dogs. Need a boost?"

"I drive a truck bigger than this back home." Jenny climbed up into the passenger seat and opened the driver-side door for him. "Need a hand up?"

"Very funny." Alexander took his seat and started the truck. "You might want to hold on to something."

"I'll be fine."

Alexander punched the accelerator, and they roared out through the front gate. Jenny grabbed the door handle as he turned sharply onto the winding dirt road through the heavy growth, then picked up more speed. Soon they were doing more than ninety miles an hour over steep, uneven, muddy roads.

"Aren't there are any, you know, speed limits out here?" she asked.

"Speed limits, yes. People to enforce them, no."

The roads grew steeper as they climbed into the foothills of the Sierra Madre. Alexander parked the truck at a small ranch, where he spoke with the owner in Spanish. The man provided them with two horses, saddled and bridled and ready to ride.

Jenny gaped at the huge animals. "I've never ridden a horse," she whispered to Alexander.

"It's easy," he said. "Just hold the reins and don't fall off. Everything else is easy."

Jenny's horse was white with large brown spots, and it regarded her with huge black eyes. She felt nervous. She checked to make sure her sleeves were pulled down to her gloves, her ankles covered by her socks and jeans. She didn't want to poison the poor creature with her touch.

The horse stepped closer to Jenny, trying to sniff at her hair. She backed away and patted his head.

Jenny looked at Alexander and the ranch owner, a wrinkled man who must have been in his sixties.

"Okay...so how do I get on?" she asked.

"Just put one foot on the stirrup and swing your leg over." Alexander indicated a leather loop at the height of Jenny's chest. She looked at it doubtfully.

"I think I left my go-go-Gadget legs at home," she said. "How do I get up there?"

"When you're comfortable enough, you'll jump." Alexander took her around the waist and picked her up. He guided her foot into the stirrup, then seated her in the saddle. "How's that?"

Jenny petted the horse while she looked around. It was strange to be so high off the ground, relying on the huge mammal beneath her not to freak out and throw her off.

"Too scary for you?" he asked.

"Oh, whatever. I can handle this."

Alexander placed the reins in her hand, and Jenny held them loosely while she watched Alexander walk back to the truck. The snarls from under the tarp grew louder, and something punched upward against it, but Jenny still couldn't see what was back there. Then Alexander lowered the tailgate.

Jenny held her breath and tightened her grip on the reins. She was expected some huge dogs to come rushing out of the darkness under the tarp, but nothing emerged. The growls grew louder, though.

Alexander left the tailgate open and jumped into the saddle of his huge black stallion. He pressed his knees into the horse's sides.

"Yah!" he said, and the horse began to trot away, towards the jungle at the edge of the ranch.

"Yah?" Jenny asked, and her horse took off after Alexander. Jenny clung tight as it bounced her up and down. Her hair blew out behind her.

A wall of tropical vegetation stood just behind the rail fence at the edge of the ranch, as if the little valley had been slashed and burned from a dense rainforest. Alexander was riding towards a trail that led up into the rainforest, towards the next mountain.

Alexander whistled. Jenny looked back to see a pair of huge beasts leap out from underneath the tarp on the truck. They weren't dogs at all, but huge cats with golden coats and dark spots. They thudded as they hit the ground—they must have weighed at least two hundred pounds each.

Jenny watched the animals race to the fence and leap over it, then disappear into the jungle.

"Jaguars?" Jenny asked. "You trained jaguars?"

"Don't be silly. Nobody can train a cat."

Alexander led the way into the jungle, where the dense canopy turned the daylight green. Insects, birds, and monkeys chattered overhead. Jenny watched a few giant mosquitoes land on her wrist, then immediately crumple up and die from her Jenny pox.

In the rainforest around them, she caught an occasional quick glimpse of the great cats darting through the foliage.

"So, if they're not trained..." Jenny said.

"Look closer." One of the jaguars leaped onto a thick tree limb overhanging the steep trail. It walked until it was directly above Jenny, then sat and licked one paw.

Jenny looked closer. The jaguar had a number of deep gashes in its skin, revealing stripes of gray muscle and bone, but none of these were bleeding. Its coat was matted and dirty.

"They're dead," she said. "You made zombie jaguars."

"Great security against man or beast," he said. "Took a while for the horses to get used to the smell."

"Do they have names?"

Alexander smiled. "I call them Pekku and Pukuh. They're named after the god of thunder and the god of death."

"Mayan gods?"

"That's right."

"You're really adapting to the locals here."

"It's not so hard," Alexander said. "We've been Mayan before."

"You and me?"

"There were great stone cities in those days," he said. "You can still find the ruins of them, here and there."

"What happened to their civilization?"

"The same that happens to all of them," Alexander said. "Men can't live in peace together. We are designed to compete, and fight, and kill."

"And what about women?" Jenny asked, with half a smile.

"Women are twice as dangerous."

Jenny snickered, thinking of Ashleigh. Behind them, the jaguar who'd posed for her leaped off the limb and disappeared into the jungle.

The trail grew steep, rough and choked with lush growth. The jaguars stayed well ahead of them on the trail, where their presence flushed out brightly colored, squawking birds that retreated high into the canopy.

"Do you control everything they do?" Jenny asked.

"I can set them to one repetitive, simple task," Alexander said. "Like walking. Anything else requires some extra focus."

"That's amazing," she said. "Your power's so much better than mine."

"I've seen you wipe out an entire army in a day. I have nothing compared to what you have, Jenny."

"It's no good for anything but hurting and killing people," Jenny said. "There's nothing positive I can do."

"Sometimes destroying the right people is a positive thing," he said. "Everything depends on the situation."

"What was I like, in my Mayan life?"

"Beautiful. Powerful. Intriguing. Frightening. Godlike. Just like you are now."

"I'm not any of those things. Well, maybe frightening."

"You were believed to be divine," Alexander said. "Which you are, of course."

"What do you mean?"

"We keep coming back, lifetime after lifetime. We wield power over everyone else. We are, in our way, immortal. We aren't entirely wrong to consider ourselves godlike."

"I don't know. I would think of a God, or gods, as being sort of wise, and kind of above everything, not stuck in the world and trying to figure things out and being clueless most of the time."

"I've never encountered such a being," Alexander said. "There is only us. We are the natural rulers of the humans, because we are so much stronger. They are the sheep. We are the shepherds and the wolves."

"And which are you?" Jenny asked. "Shepherd or wolf?"

He laughed. "I'm a builder. I despise the love-charmer because she is only a taker."

"You mean Ashleigh?"

"She's a vulture who preys on others and creates nothing herself. A scavenger with no vision."

"And what do you build?"

"It depends on the age. I had constructed for my tomb in Egypt a step pyramid, which was quite influential on later kings. I have built canals, roads, temples, arenas, harbors, depending on the age. I always leave a mark behind."

"And what mark are you making in this lifetime?"

"When you see what lies ahead, you'll see what we can accomplish."

"With cocaine?"

"That will only be the beginning of our revenue. Start-up capital. In time, we will build whatever we like. And your vision will be as important as mine."

"My vision? So what am I, if she's a scavenger, and you're a builder?"

Alexander grinned. "You're just in it for the adventure." He urged his horse on, and the stallion galloped fast along the trail. "Try to keep up!"

"Yah!" Jenny yelled, kneeing her horse. The brown and white mare picked up speed, and Jenny lowered her head. She found horseback riding came naturally, as if she'd done it a million times before.

They raced up the narrow rainforest trail, Jenny's heart pounding in her chest. The trail was mostly uphill, except for a few switchbacks along the way.

Jenny lost track of time—it might have been thirty minutes before Alexander slowed down, and Jenny did the same.

They rounded a bend in the trail and came upon a pair of men with rags tied over their faces, hiding everything but their eyes. They pointed AK-47s at the jaguars, who stood side by side on the trail, like statues.

"*Hola*," Alexander said, as he and Jenny stopped their horses just behind the jaguars.

"*Hola, El Brujo*," one of the men replied, lowering the cloth to reveal his face. The two armed men stood aside, allowing them to pass. The jaguars darted ahead on the trail. Alexander chatted with them, in a mix of Spanish and Mayan, as he and Jenny rode past.

"Why are they wearing masks?" Jenny whispered when they were out of earshot.

"If another cartel finds us, we don't want them going to their villages. Tracking them down, threatening their families."

"Threatening their families?"

"Papa Calderon has many enemies," Alexander said. "But if our work here were discovered, he would have many more."

They reached a sloped clearing, where dense, overlapping rows of coca plants grew in the shadow of ancient rainforest trees. Workers picked the leaves and dropped them into woven baskets. They moved at a painfully slow pace, but there must have been thirty or more of them harvesting the crop. They were men and women and children, their skin decayed, many with an empty eye socket or missing limb.

Jenny caught her breath. She thought she'd been prepared to see this, but it was still a horrifying sight.

"You okay?" Alexander asked her. "You just went a little pale."

"It's so weird," Jenny said. "I expect them all to turn around and attack me, like in *Army of Darkness*."

"Good movie," Alexander said.

"Not you, too."

"What's wrong with the *Evil Dead* movies?"

"Nothing. It's just my boyfriend...ex-boyfriend got obsessed with them. Towards the end of our relationship." It stung Jenny's heart to talk about Seth that way, but then she reminded herself of how he'd cheated on her, the first chance he got. Knowing Jenny could never cheat on him, because she would kill any other boy she touched.

A warm, moist wind blew through the trees, and a collective groan went up from the zombie workers as it passed through their rib cages and skulls.

"Do you think they're in pain?" Jenny asked.

"I don't think they feel anything." Alexander dropped from his horse, then helped Jenny down to the ground.

Among the workers, there were three men with cloth masks over their faces and AK-47s slung over their backs. They each held a long wooden pole. Jenny watched one of them use the pole to herd a zombie woman from one plant to the next. She shuffled sideways, her hands still plucking at the empty air, until she was positioned in front of the next plant and resumed harvesting leaves again.

Alexander walked from row to row, chatting with the three living and masked overseers as he inspected the zombies. Jenny saw a few decaying children among them, tugging the lowest leaves from the plants. She shuddered.

When they reached the highest row of coca plants on the slope, Jenny saw a pair of little monkeys shrieking and chasing each other through the trees overhead.

Alexander put a finger under her chin and turned her head to look back at the zombies. "Pay attention," he said. "Watch what happens." His fingers remained on her face, and Jenny felt the pox rush out of her, the way it did on those rare occasions when she intentionally used it against someone.

The zombies accelerated, their hands darting from plant to basket and back again. The overseers had to hustle to keep the zombies moving along the rows, but the zombies were more responsive now—one quick tap from a pole would send a zombie a few steps sideways to work on the next plant, no more need for extensive wrangling and prodding each time.

"You've got them moving," Alexander said. "They'll finish this patch in a day instead of a week."

"The Jenny pox," she said. "It's zombie fuel."

He grinned and tousled her hair. "Exactly." His hand moved to the back of her neck, maintaining his contact with her. Jenny felt tingly wherever he touched her.

Jenny reached across the row of plants to touch one of the zombies, who looked like a teenage boy with half his face decayed, leaving only grimy blackened skull. Her finger brushed his arm, and he immediately doubled his speed, stripping the plant in front of him. An overseer reached his pole from two rows away and tapped the boy to the next plant.

"They like me," Jenny said.

"You're the zombie queen."

Jenny watched the harvest quietly, feeling her connection to Alexander deepen as he drew the pox from inside her. She found herself reaching an arm across his back, feeling the muscles under his shirt. She leaned against him, her head against his chest, wanting to touch him more, suddenly frustrated by her gloves and her long sleeves. He smelled like sweat and tropical humidity and horse and cotton.

"We have to keep all this a secret," he said.

"Yeah, I'm sure," Jenny said. She looked out at the rows and rows of coca. Her father had grown a small patch of bad outdoor pot on some long-foreclosed farmland outside Fallen Oak, but it was nothing on this scale. "This is like the most illegal thing you can do."

"The Mexican feds are a concern, but not our biggest one. The real danger is the other cartels."

"Why would they care?"

"The Mexican cartels sell to the United States. They buy from cartels in Colombia, Peru, Bolivia," Alexander said. "The growers. But Papa Calderon has invested in botany, and his people developed a good strong plant that thrives here, in the extreme south of Mexico. We're not too far from Guatemala. Scattered through these mountains, we have the largest coca crop ever grown in Mexico. We can cut out the South Americans and control our own production and distribution. And that would make everyone angry. The Calderon family would be more profitable than their competitors, and the South Americans would all come down on them for setting a dangerous precedent."

"And you don't have any problem working for people like that?" Jenny asked. "Drug cartels? Violent gangs?"

"What is a government but a violent gang with a flag?" Alexander asked. "In fact, all of this violence is created by the human governments. They could end it all with a wave of their hands, simply make all the drugs legal. Then the trade would be peaceful, like the buying and selling of any legal product."

"I guess..."

"But governments feed on violence and discord, conflict, people living in fear," Alexander said. "People looking to their rulers for protection. Peace and tranquility starve the state. If the world does not offer enough threats, the state must manufacture them. With violent drug gangs in the streets, the state grows more powerful. It is the prohibition itself that slowly destroys the society, and the rulers know this, yet they like the power it grants them."

"But why are *you* doing this?" Jenny asked.

"The opportunity arose, and it interested me," Alexander said. "You see how I use my share of the revenue to help the local people. I listen to their needs and do what I can to meet them. I've told you, I'm a builder."

"Schools and clinics," Jenny said.

"Just simple groundwork. There will be greater things in time. And so far as the violence...Papa Calderon is a man of the old school. He uses violence only where necessary, to defend his business and his people. His competition is the cartel run by Pablo Toscano out of Juarez, which is the largest cartel in Mexico. Toscano is truly insane. Bombing newspapers. Heads on stakes. Entire towns pillaged and burned to make a point. So long as the world is what it is, many people would benefit, many lives would be saved if Calderon took over the market from Toscano. There are many shades of gray between good and evil, Jenny, and the lighter shades are to be preferred, if we cannot have pure white."

Jenny digested this. She still wasn't sure she agreed with him, but he clearly had a sense of morality about what he was doing, and a vision for helping to making things better for the local people.

"This all sounds pretty dangerous," Jenny finally said.

"I know. Exciting, isn't it?"

"Doesn't any of it scare you?"

"Jenny, I've suffered every terrible death you can imagine," Alexander said. "Drawn and quartered. Burned at the stake. Torn apart by tigers in front of a cheering crowd. There's nothing left on this earth that can frighten me."

She found herself gazing up at him, as if hypnotized by his dark amber eyes. She didn't move when he leaned his face close, or when his lips touched hers.

It was like an electric jolt—Jenny jumped, and had a sudden memory of Alexander in a different body, purple cape lashing around him in fierce wind, walking a battlefield by spotty moonlight. He picked among the fallen, touching one here and one there, and they raised up on their feet, wearing their bloody leather armor and broken helmets, and they hefted their shields and swords, undead warriors ready for another day in the grisly march of conquest.

Jenny opened her eyes and staggered back from him. "Wait," she said.

"Too much for you?" He smiled.

"I don't feel like myself," she said. "I feel like I'm losing control."

"You're not. You're just remembering who you really are."

Jenny took a deep breath as she looked out on the rows of workers scrambling to harvest every ripe coca leaf. Put a shovel in their hands and they could dig a ditch. Put a sword or a gun in their hands, and they became unstoppable killers.

She felt sick to her stomach, and a little dizzy. Jenny plucked a few of the coca leaves, shoved them in her mouth, and chewed on them. Alexander removed one of her gloves and took her hand in his, watching her. Soon, her head cleared and she began to feel better.

CHAPTER FOURTEEN

Seth walked through the Pioneer Square neighborhood in Seattle with a picture of Jenny in his pocket. The day was gray and overcast, the cool summer climate a definite change from the broiling humidity back home.

Jenny's father had received a postcard from Jenny, sent from Seattle just a couple of days ago. Her note had been short and shallow —*Doing great...Just felt the need to travel a little...Love it here...Hope you're doing well...*Not much information at all. And no mention of Seth, either.

The postcard confused Seth's earlier idea that Jenny must have been kidnapped by Ashleigh and the others. He'd immediately booked a flight to Seattle, and now found himself trudging through the arts district, stopping at cafes and at every pottery shop or gallery he saw, asking people if they'd seen Jenny. Nobody recognized her picture, though.

Seth could imagine Jenny enjoying this city, especially here in the arts district—the Victorian mansions built of aging brick, the old-timey streetlamps with their clusters of bulbs, the trees growing through the sidewalk, statues and public art everywhere you looked. He stopped to look at a sixty-foot totem pole, staring at the enormous eyes and hooked beak of some kind of bird.

He wished he was here with Jenny now. She'd always said she didn't like cities and was scared to travel to them, for fear of infecting people with her touch. For her to come here on her own, something must have radically changed her feelings about those things. It didn't make sense that someone terrified of a city as small as Charleston would run to a city of millions like this one.

Another thing that didn't quite fit for Seth: Jenny probably wouldn't have picked the Space Needle postcard that her dad had received. That was the one image everybody knew, from TV or the movies. Jenny would have chosen a more colorful and unexpected image, like a postcard featuring this huge totem pole in front of him. Or the giant stone troll under the George Washington Bridge. Or any of the statues of settlers, firemen, factory workers or Native Americans around town—Jenny, who enjoyed pottery and sculpture herself, would have picked any of these over something as bland as the Space Needle.

On the other hand, the postcard was exactly the sort of touch that Ashleigh would add, if she'd kidnapped Jenny and didn't want people looking for her. If that was the case, then Jenny was certainly not in Seattle, or anywhere close. She would be hundreds or thousands of miles from here.

Still, Seth didn't have any clues except for the postcard. He would continue asking around, and if nothing came up by tonight, he'd get a hotel room and start fresh in the morning. Seattle was a big city, with lots of little places to look.

He could only hope Jenny was safe. If she'd fallen into Ashleigh's hands, she would be in terrible danger. Seth couldn't stop worrying about her.

***

"Jennifer Morton's father received a postcard from her today. Postmarked Seattle," said Chantella Williams, the investigator who was Heather's contact at Homeland Security.

Heather was currently working out of a borrowed office at the Medical University of South Carolina, keeping tabs on those patients who'd exhibited symptoms of Fallen Oak syndrome after the riot. She leaned back in her chair, listening to Williams on the phone.

"Seth Barrett left on a plane for Seattle this afternoon," Williams continued.

"He went to join her?"

"We borrowed somebody from the Seattle office to tail him for a couple of hours. He was showing pictures of Jennifer to the locals, asking if they'd seen her."

"So he really doesn't know where she is," Heather said.

"Or they're going to a lot of trouble to make it look that way. He just made a hotel reservation from his phone, so it looks like he'll be staying overnight."

"Any luck on Jenny herself?"

"Nothing there. She has no credit card, just a small checking account at the Fallen Oak Merchants and Farmers Bank, with less than forty dollars. That hasn't been touched. She's traveling with cash or someone's paying her way. We have her car's VIN and tag number flagged, so we'll hear from any police who might encounter it."

"So that's it? We're just waiting?"

"We'll have our Seattle people check around some more. But until she does something to draw attention to herself..."

Heather sighed. "What about her father? What's he doing?" Neither Jenny nor her father had been home when Heather arrived with the Homeland Security people on Monday, so they had moved on to Seth's house. Later, they'd determined Darrell Morton had been hospitalized with some kind of nervous breakdown on Saturday night, checked in by his daughter Jenny. That was the end of Jenny's paper trail.

"Darrell Morton was released from the county hospital on Monday evening with a recommendation to seek psychiatric care," Williams said. "Given the state of his insurance, though, I doubt he'll follow up."

"Has he made any unusual phone calls? Or purchases?"

"If he had, I would be telling you about them, Dr. Reynard. I obviously don't have time to fill you in on everything that *didn't* happen."

"Okay, sorry, Jesus," Heather said. Williams was snappy today.

"Don't swear in my ear."

"*Fine.* What else do you have? Any luck with the hospital footage?"

"We ran it through our best image-matching software, but there wasn't much to work with. The security camera was low-resolution, he had sunglasses and hair covering most of his face, no distinguishing marks—"

"Did you find anything or not?" Heather asked.

"Nothing so far. They're still trying."

"So we don't have any idea where to find them."

"There are still a lot of cracks in the world where people can disappear, Dr. Reynard. Now, Assistant Director Lansing wants me to get an update from your end."

"The update is that it's over," Heather said. "All symptoms of Fallen Oak syndrome faded from those rioters in a few days. No infections, no scarring, and of course no pathogen. We're keeping up with them on an outpatient basis. Maybe something will crop up."

"But there is no remaining evidence that anything unusual happened in Charleston?"

"Just those videos from the hospital. And your people took them into evidence." Heather sighed. "You can tell Nelson Artleby that there's no threat to the President's poll ratings on national security."

"I don't report to Nelson Artleby."

"But he sees your reports on this situation."

"That's over my pay grade, Dr. Reynard. Do you have any further information for us?"

"Nope, just a complete regression of all symptoms."

"Okay." Williams hung up on her.

Heather resumed sifting through the megabytes of data on her laptop, everything she was allowed to know about the events in Fallen Oak and in Charleston. It looked like an endless pile of useless information, but somewhere in there could be a clue that tied together Jenny Morton, the riot in Charleston, and the mysterious young man who could apparently raise the dead.

She had no idea what that clue might look like, though.

About an hour later, her cell phone rang. It was her husband Liam, calling from Atlanta. Heather felt very jittery about answering the call. She'd managed to push her personal fears away while in her professional working mode, but now they came shoving back.

Her daughter, Tricia, had been suffering a fever and swollen glands. Liam took the four-year-old to her pediatrician, who went on to order a CBC, though he'd assured Liam that it was only a precaution.

Now, here was the call, the one where she learned whether Tricia had any abnormal blood cells.

She answered before it could ring a second time.

"How is she?" Heather asked.

"We're moving on to a lymph node biopsy," Liam said.

"Oh, God. What did he say?"

"It looks like...he said there's a very high probability..."

Heather nodded. Liam was avoiding the word *leukemia*.

"You might want to come home," he said. "If your work's not too important."

Heather felt her heart clench. She looked at her laptop, all the little folders containing medical histories and police reports. The threat of Jenny creating a massive outbreak, somewhere in the world. The investigation that led only to dead ends.

"No, my work's not important," Heather whispered, seeing Tricia's face in her mind. She was already fighting the urge to cry, but she managed to hold her voice steady. "I'm coming home."

CHAPTER FIFTEEN

Jenny and Kisa walked through a *tianguis*, an open-air market crowded with venders selling wares from rugs and tents. They were in Comitán de Domínguez, the closest city. Manuel had driven them more than two hours from Alexander's house, at high speed, barely touching the brakes the entire time they wove through the narrow, potholed mountain roads. Alexander himself was away in Tijuana, visiting with Papa Calderon himself, to give a report on their progress with the crop.

Over the past few weeks, Jenny and Alexander had traveled to one coca patch after another, to check on his zombies and to fire them up with Jenny Pox. They had greatly accelerated the harvest, and Alexander expected his boss to be pleased.

Jenny still struggled with her feelings about Alexander. She was deeply attracted to him, in a way that made her physically ache. Sometimes the thought of his dark eyes and his suntanned face kept her up at night. His hand on her skin intoxicated her. She managed to resist her feelings most of the time, though she'd broken down and kissed him more than once.

Though Alexander had been kind and taken good care of her, she found her emotions too overwhelming and dangerous. She still thought about Seth, how perfectly innocent and sweet their time together had seemed, until things went sour. She missed him, but she was angry at him.

Alexander was a lot of things, but innocent and sweet were not among them.

"Look!" Kisa said. She took Jenny's hand and drew her toward a shaded table where a man fried a pot of full of tamales. They smelled like chiles and saffron. "Are you hungry?"

Jenny's stomach was growling, so she nodded. "Good idea."

Kisa spoke with the cook in Mayan, and he served them each a tamale. Jenny bit into the fried corn crust, and the spicy pork and salsa filling spilled into her mouth.

"Yum, that's so good!" Jenny said to Kisa. She nodded to the man who'd cooked them. *"Muy buena."*

The Mayan cook scowled at her a little.

"Spanish is language of *los conquistadors*," Kisa whispered. "I don't think he likes to hear it."

"Oh!' Jenny said. "I mean, *hatsutz*. Very good."

Now the man smiled again. He poured a cloudy fluid into two small porcelain cups and offered these to the girls.

"Yum botic," Kisa said, thanking him. Then she held her cup toward Jenny and grinned. "Cheers."

"Cheers!" Jenny clinked her glass against Kisa's, then drank from her cup. It tasted very sweet, with a strong alcoholic bite. "What is this?"

"Posh," Kisa said. Her English vocabulary was slowly expanding, as was Jenny's knowledge of Mayan. They had plenty of time to teach each other, loafing around Alexander's estate. "From the sugar..." Kisa circled her thumb and fingers together and moved her hand in up and down strokes, to indicate a staff of sugar cane.

"From the sugar dick?" Jenny asked. Her head was swimming a little from the cane liquor.

"The sugar..." Kisa began to repeat, then she laughed and shrugged. "Sugar dick."

Jenny snickered while she returned her cup to the tamale vendor, and Kisa paid him from the roll of pesos Alexander had provided.

"Ka xi'ik teech utsil," the man said. *Good luck to you.* It was a way of saying goodbye.

"Béey xan teech," Jenny replied. *And to you.*

The next stall sold a combination of local textiles and tourist trinkets, including a number of t-shirts. Many shirts featured a man in what looked like a black ski mask, with the letters "EZLN" printed in red. Other shirts featured a drawing of a young girl with long braids on either side of her head. A red triangle of cloth hid most of her face, except for her eyes. The letters "EZLN" were printed in black on the cloth. The words above her face were "*Las Mujeres*," and the text beneath her face read "*Con la Dignidad Rebelde.*"

"What are these?" Jenny asked, pointing to the T-shirt.

"*Ejército Zapatista de Liberación Nacional*," Kisa told her. "The army of the revolution. Against the power in Mexico City."

"Do you like them?" Jenny asked.

Kisa nodded quickly. "Good for our people." She pointed to the text under the girl's face and translated slowly: "'Women with rebel dignity.'"

"Okay, I definitely like that," Jenny said. "Should I buy one?"

The T-shirt vendor turned to them, after completing a transaction with a group of well-dressed Mexican tourists. He was a young man with dark sunglasses, smoking a cigarette. He wore jeans and one of the black Zapatista t-shirts with the masked man. When he saw Jenny, he pushed the STOP button on his boom box and removed the Spanish-language rap CD he'd been playing. He switched it out for another disc.

"For the pretty American girl," he said. Cyndi Lauper played over the speakers, and Jenny laughed. She pointed to one of the Zapatista shirts featuring the little girl in her bandit-like mask, and the vendor quickly pushed it into her hands. Kisa paid for it. Alexander had entrusted her with the shopping money, since the locals were far less likely to overcharge a Mayan girl than a white tourist.

Jenny added her new shirt to the woven shopping bag she carried, which already held a pair of leather sandals and a mixture of Mayan and Western-style clothes she'd bought here in the open-air market. She wouldn't need to borrow Kisa's clothes anymore.

They moved on to another stall, where Kisa stopped to admire the amber jewelry. The old woman behind the table smiled, her eyes flicking over Jenny, possibly sensing a gringo tourist with money to burn.

Jenny looked back over her shoulder. Manuel was at a row of butchers' stalls, negotiating over some smoked meats.

"So nice," Kisa said, looking over the yellow and red amber pieces

136

crafted into beaded bracelets, earrings and necklaces.

"You can have one if you want." Jenny reached for a bracelet of red amber pieces, and Kisa gasped and shook her head.

"Red is very..." She rubbed her fingers together.

"Expensive?"

"Very expensive." Kisa nodded.

"Okay...what about this one?" Jenny picked up a necklace of yellow amber pieces, with one small red piece right at the front. She spread it across her palm—Jenny wore a pair of gloves Kisa had made for her with the bright colors and intricate geometric weaving of Mayan craft. They covered Jenny up to the elbow, when fully unrolled. A great gift.

Now Jenny held the amber necklace out to Kisa, who studied it with wide, admiring eyes.

"Is there enough money to buy this?" Jenny asked.

Kisa hesitated, then nodded.

"Then go ahead."

Kisa paid the jeweler, and the old woman spoke a cheerful stream of mixed Mayan and Spanish, which Jenny didn't understand. Jenny put the amber necklace over Kisa's head and pulled it down to her shoulders. Kisa lifted the single piece of red in her fingers and gazed at it, and her eyes turned moist. Then she dropped the necklace and threw her arms around Jenny.

Jenny tilted her head back to avoid any contact that might kill her friend. She hugged Kisa back, cautiously, careful not to do any harm.

"*Yum botic,*" Kisa whispered. "*'in yabitmech.*"

"*Mixba,*" Jenny replied. She knew Kisa's first phrase meant *thank you*. She wasn't sure about the rest of it.

They followed the sound of drums to an area where street performers in traditional costume put on a dance. One of them was dressed as a deer, including a deer head mounted on top of his own like the stacked faces in a totem pole. Others in black and white body paint pursued him with spears. He leaped back and forth, more and more frantic as the hunters closed in around him and the drums and flute music accelerated in tempo.

Jenny heard a strangled cry and turned to see Kisa being dragged away into a closed tent of a vendor's stall. A young man had clapped a hand over her mouth and lay a knife across her throat. Kisa looked at Jenny with wide, terrified eyes, and then the tent flap fell shut and

Jenny lost sight of her.

"Kisa!" Jenny cried. She ran into the tent after the girl.

The interior was dark, with only a little sunlight creeping in around the edges of the cloth roof. The tent was stocked with clay pots for sale, but nobody was manning the store—maybe the merchant was outside, watching the show.

The back of the tent parted for a moment, and Jenny saw the man drag Kisa outside.

"Let her go!" Jenny yelled. She ran out through the back flap of the tent, into a narrow cobblestone alley. The tent blocked the crowd's view of anything that happened here, and the drums drowned out the sound of Kisa's muffled cries. The man was dragging her along, ignoring her attempts to struggle free.

"Hey!" Jenny called out, and then someone grabbed her from behind, too. A man's hand covered her mouth, and his other arm seized her around the waist and lifted her from the pavement.

Jenny didn't hesitate: she sunk her teeth into the palm of his hand.

The man grunted and tried to let her go, but Jenny bit down and grabbed onto his wrist with her hands as he released her. She landed on her feet, still biting him, until he punched her in the side of the head with his other fist.

Jenny slammed into the stone wall behind her.

"*Puta!*" he shouted and he slapped her across the face. Jenny lost her balance and fell onto her knees. Her head was ringing with pain, and bright spots flicked across her field of vision.

He stopped to look at the pulsing, infected-looking bite wound she'd left in his hand. Jenny saw the other man holding his knife at Kisa's throat, yelling at his companion, clearly urging him to hurry. He was groping Kisa's chest as he held the girl back against him.

The man who'd attacked Jenny looked down at her. He was young, muscular and very tall, his head shaved, a nasty scar across his cheek. He licked his lips.

Jenny took her gloves off.

"Come on, motherfucker," Jenny spat. She was ready.

With one hand, he seized Jenny around the throat and lifted her to her feet. Jenny grabbed at his hand with both of hers, as if trying to peel his fingers away, and he grinned.

Jenny could feel his skin blistering under her touch. She pushed as hard as she could, filling him with the pox.

Bloody skin sloughed off the man's palm as he let her go and pulled away from her neck. Huge sores bloomed along his arm, leaking pus, and his face blistered open along one side. He gaped as he watched the bite wound open into a black, dripping hole through his hand, big enough that Jenny could see his face through it.

Jenny turned to the man who was holding Kisa. The pox ruptured open a dozen festering holes in her face, and more in her arms and hands.

"Let her go," Jenny said.

He looked at his friend, whose body was being consumed by a leprous disease. Then he shoved Kisa aside, raised his knife, and stabbed it at Jenny's throat.

Jenny ducked aside, but the blade slashed across her forearm. She swung her knee into the guy's crotch. He grunted and doubled over, and she lay her hands gently on the sides of his face. She pushed the infection into him, watching coolly as his eyes filled with dark green scum, blood ran from his nostrils, his teeth blackened and fell from his mouth.

Manuel stepped out through the back flap of the tent, waving his pistol. "*Que paso? Que paso?*"

"You're too late," Jenny told him. The man with the knife toppled over onto the cobblestone, his necrotic flesh dribbling in lumps from his face.

The man who'd grabbed Jenny was leaning back against the stone wall whimpering as the pox ate his hand, leaving only a diseased and decaying stump of an arm.

Manuel put his gun to the man's head. "Finish him?" he asked Jenny.

"I'll do it." Jenny ripped his shirt open, sending three buttons flying. They skipped and rolled away across the cobblestones.

The man shook his head, weeping, begging in Spanish while Jenny pushed her hand against his heart.

"Sorry, guy," Jenny said. "But we can't have you running around attacking girls, can we?" The muscles of his chest turned to liquid mush under her fingers. His whole body turned rigid as his heart stopped, and then he fell to the cobblestones next to his dead friend.

"Kisa?" Jenny spotted the girl halfway down the alley, cowering against one wall.

Jenny wiped the blood from her hands on the shirt of the man who'd attacked her. Then she picked up her gloves and walked toward Kisa as she put them on. She pulled the pox back inside her as much as she could, and she felt the sores in her face seal up.

"*Bix yanilech*?" Jenny asked. *How are you?*

"Okay," Kisa said, staring at Jenny and trembling.

Jenny held up a hand and managed half a smile. "No touch."

"No shit," Kisa replied.

"Manuel, I think we're done shopping for today."

Manuel nodded, looking at the diseased corpses.

Jenny turned and stepped into the pottery tent, picking up the bag of newly purchased clothes she'd dropped along the way. She held the flap open and gestured for them to follow. Manuel entered the tent and passed Jenny, while Kisa approached her slowly.

"Jenny," Kisa said. "You are a powerful *bruja*. A powerful *ah itz.*"

Jenny nodded. "I'm kind of stuck with it."

"Thank you," Kisa said.

"*Mixba*," Jenny replied with a grin. But Kisa was too shocked, or too horrified, to return her smile.

***

An hour before dawn, Jenny was awoken by a soft knock on her door.

"Hello?" Jenny whispered. She sat up on her elbows. "Kisa?"

The door cracked open. "It's Alexander. I drove all night when I heard what happened. Are you okay?"

"Yeah." Jenny had bandaged the knife wound on her. She expected it to heal as quickly as all her injuries did. She seemed to heal even faster than usual when Alexander was around.

"I'll let you sleep," he whispered.

"No, it's okay," Jenny said. "You can come in."

She watched Alexander in the moonlight as he sat down on the corner of her bed, near her feet.

"I killed two people," Jenny said.

"I hope you got some good shopping in first."

"I'm serious."

"They attacked you, didn't they?"

"And Kisa."

"So it's good you did," Alexander said. "God knows what they might have done to you girls."

"I promised myself I'd never use the pox again."

"But you had to. You shouldn't feel guilty about it, Jenny. Not for a second."

"I do feel guilty," Jenny said. "And not just because I did it, but because...I kind of *liked* it, Alexander. Like I was dealing out justice. Like I had a right to kill people if I wanted."

"You do have the right to deal justice. Somebody has to, and you're capable of it."

"Yeah, I'm definitely capable..."

"Look, Jenny, you just killed a couple of assholes. You made the world a better place."

"It doesn't really feel like it."

"It was just a small move, Jenny," Alexander said. "But in the right direction. We have to accept what we are. We have to embrace it. It's the only choice."

"But we could be different," Jenny said. "There has to be some choice, somewhere."

"Embrace it or fight it, that's the choice. It doesn't change who you are. It just makes your life more difficult and out of control if you fight it."

"You said you're a builder, and Ashleigh's a vulture. Then what is Seth?"

"The healer?" Alexander frowned. "He's just a pawn of the love-charmer. Always has been."

"But not lately," Jenny said. "I think he's been pulling away from her, hasn't he?"

"He never could. If the healer got close to you, made you think he cared about you...just trust me, the charmer bitch is behind it."

"Are you sure?"

"He might not even know it," Alexander said. "It could be a multi-lifetime plot. You can forget your memories and your purpose when you're reborn in the flesh, but they will still be there, shaping your actions. The fear-giver is often her servant. My opposite, the dear little dead-speaker, is often her servant. The healer is *always* her servant, Jenny. You see why she's so dangerous? Her power can manipulate and control not only regular people, but our kind, too."

"Except me," Jenny said. "If she touches me, I'll kill her."

"This makes you her most formidable enemy," Alexander said.

"The one she can never hope to control with her poisonous love. Unless..."

"Unless what?"

"Unless she takes your heart indirectly," Alexander said. "By sending the healer to charm it from you. He can touch you, so he can get close to you. He can trick you into loving him, trusting him—especially when you're feeling so alone because you can touch no one...and then you meet one boy you can touch—"

"Okay, I get it," Jenny said. "I don't need the whole psychoanalysis thing. So you don't think Seth really cares about me? Deep down, he's still serving Ashleigh?"

"I've seen him across a thousand lifetimes," Alexander said. "He always serves her. He always will."

Jenny thought about the girl Seth had hooked up with in Charleston, the one that looked so much like Ashleigh that Jenny had thought, for a moment, that the evil girl had somehow cheated death and returned. Why would Seth have picked a girl like that, out of all the girls in the city, unless some part of him really wanted to be with Ashleigh again?

It hurt to think that her entire relationship with Seth had been a trick to get her under Ashleigh's control...but if anyone was capable of a manipulation like that, it was Ashleigh. The thought frightened her deeply, and left her feeling very alone.

"You're quiet," Alexander whispered. "Falling asleep?"

He stood up.

"You don't have to go," Jenny whispered. She reached out and took his hand. "Stay with me. But you have to let me sleep."

"I'll stay." He lay down beside her. Jenny kissed him, then wrapped an arm around him. She buried her face against his solid, warm chest, listening to his heart. And then she fell asleep, trying not to think about Seth.

142

CHAPTER SIXTEEN

Seth sat in the reception area on a wide, soft couch, looking at a portrait of Nathan Hale that glowed under track lighting. The other art in the room had cold, modernist designs without any meaning, but the framed print of the Revolutionary War spy held the most prominent place. The latest issues of *Fortune* and the *Wall Street Journal* sat on the coffee table in front of him. Elevator music played over the speakers— Seth could swear it was the song "Thunderstruck" by AC/DC, minus the vocals, played at one-tenth the usual tempo on a violin and piccolo.

He sipped the coffee the receptionist had served him. Behind her massive round granite desk, the receptionist looked like a beauty queen in a black blazer, not much older than Seth himself. She made good coffee.

Behind the slender blond receptionist, the words HALE SECURITY GROUP were mounted in sleek, metallic letters on the wall. The company was headquartered in Manhattan, but Seth was visiting their Atlanta office, since it was much closer to his home and he might need to make follow-up visits.

He didn't have an appointment, partly because he was cautious about using his phone when he knew Homeland Security might be monitoring him. He'd been waiting here almost an hour. He wondered if people in a back room somewhere were checking out his identity.

The heavy double doors at the back of the reception area opened themselves without a sound. Another ridiculously beautiful young woman in a black coat and white blouse emerged, her hair cut into a bob. She gave Seth a glowing smile that could melt ice caps.

"Mr. Breisgau is free to see you now, Mr. Barrett," she said. "We apologize for the wait."

"No problem." Seth stood up and straightened his coat. He'd dressed in a dark gray suit with a muted earth-tone tie. He hoped he looked professional.

The young woman led him back into a midnight blue corridor with deeply piled carpeting. More modern art hung on the walls here, between office doors. Each office had a large, black-tinted window that revealed nothing about who or what was inside, though presumably the people in the offices could look out into the hall.

She led him past an empty assistant's desk, white and plain and curved into a semicircle. The wall behind it was floor-to-ceiling black-tinted glass, with a single door. She opened it and led Seth inside.

"Mr. Breisgau," she said. "This is Jonathan Barrett."

"Come on in." The man who rose behind the desk might have been in his fifties, with silver streaks in his dark hair, but the solid form beneath his tailored suit looked like it belonged to a professional boxer. His hand gripped Seth's.

"Would you like coffee? Or water?" the young woman asked.

"I already had some, thanks."

"Thank you, Misty," Breisgau said. She closed the door behind her as she left. Breisgau's blue eyes locked on Seth's, and he offered a salesman's smile. "Have a seat, Mr. Barrett."

"You can call me Seth." Seth took one of the leather-upholstered chairs in front of the man's desk.

"Then call me Jerome." Breisgau sat across from him. "Sorry about the delay. I was in a meeting. What can Hale Global do for you, Seth?"

"I saw you offer ransom and extraction services for people who've been kidnapped. Like those two oil executives in Nigeria last year."

"You've done your research." Breisgau shook his head. "Kidnap and ransom is a multibillion-dollar business around the world, unfortunately. And American businesspeople are the number one targets. Do you know somebody who's been captured?"

"Maybe," Seth said.

"Maybe?"

"It's my girlfriend, Jenny." Seth fought to stay calm. Just saying her name made him want to cry. "She disappeared a while ago. I think someone might have kidnapped her."

"How long ago?"

"A couple of weeks. There was a riot in Charleston."

Breisgau nodded. "I saw that on Fox News."

"That was the last time I saw her. She hasn't been home or called her dad, which is really strange for her."

"You think something happened to her during the riot?"

"Right."

"There's been no contact at all since? No ransom demands?"

"No," Seth said. "Well, there was a postcard, from Seattle, sent to her father."

"What did it say?"

"It claimed to be from Jenny. She said she was traveling around on her own and she was happy."

"But you don't think it was from her?" Breisgau asked.

"It didn't really sound like her," Seth said. "And the choice of the postcard...I don't know, it just feels wrong to me. Plus, she would have called her dad by now."

"Wouldn't she have called you, too?"

"She was sort of mad at me last time she saw me."

"So...maybe she's just taking a break. Going to 'find herself.'" He made finger quotes in the air. "You know. Women."

"Maybe you're right," Seth said. "I hope you're right. But..." Seth shrugged. He was feeling very nervous now, hoping they didn't turn down his case. "What if they took her?"

"Do you have any idea who might have kidnapped her?"

"I do," Seth said. He almost told the man about Ashleigh, but Ashleigh was officially dead. Her spirit had inhabited Darcy's body temporarily. He had no idea what kind of body she might have now. "There's...four of them."

Breisgau grabbed a light pen and scribbled something on his tablet PC. "Names?"

"The first one is...the only name I have for him is 'Tommy Goodling,' but that could be a fake. I can describe him for you."

146

"Where's he from?"

"I don't know."

"What do you know about him?"

"I know what he looks like."

Breisgau shook his head. "Next name?"

"Um, he might have a Mexican girl with him. I don't know her name. I've never even seen her, just heard about her."

"Mexican-American or Mexican Mexican?"

"I'm not sure. I don't know anything about her."

"What do you know about the other two?"

"One will be female," Seth said. "But I don't know her name or what she looks like. The other one is a guy, I can describe him for you."

"I suppose it would be too much for you to give me his name."

"Sorry," Seth said.

Breisgau looked at his tablet. "There's very little information here. Why do you suspect these people?"

Seth didn't know how to begin explaining that. The truth would make him sound like a crazy person. "It's just what I've heard. A group like that might have taken her."

"Heard from who?"

"People who were at the riot."

"Four suspected kidnappers," Breisgau said. "No names, except an alias. No pictures. No idea where they come from or where they could have gone."

"That's why I came here," Seth said. "You guys are supposed to be the best. Ex-CIA guys, Secret Service guys. Right?"

Breisgau nodded. "Most of our professionals have a deep background in intelligence or Special Forces. But I'm not sure that's what you need here."

"Why not?"

"So far, we're just looking for a teenage girl who went missing not far from her home," Breisgau said. "She might not even be a victim of any crime. Hiring us for this is like using a flamethrower to swat a housefly."

"You don't want to do it?"

"We'll be happy to look for her. But it's going to cost you."

"I need somebody good," Seth said. "And discreet."

"All our clients enjoy full confidentiality, of course," Breisgau said. "All of our data and communications are sealed behind the most advanced encryption available."

"Good."

"It seems to me that our first step would be to find the girl and assess whether she's in danger. If she's traveling around by choice, we'd have to leave her alone."

"And if she's not?"

"Then there's a step two—ransom and extraction."

"What if the kidnappers don't want a ransom?" Seth asked.

"Then things will get expensive fast."

"Okay." Seth had plenty of money in his college trust fund, which had opened up when he was accepted to college. He could at least afford Hale Security Group's retainer, and maybe the whole fee, from that fund. In any case, spending from there was the best chance to avoid his dad noticing the big chunk of missing money, at least for a while.

"We'll need her full name, pictures, Social Security number—"

"Jennifer Miriam Morton," Seth said. He slid a manila envelope across the desk. "I have everything here."

Breisgau opened the envelope and rifled through the pages inside. "Looks like a good start. One of our associates will probably call with follow-up questions."

"I don't know how secure my cell phone is."

"I suppose we could provide you one of our encrypted phones for our conversations, if you'd like," Breisgau said.

"I'd appreciate it."

"It's your bill." Breisgau shrugged. "We'll start looking for her right away. If she can be found, our associates will find her. We'll contact you the moment we determine her location and whether she's in danger. Until then, you'll receive a weekly report, either in writing or by telephone—"

"Use the encrypted phone," Seth said. "Wait, weekly reports? How long do you think this will take?"

"We don't know, Seth. We don't have much information yet. With any luck, we'll find her happy and content in Seattle. Speaking of which, get us a copy of that postcard and a large sample of her handwriting. We can determine whether she actually wrote that message to her father."

"Okay, that sounds good. But even if she wrote it, maybe somebody forced her to do it—"

"Always a possibility. I'll have Misty check out a secure satellite phone for you, and she'll set up the wire transfer for our retainer."

Seth nodded. While Breisgau gave his assistant instructions over the phone, Seth clenched the arms of his chair, worried about his decision to hire this platinum-grade private intelligence company. If Jenny really had struck out on her own, then she needed to lay low, because the feds were after her. Hale's investigation might draw the government's attention to her, especially considering the sort of people who worked here, lots of former spies and spooks.

Seth didn't believe Jenny was safe, though. Ashleigh Goodling had been back, somehow possessing Darcy's body and getting close to Jenny. Whatever had happened in Charleston, it had almost certainly been the result of one of Ashleigh's plots. And Seth was never going to find her on his own.

"While we wait," Breisgau said, "I happened to notice that Barrett Capital has a lot of interests in the technology sector, over in Asia, India."

"That's my dad's venture-capital obsession."

"I just want to tell you that Hale Group Asia has a number of offices in the region, and a lot of friends. Corporate intelligence, risk assessment, security design. Sometimes you have to pay a little extra fee to local officials to keep things smooth. Sometimes you can hire state police at bargain prices. We can negotiate all of this."

"Oh, yeah? I'd have to talk to my dad about that."

"I would enjoy talking to him myself." Breisgau slid a business card across the table. "We can offer a package of security and data-gathering services customized to your company's needs."

"Right. Gotcha." Seth pocketed the card, which felt like silk in his fingers. "But right now, I want to focus on Jenny."

"I'll put a team on it today," Breisgau said. "We would certainly like to see this as the beginning of a long and mutually beneficial relationship between Barrett Capital and Hale Security Group."

"We'll see," Seth said.

CHAPTER SEVENTEEN

Ashleigh stood at the window of the room at the Four Seasons Hotel, looking down through the curtains at Rodeo Drive, and the smog-heavy city stretching away to the horizon. She was naked except for a beaded necklace, with a matching bracelet and anklet. Each strand of beads included a few ovals of ivory, cut and polished from the pieces of her old skeleton—as long as the bone beads touched Esmeralda's skin, Ashleigh could continue inhabiting Esmeralda's body.

Esmeralda herself slumbered deep at the back of Ashleigh's mind, completely ensnared in the thick golden web of Ashleigh's love.

"Come back to bed," the congressman said. He lay on the bed behind her, also naked. "We only have a few more minutes."

"I think you need a bigger strategy," Ashleigh said.

He laughed. "Now you want to be my strategist? I don't think Greenburg will like that."

Ashleigh flipped her hair as she looked back at him over her shoulder. "Have I ever steered you wrong, Senator?"

"It's still Representative," Brazer said. "Let's not get cocky."

"Let's do." Ashleigh walked back and sat on the corner of his bed. "Let's get really cocky. I don't think Greenburg's ads are making the biggest impact." She gave him a sad smile and stroked his leg, pouring love into him.

Six days after she'd begun volunteering for the Brazer campaign, Eddie Brazer himself came by to chat with the volunteers. Ashleigh had shaken his hand. Three hours later, they'd been in bed together at the Four Seasons. Over the past three weeks, they had spent four lunch breaks together.

"You don't like the new ads?" Brazer asked. "'I believe in the Three E's: Education, Employment, and the Environment.' What's wrong with it?"

"It depends. Are you *trying* to put everyone to sleep?"

"You don't want to panic people," Brazer said. "They want to hear that things will keep ticking like always, only better. Remember, it's mostly the elderly who vote." He traced his fingers across her stomach, up to her breasts. "Now, enough about work..."

"I'm not kidding," Ashleigh said. She'd insinuated herself into his life, even helping revise his speechwriter's drafts. Ashleigh had helped him make simple, emotional appeals for the issues that would appeal to his base: the need to protect the environment, the continuing importance of labor unions, the right of a woman to choose what to do with her own body.

"Fine, what's your big idea?" Brazer asked.

"Are you making fun of me?" Ashleigh teased. She lay her hand on his chest.

"Never. I love it when volunteer kids tell me to remake my entire campaign, four months from the election."

"Hey, I'm on the payroll now," Ashleigh said. "If you can't trust your Social Media Coordinator, who can you trust?"

"So you really think I should ax the ads."

"It's not about the ads," Ashleigh said. "You need to do something bigger, to generate tons and tons of media. Something that will make you a household name."

"Like putting naked pictures of myself on Twitter?"

"Right, that would be a brilliant move." Ashleigh had to force herself not to glance at the slightly parted closet doors. On the top shelf, between stacks of spare pillows and blankets, she'd stashed a video camera to record the two of them together. If you were going to hook up with a congressman, you might as well get full mileage out of it. "But seriously. People need to see you as a leader. A crusader."

"Not the Muslim community."

"I mean, you need a hot issue. Something you can use to attack the President and his whole party."

"The economy. The endless wars."

"Nobody understands the economy," Ashleigh said. "And nobody cares about the wars. You need outrage. You need to make them feel threatened, and make them understand it's the President's fault."

"You are diabolical." He drew her down alongside him and kissed her. Brazer was in his mid-forties, married, reasonably good-looking, not that great in bed. "But if I'm going to be Jack the giant-killer, I'll need a pretty big ax."

"I have a couple of ideas."

"I knew you would."

"Have you heard about this thing in South Carolina? A bunch of people disappeared in some little town. Homeland Security was all over it for a minute and then went away."

"I don't think I've heard of that one."

"People are saying that a bunch of people died, hundreds of people died. There was some kind of extreme toxin. Maybe even a bioweapon kind of thing."

"What people are saying that?"

"On the Internet. A bunch of people."

"Esmeralda, you can't trust everything you read on the Internet."

"And don't talk to me like I'm some little old lady who just discovered the computer lab at her nursing home. I think there's something to this. I think somebody screwed up, and a lot of people died, and the White House used the Department of Homeland Security to cover it up."

"You don't want to go poking around national security issues," Brazer said. "That can explode in your face."

"It's not so much national security. It's incompetence, death and a cover-up to hide their mistakes. I'm telling you, there's something to this story."

"You're really attached to it."

"I've just been looking for something you could use," Ashleigh said. "This looks like a possibility to me. Lots of sloppiness and loose ends, on their part."

"It sounds risky."

"You just have someone look into it," Ashleigh said. "If it looks like a good way to take a shot at the President, accuse him of corruption and lying to the public and all that, you can take it back to the Homeland Security oversight committee with you. Launch some hearings. You get to position yourself as a reformer uncovering abuse of power." She kissed him, spiking him with more love. "If nothing else, you might scare somebody up there, and maybe they'll shovel you some money and political support in exchange for you shutting up about it."

"You think this could work?" His eyes were glazed over as he looked at Ashleigh. He was like soft clay in her fingers.

"It really could," Ashleigh said. She knew Brazer was on the House Homeland Security Committee, and his party controlled the House, though not the Senate or the White House. She was determined to use his position to help her figure out what had happened in Fallen Oak and in Charleston, and why Jenny kept getting away with her horrific crimes. She suspected it was just as she'd told Brazer—some very powerful people did not want the administration to look weak on security, not while the President only had a 35% approval rating and was in danger of losing the Senate in November.

"And who would I appoint to go investigate this for me?" Brazer asked. "It would have to be someone I can trust. The early part of the investigation needs to be low-key, well under the radar. If we hit trouble, we need to be able to close it down fast, run away, and forget all about it."

"That's why I love you, Congressman," Ashleigh said. "You're so smart."

CHAPTER EIGHTEEN

"Who are you really?" Jenny asked Alexander. It was nearly midnight, under a luminous full moon and a clear sky glowing with constellations. They sat on the beach below his house, a blanket insulating them from the wet volcanic sand. Jenny was puffing on a sizable spliff he'd rolled for them, to help settle her raw nerves.

"You know who I am better than anyone." He leaned back on his elbows and looked out at the slow, deep waves of the Pacific.

"I mean in this life. You know. How did you end up down here, doing this? Where did you start out?"

"Where was I born?"

"Yeah. Stuff like that."

"It's nothing special," he said. "It's why it's not worth talking about. My dad's an entertainment lawyer in Los Angeles. Total douchebag. So is my stepmom. My real mom lives in New York, or she did the last time I heard from her." Alexander took the joint from Jenny's fingers.

"What else?" Jenny asked. "What were you like in high school?"

He laughed. "Kind of a troublemaker. I already knew just about everything they had to teach, from my past life memories. Got into a lot of arguments with my history teachers. I was just bored."

"Me, too. Well, the bored part, not the arguing part. I was really quiet."

"That's so unlike you," Alexander said.

"So your life sucked in high school, too," Jenny said. "Then what?"

"A year at Stanford. The summer after my freshman year, I decided to go backpacking through Mexico. Nobody would come with me, because they were so scared of the drug war and the kidnappings and just the unknown. That's one problem with people these days—no courage. They just want to plug their brains into a TV or video game and escape. Nobody had the balls to take a risk."

His words actually made her think of Seth, and how he always ended up under his parents' thumb.

"So," Alexander said, "One morning, I staggered out of a bar with a brain full of tequila. Tiny little town in the Baja. I'd told some local guys I could make the dead walk, and ended up taking bets from all of them. They thought I was just some stupid drunk gringo, and they were pretty much right. There was a funeral in town that day, this poor old woman who'd been killed by a rattlesnake. And we went to that funeral, me and the four or five guys I'd been drinking with. And...well, like I said, I was just a drunken asshole."

"What did you do?"

"I shouldn't have. I wouldn't have if I'd been sober. But I walk into this lady's funeral, and I touch her hand. And then I make her corpse jump right out of the casket and dance around in front of her family and the whole village."

"That's terrible!"

"I told you it was terrible." He shook his head. "I still feel bad about that one. Everyone was horrified, screaming, praying, and I was just full of tequila and laughing. I'm not even sure if I collected on my bets. It was practically a riot."

"That was pretty mean."

"Yeah, well, that's why you shouldn't drink tequila, kids. But that's how the Calderon people heard about me. Papa Calderon collects astrologers, psychics, shamans. He's got a dozen or more on the payroll. I think they're mostly frauds, but I'm one of them, so what do I know? And it turns out I fit right into his plans to grow coca in the Sierra Madre."

"So you're happy being a drug dealer?"

"I'm not. I'm a farmer. And a public benefactor."

"Right."

"What about you, Jenny?" Alexander asked. "Any dark or boring secrets?"

"I killed a bunch of people in my hometown," Jenny said. "I mean, they tried to kill me first, but still."

"You shouldn't feel bad about defending yourself."

"I started out just defending myself, but then it was like something else took over," Jenny said. "Somebody who wanted to *punish*, not just survive."

"You were waking up," Alexander said. "I could feel it way down here in Mexico, like a psychic earthquake. I've been waiting for that all my life. Looking for you."

"How do you remember all your past lives?"

Alexander shrugged. "Broke my arm when I was a kid. The anesthesia killed me for a minute. When I came back..." He tapped the side of his head. "I don't have full consciousness in all my lives, but I think I keep my memories much more often than most of us. Maybe because my power has so much to do with death."

"Does your opposite remember her past lives, too?"

"The dead-speaker? No, Esmeralda refuses. I haven't even bothered speaking to her in several lifetimes, though it's worth knowing where your opposite is and what she's doing. Which is invariably nothing much, she has so little ambition. She usually insists there is no reincarnation, and if there is, it wouldn't be worth knowing about. She says only the present life matters. That's one philosophy she keeps, life after life." He chuckled. "It doesn't make sense to me. Why wouldn't you want to know who you really are?"

"Because who I really am is a crazed murderer," Jenny said.

"No, Jenny. That was your inner goddess coming to the fore. You're always involved in justice."

"Like when I killed the whole city of Athens?"

"Protecting the world from their brutal empire. The Athens you destroyed was not the Athens of the great philosophers and scholars— that Athens had passed long before. The Athens you destroyed was dedicated only to power and conquest."

Jenny thought about that. "But everybody in the city?"

"Our work is divine, Jenny. We shape history. We can't help but use

156

our powers, so we must use them the way we think is best."

"I feel a little sick," Jenny said. "Do you have any more of those coca leaves?"

"Not on me."

"Crap. I like that numb feeling they give me."

"I do have a little of this." Alexander lifted a drawstring pouch from his pocket, opened it, and took out a small silver spoon and a plastic baggie knotted at the top. The plastic was stuffed full of white powder. "The final product."

"What does that feel like?" Jenny eyed it with a mix of suspicion and desire. If it could lift her heavy feelings of despair, even for a minute...

"Like chewing the leaves, but ten thousand times better." He untied the plastic, dipped the spoon inside and held it out to her. Jenny stared at the spoon—it looked like a heaping teaspoon of sugar.

"Won't I get addicted?" she asked.

"You have to do it, like, hundreds of times to get addicted."

"Really?"

"Sure, it's not a big deal. Watch." Alexander held the spoon up to his nostril. She watched him block his other nostril, then snort up half the powder. Then he switched nostrils and snorted up the rest. He tilted his head back and sighed.

"What are you feeling right now?" she asked.

He sniffed a few times, rubbing his nose as he looked back at her. "Awesome. Amazing. Like Jesus on a roller coaster."

Jenny laughed. "Okay. Just a little. Don't let me take much."

He dipped out a spoonful and gave it to her. Jenny copied what he'd done, putting the powder up to her left nostril and then pressing the other nostril closed with her fingertip. She hesitated.

"It's cool," Alexander smiled. "I like it."

Jenny sniffed.

The lump of powder scorched the inside of her nose and the soft tissue behind her left eye. She blinked rapidly, and her whole head and body quickly turned numb. She coughed, tasting the cocaine as it dripped in snotty lumps down the back of her throat.

"Ugh," Jenny said.

"How do you feel?"

Jenny looked at him, then she gave a big smile. "I feel like I just ate a pillowcase full of Halloween candy."

He laughed. "Do the other nostril. Your nose feels better once it's balanced."

"My nose feels pretty awesome already." Jenny thumped the tip of her nose with her fingertip. She could barely feel the impact. It was like she was incapable of feeling pain, and giddy and hyper, and eager for more of the drug. She snorted the rest of it up her other nostril, then dropped the spoon, covered her nose, and laughed.

"Not bad?" he asked.

"I just feel so *good*." She took the smoldering roach of a joint back from him and puffed it. "It's like I want to do everything, right now. I wish we had our horses so we could ride them as fast as they can go down the beach. They're always clomping through the woods. I bet they'd love to just run out here. That would be fun. How long would it take to get the horses? It has to be before the coke wears off. This isn't wearing off already, is it?"

"You've got some time, Jenny." He smiled, looking her over. "It's way too late to bother with the horses, though."

"But what are we going to do?" Jenny jumped to her feet. Her long black hair streamed across her face in the salty breeze. "We have to do *something*. We can't just sit here."

"Then let's explore." Alexander jumped to his feet. "There's an old lighthouse down the beach. No light left, but we can go look at the ruins."

"Okay." Jenny let him take her hand as they walked down the beach. She could hear the cheerful buzz of a trillion insects singing in the night.

The beach became a volcanic maze, with jagged rock formations jutting up around them, between pits of soft, gray sand. Jenny heard her mouth rattling on, telling Alexander about how she liked to work in clay and how many great ideas she'd gotten from the pottery at the open-air market in Comitán.

"There it is." Alexander lay an arm around her and pointed. Following his index finger, Jenny saw a square clay tower, no more than three stories high, perched on the cliff overhead. In the moonlight, she could see the empty holes of its windows. "That's my property, now, too. I'm calling it the great lighthouse of Alexander. It used to warn sailors not to come crash on my beach."

"And who warns them now?"

"I'm not sure. Maybe word just got around." He led her toward a heap of boulders. "There are stairs up to it. They aren't much steeper than what you'd find on a Mayan temple."

Jenny stared at the shell of the lighthouse, outlined against the stars. It looked scary to her, or maybe just depressing, darkness and emptiness where there had once been a source of light.

"I don't want to," Jenny said. She pulled away from him, then took off her sandals and walked through the rocks on the edge of the surf. "Let's go swimming instead."

"Not here. It's too rocky."

"Are you scared?" Jenny asked. She pulled her bright, long-sleeved Mayan blouse over her head and lay it on the boulder next to her sandals. "Do you think we could go skinny dipping without you turning it into some kind of sexual thing?"

"I doubt it," he said.

"Try your best." Jenny tossed her jeans on the boulder. "Remember, I've killed bigger men than you."

"I know you have." Alexander began to undress. "Just keep your hands off me and we'll be fine."

"Ha." Jenny slipped out of her underwear and walked out into the water, until it was deep enough for her to dive in. She turned around and saw Alexander on the beach, his tall, muscular body bare in the moonlight. He strolled into the water and swam out to her.

"You're having a good time," he said.

"It's nice." She looked up at the stars. "Alexander, what are your real plans for this life? Build more pyramids? Conquer more empires?"

"No, the world's too old for that." He tread water a couple of feet in front of her. He gave a smile that, for a moment, made him look very old, too. "All I want is to carve a nice, comfortable little kingdom out of southern Mexico. Nobody else is doing anything useful with it. I could modernize, beautify, carve my initials here."

"And you think these people will let you rule them?"

"There are many ways to rule, both out front and behind the curtain."

"Tell me about some things we did in our past lives," Jenny said.

"Where do I start?"

"The beginning, maybe," Jenny said.

"You really want to hear about five hundred lifetimes of mastodon hunts?"

"Skip to when it gets interesting, then."

"The city of Megiddo," he said. "Though it wasn't called that nine thousand years ago. You were born to a family of potters and craftsmen, me to a family of shepherds and raiders." His eyes looked deep into her, and his smile was warm. "I can remember the first time I saw you in that life. Neither of us had our full memories, but I knew there was something about you. The intelligence and fearlessness in your eyes. Watching your bare hands covered in wet clay, shaping the most beautiful things out of mud." He shook his head. "I feel that way every time we meet, every life. Life doesn't really begin until we meet each other."

Jenny smiled. "So what did you do?"

"I kidnapped you from your family and made you my wife. Those were rougher days."

"You're such a monster."

"You liked it. Your parents had promised you to some other boy you hated." He took her hands and drew her closer. "You married me again and again, life after life. You killed me a couple times, too. But that's marriage. Mostly, we've been happy. I don't want another lifetime without you."

Alexander began treading water, and he pulled her against him. Jenny drowned in the wet, salty taste of his lips, the electric touch of his body...and then she opened her eyes and swam back from him.

"I told you, none of that right now," she said.

"Then I guess you'll have to kill me." He swam toward her. "You said that would be my punishment."

Jenny held up both her hands. Dark lesions ripped open all over her palms and fingers. "Try me."

He took her around the waist and pulled her to him again. He kissed her harder this time. Jenny's hands smeared blood and gore all over his face and neck as she kissed him back.

This time, she let him kiss her as long as she dared.

CHAPTER NINETEEN

At Egleston Children's Hospital in Atlanta, Heather sat in the hospital room next to Tricia's bed. The four-year-old with the untameable brown hair was mercifully asleep for the moment. A bandage covered her tiny back, where the methotrexate had entered Tricia's spinal fluid through an intralumber injection.

A week of chemo had made the girl pale and gaunt. While Tricia had started acting tired before she was diagnosed, the chemo kept her sleeping all day. When awake, she only spoke in weak whispers.

Heather's phone buzzed again inside her purse, rattling against her sunglasses. Heather sighed and took it out. Her boss Schwartzman, for the fifth time in the past two hours. Heather walked to the window and called him back, looking out at the orange light of a late July afternoon. He answered halfway through the first ring.

"Heather," he said, "How is she doing?"

"Sleeping," Heather whispered.

"We have a bad situation."

"I'm on family leave, David."

"I know.   And I'm sorry. But there's a small congressional

162

investigation going on here. It's about Fallen Oak. And they want to talk to you in person."

"Who wants to talk to me?"

"Investigators sent by the House Homeland Security Committee. It looks like Artleby doesn't have the lid screwed on as tight as he thought. They're asking a lot of questions about Fallen Oak, about Charleston—everything you've been doing."

"They can read my reports."

"I told them that, but nobody in Washington reads anymore," Schwartzman said. "Nothing longer than a headline, anyway. They said they can do it here, or come to your home—"

"I'll come in," Heather said quickly. "Is tomorrow okay?"

"It should be. They don't seem to have any intention of leaving soon. I'll let them know you're coming by in the morning. I'm so sorry to call you."

"It's fine."

"How are you holding up, Heather?"

Heather looked at her little girl, eaten up with cancer in the hospital bed, a stuffed Big Bird lying beside her. "I really don't know how to answer that, David."

Schwartzman's office was, like the man himself, slightly unkempt, the bookshelves overstuffed with thick medical texts and heaps of research journals, all of it carefully organized according to a "right-brain-generated chaotic pattern," according to him. Heather entered, looking at the Lord of the Rings figurines arranged on his desk so that they seemed to be stalking his telephone.

Schwartzman wasn't here, though—he'd sent Heather to meet with the chief investigator, who was borrowing his office. While a team of sharp-eyed young lawyers were pawing through the records, their leader was a pretty Latino girl who looked no more than twenty years old. From what Schwartzman said, she wasn't a lawyer, and she didn't appear to have any real qualifications to run a congressional investigation. Heather wondered who she was sleeping with.

"Hello, Dr. Reynard." The young woman stood up behind Schwartzman's desk and held out her hand. "I'm Esmeralda Rios. I was sent from the House Homeland Security committee. We're just trying to clear up a few things."

"Nice to meet you," Heather said automatically. She took the girl's hand, and something came over her. Her resentment at being called in to work melted away—it was clear that this young woman, Esmeralda, was just an earnest person trying to do a difficult job. Heather's heart went out to her. "I hope I can help," she added, sincerely.

"I'm sure you can, Dr. Reynard." Esmeralda sat in Schwartzman's chair, and Heather sat across the desk from her. "It sure was nice of Dr. Schwartzman to loan me his office while we're here. He's been so nice and helpful."

"I'm sure your work is important." Heather gave her a smile. She felt a strong desire to help this girl and be supportive.

"Maybe we could start with an overview," Esmeralda said. "Can you tell me what happened the day of the...outbreak...in Fallen Oak?"

"The reports say it was some kind of chemical leak," Heather said.

"I know what the reports say. But we're after the facts here." Esmeralda winked and patted Heather's hand. Heather's heat skipped a beat. She liked the touch of the girl's hand. Heather had a crazy, elated sense of falling in love with this girl. "You understand. Somebody has to get to the truth here, don't you agree?"

"I really do," Heather said, gazing into the girl's dark gray eyes. "But I was told to keep quiet..."

"By who?" Esmeralda squeezed her hand. "You don't have to keep any secrets from me."

"Homeland Security took control of the scene," Heather whispered. "The investigation, the media, everything."

"That's exactly the problem," Esmeralda said. "We're not investigating the CDC here. You guys are great. Our concern—the committee's concern—is that the Department of Homeland Security might have been used in a way that put politics ahead of the country's security. We think critical information was deliberately kept from members of Congress. We want to know the details."

Heather found herself nodding along. She wasn't happy with how the Fallen Oak situation had been handled, either. Something needed to be done, and she wanted to help, but that wasn't really what she was thinking about at the moment. She was wondering how this Esmeralda girl would react if Heather kissed her.

"So, will you help us?" Esmeralda asked. She was stroking the back of Heather's hand now, and Heather found the sensation delightful beyond words.

164

"Of course," Heather said. "Anything you want."

"What was your role in the Fallen Oak investigation?"

"I'm an epidemiologist," Heather told her. "So my job was to identify the pathogen and try to find the source."

"What did you discover?"

"There was no pathogen," Heather said. "The disease was so extreme and so rapid, I was thinking it must have been genetically engineered. I was initially worried about bioterrorism, to be honest. But there was nothing to be found. It was all symptoms, no vector. Strangest thing I've ever seen."

"Did you have any luck finding the source?"

Heather bit her lip. She wasn't sure how much she should share, when everything had been declared classified.

Then Esmeralda laced her fingers together with Heather's, and suddenly all Heather could think about was how to get alone with this girl. Esmeralda was from out of town, so she must have a hotel room. That would be easier than Heather taking the girl home to her own bed, where Liam was obviously going to ask questions.

"The source of the outbreak?" Esmeralda asked again.

"Oh...there's a girl," Heather said. She was feeling drunk now, aching to touch the girl. "Jennifer Morton."

Esmeralda's eyes narrowed. "Tell me about her."

"We...I think she's an immune carrier," Heather said. "Some reports say she can exhibit symptoms at will, she can become contagious at will. That sounds crazy, but that's what I've heard. And I'm starting to believe it." Her voice dropped to a whisper again. "Something supernatural is going on here, Esmeralda. Not many people believe it, but I do."

"So you think Jenny Mitt...Morton willingly infected and killed all those people in Fallen Oak?"

"That's what I think." Heather giggled—the girl's touch was making her lose her mind. "Don't tell anyone I said that, though. I mean, I examined Jennifer's hair and blood, and there was nothing unusual there—until I put them in contact with a control group of live blood cells. All of the cells that didn't belong to her just shriveled and died on contact. But I never saw a transfer of a pathogen. It's really not possible, what I saw. But that's what I saw."

"And where is Jenny Morton now?" Esmeralda asked.

"That's the billion-dollar question. Homeland Security is looking for her, but she's gone into hiding somewhere." Heather's fingertips stroked their way up along the inside of Esmeralda's forearm. She couldn't stop smiling at the girl. "Do you want to go get a drink with me, or...?"

"Aw, that's sweet. Maybe later." Esmeralda winked. "You don't have a clue where to find Jenny?"

"Not a one."

"What about the bodies? Where are all the bodies from Fallen Oak?"

"The bodies..." Heather had to concentrate. The desire was taking over her brain as well as her body.

"Yes, Heather," Esmeralda said. "Where are the bodies buried?"

"I'm...not really sure. They aren't buried, though. They're frozen."

"Where?"

"Some kind of secure storage facility. I think it's around here somewhere, maybe a little outside Atlanta. I know the contract went to one of Nelson Artleby's companies. You should ask him."

"The President's campaign adviser?"

"That's the one," Heather said. "He took over the investigation. Whatever Homeland Security did, they did under his orders."

"This is just what we're trying to find," Esmeralda said. "Whether the White House is guilty of lying to Congress. The House oversight committee hasn't heard a thing from Homeland Security, except for their official reports about a chemical leak in some abandoned old factory."

"Which is bullshit," Heather said.

"Of course it is. That's why I'm here." Esmeralda scrolled through a few things on her laptop. "Okay, that gives me some ideas about where to start. Thanks for coming and talking to me, Dr. Reynard. I'm sure I'll be in touch as the investigation continues."

"Call me Heather. And just let me know if I can help...or if you just need someone to talk to...or a place to spend the night..."

Esmeralda raised her eyebrows, and Heather blushed.

"Thanks so much, Heather," Esmeralda said. "You're very helpful."

Heather squirmed in her seat as she gazed at the girl.

"You can go now," Esmeralda said.

"Oh, sorry! Of course." Heather stood up. Esmeralda shook her hand again, holding it for a long moment, and Heather had to resist the temptation to draw her close in an embrace.

Heather hurried home and immediately stripped down and took a long, warm shower. It took a couple of hours for her fever of desire to finally break, and when it did, it left her feeling confused and a little ashamed. Heather had really never been attracted to other women, not that way. She wondered what it was about Esmeralda that made Heather crave her touch so badly.

CHAPTER TWENTY

Jenny woke to shouting voices from downstairs, and the sound of a woman screaming.

It took a second to get her bearings—it was late, probably long past midnight. She'd gone to bed after a late dinner with Alexander, somewhere around nine or ten o' clock. Late dinners were common here. So was a fantastic thing called a "siesta" where people napped through the hottest part of the afternoon.

Jenny dressed quickly, pulled on gloves and boots, and ran out of her room and down the back stairs. She followed the screams out to the front hall, where the front door stood open. Alexander and one of his men, Raul, stood just outside. Raul had his AK-47 off his shoulder and in his hands, and he nodded while Alexander spoke in rapid Spanish.

"What's happening?" Jenny asked.

Alexander hurried inside and embraced her. "We have a security situation. You should go back upstairs. I don't want you to see this."

"See what?" Jenny looked around his shoulder to the open door.

"They were on their way back from Zinacantan," Alexander said. "Someone strafed their truck. We think one of Toscano's men."

Jenny took a second to process this. Toscano headed the Juarez

168

cartel, the chief rival to Papa Calderon's Tijuana-based cartel. And Zinacantan was the home village of Kisa and her family. She and her brothers had gone home to visit for the week.

"Did they hurt Kisa?" Jenny asked.

Alexander looked at her for a moment, frowning. "Jenny..."

"I want to see her!" Jenny pushed her way past him and ran for the open door.

"Wait!" Alexander shouted.

"If someone's attacking us, I can help," Jenny said. She didn't stop running.

Outside, one of the trucks idled in front of the house, one headlight glowing. The windshield and one side of the truck were stippled with gaping bullet holes, and one tire was flat.

Noonsa leaned against the truck, staring into the flatbed. The old woman was screaming and crying. She had stayed at Alexander's compound instead of visiting home with her niece and nephews.

"Raul was barely able to get the truck home," Alexander said. "By the time we found them, it was too late for a doctor."

Jenny ran across the wildflowers of the front yard to the battered, slumping truck. She looked at Noonsa, who covered her face with her hands, sobbing. Then Jenny looked into the back of the truck.

Three bullet-riddled bodies lay in the pond of fresh blood in the truck's payload: Iztali, Yochi, and Kisa. The girl had died in mid-scream, eyes scrunched closed, mouth wide open. Most of her neck had been blown away, leaving only a strip of flesh connecting her head and shoulders.

"Kisa!" Jenny screamed. She shed a glove and took one of the girl's cold, blood-slick hands, finally able to touch her friend. One of the only friends she'd ever had. A pained wail erupted from Jenny's lips.

"I'm sorry, Jenny. This is what I didn't want you to see." Alexander spoke in a gentle voice and touched a cool hand to the back of her neck. He drew her close to hug her, but Jenny pushed away.

"Who did this?" Jenny snapped.

"Manuel and some others are searching for them now," Alexander said. "The shooters won't get far. But this could be the first step in an attack against this compound, so I'd like you to get back and inside. There could be gunfire."

"If the people who did this come here, they're getting hit with worse things than gunfire." Jenny looked at Kisa's body again, and her eyes burned with tears. She looked away quickly. "I mean it."

Raul approached from the house with an armload of blankets. Jenny helped Alexander and Noona wrap the bodies. Alexander said he would have someone drive them back to their village in the morning. Noonsa embraced each of her young relatives, weeping, just before the bodies were wrapped. She came away with blood all over her dress.

They moved the bodies to the blind cavern under the main house, which served as a root cellar and storage. It was the coolest place to keep them from decaying in the tropical heat.

Everyone sat on the front porch, with blood smeared all over their hands, and they waited.

Manuel returned in the Jeep about an hour later, with two other Calderon men. A fourth man huddled in the back of the Jeep at gunpoint —beaten and bruised, hands tied, blindfolded.

Manuel opened the rear door of the Jeep, and the two other men kicked the prisoner out. He grunted when he hit the dirt.

Alexander and Manuel spoke in very rapid Spanish. Jenny was picking up some words of that language, too, but people usually spoke too fast for her to follow.

"There were two men," Alexander said. "The gunner and the driver. This is the gunner."

"Where's the driver?" Jenny asked.

"Manuel killed him and fed his body to the jungle," Alexander said. "This man confesses. He was sent by Toscano to attack our people. A warning." Alexander frowned. "This means Toscano knows we have an operation going here in Chiapas."

Jenny looked at the man kicking and flailing in the dirt. "Why did they kill Kisa, too?"

"Because she was there," Alexander said. "I told you, Toscano is a psychopath. He thinks nothing of killing women and children."

"What are you going to do with him now?" Jenny asked. The man in the dirt was begging and sobbing, but she had little sympathy for the murderer.

"Put a bullet in his head and send him back to Toscano," Alexander said. "That will be our message in reply."

Jenny glared at the sobbing gunman. "That's too good for him. We can send a scarier message."

"What are you thinking, Jenny?"

Jenny knelt beside the writhing man. She took her glove off again and pulled the blindfold down to his nose. When he saw her, he renewed his shouting and beseeching in Spanish.

"You killed my friend," Jenny said.

The man wept. She doubted he could understand her, but she kept talking. He could understand her tone.

"I loved that girl," Jenny said. "You shouldn't have done this to her."

She reached a hand toward the man's face, and he stopped shouting and started blubbering, as if he thought she was granting him mercy. She wasn't.

Dark cysts popped up all over his face. Bloody abscesses opened at the corners of his eyes, nose and mouth. The infection traveled down his throat, out to his fingertips, his skin boiling and bursting open. The man cried out and struggled to inch away from her in the dirt, but Jenny moved with him, keeping her hand on him until he seized up and collapsed in the dirt, his face a corrupt, wet mass.

Jenny looked up. Manuel and his two gunmen gaped at her, and even Noonsa had stopped crying to stare in shock.

Alexander reached out a hand to Jenny, and she let him help her up. She'd been shaking with rage, but now the anger began to fade, replaced by sorrow for her lost her friend and the beginnings of guilt for killing yet another person. Even if he deserved it.

Alexander drew her against him. "You did the right thing," he said.

Jenny looked at the contorted corpse of the man who'd killed Kisa. "I think I did."

"Let's go inside," Alexander said. "The men will clean this up."

Manuel and the other two gunmen watched them leave and whispered to each other. One of the men bowed his head and crossed himself. Jenny understood. She was *la bruja*, the witch. And nothing she could do would ever change that.

CHAPTER TWENTY-ONE

Ashleigh beamed as she walked into Brazer's Los Angeles office, her briefcase case in one hand. He stood up, grinning like a fool, and Ashleigh closed the door behind her.

"Esmeralda," he breathed. She went to him and kissed him for a long minute. When he sat down again, she sat in his lap, one arm around his shoulders, the other toying with his necktie. "I missed you," Brazer said.

"I missed you, too, baby," Ashleigh said.

"What did you find?"

"It's a goldmine," Ashleigh said. "There wasn't any stupid chemical leak. It was some kind of powerful disease. Even the CDC doctors couldn't figure out what happened."

"It's still a little fuzzy to drag out in front of the public. You have to imagine the public as a huge, slobbery animal that only understands soundbites and buzzwords."

"There are dead bodies," Ashleigh said. "Hundreds of them. Show that to the media, and ask why the President covered up their deaths. Why Homeland Security gave a blatantly false cause for the event."

"I don't know..."

Ashleigh kissed him again. "This is serious stuff, Eddie. Launch some hearings in the fall so they're in everybody's minds for the election. You'll put the President on the defensive, his party will run away from him..."

"And we'll take over the Senate." Eddie looked at her glazed eyes.

"Exactly."

Eddie ran his finger across her lower lip, Ashleigh sucked his fingertip.

"Marry me, Esmeralda," he said.

"You're already married."

"But she's nothing like you. You're brilliant..." He kissed her. "Beautiful." He kissed her again. "I can't stand being away from you, even for a night."

"The wife and three little kids make a good picture," Ashleigh said. "That's what voters want to see. A divorce could make the election messy."

He slipped a hand under her starchy black skirt, up along her thigh. "Should we have lunch at the Four Seasons?"

"Of course."

"I love you, Esmeralda," he said in a low, tense voice.

"I know you do."

***

"You're fucking him, aren't you?" Tommy asked. He sat on Esmeralda's bed in his underwear, drinking a pint of cheap whiskey and watching an *A-Team* rerun on the small TV. His eyes flicked over to Ashleigh as she stripped out of her professional wear.

"Who?" Ashleigh asked.

"Come on. The politician guy. Eddie for Senate."

"First, I am not doing that." Ashleigh took off her shoe and pointed her sharp high heel at Tommy. "Second, even if I were, it would be none of your business."

"But you're my girl."

"*Esmeralda* is your girl." Ashleigh pulled on a linty polyester nightgown, possibly the least sexy thing Esmeralda owned. "I'm my own person."

"But you're using her body," Tommy said. "You can't go screwing around with other people. I bet she wouldn't be happy to hear about it."

"Tommy, just relax. I'm not doing it anyway. I just wanted to point out that I have the right do it if I want." She laid down on the bed and turned her back to him. "Good night."

"Good night?" He turned her toward him and kissed her—he tasted like bad liquor, cigarette ashes, and six-day-old morning breath. His hand pawed at her breasts.

"Stop it!" Ashleigh pulled away from him.

"Just let Esmeralda out for a minute."

"No. I'm tired."

"Maybe she's not."

"We need our sleep, Tommy."

"Damn it. You know, I can't just go out and get laid. Most women don't like the fear. You know why I wear these gloves?" Tommy held up a hand. He wore black leather gloves, with the knuckles and the back of the hand cut out.

"Because you're a gay biker?" Ashleigh asked.

"Because I can't be normal around people if they touch me. They're afraid of me."

"I thought you liked making people feel fear."

"It can be useful. But I wish I could turn it off sometimes. Just be normal instead of making everyone feel fear."

"So sorry for you." Ashleigh closed her eyes and pulled the comforter over herself. She could feel Tommy's eyes glaring at her, but she stayed still and didn't say a word.

"Fine," he said at last. He stood up, and she heard rustling as he got dressed. "I'm going down to Jack's Spot."

"Of course you are. Drink the night away."

"Hell, yeah. One of us needs to remember how to have fun."

"Shooting pool in a dark hole with the lowest of the city's lowlifes," Ashleigh said. "Sounds like a barrel of fun."

"Lowlifes? You hang out with politicians. What exactly do you do for him, anyway?"

"Social media coordinator. I told you."

"What the hell does that mean?"

"You know. I keep up his Twitter and Facebook accounts, his blog..."

"Sounds real tough."

"At least I get paid," Ashleigh said. "I don't have to rob meth heads just so I can afford to hang out in a sleazy bar."

"Fuck you, Ashleigh." Tommy slammed the bedroom door as he left.

"Not until you take a shower," Ashleigh whispered. She turned off the bedside lamp and closed her eyes again.

CHAPTER TWENTY-TWO

Jenny and Alexander hiked along a narrow, steep trail through the jungle, heading up the side of a mountain. Jenny was soaked with sweat in the steaming afternoon heat. Alexander's two zombie jaguars were ahead of them on the trail, spooking off any man or beast who might bother them.

"Need a break?" Alexander asked. They'd been hiking for more than an hour up rough terrain.

"No," Jenny said. Her legs and feet were aching. The pack on her back had felt light at first, but she could swear it grew heavier with every step. "Why? Are you tired or something?"

"I'm great." Alexander sipped from his canteen and passed it to her.

"That's what you think of yourself?" Jenny put the canteen to her lips and tried not to slurp the whole thing down.

"It's what I think of you."

Jenny rolled her eyes. "I'm great at killing people."

"Some people need killing."

"According to who? Who decides who lives and who dies?"

"You," Alexander said.

"Why should I be the judge?"

"You are, whether you want to be or not. It's always your choice."

"I'm really trying not to do that anymore, Alexander."

"How does it make it you feel?"

"How do you think?" Jenny snapped. "Sick, guilty, hating myself..."

"And...?"

Jenny didn't answer.

"Part of it feels good, doesn't it?" Alexander said. "Expressing your power. Letting your inner goddess out."

"Don't say that. It sounds like something from Oprah. 'Let out your inner goddess!'"

Alexander laughed.

They continued onward, Jenny trying not to think about Kisa. Jenny and Alexander had attended the funeral at the big stone Catholic church in Zinacantan. Jenny missed her terribly, and tried not to cry about it until she was alone.

Noonsa had left, unable to work in the place where she'd seen her nephews and niece die. Alexander had hired a couple of middle-aged *mestizo* women to replace Noonsa and Kisa's housekeeping and cooking, and he'd brought a couple of other Mayan men who'd previously guarded coca patches to help provide security at the compound. Jenny tried to avoid speaking to the new people, or to anyone. She didn't feel like making new friends yet.

The trail widened and they reached their destination.

"Here we are," Alexander said. "The lost city of Paochilan. What's left of it, anyway."

Jenny took in the crumbling stones walls, carved with reliefs and full-size animal statues. Everywhere she looked, the land was terraced, with wide stone steps choked with weeds. Entire trees grew up through the largest building, a towering pyramid like a mountain, with steps leading up to a narrow stone building at the top.

"This is amazing," Jenny said. "Doesn't anybody know about this place?"

"Just one more Mayan ruin," Alexander shrugged. He approached the pyramid. "Come on. We want to reach the top before sunset." He stepped on the first of many steep, broken stone stairs. The jaguars sat down on either side of the staircase like guards.

"Is it safe?" Jenny asked.

"Is anything?" He climbed a few more steps. "There's only two hundred steps."

"Great." Jenny placed a foot on the lowest step, and then she looked up. The staircase was so steep that it seemed like she'd be walking almost straight up. A number of the stairs were cracked and eroded, and they were all very shallow. She could barely fit her foot on one.

"Scared?" Alexander asked.

"No. If something breaks loose and I fall, I'll deserve it for listening to you."

"That's the spirit, Jenny."

They ascended. Jenny was fascinated by the carvings set into the pyramid, lots of birds and jaguars. She could have stopped to study them every step of the way, but the sun was low in the sky and she didn't want to be looking for steps in the dark.

Panting, she finally reached the top, hundreds of feet above the ground. They faced a building with three empty doorways, Mayan hieroglyphs carved into their stone lintels.

"This was the holiest place in the city," Alexander said. "Only the highest priests allowed. They received messages from the gods here."

"Didn't they do human sacrifice?"

"Some of that, too."

Jenny looked down the steep slope of the pyramid—it was a long fall to the shadowy ground below. For a moment, she could imagine thousands of Mayans standing below, looking up in awe as priests performed the ceremonies.

Then she looked out to a breathtaking view of the sunset over the Sierra Madre mountains. She could see a waterfall here and there off the mountains, disappearing into rivers that slinked away below the dense green canopy. A flock of brightly colored birds passed nearby.

"How old is this place?" Jenny asked.

"About twelve hundred years, give or take," Alexander said. "It's not one of the famous, touristy places. Most of the old ruins aren't well known. The government just picks a few, runs a lawnmower over them, and charges admission. But nobody ever comes here. We've got the place to ourselves. Let's check out our room."

Alexander led her through one of the portals, into a room lined from floor to ceiling with hieroglyphs. A thick layer of leaves and debris had accumulated on the stone-tile floor. Alexander swept an area clear with his foot, then shrugged off his hiking pack and set it down. Jenny was grateful to set hers down, too. She stretched her arms and back, all of which now felt incredibly light.

"Got any more coke?" Jenny asked him.

"Why? We're done hiking."

Jenny shrugged. "Just an idea."

"We're not doing any more of that tonight." Alexander laid out a bright, geometric-patterned Mayan blanket that covered a large portion of the cover. Then he took out a woven pouch the size of a grocery bag.

"Dinner?" Jenny asked.

He opened the bag to show her. It looked like a couple of pounds of raw mushrooms. They smelled pungent, like earth and decay.

"Tell me that's not what we're eating," she said.

"It's the only thing we're eating."

"Ugh. They look sick."

"We're not eating them for the flavor, Jenny." Alexander tossed a mushroom in his mouth and chewed on it, and he was obviously trying to hide a grimace at the taste. "These are sacred mushrooms."

"Oh...I've never done those." She looked into the bag again and wrinkled her nose. "Those can make you crazy, can't they?"

"If you use them like a party drug. Used correctly, they can open hidden doors in your mind." He held out a mushroom to her, but Jenny didn't take it.

"What kind of doors? Hallucinations and stuff?"

"In your case, the doors to who you really are," Alexander said. He popped the mushroom she'd refused into his own mouth and chewed it quickly. "After tonight, you'll remember everything, Jenny."

"You mean my past lives?"

"All of them, if we do it right. You'll remember the different ways you can use your power, too. And then you'll be fully awake. You'll remember yourself, you'll remember me, and we'll both be fully ourselves again."

"All that from a mushroom, huh?" Jenny asked. She was starting to feel afraid, but she didn't want to show it. Her real self, as Alexander called it, the primordial part of her that had reincarnated so many times, had often acted as a monster. She'd glimpsed that much already. "I'm not sure I want to see my past."

"The truth is the truth whether you learn it or not," Alexander said. "So you might as well learn it. That's my philosophy."

He offered her another mushroom.

Jenny could only think of the difficult life she'd had so far. Her father's struggle to make her a good person, his depressing disillusionment when he realized he'd failed. Ashleigh's manipulations—which might even include Jenny and Seth's entire relationship, according to Alexander.

She did know one thing—she was sick of being in the dark about what she was, and she didn't want to go through life depending on Alexander to tell her. She needed to know for herself.

Jenny took the mushroom into her mouth and bit into it. It tasted the way cow patties smelled.

"Delicious, huh?" Alexander asked.

She raised her middle finger at him while she chewed the mushroom. Then she accepted another. And another.

They walked out of the temple and sat on the highest step, watching the sun fade away while they ate their way through the mushrooms, washing them down with water. Jenny grew nervous, then anxious, then bored. The corona of the sun slid out of sight, and an ocean of stars became visible.

"I don't think these are doing anything," Jenny said.

Alexander grinned. "Tell me about your earliest memory."

"Like Egypt? Or Africa?"

"This lifetime."

"Oh." Jenny thought. "I was outside in the yard, like two or three years old. I don't remember what I was doing. But I saw this snake—a huge rattler—crawling around below this log. And for some reason, I thought it would make a fun little toy."

"You liked the rattle."

"Maybe. I thought it was kind of cute. But when I picked him up..." Jenny looked at Alexander. He could probably guess what came next, but he just waited attentively, his eyes watching hers. "Well, he died. The Jenny pox made him bleed everywhere. My dad got really pissed at me for playing with rattlesnakes."

As she told the story, she thought she could hear a sound like rattling, but at first it seemed like an echo of her childhood memory. Then the rattling grew louder and multiplied, as if the forest were filled with diamondback rattlers.

"Do you hear that?" Jenny asked.

"The sound of the jungle?"

"Not exactly..." Jenny heard the rattle behind her, loud and strong, and she whirled around to look at the temple.

A feathered serpent was carved above the doorway on the far left, its squarish jaw open and pointed tongue protruding, its scales rectangular with a dot carved inside each one. When they'd arrived, the serpent figure had been folded in on itself in stack of coils.

Now the serpent's head was sliding forward across the front of the temple, towards the middle door, while layer by layer its body unfolded and stretched out behind it. The serpent opened its jaw wide and ate the hieroglyphic birds carved on the lintel of the middle door. Then it flowed on across the face of the temple, towards the door on the right.

"Do you see that?" Jenny whispered. She looked at Alexander. His face kept shifting and melting in front of her eyes, changing from one face to another to another, all of them somehow familiar to Jenny. The only constant was his dark eyes, watching her while the rest of his face kept changing.

"I see you," Alexander said. "All of your faces like masks, nested inside each other like a Russian doll."

"I see you, too," Jenny said. "All of you."

The snake rattled again. It swallowed the hieroglyphs above the third door, then turned inward and began flowing away into the temple wall, as if it had found some hole in which to burrow.

Then its head and body curled down into the doorway, but it was no longer a stylized relief carved in stone. Instead, it was a live snake, its head as big as a lion's, its body as thick as a man. It was identical to the snake from her first memory, except that thousands of actual diamonds glittered among the scales on its back.

"Tell me you're seeing that," Jenny whispered.

The snake extended out of the doorway, its head gradually dropping lower as more of the body flowed out of the doorway, until its head was just above the stone floor.

"What are you seeing?" Alexander asked. His voice seemed to echo around her, along with the thousands and thousands of snake rattles.

"A snake," Jenny said. "It's huge. And it's coming toward us."

"Don't be afraid." Alexander took her hand.

"It's not real, is it?" she whispered. The snake moved silently across the stone tiles, towards her feet.

"It's more than real," Alexander said.

"That's not what I wanted you to say." Jenny watched the huge head approach her. The snake rose up in front of her like a charmed cobra, its bottomless black eyes staring into hers. Its rattle sounded as loud as a drum in her head.

"Don't show it any fear," Alexander's voice said, somewhere. Jenny couldn't see him, only the vast snake raising up above her now.

"Yeah...I don't know if I can do that," Jenny whispered.

The huge diamondback's head rose a few feet above Jenny, and then the snake froze, its eyes still locked on hers.

"Nice snake," Jenny whispered. Her whole body was shaking, but she knew better than to make sudden moves around a poisonous snake, even if it was just a hallucination. "Good snake..."

The snake's jaws opened, revealing fangs the size of butcher knives. Then its head darted down at Jenny, and its venomous fang sank deep into her right temple. She could feel it skewering her brain, flooding her head with hot poison.

"Alexander!" Jenny cried out. The snake tore loose, ripping away a sizable chunk of her face. Jenny screamed and toppled forward, toward the steps.

She caught her balance and found her feet sliding forward on stone. She was reminded of moments when she'd been about to go to sleep, when suddenly she would feel her feet slip out from underneath her and then feel herself falling, even though she was lying in bed. Then she would regain her sense of balance.

When Jenny regained her balance, she found herself walking along a crowded cobblestone street that reeked of horse manure, human waste and baking bread. She wore a long, rough skirt and a stiff, scratchy blouse, as well as a pair of gloves to her elbow. Her hair was tied back with a length of ribbon. The crowd jostling around her wore similar archaic, handmade clothing.

All at once, she knew that this was Paris, but not the modern city of wide boulevards and classical architecture. This was more of a medieval warren tucked behind high walls, the streets as narrow and twisted as rabbit-trails in a thick forest. It was the early seventeenth century.

Jenny heard a pained wail behind her. She looked back over her shoulder, and suddenly the crowd was gone. Instead, people huddled in doorways, shivering, their bodies swollen with thick black growths. Corpses littered the streets.

All around her, the dense crowd had turned to scattered individuals staggering their way down the street, afflicted with the horrific disease. She watched a hobbling old man drop his cane, then fall to the street motionless. The city was filled with cries of despair and muffled weeping.

"What do you see?" Alexander's voice said beside her.

"The plague," Jenny said. "Paris." She turned to look at Alexander. They were standing just where they'd been, on the top step of the Mayan pyramid. Though Jenny had been part of the street scene, it now appeared to float before her, like a television screen glowing in the vast open darkness in front of the pyramid. She could see herself in that life, pulling the hood of her cloak over her head as she hurried through the plague-ridden city.

She turned to Alexander, whose face was still shifting appearance at least once a second, one face giving way to another. His faces smiled at her.

"Look again," they said, and the sounds of countless snake rattles grew as loud as a thunderstorm.

Jenny looked. The space in front of the pyramid seemed to unfold, and with each unfolding a burst of images appeared. Ancient Greece, ancient Egypt, medieval Germany, more and more scenes woven together in a vast, animated tapestry drawn from across the millennia. Her past lives, all of them appearing to happen right now, in the present moment, parallel to each other.

Her eyes found a recent life—glimpses of herself on a circus train crossing America, and then in a shadowy tent, the pox all over her skin so that she was unrecognizable under her mask of bleeding sores. A carnival barker: *Yes, sir, yes, ma'am, pay a penny and see the world's most diseased woman...a true horror, friends, a true horror...*

"Not there." Alexander lay a finger under her chin and turned her head to a different scene. "Look there."

Jenny watched Alexander leading an army of the dead toward Babylon, thousands of years ago, Jenny at his side in some kind

184

of horse-drawn wagon. She was dressed in silks and jewels.

Elsewhere, she saw a similar scene: an army of zombies sacking a city in India.

She looked again, and saw herself hurrying down a street in nineteenth-century London, the air heavy with factory smoke. Jenny was bundled in with a coat, scarf and hat, and carrying an armload of books.

"Not there," Alexander said again. He turned her head to look at another army, both men and women this time, all of them with blue-painted skin. Jenny was one of them, and she blew a plague at an approaching Roman legion.

"Now remember me." Alexander was behind her, embracing her with both arms. She could feel the heat from his hands on her belly.

She saw the two of them together, making love in countless temples and castles and primeval forests, Alexander ravaging her, her lips crying out in passion and pleasure and pain.

Jenny reached her hand back to his hip, and she rubbed her hand up and down along his thigh. She leaned back against him, her body trembling and aching to be close to his. He kissed her neck, and she could feel every detail of it, the warm texture of his lips, his hot breath damp on her skin.

Jenny turned and kissed him back hungrily. She remembered.

"My lord," she whispered, but the language she used was a long-forgotten dialect from ancient Sumeria. "My love, my life."

"My love, my life," he whispered back.

She ripped open his shirt and kissed the muscles of his shoulders, chest, abdomen. Then she stepped back from him and took off her blouse, her sneakers, her jeans. She took off every stitch of clothing, until she was naked before him, her pale body lit by the moon and stars. Her body trembled and burned with the most painful desire she had ever felt. Her soul swam in an ocean of raw power.

Jenny shoved Alexander back through the door of the temple, and they embraced and fell together on the Mayan blanket inside.

Alexander slid out of his jeans and turned her on her back.

He climbed on top of her, and she felt him jab her in the stomach, long and hard.

"Not yet," Jenny said. She gave him a wicked smile and pressed a hand to the top of his head, pushing him down along her body. He kissed her breasts, then her stomach. Jenny spread her knees wide as she pushed his face between her legs.

His tongue entered her, and her hips jerked immediately, and she cried out. He licked her and sucked at her, his hands on her breasts, her nipples between his fingers. Her body writhed in pleasure at the touch of his tongue and lips.

Jenny cried out again, and again, her scream of pleasure echoing back from the high stone walls of the Sierra Madre.

"Now!" Jenny shouted, and he climbed on top of her. Her hands slid all over his back as she pulled him down on her. She couldn't touch him enough—each touch only made her crave him more.

She felt him enter her, and her fingernails slashed across the flesh of his back. He filled her up in a way that was both painful and unspeakably satisfying. She bit hard at his neck and cheek, drawing blood while he slid into her again and again.

When she screamed again, she though the mountains would shatter around her. For an instant, her entire body felt like fire.

"*Netjenkhet!*" she cried, and she felt the tidal wave of his orgasm inside her.

He collapsed on her, and they panted and sweated and bled.

"I love you," Jenny said.

"What do you remember?"

"Everything." She caressed his face. She was the ancient thing, the nameless being who only play-acted at being poor little Jenny Morton from Nowhere, South Carolina. She had played any number of roles, but she wasn't playing anymore. She was awake and aware, yet still in the flesh. It was a powerful feeling.

She stood and walked out into the humid night air.

"I knew you would remember," Alexander said. He stood beside her, one hand on her lower back, while she looked down the long, steep stairs to the ruins below. The sound of rattlesnakes still pulsed in her ears.

She had once been regarded as a goddess in this city, or one very similar to it, and blood sacrifices had been made to appease her.

Jenny looked up at the sky. She could see the great serpent there, coiled in its spiral, each one of its massive scales an entire glowing galaxy.

Eons ago, in a time before numbers, long before the universe was stable enough for time to be measured, their kind had existed in the formless void, the endless chaos. They had fed on a raw psychic energy, the most basic fabric of the cosmos. They developed strategies for stealing this energy from each other, strategies that would, eons later, translate into the powers they expressed when born in the flesh.

Among this chaos, the great serpent began to grow. It did not simply steal energies, but devoured the beings themselves, swallowing and incorporating them into the structure of its body. The more it grew, the more it could devour, and it soon grew massive and powerful, though this also meant it moved more and more slowly.

They did not know whether the great serpent was an invader from elsewhere, or one of their own kind, grown to titanic proportions by devouring so many of the others. As the serpent ate and grew, it left more and more open and empty space in the cosmos. The remaining beings learned to fear and hide from the great serpent so that it would not devour them.

In time, those original beings who still remained hid themselves away from the serpent, in the remaining pockets of primordial chaos too small and distant to interest the slow and titanic being. Each scale on its back was a galaxy. Its form repeated throughout its colossal body, from the serpentine shapes of the galaxies to the DNA coils that constructed plants and animals around themselves. Every living thing was its offspring, its parentage reflected in that coiled serpent at the core of every cell.

While the serpent became a highly structured universe, their kind, the remaining inhabitants of the original chaos, lived as forgotten outcasts on the fringes of the cosmos. After an immeasurable span of time, they learned to insinuate themselves like parasites into the great serpent's flesh, and to take the forms of living things. Deep down, their intention was to destroy the great serpent. By defeating their ancient enemy, they could feed on its corpse and restore the old chaos in which they had thrived.

Those humans whose minds could tap into the great serpent's dreaming superconscious were known as shamans, prophets and madmen. They had called the great serpent by a hundred thousand names: *Ngalyod, Sheshanaag, Nüwa, Tiamat, Ophion, Amduat, Ouroboros.*

Finally, many of the humans had stripped away ceremony and symbolism and simply called it *God.*

CHAPTER TWENTY-THREE

It was ungodly. I'm telling you it was evil, it was the devil. That man got crushed by that tractor, shoulda died, and the Barrett kid just touches him and reshapes him til he's fixed again. And the Morton girl threatens everyone with her, her witchcraft, that's what got the town thinking about witchcraft—

Thank you, Mr. Bowen.

Heather read those lines of transcript again and again. The talk of the devil and witchcraft came from one Sammy "The Steal" Bowen, nicknamed after his signature move from his glory days on the Fallen Oak High School baseball team. Heather knew this from earlier in the transcript, when he'd made a point of explaining his nickname in as great a detail as the interviewer would tolerate.

Sammy was now a fifty-six-year-old peach farmer on the outskirts of Fallen Oak. He'd been interviewed by a CDC physician at the temporary testing center set up at the Fallen Oak High gymnasium during the town's quarantine. He'd shown up for testing and free provisions, as everyone in town had been ordered to do.

The CDC doctor had quickly dismissed the farmer's rambling about witchcraft, as Heather herself had done when Darcy Metcalf first told her about Jenny Morton. But after the things she'd seen, Heather was much more open to talk of the bizarre and inexplicable.

Now Heather sat in Tricia's hospital room, sifting through the investigation data on her laptop—anything to keep her mind off what was happening to Tricia, and her own powerlessness to do anything about it. A couple of months of chemotherapy had brought no measurable results. Tricia lay in her bed now, a permanent grimace of pain etched on her face even as she slept, her skin white as paper.

Heather wondered how she could check out the farmer's story. The miraculous healing had supposedly happened at farm owned by a family called McNare. Their contorted, diseased bodies had been collected and frozen by the CDC, like all the fatalities in Fallen Oak, while Heather and others tried to figure out the cause of Fallen Oak syndrome.

She could try to find other witnesses, if any were still alive. Maybe she could figure out which EMS workers had been at the scene and try to get their account. Or she could call Jenny's father, who had supposedly been healed by Seth, but Heather didn't exactly have a warm friendship with Jenny's and Seth's families. In the past, she'd gone to their homes in the company of armed Homeland Security officials, some of whom had beaten up on Seth. Those were the same federal forces from which Jenny was currently hiding. Jenny and Seth hardly owed Heather any favors—to them, Heather was the villain.

On top of all that, Heather wanted to be discreet. She didn't want Homeland Security, or even Schwartzman, asking questions about why Heather was making unauthorized contact with a person of interest. The Barrett family was actually pursuing litigation against Homeland Security and the CDC for harassment, destruction of property, and assault. It probably wouldn't go anywhere, but Heather was supposed to stay hands-off for now.

Heather looked again at Tricia. A thick knot of drool slid down her cheek, and Heather carefully wiped it away with a paper towel. She had to be careful touching her daughter, because the chemo made her hypersensitive—just touching Tricia's hand could make her scream in pain. Despite the chemo, the leukemia showed no sign of stopping its advance. Tricia's time could be very short.

Despite her past conflicts with Seth, and her personal dislike for the spoiled rich kid, Heather would have to beg him for help, at the risk of losing her job, and maybe facing criminal charges if she pissed off somebody high enough. None of that really mattered, though. Tricia's life was more important than any sense of duty Heather might feel for her job and her government.

"Tricia, honey, I have to go," Heather whispered, gathering up her purse and her car keys. "I'll try to get Daddy to come sit with you."

Tricia didn't reply. Her heart monitor was the only sound in the room.

***

"Time to get crunked up from the stump up!" Wooly said. He navigated the tree-lined sidewalk of Wentworth Street, which was crowded with drunken students spilling out from the fraternity houses. "The guys said you're pretty cool. I think you're getting in."

"Good," Seth said indifferently. He followed Wooly to the front porch of a three-story blue house with wraparound porches on every level. Metallic Greek letters were nailed to the front of the house: Sigma Alpha Theta. Wooly, an old friend from Seth's Grayson Academy days, had dragged him to the formal pledge events. Tonight was an informal event, keg parties at all the houses. On Saturday, Seth would find out whether he'd been accepted into the fraternity.

"Skunker!" Wooly said, greeting one of the guys who'd attended Grayson with him and Seth. Wooly was shaking hands and clapping arms all around. "Chaderino! Rickster! This is my buddy I was telling you about, man, S-to-the-dog Barrett."

The fraternity members greeted Seth, and he didn't really bother trying to learn their names. They looked interchangeable to him: polo shirts, khaki shorts, expensive watches, shaggy hair.

"Come on, S-dog, let's hit the bar." Wooly pulled him forward through the crowd. He nodded at a group of pretty girls in skimpy tops and stretchy black pants. "You should get a taste of that tang. Those bitches are begging to spread."

"Right," Seth said. They wove through the mob, Wooly stopping to greet people left and right—apparently he'd been attending parties here throughout his senior year of high school.

Seth was barely conscious of where he was. He'd drifted his way into his freshman year at College of Charleston and let Wooly drag him through the pledge process. He was still waiting for any kind of solid information from the Hale investigators. It had been almost two months since Seth had hired them, but their weekly updates boiled down to "we're still working on it." Seth had hoped things would move much faster, though to be fair, he hadn't exactly given them a mountain of useful information for their investigation.

If Jenny had meant to disappear, she'd done an amazing job of it. If not, she was in a lot of danger.

Wooly pressed a plastic cup of beer into Seth's hand and steered him out onto the back porch of the fraternity house. Small clumps of students were out here, smoking cigarettes or pot. Wooly pulled him to one corner of the porch, away from other people.

"Time to make the magic happen," Wooly said. He popped open a brown pill bottle, then dumped out a pair of pink tablets and a few little squares of paper into the palm of his hand. "Open your mouth and get ready to flip some candy."

"What are you talking about?"

"One tab of Ex." Wooly pointed to one of the pink pills. Then his finger moved toward the squares of paper. "One or two hits of Captain Syd."

"What's that?"

"You know, like Syd Barrett, dog," Wooly said. "Why are you so slow?"

"Acid?" Seth asked.

"Just take it. Acid plus ecstasy equals a candyflip, the best night of your life."

"I don't think so," Seth said.

"Come *on*, S-dog!"

"I'm good, Wooly."

Wooly shook his head, then popped one of the pink pills. Then he placed a square of paper on his tongue. "Your loss, hombre. I'll save the rest for my bitches." Wooly returned the drugs to the pill bottle and sealed it. "Let's go inside and flip the motherfucking switches!"

"Do you always have to talk like that?" Seth asked.

"Talk like what, S-dog?" Wooly clapped a hand on his shoulder. "Let's go find some slut puppies to Hoover our hot dogs. This place is like the QuikTrip snack bar of pussy."

***

Later, Seth wandered drunkenly through the parking deck on

Meeting Street. He'd had a few more beers than he intended, mostly to help him talk, since he didn't really feel like saying a word to anyone. Seth had last seen Wooly leaving in the company of a few freshmen girls, whom Wooly had variously described to Seth as "frat groupies" and "easy meat." Seth managed to refuse Wooly's hundred insistent invitations to come back to the girls' apartment with him. Ultimately, Wooly had called Seth "a total sack-licker" and left without him.

Now, Seth was having trouble remembering where he'd parked, so he walked up every level of the graffiti-spattered concrete garage, looking from row to row for his blue Audi.

Then he saw another car he recognized: a reddish-brown 1975 Lincoln Continental, with a daisy-colored passenger door. His heart nearly stopped. It looked just like Jenny's car.

He looked closer. Shag carpet, cheetah-spotted seat covers. He even recognized the empty glass Red Rock soda bottle in the floor of the backseat. This was definitely Jenny's car.

Seth leaned against it, looking around, as if Jenny was going to pop up from behind one of the other cars at any moment. If her car was here, that meant she was back in Charleston. All he had to do was wait for her to come back. He smiled.

After a minute, he thought of another, more chilling possibility: maybe her car had been sitting here, in the back corner of the fourth level of this parking deck, ever since the night of the riot. Which would mean she had definitely been kidnapped.

He tugged on each of the door handles, but the car was locked up. He wouldn't get inside without smashing a window, or acquiring some car-thief skills.

Seth looked into the driver-side window and cupped his hands around his eyes to block the fluorescent glare from the overhead lights. On the driver's seat, he could see the narrow paper coupon printed out by the machine at the parking deck entrance, the one that told the attendant when you'd arrived and, consequently, how much you owed. The print was tiny and faint.

Seth squinted his eyes and tried hard to focus, but the printout was just too small to read. Seth banged his fist on the roof of the car. He needed to see that piece of paper.

He looked for security cameras, but didn't see any. Security couldn't be that great in a place that let an abandoned car sit this long, he thought.

194

Seth balled up his fist, closed his eyes, and punched through the driver-side window, slashing open all of his fingers. He reached his bloody hand into the car and pulled up the knob for the door lock.

Seth opened the door and grabbed the printout with his non-bleeding hand. He squinted. It had been printed in June, almost three months ago, the same day as the riot. The car had been sitting here since then.

Jenny was definitely in trouble.

He hurried along, still trying to find his car. Splinters of glass dripped from his injured hand as the sinew and skin regrew, pushing out the foreign objects. By the time he found his car, the hand was completely healed, though still slick with blood.

Seth drove as fast as he dared through the city. The secure phone that Hale had issued him was back at his apartment, and he would need to call them with this new information so they would know they were looking at a kidnapping. Maybe they could use forensics and find some clues in Jenny's car.

Seth's apartment was actually a rented condo in a French Quarter building, near the waterfront. The building was brick, four stories high, and had begun its life as a dock warehouse in the 1920s. Seth's father had wanted him to live in a dorm his freshman year, but Seth insisted on an apartment. He still clung to the idea that Jenny would one day come and live with him, so he needed a place for the two of them. If he'd moved into a dorm, that would have meant he'd given up hope.

Seth parked in the building's underground garage, then took the elevator up to his floor, pacing back and forth the whole trip. The elevator opened on a hallway that he shared with the floor's other tenant. Seth hurried to his apartment door.

The place had vaulted ceilings and sculpted masonry, with the occasional wall left bare brick for character. His mother had taken the initiative in furnishing and decorating his apartment, before his parents went back to their usual extended retreat in Florida.

Seth found the Hale phone in his bedroom and left a voicemail for Jerome Breisgau, explaining that he'd found Jenny's car. He hoped his voice wasn't too slurred to make any sense.

He sat on a wingback chair in front of a huge window overlooking the harbor, drumming his fingers, half-hoping the man would call him back right away, though it was only about five in the morning. He closed his eyes and waited.

A buzzing sound startled him awake a few hours later, and he raised a hand to block the searing sunrise over the harbor. The buzz sounded again. The front gate.

Seth turned on his television and flipped it to the channel that showed the feed from the security cameras at every entrance. The person buzzing him was a woman in a car, trying to get into the parking garage. Seth recognized her right away, and he suddenly felt very cold. She was the CDC doctor who'd done so much to turn his life, and Jenny's, into sheer hell.

He walked to the security unit by the door, which also had a small video screen. He pressed the intercom button. "Who's there?"

"Seth?" Dr. Reynard asked. "Seth Barrett?"

"Your name is Seth Barrett?" Seth asked.

"No. Sorry. It's been a long drive. I'm Dr. Heather Reynard with the CDC. Can you buzz me? We need to talk."

"Oh, I remember you," Seth said. "I'm not supposed to talk to you without a lawyer."

"I just need to talk for one minute," Dr. Reynard said. "Just let me in. Please? It's really important."

"Why don't you just have your friends bash down my door?"

"I'm not here on official business. And I didn't agree with how they handled the search of your house."

"I don't remember you complaining when they were slamming me into the floor. What do you want?"

"It's personal, Seth. Not official."

"Personally, I think you can go fuck off," Seth said. "Officially, too."

"Seth, I need your help!" She looked like she was about to cry, but it could have been an act. "I know you can heal people. That's why you can be with Jenny, isn't it? She spreads disease, you heal."

How the hell does she know? Seth wondered. He said, "You're crazy."

"My daughter has leukemia, Seth. She's only four. The treatments aren't working."

Seth studied the doctor's face. This could be a trick. It probably was a trick. He didn't trust her at all.

On the other hand, she looked desperate and scared...if she was acting, she was good at it.

Against his better judgment, he said, "Okay. You can come in for five minutes. Ten if you brought coffee." He pressed the button to open the gate.

CHAPTER TWENTY-FOUR

Ashleigh stopped by Esmeralda's apartment with a few cardboard boxes to collect some more of her clothes. When she walked inside, she found Tommy sitting at the kitchen table, while Esmeralda's mother served him frijoles and rice from the stove. Esmeralda's mother looked at Ashleigh over Tommy's shoulders and mouthed *help me* in Spanish. Ashleigh just smiled. She hadn't been here in a couple of weeks, and she wondered what life was like back in Esmeralda's apartment.

"Tommy, when you're done eating, I need you to carry some boxes out for me."

"That's it?" Tommy asked. "I don't hear from you for a month, and when you finally show up, that's all you have to say to me."

"It hasn't been a month. Two weeks, maybe. I'll be packing." Ashleigh carried the empty boxes toward Esmeralda's room.

"Damn it!" Tommy overturned his plate, and it shattered on the floor. Esmeralda's mother shrieked. Tommy stood up and followed Ashleigh. "Where have you been this time?"

"Oh, you know." Ashleigh shrugged while she pulled clothes from Esmeralda's hangers and dropped them in a box. "Washington and Atlanta, mainly. Plus Sacramento, San Francisco...we have a whole state to cover, you know."

"You and Eddie."

"It's my job, Tommy." She began packing shoes.

"Are we moving out?" Tommy asked. "I think Esmeralda's mom is finally starting to like me. I've listened to all her stories about Esmeralda."

"We're not moving. I'm just picking up a few things."

"You're taking all the clothes."

"No, I'm not. I'm leaving those tube tops."

Tommy grabbed her shoulders and turned her around to face him. "I want to talk to Esmeralda."

"Tommy, not now." Ashleigh sighed. "We're on a tight schedule. The cab's waiting for me."

Tommy knocked the box from her hand. "I don't care about your schedule. I want to see her."

Ashleigh sighed. "Okay. Five minutes, no more."

"Hurry up."

Ashleigh closed her eyes. She slowly rolled her head around on her neck, then opened her eyes again.

"Tommy," she said. She kissed him. "I missed you so much."

"I miss you, too." Tommy held her close. "Don't you think it's time we find a permanent body for Ashleigh? Then you and me can be together."

"And I want us to be together. But we have to wait until after the election, okay? Because Ashleigh knows how to do this work for the congressman, a lot better than I do. I don't want to get stuck with all her work."

"What do you care about any of that?" Tommy asked. "You say you love me. But you don't even try to stay with me. You let Ashleigh control you all the time."

"I love Ashleigh."

Tommy grimaced. "What's to love?"

Ashleigh scowled at him. "Fuck you, Tommy." She pushed away from him and reached for the box he'd knocked to the floor.

"Do you love me or not?"

"Of course I do. We're just very busy right now."

Tommy pulled her back to him and stared into her eyes. "You don't sound like Esmeralda."

"What the fuck are you talking about? It's me, Tommy."

Tommy stared at her a minute longer. "Do you remember the gold coin I gave you?"

Ashleigh had no idea what he was talking about. "Of course I do, baby. It was really sweet."

"Do you remember the year on the coin?"

"The year?" She giggled. "What are you talking about?"

"What was on the coin? Which president?"

"Tommy, just tell me what's wrong."

"Just answer the question."

Ashleigh sighed. "I don't remember."

"Try."

"Was it...Washington?"

"There wasn't a president, Ashleigh. It was an Indian chief."

"Oh. Hey, you called me Ashleigh. Silly boy." She tried to kiss him again, but he pushed her back.

"You are Ashleigh, aren't you?" he said. "You're trying to trick me."

"Tommy, no, I just couldn't remember—"

"Esmeralda would remember. Has she ever been with me, since she let you take over her body?" A snarl curled his lips. "Have you been tricking me the whole time we've been here?"

"Tommy, you're crazy."

"I am not crazy!" He slammed her back against the wall, and grasped her throat in one hand. "You are a liar. I've seen how you tricked everyone. Darcy. Jenny. You lie to everyone. And most people are stupid enough to believe you."

"Tommy, let me go. That hurts."

"It's supposed to hurt." He squeezed her throat tighter. "You don't think you've hurt me, Ashleigh? Or do you just not care?"

Ashleigh couldn't breath. She slammed her knee up into Tommy's crotch, and he howled and staggered back.

"Bitch!" he snapped.

Ashleigh grabbed the lamp on Esmeralda's bedside table. She swung it around, cracking the ceramic base into the side of Tommy's face. Then she drew it back and slammed it into his nose, breaking off a chunk of the lamp's base. She hit him again and again, staying close while he tried to back away. When the base of the lamp was completely broken, she swung the lamp like a baseball bat, denting the aluminum tube of its body against Tommy's jaw.

He knocked the lamp aside, grabbed the front of her shirt and raised his fist.

"Don't hurt me, Tommy!" Ashleigh screamed, in what she hoped sounded like Esmeralda's voice.

Tommy hesitated. Blood trickled from his nose and mouth, and one of his eyes was swelling up. Ashleigh knew he would be feeling conflicted, between his desire to punish Ashleigh and his affection for Esmeralda.

"If you hurt me, Esmeralda will stop loving you," Ashleigh said in a low, calm voice. "You know she will."

Tommy let go of her and lowered his fist. He sank to the bed. "I just want her back. And I want you gone."

"Aren't you a sweetheart?" Ashleigh picked up the box of clothes again. "You're going to get half your wish right now."

She turned her back on him and walked out of the bedroom. Esmeralda's mother was hurriedly cleaning the kitchen. She ran up to Ashleigh.

"You must get that evil boy out of here," she said to Ashleigh, in Spanish. "It is like living with the devil."

"Too bad," Ashleigh said. She nudged the older woman aside, and she walked out the front door.

CHAPTER TWENTY-FIVE

Jenny watched as Alexander's men assembled the row of wood and cloth dummies near the crumbling back wall of the compound, towards the ocean.

"I haven't used these modern guns before," Alexander said, nodding to the row of zombies with AK-47s at their feet. "They say these AKs are the easiest machine guns to use."

"So easy a zombie could do it?" Jenny asked.

"I hope so." He touched her hand. "When your power is feeding mine, I could probably get them to dance a ballet, if I wanted to."

"That would just be grotesque," Jenny said.

"I thought you liked grotesque," he said, and Jenny smiled.

It had been about two months since her awakening. She understood how much she and Alexander belonged together, how many lifetimes they had spent as companions and lovers since learning to incarnate in human flesh. Her recent attachment to the healer was almost certainly a trick by the love-charmer. The healer had served the charmer since their earliest incarnations among the primates of this world.

Her recent time with Alexander had been the most delightful in this entire incarnation. She had cast aside the mask of poor little Jenny

Morton and become her true, ancient self, to whom human life was just an amusing game. Her senses seemed sharper, her ability to experience pleasure greatly enhanced. They had attended concerts and plays in San Cristobal, a beautiful city with several centuries' worth of European-style architecture and a population of expatriate artists and dilettantes from around the world. She no longer feared cities at all—it was others who needed to fear her, after all. Jenny was learning to enjoy life without fear.

She'd also ditched the jeans-and-sneakers look, insisting on fashions imported from Italy and France, and jewelry to match. Alexander was happy to indulge her resurrected sense of taste and style, honed over the millennia.

"Let's give them a try," Alexander said. He clasped his hand tight around hers, and Jenny felt the dark energy flowing from her into him.

Ten zombies stepped forward, picked up their AK-47s, and fired at the wooden dummies. Some of them were firing wild, their bullets chipping at the rock wall or sailing away over the ocean. Alexander looked at each one in turn, making them adjust their stances and grips until they were shooting at the targets. The bullets sliced the dummies to pieces.

Alexander raised a hand, and they all stopped firing, their dead eyes expressionless.

"What do you think?" Jenny asked.

"Much better than muskets," Alexander said. "Imagine trying to get them all to clean, reload, add powder. This is just point and shoot."

"How many can you control at once?"

"I could do thousands of them, with a little practice. And calories, lots and lots of calories. Are you hungry yet?"

"We just ate an hour ago. How far do you plan to conquer this time?"

"Conquest is slippery in the modern world. A mass of soldiers can be bombed from the sky. We will construct our empire with bribery, diplomacy and deception, as well as fear and force. Our immortals will only be one part of the strategy."

"And what great monument to your vanity will you leave behind?"

Alexander smiled. "Perhaps it will be a great monument to your beauty."

"Beauty is not my strong point in this lifetime."

"I disagree." He drew her close and kissed her.

"*Alejandro*," a man said. "We must talk."

Jenny saw Ernesto Calderon, the big boss's nephew, crossing the lawn, his usual entourage of gunmen in tow. Ernesto, she'd learned, was the regular contact between Alexander in Chiapas and Papa Calderon in Tijuana, hundreds of miles away.

Alexander released Jenny. "Then let's talk."

"Privately." Ernesto glanced at Jenny.

"One second, Jenny." Alexander kissed her again before going into the house with Ernesto.

Ernesto's gunmen lingered behind, looking at the corpses holding their AK-47s, and then at the shattered targets.

"Where did you get these men?" one of them whispered to Jenny. "They look...strange."

"They look strange because they are dead," Jenny said. "The bodies are swept up from the streets of Juarez."

"How do you make them walk?" he asked.

Jenny held up a hand. Bloody lesions opened all over her fingers and palm. "Come closer, and I will make you into one of them. Then you will understand."

One of the men crossed himself, and all three backed away toward the main house.

"Come on," Jenny said. She stalked toward them, letting more blisters open on her face and throat. "Doesn't anyone want to try?"

The men ran inside the house, whispering the word *bruja* to each other, and Jenny laughed at the terrified looks on their faces.

***

In his office, Alexander poured a small glass of local mezcal for Ernesto, then another for himself. They sat on facing couches.

"How was your trip from Ciudad de Mexico?" Alexander asked.

"I am always traveling." Ernesto shook his head and sipped his mezcal. "It seems the whole country is full of people I must see."

"That's why I like it down here. Summer all year, the beach, not many people around."

"Except for the dead."

"The dead never make problems. Nice and quiet."

"The girl? Does she seem trustworthy?"

"She is. We could not accomplish so much without her."

204

"And my uncle is pleased with the size and speed of the harvest," Ernesto said. "He wanted me to convey this."

"Is that the reason for your visit today?"

"No." Ernesto sipped mezcal again. "This is good."

"It's made about twenty miles from here."

"There is a man you must meet," Ernesto said. "Felix Arellano Francisco."

"And he is...?"

"Among many things, an agent with CISEN."

Alexander raised his eyebrows. The Centro de Investigación y Seguridad Nacional, or CISEN, was the country's intelligence agency, the Mexican equivalent of the CIA. "Is he investigating us?"

Ernesto laughed. "He is an important friend. He keeps several units of the Mexican military friendly to us."

"He hands out bribes for us."

Ernesto smiled. "We wish to keep him as a close friend."

"Then what does he want with me?"

"Only to speak."

"About what?"

"He says it is personal."

"I've never heard of him before," Alexander said. "How can it be personal?"

"You will have to ask him yourself. Do not upset him."

"But you're certain we can trust him?"

"I am not certain of that with anyone. Least of all government agents. Or sorcerers who use the witchcraft to raise the dead. But we all do what we must."

Alexander nodded. "Tell me where to meet him."

CHAPTER TWENTY-SIX

Seth rode in Heather's car all the way to Atlanta. If he hadn't been groggy, tired and more than a little hung over, he might have driven separately, but he was already struggling to keep his eyes open.

He didn't trust the doctor, but she had showed him pictures of her daughter Tricia, including a couple of cell phone pictures of the tiny girl wasting away in the hospital. Heather did seem desperate. If this was a trap, they'd put it together very well.

He'd already asked if Heather knew where to find Jenny, but Heather claimed nobody knew.

Seth watched the mile markers and cow pastures whip by—Heather was really pressing the gas pedal. She didn't speak much, just stared at the road. Her radio was tuned to NPR, which had a very long report about a struggling sweater factory in New Hampshire.

"What's it like?" Heather asked, after a long period of silence.

"What's what like?" Seth opened his eyes.

"Healing people."

"It's draining," Seth said. "I get hungry and tired."

"But how does it feel, knowing you can do that?"

"It feels like I'm a freak."

"That's all?"

"No, it's not all!" he snapped. "I have to worry about people finding out."

"Would that be so bad? You could heal lots of people—"

"—until someone like you comes along and wants to lock me up somewhere so you can study me. Then I couldn't help anyone."

Heather was quiet for a minute. "And what about Jenny killing those people in your town? How do you feel about that? You think that's okay?"

"You weren't there," Seth said. "It was a lynch mob. They were trying to kill her. They killed me."

Heather looked at him.

"I got better," Seth said. That was Jenny's usual comment, when she talked about how she and Seth had died and come back the night of Easter. "They didn't kill me enough. I was able to heal. Then I had to heal her, because she was dead by then."

"You brought her back from the dead? Like your friend at the hospital, with the zombies?"

"Not exactly. And he's not a friend. I have no idea who he is." Seth was only lying a little bit. He suspected the zombie master was the reincarnation of his own great-grandfather, a scary and evil man. "There are others like us, you know. And you may think we're evil, but they're truly evil."

"What others?"

"There's a guy whose touch makes you feel fear," Seth said. "I think he might have started the riot in Charleston. And there's a girl who can make people feel love. She's the one who sent the mob against Jenny—she had the town in the palm of her hand since she was a kid. The preacher's daughter."

"One who can make you feel love?" Heather's eyes grew distant, as if she were thinking of something. "Do you mean love, or lust?"

"That depends on how high she turns it up."

"What's her name?"

"It doesn't matter. She's not using it anymore."

"What does she look like?"

"She's..." Seth thought of Ashleigh, but Ashleigh's old body was dead, destroyed by the Jenny pox. Somehow, her spirit had possessed Darcy Metcalf, but now Ashleigh had left Darcy to pick up the wreckage of her life. Ashleigh might still be out there, in another body, but Seth wouldn't know what that one looked like. "I don't know," he said.

"Are you trying to protect her, too?"

"Hell, no," Seth said. "You can put her in a lab cage if you find her. I don't care."

"What are you, exactly?" Heather asked.

"I'm a freshman at Charleston, a pledge at Sigma Alpha Theta, an endless source of disappointment to my parents—"

"You know what I mean."

"I only got a glimpse of that when I was dead," he said. "And it's hard to remember the pieces I saw. Your mind kind of works differently when it's not attached to a brain."

Heather just stared at him.

"I can't answer the question," Seth said. "We're born with these abilities. We reincarnate."

Heather shook her head. Seth closed his eyes, leaned back, and listened to the NPR reporters interview the children of laid-off sweater makers.

***

Heather's daughter was at a children's hospital in Atlanta, called Egleston. She didn't say a word as they walked down the hall of the cancer ward. Seth looked into some of the rooms they passed, seeing pale, sick children slowly wasting in their beds. He felt terribly sad at the sight of them.

"Here," Heather whispered.

He followed her into a hospital room shared by two little girls, their beds separated by a curtain. Heather's daughter Tricia looked tiny and pale in her bed, dwarfed by the monitoring machines around her. Her little head was shaved bare. Her eyes were closed.

Seth reached out a hand. His first instinct was to touch the girl and heal her right away, but he stopped himself, folded his arms, and stepped back from the hospital bed.

"I'm not doing this for free, you know," Seth said. "I don't owe you any favors."

"You want money?" Heather asked.

"I want you people to leave us alone. Me and Jenny both."

"I don't have that kind of power," Heather said. "Homeland

208

Security is involved. The White House is involved. If you've ever seen an alien-invasion movie, you know that the guys with guns don't usually listen to the guys with microscopes."

"I expect you to help us," Seth said.

"I would. I will. I just don't know what I can do."

"I don't have to help you, either," Seth said.

"Just tell me what you want me to do," Heather said.

"Use whatever influence you do have to make it seem like Jenny isn't a threat," Seth said.

"I'll try, but I've already filed reports—"

"Tell them your reports were wrong."

"They'll think I'm crazy."

"That's fine with me."

"Will you help her now?" Heather asked. She looked like she was on the verge of tears.

"If I do this, you work for me from now on," Seth said. "If I need you to steal information from your job, you'll do it. If I need you to falsify reports, you'll do it."

Heather looked at her daughter. "Of course I will," she whispered.

"If I need you to commit a crime, kill somebody, or soak yourself in gasoline and light a match, you'll do that, too."

Heather gaped at him.

"I'm not joking," Seth said. "If I save her, you owe me everything."

Heather frowned, but she nodded her head. "I'll do anything for her."

Seth stared at her for a minute longer, then he took a breath and turned toward the little girl in the bed. He took one of Tricia's hands, and Tricia winced at the pain of being touched. Her eyes opened.

"Are you a doctor?" Tricia whispered.

"Not exactly," Seth said.

"It's okay, honey," Heather said.

Seth could feel the healing energy flow out of him and into the girl. He pushed it harder—the girl would need a lot of help.

Tricia gasped and squeezed her fingers tight around his. Seth took her other hand and concentrated.

Her little green eyes grew wide as the color returned to her skin. Her heart monitor accelerated its beeping. Seth could feel the energy draining from him, filling up the girl, dissolving the disease inside her.

After a few minutes, he staggered back and dropped into one of the room's chairs, exhausted. Tricia sat up in bed, smiling, looking radiant.

"Tricia?" Heather asked. "How do you feel, honey?"

"I want to go to Six Flags," Tricia said.

Heather laughed and hugged her daughter."You look so good, sweetie."

"That should do it," Seth said. "Have them test her as soon as you can, so she can get off the chemo."

"Oh, thank you." Heather turned to Seth, her face covered in tears now. She leaned down and hugged him tight, inadvertently burying Seth's face in her breasts. "Thank you so much."

"Just remember our agreement." Seth's voice was muffled against her shirt.

"I won't forget. Anything you want." Heather beamed at him for a minute, then turned back to her daughter, who was wide awake and cheerful, talking about a dream she'd just had involving a Panda bear and a roller coaster.

When Seth felt a little better, he stood up and stretched. He walked around the curtain, to where the other little girl lay sleeping. She looked like she was wasting away.

Seth touched the girl whose name he didn't know, and again felt the healing energy drain out of him, repairing and healing her body.

He glanced back at Heather, who was talking happily with her daughter. Then Seth wandered out of the room.

He moved into the next room, and then the next, healing every cancer-stricken child in the ward. By the time he finished the last one, his body felt hollowed out, his eyes sunken, his muscles like scraps of rags.

As he stumbled out of the last room, two nurses confronted him.

"Can we help you?" one asked.

"Oh, no," Seth said. "I'm fine."

"I've just seen you go in and out of three different rooms," the nurse said. "What are you doing?"

"Just visiting the kids," Seth said. He was so exhausted that he was about to pass out. He wondered how he looked to them—like some crazed drug addict, probably. He leaned against the wall, working to keep his balance.

"We're going to need you to leave this hospital," the nurse said. "Immediately."

"No, wait," Seth said. "Heather, tell them I'm okay. Heather?"

Tricia's room was at the other end of the hall, though, and Seth was too tired to speak very loudly. It looked like he was speaking to an imaginary person, which didn't help increase his credibility with the nurses.

"I'm paging security," the nurse said.

"No, I'll go," Seth said. "Just tell Heather I'm outside."

The nurses stayed close behind him until he stepped onto the elevator. Seth made it to a bench outside the hospital's sliding front doors, and then he sat and waited.

Heather emerged about twenty minutes later. "Getting some air?" she asked.

"I got kicked out."

"Why?"

"I went into every kid's room on the cancer floor."

Heather smiled at him and shook her head. "You're so sweet. I owe you everything."

"Don't forget it."

"You look drained. What can I do for you?"

"Take me to Checkers," Seth said. "I need about eight hamburgers. And a shake. And lots of fries."

"I'll buy you everything on the menu," Heather said. "Tricia's hungry, too, thank God. I can't remember the last time she said that."

Heather took Seth's hand, and he leaned heavily on her, walking like an old man while she helped him to her car.

CHAPTER TWENTY-SEVEN

The intelligence agent Felix Arellano Francisco wanted Alexander to meet him at a tin-roof cinderblock cantina outside Mexico City. The sign out front forbade women and government officials in uniform from entering.

Alexander took a table in the back of the smoke-filled bar and ordered a beer. While he waited, he watched the topless dancers come and go on the central stage. Occasionally, one of the dancers would lead a customer through a curtain to some kind of back room. He watched one proposition a couple of elderly men playing dominoes, who waved her away.

Alexander bought a cigar from a waitress and puffed on it. Francisco was taking his time.

So far, he thought everything was going well. The plague-bringer was his again, letting her power flow freely into him. She remembered the many lives they'd spent together, remembered that she belonged with Alexander.

The zombie workers were productive, and money was pouring in thick and fast. Alexander couldn't ask for much more, beyond a few minor details that still needed attending.

A man in a suit entered the cantina, spotted Alexander, and took the chair across from him.

"You are *El Brujo*," he said.

"How could you guess?"

"The only gringo in the bar." Francisco ordered whiskey from a passing waitress and patted her ass when she delivered it. "Nice place, no? Good for discrete conversation, since no man wants to admit publicly he was here. See that girl onstage now, Carmen? She gives the best head in three states. Should I call her over?"

"No, thanks."

"More for me." Francisco sipped his drink. "Though I am suspicious of men who do not indulge in pleasures."

"I indulge plenty," Alexander said. "But I have a busy schedule today."

"We should not be prisoners of our work."

Alexander just nodded and puffed his cigar.

"All business, then," Francisco said. "I have a few good friends up north who have asked for my help."

"With what?"

"They need to open a line of communication with the man who is said to make the dead walk."

"I don't know any such man," Alexander said.

Francisco laughed, revealing several gold-capped teeth. "Then Ernesto must be punished for making a fool of me. It is said that Papa Calderon has a man who captured four of Pablo Toscano's men, killed three, and brought their corpses to life to bite and terrify the fourth Toscano man. They say that his message to Toscano was that any interference with Calderon business would be punished with terrifying black magic. They say he is a gringo who goes by the name *El Brujo*. Ernesto assured me he would send this man to meet me today. And here I am, with a gringo who pretends I do not know what I am talking about."

"In that case, I guess you have the right person."

"Is it true?"

"Is what true?"

"You can made the dead walk? Is it a trick?"

"Of course it's a trick," Alexander said. "But many people are superstitious and will believe such illusions."

Francisco laughed again and started his second whiskey.

"Psychological warfare."

Alexander gave a small nod. "So who are these people? Not DEA, I hope?"

"Of course not. I am to keep such people away from Papa Calderon's business, not bring them into it. These are former associates of mine who now work in private industry."

"Can you be slightly more specific?"

"Corporate intelligence. High net-worth individuals."

"I suppose that's better."

"They simply need a few minor questions answered. They say they are concerned about some American girl."

"And you're certain they aren't working under government contract? Homeland Security, maybe?"

"These men have moved on from working for the state," Francisco said. "From what they told me, I believe they are working for the girl's family."

"What girl?"

"Her name is...Julia? No. Jennifer." Francisco unfolded a sheet of paper. Jenny's high school yearbook picture was printed on it. "Jennifer Morton. Does she look familiar to you?"

Alexander studied the picture. "You say they're working for her family?"

"If the U. S. government were involved, I would not bring this to you. I would say I could not help them. It is her family looking for her."

Alexander knew Jenny's father couldn't afford any such investigation. Jenny's boyfriend, though—the healer. The Barrett family had plenty of money, most of it from investments Alexander had made himself, when he wore a different body. He was curious how it had compounded over time. He wished to see the house he'd built, the family graveyard he'd ordered constructed when he was already half-senile.

That previous incarnation had lacked the clarity of this one, probably because Jonathan Barrett the First hadn't died under anesthesia as a child, and then gotten revived. Alexander Scipioni, son of a Beverly Hills entertainment lawyer and drunken plastic surgery addict, sure the hell had. Alexander had nearly gone insane, but he'd come back with his mind wide open, fully understanding the past-life glimpses and dreams he'd been having since he was born. With further research, he'd decided to use a more natural alternative for Jenny, and that had worked out just the way he wanted it to.

"Do you know where to find the girl?" Francisco asked.

"I have her," Alexander said.

"Really?" Francisco waited for more, but Alexander volunteered nothing. "You have her?"

"Yes."

"I see. In that case, my friends want me to ask about a ransom. A great deal of money is available to pay for her return."

"There is no ransom," Alexander told him. "The girl will not be returned."

"I see." Francisco downed his whiskey. "Can you give some evidence that she is with you of her own free will? Have her send us a note?"

"No."

Francisco studied Alexander. A minute passed, while Alexander listened to the brassy horn music playing over the cantina's scratchy speakers.

"I do not know if this will satisfy my friends." Francisco finally said. "They suspect kidnapping. They want assurance that she is willing to be where she currently is, and that she is not a prisoner."

"I can offer no such assurance," Alexander said. "And there will be no ransom."

"You might make them angry with you. Should I deny the girl is with you? I don't want this to lead to trouble for Papa Calderon."

"Do not deny it," Alexander said. "Tell them you found me. Tell them I have the girl, and I do not desire a ransom, and I will not provide proof of her well-being."

Francisco scratched his head and sat back in his chair. "I will tell them what you say. Anything else you want passed along?"

Alexander shook his head.

"Then our business is concluded." Francisco whistled to the dancer he'd admired earlier, who was now over at the bar. "Carmen! Come and see us."

Alexander stood up and left pesos on the table for the waitress.

"You don't want to miss this." Francisco gave another gold-toothed grin while the girl approached the table.

"I'll pass," Alexander said. "Busy schedule." He stepped away from the table.

"Watch your ass, *Brujo*," Francisco said as he left. "You don't want this to become trouble. Not for Papa Calderon, and not for me."

"No trouble," Alexander said. He put on his sunglasses and stepped into the hot, dusty afternoon outside the cantina.

CHAPTER TWENTY-EIGHT

Seth found himself back in Atlanta only a couple of days later, after receiving an urgent call from Jerome Breisgau at Hale Security Group. He'd spent most of the intervening time sleeping, eating and recovering from all the healing he'd done at the cancer ward. He'd missed two days of classes, but he didn't really care.

The receptionist took Seth to Breisgau's office as soon as he gave his name.

"Have a seat, Mr. Barrett," Breisgau said as he shook his hand. Seth took the chair, feeling a little weird about a man decades older than himself calling him *Mister.* "Coffee?"

"She already offered, thanks."

Breisgau sat across from him and seemed to study him for a moment. "Your girlfriend seems to be running with a rough crowd."

"You found her?" His heart began to race.

"Possibly. Since you mentioned a Mexican girl was involved, we went ahead and reached out to a few associates south of the border. Someone told us a rumor about a certain person who can supposedly raise the dead. Exactly the rumor you told us to watch out for."

"Then let's check it out," Seth said. He was leaning forward in his chair now, impatient.

"We have. The man is called *El Brujo*. In Spanish, that means a sorcerer, a male witch. Unfortunately—and this where things get complicated—he's a part of the Calderon cartel." Breisgau watched Seth for a reaction.

"What's that?"

"One of the two biggest drug trafficking organizations in Mexico today." Breisgau set a tablet PC on his desk. It displayed a map of Mexico, with areas highlighted near the United States border. "The largest is the Juarez cartel, smuggling into Texas, run by a man named Pablo Toscano. The second largest is the Tijuana cartel, smuggling into California, run by a man named Ricardo Angel Calderon, or 'Papa' Calderon. The two cartels are mortal enemies."

"Okay," Seth said. "And the zombie master guy works for the...Calderon...people in Tijuana."

"Right. Now, we had an associate in a Mexican intelligence agency reach out to him. This associate is familiar with players in the underworld down there. And our associate actually had a sit-down with this man called *El Brujo*."

"And what happened?" Seth wished the guy would hurry up. "Did you find Jenny?"

"He admits that Jenny is with him," Breisgau said. "But he will neither accept a ransom nor provide anything to show that she's with him of her own free will. It looks to us like she's been kidnapped, but the man has no intention of ever returning her home."

He probably wants to use her power, Seth thought. Out loud, he said, "What do we do?"

"Frankly, there aren't a lot of options, Mr. Barrett. He won't let Jenny communicate with the outside world."

"I understand that. She's his prisoner."

"That would seem to be the case."

"So now what? You guys are supposed to be the experts on kidnapping."

"And normally that ends with a ransom solution," Breisgau said. "In only a few cases do we need to consider the next step."

"Which is?"

"Forcible extraction."

"That sounds dangerous," Seth said.

"It is. And highly expensive. But it looks like the only option we have left." Breisgau touched something behind his desk, and large plasma screen mounted on the wall came to life. He stood up and began to pace. "Here's what we can do. We can put together a team of six to eight men, all highly trained—former Green Berets, Navy SEALs. We raid the house where he's keeping Jenny, and we helicopter her out of there." On the screen behind him, some kind of Hale corporate marketing video played, the sound turned off. It showed men in black armor stamped with the Hale logo leaping from a helicopter, in a desert somewhere. They surrounded some men in turbans, who quickly held up their hands and surrendered. They escorted a white woman in a business suit back to the helicopter.

"You know where he's keeping her?"

"We have a pretty good idea that it's a property belonging to Calderon, via a dummy corporation, here in Chiapas." On the digital tablet, Breisgau pointed to the extreme south of Mexico, near the Guatemalan border. "He must be watching the pipeline for Calderon. Cocaine flows up from Peru, Colombia, Bolivia, through Guatemala, into Mexico. From there, it goes to Tijuana, and then California."

"So we just raid his house? That can't be legal."

Breisgau grinned. "That's where you're in luck, Mr. Barrett. Chiapas does not exactly have a stable system of governance. The Zapatistas—local rebels, Communists—asserted themselves in the early nineties and took over several chunks of Chiapas. The Mexican national government has failed to regain control of these areas. As you can see, the government of the state of Chiapas is a very loose affair. A few well-placed bribes will be sufficient to turn any necessary heads away from our actions."

"So that's the plan?" Seth asked. "We just go in and take her."

"That appears to be the only way to bring her back," Breisgau said. "We could, of course, try to get the local police down there to help us, but they are likely to be in the pay of the drug cartels, too. What I'm offering will be efficient and effective. You could have her back very soon...if you're willing to pay for it."

Seth thought it over. He was sure his college trust account did not have the kind of money Breisgau was talking about. On the other hand, he did know where to find the index card in his father's desk drawer in the Fallen Oak house, the one where his father jotted down passwords. Seth could access his father's accounts and steal however much money Hale Security wanted for the rescue operation. Obviously, his father would kill him for it, but that hardly mattered.

"Okay," Seth said. "But I want to come along when they go in."

"Not a good idea," Breisgau said. "We'd have to add an extra security detail to keep you safe. Any number of things could go wrong."

"I know that. But I want to be there." Seth was eager to see Jenny, but beyond that, he doubted whether Hale would be ready to deal with the supernatural aspects of this mission. If the man who'd kidnapped Jenny wanted her for her powers, it was possible that he'd tracked down others of their kind, too. Seth didn't know what they might be facing.

"It's going to cost extra for you to go along," Breisgau said. "Significantly more. And you'll have to do exactly what our professionals tell you, when they tell you, for your own protection. And sign a full liability waiver."

"I understand."

Breisgau returned to his chair and grinned at Seth. "All right, then. We'll just pull together the paperwork and discuss the fee."

"Let's get to work," Seth said.

CHAPTER TWENTY-NINE

Jenny was slumbering in Alexander's bed when she heard the approaching *whump-whump-whump* from the back of the house. She felt Alexander slip out of bed.

"What's happening?" she whispered. It was still dark outside. Jenny reached for the lamp.

"Leave the light off," Alexander said. He was getting dressed.

"What time is it?"

"Almost dawn."

The *whump-whump-whump* sound drew closer, and the glass in the windows rattled.

"What's that sound?" Jenny asked.

"I'm going to check it out."

"Wait," she said, but Alexander had already left the room through the terrace door. "Fuck." Jenny got out of bed and hurriedly threw on a dress. She was groggy and tired. They'd only gone to sleep a couple of hours earlier, after about three hours of very intense lovemaking. The complementary nature of their powers seemed to feed both their desires and their endurance. Jenny wanted Alexander more every day.

She followed him to the terrace outside his room, and found herself watching a black helicopter descend into Alexander's back yard, inside his walls. The hot wind from the whirling blades blew their hair back.

Alexander took Jenny by the arm and pulled her down beside him as he squatted behind the low stucco wall of his terrace.

"Friends of yours?" Jenny shouted over the thumping din.

"Afraid not," Alexander said. He raised a walkie-talkie to his mouth. "Manuel! Get everyone moving. We are under attack this morning."

"Is it Toscano's people?" Jenny asked.

"Could be. You better get inside."

"I'm sticking with you," Jenny said. "Want me to kill them?"

"No, thanks. Sweet of you to offer, though. Manuel!" he shouted into the walkie-talkie.

"Yes, yes, we're moving!" Manuel's voice crackled back.

"I want everybody with a pulse to stay inside the house and lay low. Don't shoot unless they reach the doors or windows." Alexander said. "But get ready to move together. And somebody bring me the Thumper."

Jenny watched the helicopter descend. It would be on the ground in less than a minute.

Alexander had ramped up his security after a recent trip to Mexico City, saying there was a growing threat from Toscano's Juarez-based cartel. He now kept eight or ten gunmen around the house at all times, under Manuel's direction.

One of the young new gunmen raced out onto the balcony, keeping his head low. He slid Alexander something that looked like a green guitar case, then watched Alexander expectantly.

"Go on back with Manuel," Alexander ordered him. The young man frowned, cast a longing look at the green case, then returned inside.

When the helicopter was a few feet from the ground, men began jumping out of it, one after the other. They wore black armor, helmets, and goggles, and carried assault rifles. They broke out into four teams of two that fanned across the yard toward the house, moving like wildfire.

"Holy shit," Alexander said. "Israeli Tavor rifles. That's *not* Toscano."

He grabbed Jenny's hand, then pointed with his other hand at the dilapidated building where he kept his two reanimated jaguars. A row of zombies rushed out and opened fire with their AK-47s.

The men in armor dropped instantly to the ground, flat on their bellies, returning fire. Jenny saw a bullet shatter a zombie's skull, but the zombie kept advancing and shooting.

"Over there!" Jenny pointed to a pair of black-armored men that were on the move, running with their heads low. They were dangerously close to the house—a few more yards and they would be underneath the second-story terrace, out of sight.

Four zombies turned and sprayed bullets at the breakaway pair, who then had to drop to the ground and return fire. The invaders' guns slowed the ragged row of zombies, gradually chipping away at them. The zombies, for their part, depended on Alexander for directions and so weren't the most precise shooters. They used a lot of long, wild bursts.

Then a series of booms echoed across the lawn, and the row of zombies were quickly sliced to pieces. A massive machine gun on a mount had swiveled out from within the helicopter, and now it provided cover for the eight men, pulverizing the zombies with hundreds of rounds. The invaders advanced.

"What a mess," Alexander said. He lifted the lid on the green case and drew out what looked like a sawed-off shotgun. He broke it open and cocked the hammer at the back, then slid in a single round that looked like the Bluebird juice cans Jenny used to drink in elementary school. He snapped the gun closed.

"That's a big bullet," Jenny said.

"That's because it's a grenade," Alexander said. He flipped up the sight and took aim at the helicopter below. There was a hollow popping sound that reminded Jenny of blowing air across a glass Coke bottle. The grenade punched the ground in front of the helicopter and detonated, throwing up a huge cloud of dirt.

The invaders hit the ground at the explosion. Alexander broke the grenade launcher open and handed it to Jenny. "Reload."

"Um...okay." Jenny copied what he had done, taking one of the cylindrical grenades and feeding it in. She cocked the hammer back and closed the breech.

While she did this, Alexander pointed to the dilapidated building again. A second string of zombies grabbed up the AK-47s and fired at the invaders. The rest of the zombies, seven or eight of them, charged the helicopter, unarmed.

Alexander fired another grenade at the helicopter, and this one struck the whirling blades at the top. The helicopter blades shattered and shot out in every direction. One fragment sliced an approaching zombie in half. Another skewered one of the invading men.

Jenny watched as one big chunk of blade sped towards them. "Watch out!" she screamed, grabbing his arm. They dropped to the floor together. The helicopter blade skipped off the low outer wall of the terrace, then smashed through Alexander's bedroom window.

"That was pretty cool," Jenny said.

Alexander reloaded the grenade launcher, and this time he aimed for a pair of black-armored men. The grenade struck the ground between them, blasting the two men away from each other. They landed heavily on the ground. The two zombie jaguars leaped out of the shadows, pounced on the two blasted men, and began ripping them to pieces.

"It's fun to be a grenadier," Alexander said. He held out the launcher to her. "Want to try?"

"Sure." Jenny reloaded the weapon, then got up on her knees and looked over the wall. She lined up the helicopter in her crosshairs.

The zombies swarmed the helicopter like ants on a rotten squirrel. They hauled out another black-armored man and chomped on his throat, which the bulletproof armor left bare.

"Get moving, Manuel," Alexander said into his walkie-talkie. "Clean up."

Below, Manuel and his men opened fire on the few remaining invaders, who found themselves under fire from two directions, the house and the lurching knot of armed zombies.

"Are you going to shoot?" he asked.

"If it's not Toscano, who the hell is it?" Jenny asked. "The government?"

"Does it matter right now?"

Manuel and his men walked among the fallen invaders, shooting the wounded.

"Manuel, the helicopter," Alexander said. "See if we can get a prisoner or two. Find out who these people are."

Manuel's team advanced on the helicopter. The zombies stumbled out, clearing the way for them, and then Manuel and two other men stepped inside.

They hauled out another man in a black helmet and matching

armor. Manuel stripped off their captive's helmet, revealing a young man with strawberry blond hair. Manuel turned him to face Alexander and Jenny on the terrace.

It was Seth.

"The healer," Alexander said. "He's the one behind the attack."

"That asshole," Jenny said.

CHAPTER THIRTY

Jenny followed Alexander down to an underground room below the main house. Seth was there, stripped of his helmet and gloves and armor, his face beaten but already healing. He wore only black fatigues now, and he was barefoot. His hands were bound by ropes, each of which was anchored in a hook in the wall, so that he had to remain standing.

A folding table had been set up in front of him. On its surface were several blades and a hacksaw.

Seth's head lifted when Jenny entered, and he managed to smile. "Jenny."

Jenny looked at him coldly. Alexander had given her the task of dealing with Seth, and now he stood back with Manuel and two of the Tijuana gunmen, while Jenny approached the prisoner.

"What were you thinking, Seth?" Jenny asked. "That you could come and take me at gunpoint? You didn't think we would fight back?"

"I thought you were kidnapped," Seth said.

Jenny laughed. "As if anybody could force me to act against my will."

Seth gave her a puzzled look. "Are you feeling okay, Jenny?"

"I'm not feeling okay. I'm feeling great." Jenny wiped her nose—she'd just snorted up two thick lines of coke to get herself ready. "Top of the fucking world, Seth. But, you know, I have just a few questions for you, before I kill you."

"Before you do what?" Seth asked, and Alexander chuckled.

Jenny took a scalpel from the table. She prodded the tip into the hollow of Seth's throat. "First. Who was that girl in Charleston?"

"The girl? Jenny, that was a mistake. I'm sorry."

"It was definitely a mistake. And then you decided to attack me here. That was a mistake, too."

"I came to rescue you."

"Rescue me?" Jenny smirked as she dragged the blade down across his chest, slicing open flesh and muscle.

"Jenny, stop!" Seth yelled. "What's wrong with you? What happened to you?" He looked at Alexander.

"There's nothing wrong with me," Jenny said. "I remember so many past lives now. Alexander remembers all of his, too. He showed me how. I remember what I am, and what all of us are."

"I know what I am," Seth said. "I'm the person who loves you."

Jenny snickered. "You're the charmer's tool. She sent you to seduce me." Jenny slashed the blade diagonally across his stomach, and Seth gasped in pain. "You thought you could trick me."

"What are you talking about, Jenny? I've always been honest with you. I'm not playing any trick."

She scowled. "Maybe that's what you think, healer. But sometimes, you can hold such a strong intention when you incarnate that your little incarnated personality works to carry out your purpose, without really knowing why. So maybe you are still caught in the illusion of being Seth Barrett, as I was caught in the illusion of being Jenny Morton. But you are not him, and I am not her." Jenny moved closer, lifting his chin with the tip of the blade. "Don't you remember anything?"

"I remember all the time we spent together," Seth said. "I remember that we loved each other. You're the one who's forgotten."

"That was only a game," Jenny said. "The charmer wanted you to get close to me. That's why you think you love me. That was a plot etched deep in your soul. But our kind don't truly love, Seth. We don't have human souls. We are older than love itself."

"That's not true!" Seth said. "We love each other. We're learning to be human."

"We cannot learn to be what we are not. You are a serpent, trying to play monkey."

"That's not true, either," Seth said. "I don't know what you think you remember—"

"My memories are very clear," Jenny said.

"And they tell you...what? That you belong with this guy?" Seth nodded to Alexander. "He's my great-grandfather. Did you know that? Jonathan Seth Barrett I. He made his first fortune with plantations worked by zombies. What are you doing with them this lifetime, Gramps?"

Alexander smirked.

"Is that true?" Jenny asked Alexander.

"Fallen Oak was my sandbox first," Alexander said. "I left my mark."

Jenny thought of the picture of the first Jonathan Seth Barrett shaking hands with Woodrow Wilson, his eyes like dark steel. The man who'd built the family graveyard and so obsessively laid out instructions for how he was to be remembered by succeeding generations, and how they were to act. It was a pathetic echo of how an Egyptian pharaoh created his own glorious funerary complex and priestly cult, all to maintain his memory and encourage people to worship him after death. All to avoid being forgotten.

"Cheap zombie labor," Seth said to Alexander. "I'm guessing you have zombies growing drugs for this cartel you've joined. Cheap zombie labor. That's how you keep margins up on a plantation, am I right, Gramps? That's what you told my dad."

Alexander answered with a short, cold laugh, and his dark eyes did not look amused.

"When you look at the big picture, you're just stuck doing the same thing, over and over again, one lifetime to the next, aren't you?" Seth asked. "Caught in the same loop. Can't do anything new."

"You don't know what you're talking about, healer," Alexander said.

"I think I do, zombie guy," Seth said. "I was dead for a while. Maybe I don't remember everything, but I saw enough to realize the past isn't worth remembering. I don't want to go back and be who I was before. I'm alive now, I make my choices now. And leaving the past behind makes us better than what we were."

"You can't leave it behind. Your past is what you are," Jenny said.

"No, it isn't," Seth said. "What you do right now, that's what you really are."

"Just kill him, Jenny," Alexander said. "I've had enough of this conversation."

"You take orders from him now?" Seth asked.

"No one gives me orders," Jenny said. "And I'm in no hurry to kill you. I want to watch you suffer first. Your punishment for tricking me into loving you."

"It wasn't a trick!" Seth snapped. Jenny punched him in the mouth.

"Stop," she hissed. "Stop lying. You've always served the love-charmer."

"Even if that's true, I don't serve her anymore," Seth said. "I'm not a prisoner of my past. Unlike zombie boy over there. And now you let him trick you into being his slave—"

"Quiet!" Jenny plunged the knife into his stomach.

"Ow, stop, Jenny!" Seth said. "That's going to take a minute to heal."

"I know."

Seth glanced at Alexander, then back at Jenny. "So that's it. You're going to kill me and run off with him."

"Alexander and I have always been together," Jenny said. "You belong with Ashleigh. That is how it has always been."

"Always?" Seth asked. "I may not remember much, but I did see our last few lives together. You weren't with him then. You were with me."

"I don't think so..." Jenny began, but the intense look in Seth's eyes triggered something inside her. She remembered when Alexander had opened up her past-life memories, there were a couple that he steered her right past without looking. Her most recent lives.

"Jenny, we need to hurry up and kill him," Alexander said. "We have to dispose of all these bodies."

"One second. I'm just trying to decide how I want to do it." Jenny remembered herself in early industrial London, hurrying up a narrow, crowded street with an armload of books whose subjects ranged from scientific medical treatises to kabbalistic magic. She was going to meet Seth in the small, dusty loft where he lived. They were working together, trying to figure out the meaning of their powers. The anticipation of seeing him made her face flush.

Then another life, decades later. Jenny was part of a traveling circus in America in the early twentieth century. She was part of the freak show—people would pay pennies to see "The Most Diseased Woman in the World." One week, the circus pitched its tents in a field alongside a tent revival, where she met a boy who, according to the preacher that he traveled with, could heal any ailment for a quarter. Once they met, they never parted again.

Now, the last piece of herself fell into place. Her relationship with the healer was no trick. She had chosen to pull away from the dead-raiser...just as the healer had chosen to pull away from the charmer.

"Jenny," Alexander said.

"This is no good," Jenny said. "I can cut him up all night, but he heals too fast. If you're really in a hurry, I need to burn him."

"Jenny!" Seth said. "What's wrong with you?"

"Shut up, healer," Jenny said. She turned to Manuel and the two gunmen, who were off to her right, near the door. "Someone bring me a pan of hot coals. And tongs."

Manuel looked to Alexander, who was on Jenny's left. Alexander gave a quick nod, and Manuel gestured for his two gunmen to go. They both hurried out of the room.

"Seth, Seth, Seth..." Jenny traced her scalpel down along his rib cage, drawing a thin line of blood. "You really had me fooled for a while. I thought you loved me."

"I did love you."

Jenny snarled. "You're pathetic. I want you to beg me for mercy."

"Mercy?" Seth asked. "I don't want it. If you really want me dead, Jenny, go ahead and do it. My life isn't worth living if you don't love me."

She smiled. "Then you've made your choice. And here's what I'm going to do." Jenny slashed a deep cut along the top of each of his arms, which were extended out to his sides. "First, we make our incisions. Then we fill them with fire to keep the wounds open."

"I can't believe this is what you are now," Seth whispered.

"Here they are," Jenny said. The gunmen returned, one of them carrying, with oven mitts, a cast-iron skillet full of burning charcoal. "Could you guys have taken a little longer? What did you do, stop for a drink on the way?"

"We hurried, *la bruja*," one of the men said.

"Quiet." Jenny took the tongs from the other gunman, the one who wasn't holding the black skillet. She pinched out a few red-hot pieces of charcoal. She scattered these along one of Seth's arms. He screamed, rocking back from her as far as the ropes would allow.

"You fucking bitch!" Seth screamed.

"Hold still," Jenny whispered. She dropped most of the charcoal onto the coil of rope binding his wrist. Louder, she said: "Can you feel that burning, Seth? That's what my hate for you feels like."

She sprinkled more hot coals along his other arm, again saving most of them to drop on the rope at his wrist. He thrashed and screamed, trying to get back and away from her. "Now, this next part is going to get messy," Jenny said.

Jenny took a deep breath, and summoned up the pox inside her until she felt it swirling in her guts, in her lungs. Then she turned her head and breathed out a thick cloud of black spores, which flowed over the two gunmen.

Their skin ruptured open into lesions and dripping boils. The men screamed and staggered back. The pan of coals dropped to the floor, and half the burning coals scattered across the clay tiles. They spattered onto Seth's bare feet, and he cried out and stumbled back. His hands tore free of the burning ropes, and he collapsed to the floor and rolled, trying to put himself out.

Manuel let out a long, wet cough. He lurched toward the door, leaning on the wall and leaving a long smear of a bloody handprint behind him. Open sores festered all over his face.

He raised his other hand, which held his pistol. His eyes were burning directly at Jenny.

"*Vaya con dios...puta del Diablo*," he managed to say through his wheezing, and he pulled the trigger.

Jenny screamed and ducked. She felt a hot slash across the right side of her head and smelled her hair burning. Another bullet plowed through her right shoulder, shattering bone, and she cried out again.

She fell to the floor and quickly looked up at Manuel. Fortunately, the man had made his way to the door and was on his way upstairs. Unfortunately, he had a lot of friends with guns up there. Jenny could already hear their footsteps and voices rallying in response to the gunshot below.

"You traitor," Alexander sneered. He grabbed one of the long scalpels from the table and approached her. "You choose him? The love-charmer's weak little pet? You're choosing him over me?"

Jenny looked to Seth, who lay on the floor a few feet away. "Help me, Seth. The pox doesn't hurt him."

Seth gaped at her, then at Alexander raising the blade. His eyes darted around the floor, and then he rose up on his knees and picked up the iron pan, still half-filled with hot coals. The skin of his palms sizzled on the iron handle, and Seth gritted his teeth.

He flung the coals into Alexander's face, raining bits of fire all over his face, hair and shirt. Alexander howled and stumbled away. Seth flung the hot pan after him, and it cracked against Alexander's head. Alexander dropped to the floor.

Seth leaned his forearms on his thighs and pushed himself to his feet, wincing in pain. His fingers were curled up, his hands blackened from the scorching they'd taken, both from Jenny and from the pan.

"Seth, we have to get out of here." Jenny leaned on her good arm and managed to get to her feet.

"So...what the hell just happened?" Seth asked.

The voices grew louder upstairs.

"Manuel's coming back with a bunch of people who will want to put bullets in us," Jenny said.

"Wait." Seth looked at Alexander on the floor, then at the blades on the table. "I should finish him off."

"Trust me, Seth, you don't want to be a killer like me," Jenny said.

Seth tried to pick up a boxcutter, but his blackened fingers appeared frozen, the nerves still dead.

"Come on!" Jenny grabbed his arm and pulled him toward the door.

They hurried up the narrow staircase. Jenny let the pox break out on her face until she was a mask of disease.

"Are you going to infect them all?" Seth asked.

"I'm hoping to avoid that."

The door at the top of the stairs opened on the back hall of the house, where seven gunmen stood with their pistols out. They were staring at Manuel's convulsing, dying body on the floor. Jenny and Seth would have to get past them to escape the house.

All of them looked up at Jenny.

Jenny held her hands in front of her, palms out. She let oozing sores break open as the men watched.

"You know I am a witch," Jenny said in Spanish. "Tonight you see my deadliest curse, the...Devil's plague. I have already killed three of you. With one breath, I can kill all of you that remain. You may choose to leave this house now, or you may choose to stay here and die."

The men looked at each other, then hurried away. After a minute, she heard the sounds of truck engines.

"What did you say to them?" Seth asked, as he and Jenny limped toward the back door.

"I just asked them nicely to leave."

"Right." Seth stepped out to the back terrace with her. He brushed her hair back with one burnt, curled hand. "You're bleeding pretty badly."

"It's just a bullet to the head."

"Let me heal you."

"Heal yourself first, Seth." They crossed the back lawn, toward the barn, where the door stood wide open. Most of the trucks were gone. "And I'm sorry for setting you on fire. It was the only way to free you without alerting them. I figured they wouldn't see pouring burning coals on your wrists as an attempt to help you."

"Yeah," Seth said. "Most people wouldn't see it that way."

Jenny stopped him at the door of the barn. She reached her arms around his neck and kissed him.

"Thanks for coming to rescue me," Jenny said. "That was really sweet."

"Anytime."

Jenny approached an Army-green Jeep. "This is what I arrived in," Jenny said. "It might be poetic to leave in it, too."

"Sort of looks like Ashleigh's Jeep," Seth said.

"Actually, let's take that big Dodge truck over there," Jenny said. "Reminds of my dad's Ram."

She found the keyring on a row of hooks on the wall. Jenny drove, since Seth's hands weren't healed yet. Seth looked out the window as they drove past the main house.

"Jenny, what have you been doing down here?"

"Terrible things. What about you? Since when do you have helicopters and ninjas?"

Seth laughed. "They're a private security company. A bunch of ex-CIA guys."

"Wow. How'd you pull that off?" Jenny drove out through the front gate, which the others had left wide open.

"I stole a bunch of money from my dad."

Jenny laughed. "Your mom was right. I am a bad influence on

you."

"That's not possible." He looked at her. "I missed you a lot, Jenny."

"You know I'm not the same person," she said. "Jenny is just a small part of who I am."

"My favorite part, so far," Seth said.

"Mine, too, I think," Jenny said with a smile. "Especially since I met you. Alexander managed my past-life recall thing, and he tried to keep me from seeing the last few lives. In a thousand lifetimes, in all of eternity, I've never been happier than the time you and I have spent together as these simple human beings."

"Some of us are more simple than others."

"Ha. And that's what Alexander didn't want me to know. What he and I have is an ancient alliance stretching back forever. Our powers complement each other—the Jenny pox enhances his power. And I have to admit, it was nice seeing the pox could be used for something that isn't totally destructive."

"Like what?"

"They fueled his zombies so they could work hard in the fields, growing coke. And use complex tools like machine guns. Okay, maybe not the best example of things that aren't totally destructive. But you get what I mean."

"Why did you run off with him in the first place?"

"I recognized him from my dreams of past lives. And he remembers his past incarnations. I thought I could learn a lot from him, and I did."

"Were you close with him?" Seth looked at her carefully.

"He brought up a lot of old feelings. I had this very intense, kind of uncontrollable attraction to him—"

"That's just what I wanted to hear."

"—but love is something different from that. What you and I have is new, Seth. It's something that's grown between us and helped us become more human. It's something...precious and rare and alien to what we are. Spending all this time as humans has taught us so much. And I nearly lost that because of how Alexander handled my memories."

Seth looked at the dirt road ahead. "I assume you know where you're going now."

"I don't really, Seth. But I know I'm going with you."

"I meant, more specifically, this road we're driving on."

"Oh. Sure, eventually we get to the highway, and just take that north. Back to America."

"You have a passport?" Seth asked.

"Um..."

"We could have a little trouble slipping back in. Especially with Homeland Security looking for you. We're not out of the woods on that."

"We're not going to be free from Alexander, either. He'll come back for me."

"You should have let me kill him."

"Your hands weren't working," Jenny said. "How are they now?"

Seth held them up. The burns had shrunk to smaller patches as new skin grew into place. "Coming along." He reached a hand to touch her bleeding head and shattered shoulder, but Jenny pulled away, wincing.

"Not until you're healed," Jenny said.

"Here's what we need to do. Find a flat area, like a farm, a little bit out of the way where we can spend a little time." Seth unbuttoned his black fatigues.

"Seth, I think we have more urgent things to think about..."

"I know." He pushed his pants down to his knees. "I want to show you something."

"I've seen it before."

"Ha ha." Seth tugged back the leg of his boxer shorts to reveal a black band around one thigh with a circular device mounted on it. It reminded Jenny of a wristwatch.

"What's that?" she asked.

Seth lifted a cap on the black circle, revealing a small red button. "It's GPS. Hale Security can track me by satellite. When I push this button, that signals I'm ready to be picked up. We need to find a place a helicopter can land, though."

"You thought of everything."

"It's a standard Executive Personal Emergency device, apparently."

"Won't I still need a passport?" Jenny asked.

"Not with these guys. They're experts on how the American government works. They'll know how to slip us between the cracks. I've got it all taken care of."

Jenny smiled. "I'm so glad you came."

"I could tell by the way you were torturing me."

"I'm sorry! That's what he wanted me to do. I did save your life a little."

"A little."

"As soon as I saw it was you, when they pulled you out of the helicopter...I could start to feel something was wrong. You upset me, bringing up all these feelings of love, when Alexander had convinced me our relationship was probably a scheme by the charmer. By Ashleigh, I mean."

"And you believed him?"

"It made sense, looking back on all the past lives. You were allied with her more often than not. I was allied with him. Our factions have made war on each other forever. He knows that you and I getting together means I won't be his, and so his power stays limited. And Ashleigh hated me for drawing you away from her over the last few lifetimes—she hated me from the beginning of this life, even if she didn't know why."

"It's weird that our lives are shaped by so many things we don't even remember," Seth said.

"But they're not," Jenny said. "That's what I really learned. More important than remembering all the ancient stuff was understanding that this new thing, between you and me, is what really matters. I love you, Seth. I hope you still love me."

"Does this mean I should take my pants all the way off?"

She laughed and shook her head.

"We're going to need a plan," Jenny said. "How to deal with Alexander when he comes back for me. And how to deal with Homeland Security."

"I can help a little there. That CDC doctor, the one who came to your house? She's on our side now. She sort of figured us out."

"I don't think we can trust somebody like that."

"I healed her daughter from cancer."

Jenny nodded. "Okay. So let's figure something out."

CHAPTER THIRTY-ONE

The Hale rescue helicopter refueled in Cancun, so Jenny and Seth ate lunch in an open-air restaurant on the beach while one of the Hale guys kept an eye on them from the bar. They had swordfish, shrimp and oysters, along with rice and beans and Mexican wine. Jenny watched Seth's burn wounds disappear as he ate. Then he took her hand and looked quietly into her eyes while her gunshot wounds healed, underneath the bandaging the Hale men had applied.

Seth had to explain to the Hale men that none of the extraction team had survived, which made the mood in the helicopter quiet and somber. The helicopter pilot, in turn, explained that Seth's father had tracked the stolen money through Seth's account to Hale Security Group, so they would be landing in Florida instead of South Carolina.

Jenny and Seth stayed quiet for most of the ride, since the things they were eager to discuss couldn't be said in front of strangers. Jenny lay her head on Seth's shoulder as they flew north along the Florida coastline, while the sun set over the land to their left.

They dropped low just outside St. Augustine, landing on a helipad inside the gated community where Seth's parents lived. Seth's parents were already waiting for them. Seth's dad seemed to have a lot more gray hair than Jenny remembered.

"This is going to be fun," Seth said, as the pilot opened the door for them. "If they kill me, say hi to Rocky for me." He stepped out of the helicopter and offered Jenny his hand. She took it, though she didn't really need it. It was nice to touch him again.

Seth shook hands with the two Hale men that had picked them up, then he and Jenny ducked low as they walked under the whirling blades towards Seth's parents. It was growing dark, and a few streetlamps flickered to life.

"Jonathan Seth Barrett," his mother said. She looked him over. "Where have you been?"

"I had to rescue Jenny," Seth said. He looked at his dad, but the man was just glowering at him, flexing his jaw.

"Get in the car," Seth's dad said. He turned away and walked over to the parking slots by the helipad, where his black Lexus SUV was waiting.

Seth's mother was scowling at Jenny, a look of pure hate in her eyes. Seth grabbed Jenny's hand and led her toward the car.

"Everything will be fine," Seth told Jenny.

"Everything certainly will not," Seth's mom said. "I just have no words for what you've done. All that money you took."

"I needed it," Seth said.

"Haven't we taught you anything about values?" his mother asked, as she opened the passenger-side door. "About morals?"

"Not really," Seth said.

Jenny didn't know what to say—it was clear she wasn't welcome here, and she felt like anything she said would only make it worse. So she kept quiet in the back seat and gripped Seth's hand tight as they drove through the community. The homes here looked huge to her, but they were mostly concealed behind stone walls and groves of trees.

They parked in front of a three-story house with little spires and gables, white stonework and blue trim, and lots of windows. Jenny followed them inside. The interior had huge cathedral ceilings, glass walls looking out on the ocean, lots of bright colors , blond wood, comfy overstuffed furniture, and a few indoor trees. It seemed like Seth's parents had taken pains to make this house as different as it could be from the Fallen Oak house. Jenny didn't blame them—even at its best, Barrett House was about as cozy as a Transylvanian mortuary.

They entered a spacious, atrium-like living room with broad

skylights, which now showed a few stars instead of the sun.

"Seth, my office," Seth's dad said, approaching an open-air staircase to the second floor.

"No," Seth replied.

His dad stopped and looked back at him. "Let's go."

"This involves everyone," Seth said. He walked to the wet bar at the corner of the living room. "And it requires drinks." Seth opened a bottle of Woodford Reserve and splashed it into two glasses. He reached for a bottle of Grey Goose. "Vodka for Mom..."

"What the hell do you think you're doing?" Seth's dad asked. His face was glowing red, reminding Jenny of the pan of hot coals. Jenny glanced at Seth's mom, who looked angry, too. For a moment, the four of them stood scattered around the living room, saying nothing.

"Jenny, you want a Grey Goose?" Seth asked.

"Um...If everyone else is..." Jenny looked at Seth's mom, but the woman was ignoring her and staring at Seth. Jenny shrugged, but Seth had already poured her a drink and placed the four glasses on a tray.

His parents stared as he carried them to the center of the room, where a huge loveseat faced a matching sofa. He placed the tray on the coffee table, between two vases of fresh-cut flowers. Then he sat down on the loveseat and sipped his drink.

He looked around the room. "What's everybody waiting for?"

Jenny walked over and sat down beside Seth, but she didn't touch the vodka waiting on the table for her. She would be the last one to drink, if she did. Mrs. Barrett already hated her enough.

Gradually, Seth's parents made their way to the sofa and sat down, sharing worried, puzzled looks with each other.

Seth raised a glass. "To Florida. It might be a cheesy place, but it beats the hell out of Chiapas."

Nobody joined his toast, but Seth drank as if they had. He set down his glass.

"Okay," he said. "Mom. Dad. Here's the thing. Jenny and I have, like, powers."

His parents gave him blank looks.

"What the hell are you talking about?" his dad finally asked.

"Of course, you're not going to believe me," Seth said. "So, um...Jenny, can you go over to the kitchen and grab, say, a butcher knife? And a towel? Not one of the monogrammed ones, though. Mom just uses those to decorate."

"Okay..." Jenny walked past a pair of columns and into the brick kitchen, where the tall windows were open to the ocean breeze. She found the block of knives and a dish towel featuring a grinning cartoon duck wearing sunglasses. She had a pretty good idea of what Seth had in mind, and this looked like a towel Mrs. Barrett might not mind losing to bloodstains.

Jenny returned to the living room and set the butcher knife and towel on the coffee table in front of Seth.

"What is this about?" Seth's dad asked.

"I'll have to show you so you'll believe me." Seth reached out his left hand toward them, turning it back and forth. "This is my real hand. What you're about to see is completely real. There's nothing up my sleeve, obviously, since I'm wearing this cheap tourist T-shirt from Cancun."

Seth folded the towel and lay his left hand on it. With his right hand, he raised the butcher knife, point down.

"Seth, what are you doing?" his mom asked.

"Just watch." Seth took a deep breath, then plunged the butcher knife through the center of his hand.

"Seth!" his mom screamed, reaching for him.

"It'll be okay." Seth winced as he ripped the butcher knife forward and out between his knuckles, cutting most of his hand in half. Blood soaked the sunglasses-wearing duck.

"Oh, my God!" Seth's mom screamed, reaching toward him, but Seth pulled away.

"Have you lost your mind?" his dad asked.

"No, it's fine. Look." Seth held up his hand and spread his fingers wide, looking at his parents through the wide, bloody "V" in the middle of his hand. He furrowed his brow and concentrated. His parents watched with wide eyes as strings of sinew and muscle bridged the wound and pulled the two halves of his hand together.

Seth wiped the blood from his hand with the towel, then showed them the front and back of his hand again, making it clear there wasn't even a scratch.

"What was that?" Seth's mom grabbed his hand and inspected it more closely.

"Didn't you ever wonder why I never got sick? Why I never got hurt, even when I fell twenty feet from that tree in the front yard?"

"We thought we were just lucky," Seth's mom said. "What else were we supposed to think?" She looked at Seth's father, who was just staring at Seth with a cold, distant look in his eyes. "Jonathan?"

Seth's father didn't say a thing.

"I can heal other people, too," Seth said. "Jenny's father was crushed by a tractor last year, and I healed him. There were witnesses. That's when the town started all the talk about witchcraft."

"Witchcraft? I don't remember any talk about that," his mom said.

"That's because you two were here," Seth said. "You would have heard if you were around, and especially if you were still going to Fallen Oak Baptist. The Goodlings really stirred everybody up about it. Ashleigh Goodling had a power, too. Her touch made people feel love. And she used it to be a very effective evil bitch."

"Don't say that!" Seth's mom said. "Ashleigh's such a nice girl."

"No, she's not," Seth said. "She just had everyone under her spell. That's how she raised a mob to kill me and Jenny."

"What? When did this happen?" his mom asked.

"Easter. Ashleigh got me through the chest with a shotgun. Then they tried to hang Jenny from that old oak tree in front of the courthouse."

Jenny looked at Seth, not sure if she wanted things to go this far.

"Easter..." his dad said.

"And Jenny's my other half," Seth said. "Her touch doesn't heal, but..." Seth looked at her.

Jenny looked from Seth to his parents, who were staring at her. *Fuck it*, she thought. She took off a glove and raised her hand, then she made pulsing blisters and a dark rash appear on her hand. She quickly drew it back in, leaving no sign of disease.

"Ugh," Seth's mother said, and Jenny felt a little hurt, and a little angry at Seth for revealing her secret.

"Jenny and I belong together," Seth said. "And we could be together for the rest of my life, as far as I'm concerned. I'm not going to live without her again."

Jenny felt unexpectedly touched, and lowered her head to hide her eyes behind her hair, until she could swallow back the tears that threatened to form. It felt good to be back with Seth, even with all the vulnerable emotions he stirred in her. She liked feeling human with him more than she'd enjoyed feeling like a goddess with Alexander.

Seth's parents stared at them in shock.

"So, that takes care of that." Seth downed more of his whiskey.

"We have two pretty urgent problems. One, the United States government—I mean CDC, Homeland Security, all the way up to the White House—they wanted to capture Jenny and me, and make us their lab rats for the rest of our lives. They might lie and tell you they're only after Jenny, but they want us both. I think the only reason they haven't come for me yet is because they were waiting for me to find Jenny. So, we have to deal with that.

"And on top of that," Seth continued, "There are others like us, and they're not the nicest people out there. One of them is...has Great-grandfather's ability, Dad. He can raise the dead and make them into zombies."

"You told him about that?" Seth's mom snapped at his dad. "I thought we agreed to keep all that away from Seth."

"We did agree. And it clearly didn't help," Seth's dad said.

"It turns out Jenny's power enhances the zombies," Seth said. "It's like a fuel. Or an upgrade. Or both."

Jenny nodded when Seth's dad looked at her.

"He's not going to leave Jenny alone," Seth said. "He wants her power, and he'll be back for her. Probably with a big pack of rabid zombies. We need to get ready for that."

His parents stared at him in silence for a long time. Jenny felt increasingly nervous. She glanced at her vodka on the table, but she still didn't want to make a bad impression.

"Well, this is a beautiful house, Mrs. Barrett," Jenny said, by way of breaking the tension.

Seth's mom just blinked at her. Jenny sank a little in her chair.

"We can do this with your help or without it, but our chance of surviving and escaping will be a lot better if you help us," Seth told his parents. "We need you."

His parents looked at each other.

***

Later, Jenny and Seth sat on the dock under the stars, looking out at the dark waters of the Atlantic. Jenny leaned back on him, loving the feeling of his warm hands, which he'd slipped underneath her shirt to rest on her belly.

"Did you really mean what you said?" Jenny asked.

"Which part?"

"About wanting to spend the rest of your life with me?"

"I definitely meant that. It was terrible being without you. I felt like a big part of myself was gone." He pulled her closer against him. "I missed everything about you, Jenny. Do you remember how much fun we used to have, before everything went crazy?"

Jenny smiled and lay her hand on his. "I remember. It seems like a million years ago, our first date. Halloween."

"Remember how you puked on me after our first kiss?"

"You just have that effect on people."

"I miss the sound of you breathing beside me when you sleep," Seth said. "I would just look at your face and think how lucky I was to find somebody so funny, and smart, and kind, and beautiful..."

"Oh, come on."

"I mean it. It would kill me if anything happened to you." His fingers flexed on her stomach. "You should have let me kill Alexander when we had the chance. Then you'd be safe."

"You weren't in any condition for that. And we had to get out of there fast."

"I could have done it." Seth was quiet for a minute. "Are you sure you didn't want him left alive because of your feelings for him?"

"Seth!" Jenny elbowed him. "That's not it." Jenny wondered, though. She had a felt an intense, magnetic attraction to Alexander. And his understanding of their kind made her feel secure. Maybe she hadn't been ready to see him die.

"Why didn't you let me do it?" he whispered.

"I don't know, Seth. I just got out of his bed a couple hours before that. Killing him on the same day seemed a little...black widowish."

"You were sleeping with him?"

"What are you so outraged about? You slept with that girl who looked like Ashleigh."

"I told you, Ashleigh was behind that. She was possessing Darcy Metcalf."

"And you're so lucky I believe you about that," Jenny said. "She did a good job acting lonely and pathetic, though. And then she *knew* I would see you with that girl and think that you were still secretly in love in Ashleigh."

"And that's why you ran off with Zombie Xander."

"It helped me decide. But you know, I had to escape from the riot Tommy set up. And from Homeland Security. The National Guard. He saved my life from that mob, you know. I decided I'd rather let them kill me than repeat that terrible Easter again."

"Then I'm glad he saved you. I wish I'd been there to do it. I feel like I'm never there to help the people I love." A sad look crossed his face, and Jenny knew he was thinking about his brother Carter.

"It's not your fault. And you didn't have a gang of zombies to help out," Jenny said.

"I wouldn't need one, if I saw you in danger."

"Aw."

"So, about sleeping with this other guy..."

"I thought you'd cheated on me. And he was my companion for a thousand lives. See, I'm more like a normal girl now, Seth. I have a psycho stalker ex-boyfriend."

"But did you love him?" Seth asked.

"I..." Jenny looked him in the eyes. "No, Seth. I didn't love him."

"Tell me how you hated being with him."

Jenny couldn't help but think of her long nights with Alexander, how he'd known exactly what to do with his fingers, his tongue... "He did have a thousand lifetimes of experience," Jenny said.

"Big deal. I just need more practice."

Jenny turned her head to face him. "Then we'd better practice," she said.

He kissed her, long and slow.

CHAPTER THIRTY-TWO

Ashleigh was working late in her corner office at the Los Angeles campaign headquarters when he came to see her.

"Ashleigh," his voice said.

She looked up, startled. He'd entered without a sound. The young man was tall, muscular, with shaggy brown hair, handsome except for the tiny burn scars that dotted his face and neck. He was dressed Rodeo casual, T-shirt and jeans and sneakers that must have cost a thousand dollars. He took off his Fendi sunglasses as he regarded her. His dark eyes seemed to laugh at Ashleigh.

"Ashleigh Goodling?" he asked.

"How did you get in here?"

His eyes locked onto hers. "I can get into anyplace I want."

Ashleigh felt uneasy. Her fingers drifted toward the SECURITY button on her desk phone. "You have the wrong person," she said. "My name is Esmeralda."

"I don't think it is." He dropped into the chair across from her and leaned back, swinging idly from side to side like a bored child. "Esmeralda Medina Rios was a funerary cosmetician. I kept tabs on her. She didn't care for politics. The love-charmer, though—politics are an

248

irresistible nectar to her. The power. The blood. That's why I believe
you are not Esmeralda Rios, but Ashleigh Goodling, riding Esmeralda's
body like a horse. And if I know you, love-charmer, you're not sharing.
You're possessing. Because that's what you love to do most of all,
possess."

Ashleigh gaped at him. "Who are you?"

"Esmeralda is my opposite. It's always interesting to keep tabs on
your opposites, isn't it, love-charmer? And how is your Tommy? Using
his abilities in the most unfocused and unproductive ways, as usual?"

Ashleigh couldn't help but laugh.

"They can require such guidance and hand-holding, can't they?" he
asked. "So few of us are masters. So few of us remember what we truly
are."

Ashleigh, completely caught off-guard and a little frightened,
could only stare at him.

"You may now reply," he said, with half a smile.

"Oh!" Ashleigh was feeling flustered. "Then, what do you want
with me?"

"Don't be afraid," he said. "I'm not going to cast you from
Esmeralda's body like Christ and his demons. I could, though.
Opposites have special influence over one another, as you know." He
reached across her desk, and Ashleigh shrank back from him. She
covered the bracelet on her hand, the one that contained pieces of
Ashleigh-bone, keeping her connected to Esmeralda's body.

"But I won't," he continued. He reclined in the chair and put his
hands behind his head. "Esmeralda is as useless to me as your Tommy
is to you. No imagination. No ambition. Forget her for now. It's your
help I would enjoy, Aphrodite."

"Cute," she said. From her large swaths of past-life memory,
Ashleigh was beginning to recognize who this man was. A brutal
conqueror, an iron-fisted ruler of humans, whom he regarded as cattle.
He had been her enemy often, though not always. She needed to be
wary. He seemed to radiate power.

"What is your name, this lifetime?" she asked.

"Alexander. You may remember the wars we have enjoyed waging
against each other in the past, with our armies of human pawns. But,
regardless of our previous conflicts, we now share a common problem,"
he said. "The healer and the plague-bringer."

"Jenny? Do you know where she is?"

"She has been with me these past months," he said. "Until, as is increasingly the problem in recent lives, she ran off with your servant, the healer."

"She's with Seth?" Ashleigh sat up. "You know where to find them?"

"Of course, with him," Alexander said. "They grow closer together each lifetime, and further from us. We must reclaim our slaves. Our property must be returned to us."

"I don't want to reclaim Seth," Ashleigh said. "I want him dead, maybe, but not back in my life."

"Of course, they must be punished for their insulting disloyalty in this lifetime," Alexander said. "That is understandable. But we have eternity to think about. Countless lifetimes when they could be serving us. Or we can let them draw together and become our enemies."

"What did you have in mind?" Ashleigh asked.

"I want to destroy them. I want to give them both a death so horrific it leaves them scarred for lifetimes. And if there is anyone who knows how to maximize the suffering of others, it's you, charmer."

Ashleigh stood and walked around the desk. She leaned against the front of it, looking down at him. "I like how you think. We'll punish them with the worst death we can design." She offered her hand.

Alexander drew on a black glove. "Sorry, I don't feel like getting charmed today." He shook her hand.

"There's just one little loose end I need to tie up," Ashleigh said.

Alexander had arrived in a cab, so they left in Esmeralda's mother's car, an old Toyota Corolla. Ashleigh had lovingly convinced Esmeralda's mother that she should start taking the bus to work, leaving her car for her daughter to use. After the election, Eddie was supposed to buy her a new BMW convertible. Until then, it was best to avoid anything that might draw attention to the congressman's affair with her.

They drove towards a private airport, where Alexander had a plane waiting. Ashleigh stopped at rundown Citgo along the way.

"Where are you going?"

"Just one second." Ashleigh got out of the car and approached the two payphone boxes outside the store. Both were covered in years of spraypainted messages, and one of the phones was gone, with only a frayed wire where it had been.

Ashleigh picked up the remaining phone, holding it a few inches from ear, since it was thick with grime and filth. She fed in a few quarters, then called 911.

"I want to report an escaped convict," Ashleigh said. "He usually goes by Thomas Krueger, but I think his legal name is actually Thomas White. He escaped from Riverbend Prison in Louisiana a few months ago. He says he's killed two people since then. He's always armed. You can find him after 10 p.m. every night at Jack's Spot on Sepulveda."

The operator tried to take her information, but Ashleigh said, "This has to be anonymous. He'll kill me if he knows I reported him. He's very, very dangerous and violent. He's high on meth most of the time, so expect him to fight back or shoot at the police when they go to arrest him. Thank you!"

Ashleigh hung up the phone and returned to her car.

"Everything good?" Alexander asked when she sat down.

"All squared away." Ashleigh beamed at him. She tried not to think about the intense attraction she felt for Alexander, which almost made her squirm. He was strong, powerful, the first guy she'd met that she might not be able to manipulate at all. It seriously turned her on.

"Then let's drive," Alexander said.

"Sorry!" Ashleigh cranked the car, blushing. "I can't wait to see that bitch's face when I finally destroy her."

CHAPTER THIRTY-THREE

Jenny and Seth took a quick charter plane ride to Charleston, where they picked up Jenny's old Lincoln. The clerk at the parking deck booth was amazed to see the car had checked in more than three months earlier, and said she needed to contact her supervisor. Seth shoveled cash at her until she decided it wasn't such a big problem, after all, and raised the arm for them to exit.

Jenny let Seth drive, content to watch the familiar South Carolina countryside. She'd missed the long, crooked limbs of the oak trees, the little cypress swamps, the familiar mats of moss that grew everywhere.

They arrived in Fallen Oak and drove straight to Jenny's house. Jenny felt nervous as she got out of the car—she hadn't spoken to her dad in months, and he hadn't exactly been happy with her then.

As they walked up the front porch steps, her dad appeared behind the screen door. The main door was open to catch the breeze, as it usually was between May and October.

"Jenny?" he said.

"Hi, Dad." Jenny smiled.

He opened the door, and Jenny embraced him, careful to keep her head away from his. After a minute, he squeezed her tight.

"I missed you so much," he whispered. "My little baby girl."

"I missed you, too, Daddy."

He stepped back, looking her up and down. "You been okay?"

"Yes. How about you?"

"Where you been?"

"Um, Chiapas," Jenny said. "In Mexico."

"Doing what?"

"Helping zombies grow cocaine for a big cartel."

"Goddamn, you do know how to find trouble. Did you know about this, Seth?"

"I went to get her as soon as I could track her down," Seth said.

"Well, come on in, you two. Dang gnats are still thick as gravy out here."

Inside, he led them to the kitchen. "I was just fixing to fry up some bacon," he said. "Guess I'll cook the whole mess, now."

Rocky lay in a patch of sun on the kitchen floor. His head raised and his tail thumped at the sound of her dad's voice.

"Whoa, Rocky comes inside now?" Jenny asked.

"Hell, I can barely get him outside anymore," her dad said. He set a black pan on the stove, ignited the gas burner with a match. "He sleeps on my feet at night."

"That's good, Rocky." Jenny knelt beside him and petted him with a gloved hand. He put a paw on her knee, wagging his tail. Jenny felt tears in her eyes and tried to swallow them back. Rocky had finally gotten over his fear of people. "I'm so proud of you," she whispered.

"Well, guess I'll appreciate it come winter," her dad said. He tossed in a pack of bacon, then cracked eggs into another pan. "Right now, it's too dang hot for that. He don't listen, though."

"Are you still seeing June?" Jenny asked.

"Yep. She's working a shift at the Waffle House in Varnville today."

"Can I help you cook, Mr. Morton?" Seth asked.

"Ain't really cooking. Just eggs and bacon. Y'all have a seat."

Jenny and Seth sat in the mismatched chairs at the old table in the kitchen.

"You planning to stay long?" her dad asked, while stirring the eggs with a spatula. His back was to them, but Jenny could hear a little sadness in his voice.

"I'm sorry, Daddy," Jenny said. "We got problems to deal with."

"Homeland Security," her dad said. "They done been here three, four times asking questions about you."

"That's one problem," Jenny said.

He served them the eggs and bacon on his chipped dinnerware. Jenny went to the fridge and poured orange juice into the vintage *Happy Days* glasses and brought them to the table.

Her dad cleared his throat as he sat down. "Okay. Tell me what else you got to deal with."

"There's another guy like us," Jenny said. "But he can touch dead people and make them do stuff for him. Farm. Fight."

"Sounds like them *Living Dead* movies," her dad said. "Your momma and I saw one at the old Star-Nite drive-in off 278. Guess you don't remember that. Closed up in '90-something."

"The sign's still there," Jenny said.

"Old Roy Cramer kept that thing goin' a long time, though," her dad said. "Used to be the place to go on Friday nights. Had them a Pac-Man, a foosball table, just about everything you could want. Your momma liked the popcorn. Had to get one with extra salt and butter every time." His eyes were distant now. He was obviously thinking about Jenny's mother. Jenny wondered if he was thinking how much happier he would have been if Jenny had never been born.

"This guy's going to come back for Jenny," Seth said. "He feeds on her power. He won't let her escape long."

"So you're going back on the run," Jenny's dad said.

"Not exactly," Jenny told him. "We're going to let him come to us first, here in Fallen Oak. We've already talked it over with Seth's parents. But I was hoping you could help us, Daddy. We have a few things to prepare."

"Want a slice of hoop cheese?" Her dad stood up and lifted the glass bowl from a half-eaten hoop of cheddar on the cutting board.

"I'm full. This was really good, Daddy, thanks." Jenny gathered up the dishes.

"So, can you help us?" Seth asked. Jenny scowled at him for rushing things.

Her dad bit into a slice of cheese and chewed it slowly.

"You know, Jenny," he said. "Whatever the hell you kids are, you're still my little girl. I'll help you if I can. I'm just worried for you."

"Let me tell you what Seth and I have planned," Jenny said. "Then you can decide."

254

"I already decided," he said. "Can we talk about it later on tonight? I want a little while when I can just be happy you're home. I'm not ready to think about you leaving again, Jenny." He scraped a few scraps of bacon and egg from the pan into Rocky's food dish, which was now in a corner of the kitchen instead of out in the shed. Rocky bounded over to it, his tail whipping.

"Okay," Jenny said. "It's good to see you again, Daddy."

"Used to see you every day." He looked out the window, into the thick woods behind the house. "Guess it won't be like that no more."

"I guess not. I'm sorry, Daddy."

***

Later, her dad went to the Piggly Wiggly to buy some ribs to grill, and Jenny and Seth sat on the bed in Jenny's room. Rocky napped on the floor nearby.

"It's so strange," Jenny said, looking around at her country music posters, stuffed animals, misshapen attempts at pottery. "It's like this is just one more past life. It's never going to be the same, is it?"

"We're not kids anymore," Seth said. "I'm going to miss my parents, too. But I'll be happy as long as we're together. I love you more than anything in the world, Jenny."

"I love you, too, Seth."

"Even if you stab me with a scalpel and set me on fire, I'll still love you."

"Hey, it got us out of there. I need an album cover." Jenny fished a record out of a milk crate full of dusty, wrinkled LP sleeves. All of them had belonged to her mother, another lifetime ago. Jenny looked at her mother's picture on the wall, where Miriam stood against the neon signs in McCronkin's Pub, raising a Bud Light and smiling. Jenny liked this picture because it made her imagine that her mother had spent her short life being wildly happy, surrounded by friends.

Jenny slipped the record out of its cover and dropped it on her tabletop record player. The scratchy speakers hissed.

"Hey, this one's for you, Seth," Jenny said. She placed the needle in the groove, and the long-ago voices of a very young Johnny Cash and June Carter sang "Darling Companion."

Jenny sat beside him on the bed, laid the old water-stained album cover on her lap, and crumbled the bud of weed she'd liberated from the cigar box in her dad's room. This was probably part of the harvest from the patch he grew out on neglected, bank-owned land outside of town. The money mostly went to cover the property taxes on the Morton family land. He broke the government's law in order to pay the government's bill.

"I thought you said you were quitting the drugs," Seth said.

"Yeah, I'm never touching coke again. That stuff makes you into a real asshole."

"It sure does." Seth brushed her hair from her face and kissed her. "I'm glad you came back."

"I'm glad you came swooping in to take me," Jenny said. "My hero. How sexy of you."

"I think it was very sexy, personally." Seth kissed her. "You're so lucky to have me."

"And you're so unlucky that my last boyfriend wants you dead. He's a gangster, you know."

"You're a dangerous girl."

"Obviously." Jenny licked and twisted the joint in her fingers. "Rocky, want to go for a walk?"

Rocky, who had by all appearances been deep in a coma under the window, jumped to all four feet and scampered to the door, tail wagging.

Jenny and Seth walked along the trail into the hilly woods behind her house. They reached the heap of boulders where they had spent lazy afternoons and a few very hot evenings together, but Jenny led him on past the big rock.

"Where are we going?" Seth asked.

"Further."

She led him up and over a steep ridge and through a stand of old, coiled oak trees to a small patch of sunlit meadow, full of fall wildflowers, purple asters, goldenrods in bloom.

"Here." Jenny took his hand and led him a little pyramid of creek-smoothed stones at the center of the meadow. "This is where my dad buried my mom."

"Oh." Seth gazed at the stone cairn. "I didn't know she was here."

"Officially, she's still 'missing,'" Jenny said. "My dad hid her body so they wouldn't identify her cause of death. Which was me. It's my fault she died. I ruined their lives, my mom and dad. They used to be happy people."

"It's not your fault."

"It is. I've started figuring out a way I can avoid killing my...killing my mothers, when I'm born. It happened by accident the first time. If I'm born in a caul, that will protect them."

"What's a caul?"

"It's a membrane from inside the womb. The amniotic sac, is what it's called. Some bodies are born wrapped in it. Looks like a shroud of skin."

"That sounds creepy."

"Most people think it's something sacred."

"But you can't control that, can you?" Seth asked.

"If I'm careful enough, and enter the fetus early enough, and I really concentrate...I think I can. I messed it up last time, but I've done it a couple times before. I was in too much of a rush, and we'd been searching for Ashleigh between incarnations, because she was hiding from us—I don't think I moved into this body early enough to influence the womb like that." She looked at her mother's grave. "I promise I'll never make that mistake again, Momma."

"Moving into the body?" Seth asked. "Is that what we do? Find some developing baby in the womb and...what? Possess it like a ghost? Are we taking over lives that were supposed to be lived by someone else?"

"From what I can remember, the regular human souls can move in anytime during pregnancy, up until right before the birth. So we just have to find an empty vessel nobody's claimed yet. It's like parking at the mall. You hope for a good spot, but you take what you can get."

"Where do all the human souls come from, anyway?" Seth asked. "Do you remember that?"

"I'm not sure I ever knew that." Jenny knelt by the cairn of stones, straightening a few that had slipped loose. "But, I think I'm kind of jealous of them. Maybe they reincarnate for a while. But ultimately they come from somewhere, they move on to somewhere. Not us. We're just stuck here, over and over again. I don't know if we ever get to move on."

"I don't mind being stuck here, as long we can live our lives together. Think of everything we might see, in all those lifetimes to come." Seth knelt beside her, rubbing her back. "I'm sorry about your mom, Jenny."

"I know." She leaned her head on his shoulder. "You lost your brother. That must have been rough."

"Yeah."

"I can almost see why people like Ashleigh and Alexander resist getting too human," Jenny said. "It can hurt so much. There's a lot of suffering involved once you start to care about people. Love makes you vulnerable to the worst kinds of pain."

"It does," Seth said. "But it's worth it. I think it's worth it. Don't you?"

Jenny smiled and kissed him again.

CHAPTER THIRTY-FOUR

"What you want to do is hit them just before closing time," Tommy said. "That's when they've got the most cash. It's easier to escape late at night, too. No traffic."

"That's when they expect to get hit," said Booker, one of the two guys with whom Tommy was drinking. They were at Jack's Spot, a filthy little bar with several pool tables and extremely cheap beer. "You want to go sometime they don't expect. Like first thing in the morning."

"Yeah, he's got a point." Booker's friend Chucky nodded. "They don't expect shit right when they open."

"They don't have any goddamn money yet, either." Tommy jabbed his index and middle fingers at Booker. The Marlboro between his fingertips had grown a long ash. "You have to let them make sales all day so the cash register's stuffed."

"Ought to hit a Korean place, too, 'cause they can't tell white people apart," Chucky said. He was about three hundred pounds, close to thirty years old, with a kerchief featured flaming skulls tied onto his head. Chucky scratched his beard stubble reflectively. "Or an Arab. Nobody gives a shit about Arabs, right?"

"I'm not robbing some Arab," Booker said. "They'll come back and suicide-bomb your ass."

"Forget it." Tommy downed his plastic cup of Milwaukee's Best. "I'm not doing a job with anybody as stupid as you two."

"Stupid?" Booker slammed his cup on the table, next to the empty pitcher. "Let's go outside and see who's stupid."

"You go first, I'll be there in a minute," Tommy said.

"You'll be there now!" Booker shouted. Heads turned. The crowd was looking to see if there was a fight, and which guy they'd bet on if one broke out.

"Fuck off, Booker," Tommy said. "You're shitfaced. You'll probably pass out before you make it to the sidewalk."

Chucky laughed, and Booker bared his teeth at him.

The crowd grew quiet. Tommy looked up and saw four uniformed cops entering the front door. One of them pointed at Tommy, and the other nodded. Tommy stood up and glanced toward the restrooms, where the rear exit was located. Two more cops were coming in from that direction.

"Shit," Tommy whispered.

"You! Stay right there!" one of the cops shouted at Tommy. "Keep your hands where we can see them."

"Well, boys," Tommy said to Booker and Chucky. "Playtime's over. It's been nice drinking with you scumbags." He took a deep breath.

"You calling me a scumbag now?" Booker stepped closer, swerving unsteadily on his feet. He raised two meaty fists.

Tommy exhaled a cloud of blood-red spores that filled the room like mist. People stood up, shouting, as spores landed on their skin and dissolved, and more spores disappeared into their mouths and noses.

"Look!" Tommy shouted, pointing at the four police officers. "Terrorists! Terrorists disguised as cops! They're going to kill us all!"

The crowd turned on the police, looking frightened.

"We can stop them if we all work together!" Tommy yelled. "Let's get these fuckers!"

The mob closed in around the police. At the same time, the police turned on each other, beating each other with fists and nightsticks. Then the mob fell on the police, punching and kicking at them from every side.

Tommy made his way through the small riot to the door, dodging flying bottles and broken table legs. He stepped out into the street, put on his sunglasses, and walked to his motorcycle.

He knew what had happened. Tommy was too small-time to bring on a nationwide manhunt. Plus, he'd been careful, staying at Esmeralda's mother's apartment, never telling anyone his legal name, Thomas White.

Except for Esmeralda. And Esmeralda wasn't really Esmeralda, and she never had been since she let Ashleigh take over her body in Charleston. The entire time they'd been in California, it was Ashleigh, tricking him.

Tommy had watched Ashleigh manipulate, use and discard one person after another. She'd pretended to be Jenny's friend in order to control her. She'd taken over Esmeralda's body, and she was never giving it back—a very sneaky kind of murder.

Now it was Tommy's turn to get screwed by Ashleigh. She was clearly done with him, had been done with him for weeks. Too wrapped up in her new politician boyfriend. Too concerned that it might "look bad" if she were seen with a lowlife like Tommy. Now she was kicking him out of her life the easiest way she could. As wicked as she was, Tommy hadn't expected Ashleigh to narc him out to the cops. He'd only broken out of prison in the first place because of her ghost harassing him in his dreams. Now she wanted him back there, out of her way.

Tommy pulled onto the freeway and gunned the engine. He wasn't going to get out of her way at all. He knew well enough what Ashleigh was after, and where he would eventually find her. He even knew the fastest way from Los Angeles to South Carolina.

***

Alexander glanced out the side at the Great Plains sprawling below in vast green and tan squares. It was a clear day, great for flying.

Ashleigh was beside him, catching up on the newspapers she'd downloaded to her Kindle before takeoff. She was keeping tabs on Eddie Brazer's campaign. It looked like the love-charmer intended to make the congressman her pet and her stepping stone, and naturally she was doing a fine job of it. He hated the charmer, but he respected her. You had to respect her, or you could find yourself with a poisoned dagger in your back.

For that matter, the plague-bringer had stabbed Alexander in the back, too, after he'd gone to all the trouble of saving her life and then waking her up to her own past lives. That had been a complicated, multi-stage process, which required her to get in touch with her power, just when she'd decided to never use it again.

So, step one had been to make Jenny use the pox in self-defense. He'd arranged that by having Jenny and Kisa attacked in the city, by a couple of toughs who had been instructed to kidnap and rape the two girls. They'd been paid a lump of cash and told that the attack was meant to be a "message" to somebody. Alexander had assumed that nobody would get too far with trying that on Jenny. And it had worked.

Then, step two: have Jenny kill someone out of vengeance. That was easy enough. Alexander had Manuel kill Kisa and her brothers, and one of Manuel's people picked up a random man from the barrio to blame for the crime. Jenny had killed an innocent man, but the most important thing was that she'd done it out of anger instead of self-defense, putting her in closer touch with who she really was.

Step three: once she was loosened up, blow the doors off her mind with the psychedelics. The more memories she could access, the more like herself she could become.

Step four had been to have Jenny kill someone in cold blood. Unfortunately, the healer had acted with greater speed, intelligence, and resourcefulness than Alexander had predicted, so Alexander had attempted to combine step four with step five: have Jenny kill the healer.

If she'd done that, it would have severed Jenny and Seth's connection for this lifetime. More importantly, it would drive a wedge through the strange, eerily human relationship they'd been forming in their last few lives. They'd spent so long incarnating as humans that they were close to going native, letting their humanity overtake their ancient nature. They were like wolves who'd stalked the sheep until they believed they were sheep themselves.

Instead, she'd betrayed him and left with the healer. For that, he would have to make her suffer. Alexander smiled.

"What are you thinking about?" Ashleigh asked. She was giving him a coy, flirty smile, which he knew better than to trust. He kept his gloves on for a reason.

"How much I look forward to destroying those two," Alexander said. "I like your ideas. We're going to use them."

"See, I can be useful." She leaned closer to him and laid her hand on his arm, her smile faltering a little when she realized it was completely covered by his jacket sleeve. "We would make a powerful alliance, wouldn't we, Alexander? The world would be ours."

"We've tried it before, my sweet little charmer," he said. "We always end up trying to kill each other."

"We could try it again." She gave him another coy smile, and now he felt a sudden surge of desire for her. He hated her. She fascinated him. He wanted to take her to bed, dominate the powerful little bitch, but he'd already made the mistake of trying that in past lives. Not this time.

"We'll see," Alexander said, and she pulled back, frowning and staring at him.

CHAPTER THIRTY-FIVE

"This seems like such a bad idea," Jenny said, as Seth parked Jenny's Lincoln on the street a few houses down from their destination, a two-story brick house surrounded by old-growth trees. They were in the Virginia Highlands, an upscale neighborhood in Atlanta not far from the CDC.

"She owes me," Seth said. He turned off the car, but he didn't seem to be in a hurry to get out. "I told you about her daughter."

"And that little girl is already healed, so this lady doesn't really have a reason to help you now."

"Except gratitude."

"That's a lot to hope for."

"And I made her promise."

"So everything depends on her keeping her promises," Jenny said. "Great."

"Let's see what she says." Seth got out of the car, and Jenny followed.

They tiptoed up to the front window, where they saw Dr. Heather Reynard and a man who Jenny guessed was her husband. They were both reading. A small girl with a short, fuzzy haircut slept on the couch

266

next to the man.

"That's the little girl?" Jenny whispered.

"That's her. I cured her cancer."

Jenny couldn't help giving him a quick kiss. "Okay, do we knock on the door?"

"We should wait for a chance to talk to her alone," Seth said. "We're kidnapping her, remember?"

"But...oh. Her husband won't be in on it."

"Not yet," Seth said. "It has to look believable. Let's go hide in the back yard before some neighbor calls the cops on us."

They walked around the house, moving as quietly as they could. The back yard was small, but fortunately two of the neighbors had fences, making it less likely that Jenny and Seth would be noticed. They found a window at the back through which they could see the family in the front parlor.

And they waited.

Eventually, the little girl stirred. Heather's husband smiled, said something to Heather, picked up the girl. He carried her toward the window where Jenny and Seth were hiding. They ducked, then Jenny peeked in again after a few seconds, to see the man carrying the girl upstairs.

"Okay, this is the best chance we're going to get," Jenny whispered.

They stood and tiptoed across the patio to the sliding glass door. Seth took the handle.

"Let's hope it's unlocked," he whispered.

He pulled, and the door slid open.

They crept through the kitchen. As they approached the front room, Seth spoke in a stage whisper: "Heather. It's Seth."

Heather jumped as Seth and Jenny stepped into her parlor. Heather's eyes shifted from Seth to Jenny, and then she glanced at the ceiling. Jenny could guess what she was thinking—she didn't like the idea of having Jenny in her house, so close to her daughter.

"What are you—?" Heather began to ask, but Seth pressed a finger to his lips. "What are you doing here?" she whispered.

Seth made a gun with his thumb and forefinger, and he pointed it at Heather with a grin. "We're kidnapping you."

"What?" Heather looked between them, panicked. "Why?"

"Because I need your help," Seth said.

"I can't right now. I have to work in the morning."

"But you won't show up, because you've been kidnapped," Seth said. "See? It all works out."

"Why do you keep saying that?"

"Because that's going to be the story," Seth said. "Jenny and I kidnapped you, determined to make our side of the story clear."

"You can just tell me your side of the story right here," Heather whispered. "I'll listen."

"That's not the real reason we're taking you. That's going to be your story, though."

"Where are we going?"

"Fallen Oak," Seth told her.

"For how long?"

"We don't know," Seth said. "Until things happen."

"It won't be long," Jenny said. "I know Alexander. I've spent enough time in his campaign tents, watching him plan battles. He's going to move fast and with overwhelming force. We're lucky we've had so much time already."

"Who is Alexander?" Heather asked.

"The zombie master," Seth said. "He's coming back for Jenny, and he wants me dead."

"What do you want me to do?" Heather asked. Floorboards creaked overhead—it sounded like her husband was returning to the stairs.

"We have to get going," Jenny said. "There's plenty of time to explain on the way."

Heather looked at Seth, then sighed. "Fine. Let me just tell Liam where I'm going." She stood up and walked toward the stairs, but Seth stopped her with a hand on her shoulder.

"You can't," Seth said. "You're being kidnapped, remember?"

"He's going to worry. He might call the police."

"He should do whatever he would normally do if you went missing," Jenny said. "That will make your story more believable. We want people to think you were taken against your will."

"That's not far off from the truth," Heather said. Liam's footsteps approached down the steps.

"Let's go," Seth said.

They left through the front door. Jenny quietly closed it behind them just as Liam reached the bottom floor.

268

Seth hurried Heather across the front yard and down the sidewalk. They'd come in Jenny's car, since Seth's Roadster didn't have much in the way of a back seat. Jenny's dad had fixed the window that Seth had smashed out with his fist.

Seth opened the passenger side door for Heather.

"You're such a gentleman about your kidnapping," Heather said, and Seth grinned at her. Jenny felt just a twinge of jealousy at the look they shared. Heather seemed a little attracted to Seth, the handsome miracle worker who'd saved her daughter's life.

"You keep driving," Jenny told Seth while she climbed into the back of her car and stretched her legs. "I hate driving in the city."

It was four hours to Fallen Oak.

***

Alexander pulled up to the gate of the warehouse. They were in a rundown industrial area just east of Atlanta, off Jimmy Carter Boulevard, and they were driving a large refrigerated box truck with a cartoon pig on the side. The pig had a bib and a crazed, elated expression as he was about to dig into a pile of barbecue. "Larry's Best Pork – Reheats in Minutes!" was painted under the logo.

The truck's original driver was probably still in a rental shower stall at the truck stop, waiting for Ashleigh's promised rendezvous with him.

"Can I help you?" the guard asked, stepping out of the gate booth. He cast a dubious look at the pig on the side of the truck. He was chunky, balding man in his late forties, wearing a black security uniform. The logo on his badge read "SyntaCorp, LLC."

"We're supposed to make a delivery," Alexander told him.

"I don't have anything on the clipboard. You sure you got the right place? We're not in the grocery business here."

"Neither am I," Alexander said. "SyntaCorp just wanted to keep things discreet."

"Oh, gotcha." The guard relaxed a little. "Just hand me your corporate ID card, and I'll swipe it for the records."

"I have it, sorry." Ashleigh took a deep breath and climbed over Alexander to smile at the guard through the window. She'd opened the top four buttons of her shirt, and the bait worked—the guard took in the very generous view of her breasts.

Ashleigh breathed out a cloud of spores that looked like pink dandelion heads. They snowed down on the guard's hair, face and uniform, and his mouth gaped open.

Alexander held his breath and tried to avoid breathing in the airborne love charms, but a few landed on his face, intensifying his genuine desire for Ashleigh. It took all his willpower to keep his hands off her—grabbing for her would let her know the charm had worked on Alexander. Although, he thought, he didn't really need to hide things from Ashleigh. They were friends now, and with any luck, they'd be lovers soon. He could probably trust her now. He was kind of in love with her.

Alexander shook his head, trying to fight back those feelings.

The security guard was staring at Ashleigh with a dazed, wide-eyed look.

"Can I see your ID card?" Ashleigh asked, with a fake giggle. "I bet your picture is so cute."

"Cute?" As if hypnotized, the guard took a plastic card from a sleeve clipped to his shirt. It showed a picture of the guard, looking bored and washed out under fluorescent light.

"Aw, it's just like I thought," Ashleigh said. "You're so hot, you know that?"

The guard gave her a goofy smile.

"Let's get together tonight," Ashleigh said. "We have this stupid little errand to do, but then I'm off work. Will you take me for a late dinner? Or early breakfast?" She winked. "Or maybe a late breakfast? We'll have to go to your place so I can change and maybe take a long, hot shower. Is that okay with you?"

"My place?" the guard asked.

"Yeah. You're just the kind of guy I've been looking for."

The guard glanced at Alexander, then back at Ashleigh. "Um, yeah. Okay?"

"Okay," Ashleigh said. "Just let us make this quick drop-off, and I'll be ready for you. Get it hard for me, will you? I don't want to wait long. I'm going to give you a screwing like you've never had before."

The guard gaped at her.

"Oh, you forgot to open the gate," Ashleigh said.

"Sorry!" The guard blushed and reached inside his booth. The two heavy steel gates swung open.

"Thanks, honey," Ashleigh said. "You won't change your mind

about me coming home with you, right?"

"Oh, no," he breathed. He was practically panting.

Alexander drove inside the gate, while the guard stared after them like a lonely puppy.

"You're such a charmer," Alexander said.

"I didn't get any on you, did I?" Ashleigh asked.

"I think we're safe."

"Pull around to that loading dock," Ashleigh said. "That's going to be the closest exit, I think."

Alexander parked, and they used the guard's ID to open the locked door by the loading dock.

The interior of the warehouse was all empty space and blank concrete, except for a rectangular metal structure at the center, which was about the size of an eighteen-wheeler truck.

"That must be it," Alexander said.

They opened the door at one end of the structure. The interior was freezing cold, and pitch black until Ashleigh found the light switch.

Shelves lined both sides of the freezer, six high, all the way to the back. The shelves were full of large objects sealed in plastic.

Ashleigh unzipped the nearest one. It contained the corpse of a teenage girl with red hair and freckles, eaten up by disease before it was frozen.

"Hey there, Cassie!" Ashleigh chirped. "Want to come out and play one more time?"

"You know her?" Alexander asked.

"She was my best friend before Jenny killed her," Ashleigh said. "But I know everybody here. This is my town."

Alexander touched Cassie's body. Cassie let out a groan and slowly, stiffly rolled over to the edge of the shelf. She planted her feet on the floor and stood up, slouching heavily. Her green eyes were blank, her jaw slack, her hair falling off with pieces of her scalp. Ashleigh snapped her fingers in front of Cassie's face, but the dead girl didn't react.

"Come on, Cass-Cass," Ashleigh said. "It's time Jenny Mittens got her payback."

Alexander was unzipping the next body, and the next. Ashleigh helped. She found Cassie's boyfriend, Everett Lawson, the obese Coach Humbee, Mayor Winder, Dick Baker ("The Attorney/Realtor You Trust"), several ladies from the steering committee at Fallen Oak

Baptists, assorted kids from the football team, and all the cheerleaders. Neesha, Ashleigh's other best friend, was barely recognizable with her collapsed face.

Ashleigh unzipped a body at the back and found herself looking at the leprous dead face of her mother. Then she unzipped her father's corpse, lying next to it. Jenny had infected the Goodlings pretty badly.

"You look like shit, Mom and Dad," Ashleigh said. "Come on, get moving."

"Your parents?" Alexander asked. "Want to leave them here?"

"Hell, no," Ashleigh said. "I want Jenny to see what she's done to every one of these people. If she's all mopey about it like you say, this should be a nice and horrible way for her to die."

"Your call." Alexander shrugged. He grabbed one of Ashleigh's dead parents with each hand and pulled them off the shelf. They fell to the floor, then slowly stood, creaking with every move.

Ashleigh looked back over her shoulder and saw scores of people, her old neighbors and classmates, shuffling out the door of the freezer.

"Are they going to move any faster?" Ashleigh asked.

"I'm still fully charged with Jenny's energy," Alexander said. "They can move fast, but they'll have to thaw first."

"Oh, that's going to reek." Ashleigh crinkled her nose.

They herded the zombies out to the loading dock. Alexander had the zombies empty the truck out, leaving a towering heap of frozen pork butts and sealed buckets of pulled pork and Brunswick stew on the dock. Then the zombies shuffled up the ramp into the box truck, lying down on top of each other, packing themselves in like sardines.

Alexander closed the rear door of the truck. The latch fell into place with a heavy thunk.

"I knew my investigation would pay off," Ashleigh said. "I can't say I expected things to work out this way, though."

"We'd better get going," Alexander said. "Unless you really want to stay and hook up with that guard."

"Ew," Ashleigh said. "I told him I'd give him the screwing of his life. He's going to get it as soon as his boss finds out what happened."

"I think he liked you," Alexander said.

"Shut up!" Ashleigh's eyes flicked up and down Alexander's body. "Why would I do that? I have much better options available."

"Who said I'm available?" Alexander asked.

"Who said I was talking about you?"

Alexander found himself reaching for her, intending to draw her close. He closed his fists and resisted the urge. "Let's just get in the truck."

"Whatever you say, baby," Ashleigh said.

Alexander climbed into the driver's seat. Ashleigh tuned the radio to a pop-country station.

"Jenny fucking Mittens," Ashleigh said, her eyes gleaming. "I warned her not to fuck with me, didn't I?"

"I'm sure you did," Alexander said. "It sounds like something you would say."

They pulled away from the warehouse, with two hundred reanimated bodies in the back of the truck.

CHAPTER THIRTY-SIX

Jenny and Seth sat on the floor of a guest room in Seth's house, the room with the curtained bed made from an old wooden sailing ship. The windows were open and their screens removed, so the breeze from outside flapped the canvas bed curtains. If you wanted to drop something onto a horde of zombies lurching up the front walk, this was one of the best vantage points from which to do it.

Heather sat in a chair in the corner of the room, watching nervously as Seth poured gasoline through a funnel into a glass beer bottle. Then he sealed it with a small, lever-operated bottle capper. Both the bottles and caps had been purchased at a home-brewing hobby shop on their way out of Atlanta.

Jenny set a pair of long kitchen matches on either side of the bottle, then wrapped it with a strip of duct tape to hold the matches in place. She carefully set it down in a cardboard box with a dozen other completed bottles. They would stay here beside the window until they were lit and dropped out. Nobody wanted to move the whole box around at once, for fear something would break and leak fuel everywhere.

"Are sure you know what you're doing?" Heather asked.

"Yeah," Seth said. "I read a whole website about Molotov cocktails."

"That makes me feel so much better," Heather said.

"Can you think of a faster way to cut down a horde of zombies?" Jenny asked.

"How do you know he's coming with a horde?" Heather asked. "Why doesn't he just bring a gun and shoot you?"

"That's not good enough, because Seth could heal us easily from gunshot wounds," Jenny said. "Besides, he'll want to make a big, dramatic point. He won't just want us dead, he'll want us ripped to pieces."

"Me, anyway," Seth said. "He wants to keep you, Jenny."

"We'll see what he wants," Jenny said. "I'm assuming the worst."

"Which would be worse?" Seth asked. "Dying, or going back with him?"

"What do you think?" Jenny scowled.

"Okay, I got you all set up." Jenny's dad walked into the room, wearing a deep, worried frown. Jenny didn't think she'd ever seen him so unhappy before.

Her dad held two remote controls from Radio Shack, which were meant to power little motorized race cars. He set them down on the dresser.

"There you go," he said. "You got to mash both switches at once to make it go. So we don't have any accidents."

"Thanks, Daddy." Jenny stood up.

"Whew, you sure smell like gas," he said. He glanced at the box full of bottles. "Y'all be careful. I don't like any of this."

"We'll be fine," Jenny said.

"I really think I ought to stick around, if this fella's coming for you," her dad said. He looked at Seth and Heather. "Y'all don't have a lot of people."

"The story will go smoother if you're not here," Jenny said. "Just head over to June's place, in case they come searching for me at home."

"You don't think they're coming tonight, do you?" he asked.

"It'll be within a few days, I bet. We're lucky we've had this much time."

"I'm staying." He folded his arms.

Jenny sighed. She closed her eyes and summoned up the pox from deep inside her, until face oozed with sores. She opened her eyes again, and spoke in the dark, ancient voice of her soul. "I am not simply your daughter. I have ruled kingdoms without number. I have slaughtered cities and armies. I have raised empires and destroyed them. I am the plague-bringer."

Her dad gaped at her. So did Seth and Heather.

"You know what, Jenny?" her dad finally said, in a much quieter voice. "I think I'll just stay out of your way on this one."

Jenny pulled in the pox until she looked like her normal self. "Thanks, Daddy." She hugged him, but he seemed distant. She hated that she'd had to do that, but she needed him safe and far away. "Take care of Rocky, okay?"

"Yeah." He nodded at Seth. "You two take care of each other."

"We will, Mr. Morton," Seth said.

Jenny's dad took a long, final look at her. "I hope to see you again, Jenny."

"Me, too, Daddy."

He hugged Jenny again, and this time it was genuine. Jenny felt like crying.

"Get over to June's," Jenny said. "Be safe. I love you, Daddy."

"I love you too, Jenny," he said, and he looked a little choked up, too. Jenny wondered if she would ever be able to return home.

***

A little after midnight, Jenny sat behind the desk in Seth's dad's office. Seth's parents had stayed in Florida, again to keep the cover story simple. The less involved their parents were, the less Homeland Security would be able to wring out of them.

The flat-screen monitor showed the viewpoints of the cameras mounted at the two gates in the walls of Barrett House. Her father had welded the back gate shut, so Alexander would have to come in through the front. Seth had activated the full security system, including motion detectors. If anything came over the wall, the software would give an alert.

At the same time, they'd left the front gates unlocked, so that anyone could push them open. They wanted Alexander coming in through the front, where they'd made some preparations for taking down the zombies.

Jenny walked out of the office and just down the hall to the library.

Seth and Heather were both sleeping on the old leather couches there, Heather with a pillow and blanket Seth had provided. It was their first chance to sleep since they'd picked up Heather the night before. Jenny felt tired, too. She hoped she had some extra time to rest before Alexander arrived, but she knew he was on his way. She could feel it.

She poured herself a glass of iced tea in the kitchen, then returned to the office to watch the monitor.

CHAPTER THIRTY-SEVEN

Tommy watched Jenny's house from the woods. The girl was Ashleigh's obsession, and if Tommy kept an eye on her, he knew Ashleigh would arrive sooner or later. He was patient. He'd sat here all afternoon, through the sunset, and for a few hours since then.

Jenny's father had come and gone a few times, but there was no sign of Jenny. Her father had left for the last time in the early evening, taking the dog with him, and not returned. At this point, he was either having a late night at a redneck bar somewhere, or he was spending the night away.

He suspected Ashleigh might be here, soon—something had made her decide to cut him loose. Maybe she was just moving to Washington, to a nice silk-lined mistress nest provided by her pet congressman, but Tommy didn't think so. He and Ashleigh were connected, like two broken halves of the same twisted soul. He could sense something powerful stirring inside her, much bigger than just the predictable unfolding of her seduction of Representative Eddie Brazer.

Tommy began to feel antsy and restless, like the action was happening somewhere else and he was missing it.

Since it didn't look like anybody was coming back, Tommy made his way out of the woods to the rickety little house. The front door was locked, but Tommy knew how to pick cheap residential locks.

The house smelled like dog and the ghosts of old cigarettes. Tommy rummaged through the bills on the table, glanced in the fridge for anything interesting, cut himself a slice of some really good hoop cheese he found under a glass dome on a cutting board.

The old cassette-tape answering machine was almost as big as a shoebox—it took Tommy a moment to even figure out what the boxy device next to the telephone was. He pressed the PLAY button, but all the messages had been erased.

He'd been here twice before. The first time, he'd come in search of Ashleigh's killers, but he hadn't known about the Jenny pox and had come away sick and scarred. The second time, Ashleigh had sent him to fill Jenny's father's mind with fear until it popped, and to leave a note Ashleigh had made for Jenny.

On this visit, he was in no hurry. He walked through the dining room, looking at the clay pots and simple sculptures on the table. He glanced into the hall bathroom, and then he found Jenny's room.

Tommy sat on her bed, looking around at the old cabinet-style record player, the dresser with the fire scars at one end. He looked at himself in the mirror, and there he saw the photographs tacked on the wall alongside Jenny's bed.

He turned to look at them. They were pictures of the boyfriend, Seth, who Ashleigh also hated deeply. Of course, Tommy thought. Why would Jenny hang around this pathetic dump when she had a boyfriend with a mansion across town? Since nothing was happening here, Seth's place seemed like a good place to look. He was going to die of boredom and his growing anxiety if he had to sit around doing nothing the rest of the night.

Tommy returned outside and rolled his bike out of the woods. He cranked it up in Jenny's driveway, and then he pulled out onto the paved road.

***

The meat truck rattled and shook as it crawled along the dirt road, which was really just a pair of weedy, sandy ruts through endless acres of dense pine trees. It came to a stop at a fork in the road.

"I think this is it," Alexander said.

"You thought that the last ten times," Ashleigh said.

"I've only stopped twice."

"Now it's three times."

"Just give me a minute." Alexander grabbed the flashlight and climbed out of the car.

"See if there's a bathroom," Ashleigh called after him.

Alexander ignored her. He thought he could discern the faint traces of the overgrown trail here. Plenty had changed in the decades since he last lived in Fallen Oak, but he had once known every inch of the town and its countryside.

He bashed aside limbs with the flashlight, stomped down thick brambles with his shoes, slowly making his way deeper into the woods.

He was beginning to think he'd stopped at the wrong place yet again when his flashlight found the brick chimney jutting up among the brambles. It had sunk into the earth a few feet over the years, and it leaned far to one side, but it was still there, surrounded by rubble masked by thorns and weeds.

Alexander dashed back to the truck. He unlatched the rear door and pulled down the ramp. Zombies marched out one after the other, carrying axes, shovels, and picks looted from a hardware store a few towns away. Alexander and Ashleigh had also gorged themselves on Waffle House food to stock up on calories. Ashleigh's purse was stuffed full of Power Bars in case they needed more.

Ashleigh leaned out the driver-side window. "Does this mean we're here?" she asked.

"We're here."

The zombies hacked open the trail with their tools. They worked reasonably fast. After spending so much time feeding on Jenny's energy, Alexander was at the most powerful he'd ever been in this lifetime. The zombies themselves were finally defrosting. He'd kept the temperature in the rear of the truck around forty-five degrees, enough to loosen them up without bringing on rot.

Soon, a wide, clear path connected the dirt road to the rubble. Ashleigh jumped down from the truck to join him next to the old chimney.

"This place is a wreck," Ashleigh said.

"We're just passing through," Alexander said. "We're not renting a room." He waved a hand, and the zombies attacked the rubble, slashing away thorns and weeds, shoveling bricks aside. Once, there had been a small cottage here, a good place to retreat for reading books and writing letters. It looked like it had been completely forgotten, which was fortunate for him.

After a few minutes of digging and scratching, a few of the zombies sank through the sandy earth and tumbled out of sight. Alexander approached the hole, which had once been hidden under the floor of the cottage. The zombies were piled on each other down on the dirt floor below, still making digging motions with their hands. Alexander had them stop and stand up. He pointed into the pit with his flashlight.

"Ladies first," Alexander said.

Ashleigh looked into the rough dirt hole. "No, thanks. I'll wait."

"Suit yourself." Alexander shrugged and jumped down into the hole. The zombies who had fallen through were teenage girls. Ashleigh had identified them as her cheerleader friends, back when they were alive.

Alexander shined his flashlight ahead of him. The dirt tunnel looked like it was still intact. He would have to duck to walk through it, but he was glad it hadn't collapsed.

"Nice work, ladies," Alexander said, slapping a zombie girl's butt.

"How's it look?" Ashleigh called down.

"Come and see."

A couple of dead football players picked Ashleigh up and lowered her into the hole, where Ashleigh's cheerleader friends took hold of her and gently lowered her to the floor. Ashleigh scowled as she looked around. "This is it?"

"It's perfectly safe." Alexander shined his flashlight across one of the wooden buttresses. It was covered in mushrooms and mold, and a tree root had partially cracked it.

"You call that safe?"

"I'm sure it'll hold up for a few minutes." Alexander sent the girl zombies ahead. More zombies dropped into the hole and followed them.

"Where does this lead?" Ashleigh asked.

"Somewhere safe. We'll be inside the walls of my estate, so they won't see us coming."

"Your estate?"

Alexander gave her half a smile. "We'd better get moving. There's a lot of work ahead, and our enemies aren't going to punish themselves."

CHAPTER THIRTY-EIGHT

Jenny awoke to the sound of breaking glass. She was lying on a couch in the library, napping while Seth took a turn watching the monitor. Heather was still asleep.

"Seth?" Jenny asked. She stood up and stretched, and she heard more shattering and breaking sounds.

Jenny walked along the hall, toward the kitchen, but then she heard the sound again. It wasn't coming from the kitchen.

"Seth, where are you?" Jenny tiptoed further along the hall, toward the gallery at the back of the house. She froze in mid-step when she saw the three sets of French doors.

Pale, diseased arms smashed in through the panes. Dead faces stared at her, and she recognized all of them. Cassie Winder, Neesha Bailey and other cheerleaders were reaching in through one set of doors, while a few big guys from the football team smashed down another. The third set of doors was broken to pieces by Coach Humbee, Mayor Winder, and Dick Baker, all of them wielding axes. The zombies surged into the house.

She had killed all of these people, and now they were coming back for her.

Jenny let out a long, high scream that rang and echoed through the house.

"What's happening?" Heather asked somewhere behind her, but Jenny was too horrified to speak. "Jenny?"

Jenny couldn't budge. Her feet felt cemented to the floor. She couldn't even think, she could only stare at the approaching horde.

Heather gasped. She placed a tentative hand on Jenny's back, and Jenny let out another scream. This one seemed to unstick her feet and her brain.

"Where the hell is Seth?" Jenny asked, whirling around to face Heather. The two of them ran to the open door of the office. Seth was there, reclined in the desk chair, bobbing his head to earphones while he watched the monitor.

"Seth!" Jenny shouted. He didn't respond, so she grabbed the earphones out of his ears. An old song by Rage Against the Machine thudded out from the little speakers.

"Jenny!" Seth looked up, startled. "What's wrong?"

"Why weren't you watching?" Jenny snapped.

"I've been watching." Seth looked at the monitor. "Nothing's happening."

"Really?" Jenny snapped. "Nothing?"

"Not as far as I can—"

"Come here!" Jenny grabbed his arm and wrenched it, pulling him to his feet. She pulled him out into the hall, where the zombies of the mayor, the lawyer and the football coach lurched forward with their axes, followed by dozens of others.

"Oh," Seth whispered. "Holy shit, it's everybody."

"They're back," Jenny said.

"They didn't come through the gate," Seth said. "This really wrecks our plans."

"Can we get moving somewhere?" Heather asked. "They look like they're picking up speed."

Jenny looked. The zombies were stepping faster down the hall.

"Upstairs," Seth said. "The Molotovs."

The three of them ran out into the dark foyer and up the wide front steps. In the guest room with the old ship theme, they each grabbed two of the bottles, and Jenny took the grill firestarter with the long snout. Seth shoved the remote controls into the pockets of his cargo pants, which he was wearing for that purpose.

They hurried down the hall into Seth's room, and Jenny opened a window looking out onto the back yard. Seth pounded it with both fists until it broke loose and fell.

In the moonlight, they could see the hill set back in the yard. The gate to the Barrett family cemetery was wide open, and few straggling zombies were still trickling out.

"How can they be coming from there?" Seth asked. "That's not possible."

"Is there some kind of tunnel or passage underneath the graveyard?" Jenny asked.

"Not that I know of."

"I think you might know of one now." Jenny lit the two matches taped to the bottle in her hand, and she hurled it at the mob below. It exploded, setting two elderly church ladies ablaze. She and Seth took turns hurling the bottles, setting fire to the zombies at the back of the horde, but it seemed like most of the undead had already made their way inside the house.

"Let's go get the rest of the bombs," Seth said. He and Jenny hurried out into the hall, with Heather close behind, but it was too late. Seth's buddies from the football team led a mob of zombies, which was already close enough to block off the door to the guest room with the Molotovs.

"Jenny Mittens, drowning kittens..." a young woman's voice sang. Another group of zombies approached from the opposite direction, led by several very decayed bodies, most of them little more than skeletons. Behind the walking skeletons, Jenny saw Alexander, who was smirking. He was accompanied by a Latino girl Jenny didn't recognize. The Latino girl was the one singing, wearing a very wide smile. "...she's so stupid...so says Cupid...."

"Ashleigh?" Jenny asked. She remembered Seth's story about how a Mexican girl had placed Ashleigh's soul into Darcy Metcalf. This must be that girl.

"Everybody missed you, Jenny Mittens," the girl said. "They all wanted to come back from the grave and see you. Including me. You think you can just kill me and get away with it?"

"You are Ashleigh," Jenny said. She could recognize the self-righteous voice.

"You left me in a very rude fashion, Jenny," Alexander said. "I don't think this relationship is going to work out. Unless, of course, you find your way to your knees and beg for mercy."

"Oh, go to hell, Alexander," Jenny said.

"I know you have an unstable temper, Jenny," he said. "But honestly, what did I ever do to deserve this heartbreak at your hands?"

"You tried to make me a monster," Jenny said.

"You are a monster." Alexander gestured around at all of them. "We are all monsters, the four of us. I was only helping you remember."

"Except the things you wanted me to forget," Jenny said. "Like Seth."

"Oh, yes, little Jonny the Fourth." Alexander looked Seth over. "We brought special visitors for you, too. I have to say, as heir to my name and my fortune, you're quite a disappointment. Don't you agree, Jonathan the First?" Alexander nudged one of the skeletal bodies, and it raised a hand and waved as if greeting Seth. Alexander put an arm around it. "Say hi to your great-grandfather, Seth. Time has certainly not been kind to my old body, has it? You know, it's interesting. I had my friends here dig up most of our family's bodies, but with my corpse, I simply called out to it and it came digging up to meet me. Isn't that interesting?"

Seth stared at him. "My relatives? You brought up my dead ancestors?"

"Don't be so offended," Alexander said. "They are my family, too. Oh, here's a special treat, just for you." Alexander stood aside, and another zombie stepped forward. The embalming fluid had done its work—Jenny could recognize the partially decayed face of Carter, Seth's dead brother, from pictures around Seth's house.

"You fucking bastard!" Seth leaped toward Alexander, and Jenny grabbed his arm to stop him. Fortunately, Heather followed suit, grabbing his other arm, and together they managed to restrain Seth from diving into the crowd of zombies to get at Alexander.

"Seth, no!" Jenny shouted. "Don't let him get to you."

"I'm afraid I've already gotten to all of you," Alexander said. "I'm going to watch your friends and family tear you apart, Seth, Jenny...whoever you are." He was looking at Heather.

"She knows who I am." Heather pointed to Ashleigh. "Does the Homeland Security Committee know you're here?"

"She's a CDC doctor," Ashleigh told Alexander. "The one who's been studying Jenny."

"That's very interesting." Alexander yawned. "Now, if you don't mind, we all have our lives to get back to. Well, some of us do." He made a gesture like he was throwing a ball.

The zombies charged forward from both sides, the football team leading the attack from one end, Seth's dead relatives leading from the other.

"Come on!" Jenny screamed, pulling Seth's arm. She opened the door to third-floor staircase and pulled Seth in with her. Nobody had to tell Heather to get moving. She followed them through, then slammed and locked the door, while fists pounded on the other side.

They picked up Louisville Sluggers that were waiting on the third step. After much discussion, they had determined that a baseball bat would be the most effective and convenient tool for bashing back a horde of zombies at close range, once Jenny explained that guns were essentially useless against them.

The door cracked and splintered, and then two sledge hammers crashed through it. Dr. and Mrs. Goodling broke down the doors and then charged up the steps gripping the large hammers, their eyes blank. The football players followed them through the shattered door.

Seth cracked his bat into Dr. Goodling's arm, then into Mrs. Goodling's, breaking their arm bones so that they dropped the sledge hammers.

Jenny, Seth and Heather backed up the staircase while beating the horde back. The idea was to lead them up into the third floor, which Seth's grandfather had redesigned as a maze of narrow hallways to trick his great-grandfather's ghost. It would ensure they would only have to confront a few zombies at a time, and hopefully a number of zombies would get lost or distracted down some of the dead-end corridors.

Seth's grandfather had long ago nailed shut and walled over all the windows on the third floor. Several hours ago, Seth and Jenny's dad had broken a hole in one of these walls with a hammer and pried the window open. That window would be the escape route for Seth, Jenny, and Heather, but they had to cross the maze first, trapping the zombie horde inside.

They reached the top of the stairs and backed through the maze while the zombies pressed forward. Seth led the way, down one narrow, dim passage and back up another.

Jenny pounded at the zombies, even taking the head off of Seth's dead grandfather.

Then the roar of a motor sounded, and a chainsaw ripped out

through the wall next to Jenny, barely missing her head. She cried out and reeled back. Seth caught her.

The chainsaw ripped a diagonal slash through the maze wall. Another chainsaw carved through the wall farther down, shattering mirrors along the wall.

"Hey, zombies can't use chainsaws!" Seth protested.

Axes and sledgehammers brought down the carved wall in a crash of plaster and dust, and zombie cheerleaders swarmed forward, swinging their tools. Jenny, Seth and Heather barely made it around the next corner. Some of the zombies followed, but more of them were focused on destroying the maze, wall by wall.

Seth led them up the next hall, but seven or eight of the football players had gotten ahead of them through a hole in one wall or another, and now charged towards them. Alexander had them trapped.

"This way!" Seth led them through a door into his great-grandfather's bedroom, which got them out of the most immediate danger, but it was the worst place to be. There was no other door in the room. When Seth's grandfather had rebuilt the third floor, he'd shrunk this bedroom to make sure it didn't touch any exterior walls, so that there was no easy exit for the ghost. The room was surrounded by the maze on all sides.

Then one wall of the bedroom came down, and the zombies flooded the room. Alexander and Ashleigh strolled in with them, Alexander looking with an amused smile at the spartan bed, the yellowed photographs, the antique adding machine with the gold and silver coins beside it.

"You've preserved my room in such perfect condition," Alexander said. "I'm touched, Seth. I bet your whole family lives in fear of me, don't they, Seth? Amusing little humans."

"Fuck you, Great-grandpa," Seth said.

Church deacons and football players seized Heather, biting and ripping at her, while Cassie and Neesha and the rest of the zombie cheerleader squad swarmed in tight around Jenny and pulled her away from Seth. Jenny didn't even have room to raise the Slugger, and teeth bit into her fingers and wrists. Somebody pulled the bat away, leaving her empty-handed.

Jenny struggled and kicked against the dead cheerleaders, but she felt their grips tightening, as if the girls' hands were iron. She realized what was happening—the zombies were growing stronger as they

touched her, feeding off the dark magic of the Jenny pox. She felt her
ribs cracking under the pressure. They tore at her clothes, and teeth bit
down all over her.

"Seth!" Jenny cried out. She managed to turn her head until she
saw him.

None of the zombies were attacking Seth. Instead, Alexander was
grappling with him, clenching Seth's arms in his black-gloved hands.
Ashleigh exhaled a cloud of fluffy pink spores that clung to Seth and
Alexander's flesh for a moment before dissolving. Ashleigh, like Jenny,
must have figured out how to make her power airborne.

Ashleigh lay a hand on Seth's face. "Sweet boy," she said. "Deep
down, you still love me, don't you?"

"Seth, fight it!" Jenny said. She was having trouble breathing. The
zombie cheerleaders were crushing her to death. Somewhere off to her
side, she heard Heather screaming in pain.

Alexander released Seth, who stood where he was, staring at
Ashleigh with a big, goofy smile.

"Come on, Seth," Ashleigh said. "You know you belong to me.
You know I love you more than I could ever love anyone else." She
took his hand. "Forget about Jenny. Stay with me. Forever."

Seth gazed at her as if hypnotized.

Jenny remembered she had a solution to this—she'd developed a
strain of Jenny pox specifically to attack Ashleigh's power. She'd
liberated Seth from her spell before.

Jenny imagined black flies devouring golden thread. She conjured
up the Ashleigh pox inside her, and then she blew out a cloud of spores.

The black spores whirled around Seth, Ashleigh and Alexander.
Seth and Alexander looked disoriented, while Ashleigh suffered an
intense cough fit, spitting up gobs of dirty yellow fluid, and fell to her
knees.

Something clicked in Jenny's mind. Back in Chiapas, Alexander
had sent the zombies after all the Hale Security men, but he'd sent living
people to collect Seth from the helicopter. And now, even though he had
a couple hundred zombies on hand, he didn't send one of them to attack
or restrain Seth.

"Seth," Jenny said, barely able to draw a breath as the cheerleader
zombies crushed her. "Seth, I make the zombies stronger. But you're my
opposite."

Seth looked at her for a moment, and then tore into the dense crowd of zombies surrounding her. They were like matchsticks in his hands. He ripped off heads, tore limbs from sockets, flung zombies across the room. The zombies crumbled in his hands.

All the zombies crushed in around Jenny, throwing up a mob between her and Seth, pushing back across the room and away from him like an evil tide drawing her out to sea.

"Seth, it won't work," Jenny said. "You have to... turn it up. Breathe it." She coughed out a few dark spores.

"I'll try," Seth said. He closed his eyes.

His skin began to glow an eerie, bioluminescent white.

"Hurry," Jenny whispered. She was starting to black out from the pain. The zombies were still tearing at her, still biting her, and she was covered in her own blood.

Seth opened his eyes. His blue irises had an electric glow.

Then Seth exhaled, and a blinding white fire billowed out from his mouth. This broke into ten thousands tongues of white flame that rained down on the zombies like phosphorous. Jenny thought for a moment of the Pentecost, the holy flames descending on the heads of the disciples. He had created Seth pox.

The mob of zombies screeched and twisted, collapsed, writing on the floor, breaking apart. The dead cheerleaders fell away from Jenny and she dropped to the floor. Wherever the white flames landed on Jenny, her injuries were healed.

Seth coughed out a few more drips of white fire. He doubled over, leaning heavily on his knees, ready to crash to the floor himself.

Behind him, Alexander had picked up an ax. He approached Seth, raising the ax over his head, glaring at Seth's back with a look of raw hate.

"Seth," Jenny said, but her voice was too weak. She pushed herself up to her hands and knees. "Seth, look—"

Alexander swung the ax down towards Seth's neck to decapitate him. Jenny cried out hoarsely, reaching a hand forward. Seth's eyes looked up and met Jenny's just before the ax hit him.

Heather screamed and ran at Alexander. She swung a sledgehammer into Alexander's knee, putting her whole back into it. There was a loud crack and Alexander's entire leg broke and bent backwards, and Alexander screamed and fell to the floor. Heather dropped the sledgehammer and staggered back until she was resting against a wall, panting. Like Jenny, she was beaten, torn, and bitten all over, blood soaking the tattered remains of her clothes.

The falling ax couldn't be stopped, but Heather's blow had knocked him aside just enough that the ax head bit deep into the muscle and sinew between Seth's neck and shoulder. Seth gave a surprised yell and dropped to the floor next to Alexander.

Jenny crawled toward Seth. "Seth, are you okay? Seth?"

"He is not," Alexander hissed. "We are all damned, all of our kind, Jenny."

Jenny helped Seth lift the ax from his shoulder. The white glow of Seth's skin grew brighter, and the ax wound healed instantly.

Seth turned to face Alexander.

"Kill me if you want," Alexander said. "I'll be back again, and again."

"Dead-raiser," Seth's voice rang out, and it was not his usual voice. Jenny knew what it was: the ancient, powerful voice of his soul. "The plague-bringer does not belong to you anymore. We only belong to each other. Remember that, if your memories remain in your next life. And remember that she may be your complement, but I am your cross, and I will destroy you."

Seth raised a hand, which glowed so bright Jenny could barely look at it. He seized Alexander's throat, and he squeezed.

Alexander convulsed, his fingers scrabbling across the floorboards, his entire body shuddering so fast it seemed to vibrate. He levitated off the floor a few inches, then crashed down again, and he ceased all movement.

Alexander's entire body had turned bleach-white, even his hair and the pupils of his eyes. He looked almost like a plaster mold of himself, a discarded shell.

"Is he dead?" Heather asked, from where she leaned against the wall.

"Dead," Seth said. "Gone from this earth." He looked at Jenny, and then both of them looked at Ashleigh.

The girl was kneeling on the floor, coughing more glops of yellow fluid. Jenny had seen that before, when she spread Ashleigh pox through the crowd of pregnant girls on Easter, breaking Ashleigh's spell. That was Ashleigh's golden bonds dissolving.

Jenny pushed herself to her feet and approached the girl.

"No!" the girl shouted. "No, please. I am not Ashleigh."

"Then who are you?" Jenny asked.

"I'm Esmeralda. See?" She hooked a finger under her necklace, then snapped the strand. Beads showered onto the floor. "The little bones. That's how she stayed in touch with me." The girl broke the beaded bracelet she wore, then lifted the cuff of her pants and broke an anklet there. The beads scattered everywhere. "Don't hurt me, please."

"You're Alexander's opposite," Seth said. "You're the channel she used to come back from the dead."

"Who is Alexander?" Esmeralda asked.

Seth glanced at the white husk of Alexander's corpse. "He's nothing, now."

"Please, you have to understand," Esmeralda said. "I didn't want any of this. There's a boy, Tommy—I came here to be with him, not Ashleigh. Ashleigh's magic tricked me. I feel like I've been wrapped up in a golden cocoon this whole time. At first, it was pleasant, but..."

"But then you realize you're her slave," Seth said, nodding.

"Yes. So please." Esmeralda rose to her feet, looking at the dead bodies all around them. "Please let me go."

Then she turned and ran down the stairs.

"Should we go after her?" Seth asked Jenny.

"I don't see why," Jenny said. "She's just one more of Ashleigh's victims. Let her go pick up whatever pieces of her life Ashleigh didn't ruin."

Jenny helped Seth to his feet. "You really wiped out those zombies," she said. "My hero."

"Ha. I didn't know I could do it."

"Should we keep going with our plan?" Jenny asked. She picked up Esmeralda's purse, which was stuffed with Power Bars. "Oh, yum. I'm so hungry."

"I'm starving. Give me one," Seth said.

"We have to. Homeland Security is still after us."

They both looked at Heather, whose face was pale, her eyelids drooping.

"Heather, are you okay?" Seth asked.

Heather looked around at the twisted and dismembered zombies, the colorless corpse of Alexander, and slowly shook her head. "I'm still just trying to adjust to all this. Zombies. Ghosts. Paranormal teenagers." She sighed. "You know, the world just isn't the kind of place I thought it was."

"It never is," Jenny said.

CHAPTER THIRTY-NINE

Tommy found the front gates at Barrett House unlocked, so he pulled one gate open and rolled his bike inside. He eased the gate back into place.

He walked the bike up the curving front drive toward the dark, looming house, looking for a good place to hide it among the trees lining the drive. He wanted to sneak around, take a look, get an update on what Jenny and Seth were doing. That would help him plan for Ashleigh's inevitable arrival.

Footsteps sounded up ahead. Tommy didn't have time to hide before he saw the figure of a girl running towards him.

He touched the dagger sheathed at his hip. He'd stopped at a gun and knife expo in Missouri, searching for the perfect weapon with which to kill Ashleigh Goodling. The one he'd picked out was a long black blade with a silver serpent design etched into the handle. It was a bit of a poetic choice—Ashleigh herself was a snake with a forked tongue. It felt very right.

"Tommy!" the girl shouted. It was Ashleigh, running towards him now, a panicked and desperate look in her eyes.

"Ashleigh," Tommy said. He gave her a wicked grin. "I didn't expect to find you so fast."

"Thank God, Tommy. Thank God you're here." She reached up her arms to hug him, but Tommy blocked her and backed away. She looked confused and hurt, being her usual manipulative self. "We have to go. All of these people are crazy."

"And where do you want to go?" Tommy asked.

"I just want to go home," Esmeralda said. "I miss my mother."

Tommy snorted. "You miss Esmeralda's mom?"

"I am Esmeralda."

"Right."

She frowned. "I mean it, Tommy. Just help me get out of here. We are still friends, aren't we?"

"You must think I'm pretty stupid. I know it's you, Ashleigh. There's no point trying to trick me anymore." Tommy raised the blade. "You took Esmeralda from me."

"What? Tommy, Ashleigh's gone. She won't be back. It's really me. Please, Tommy."

Tommy hesitated, taken in by the frightened expression on her face. For a moment, he saw her the way he'd first seen her, a beautiful and unhappy girl with a glittering butterfly on her T-shirt. He felt how his heart had swelled to the point of breaking as he looked on her.

Then he pushed those feelings back. No matter what she said, this wasn't Esmeralda, it was Ashleigh. He couldn't trust his feelings, and he certainly couldn't take the risk of trusting her again.

"You won't win this time, Ashleigh," Tommy said. "You think you're all-powerful, but love doesn't always conquer all." He tapped his chest with the blade. "Sometimes fear defeats love." He moved toward her, raising the blade.

"You want to kill me?" Esmeralda pulled open the front of her shirt. "Look, Tommy."

Tommy looked. The beaded necklace that held bits of Ashleigh's bone were gone. His gaze darted to her wrists. Those were bare, too.

"Show me your ankles," Tommy said.

Esmeralda pulled up the legs of her slacks. The anklet was gone, too.

"I told you," Esmeralda said. "I got rid of her. Actually, it was that girl...Jenny. She burned Ashleigh out of me. I'm free, Tommy. It's me."

"Not Ashleigh?"

"I fucking hate Ashleigh," Esmeralda said.

"Good," Tommy said. "Then you'll be glad to know I dropped the rest of her bones into the Mississippi River on my way here. Nobody will ever find them again. They can't be found."

"That's perfect," Esmeralda said.

Tommy looked into her eyes—dark brown, no longer with a hint of gray. She didn't seem at all upset that he'd destroyed most of Ashleigh's remaining connection to the physical world.

"I'm the same girl you met that night at the farm," Esmeralda said. "Remember? We were just kids? You gave me that gold coin...I've lost it now. But I've always kept it near me."

Tommy wanted to believe her. She did seem like a different person now. It could be a trick...but he felt a lot of affection for Esmeralda. It would be a risk to trust her. But if there was a chance he could finally have Esmeralda back, that might be worth taking.

"Okay," Tommy said. He dropped the dagger. "You want to get out of here?"

"Please!" Esmeralda embraced him.

They rode out from Barrett House, Esmeralda clinging to his back on the bike while Tommy opened up the throttle. They roared out into the darkness together.

***

Jenny, Seth and Heather had to push their way through heaps of dead bodies choking the second-story hall. All the zombies who had never made it up to the third floor had simply fallen over, lifeless, with Alexander's death.

Since the zombies had ripped Jenny and Heather's clothes to shreds, Jenny took her by a big walk-in closet full of vintage clothes. They changed quickly. Jenny saw bite wounds all over Heather's body. One of Heather's eyes was swelling shut.

The three of them descended the front stairway, stepping over dead bodies the whole way down. Jenny shivered. It was so much like that Easter night, which seemed like it had happened both a million years ago and just yesterday. She vowed to herself to never use the Jenny pox again.

They walked out through the mud room to the garage, where they climbed into Seth's Audi. They had left Jenny's car in Jenny's back yard, behind the fence, in case her dad wanted to sell it or use it for parts. Seth's car was smaller, faster and less conspicuous, so it made a better getaway vehicle.

Heather sat in the passenger seat, while Jenny sat in Seth's lap. Seth opened the garage door with a remote clipped to his sun visor, then drove outside. He braked at the top of his driveway for a last look at his home. Jenny rubbed his neck with her hand.

"What are you thinking about?" Jenny asked.

"How glad my dad's going to be," Seth said. "We're finally free of Alexander's sadistic game. The family curse. The ghost of great-grandfather." Seth snorted. "He did all that just to amuse himself, didn't he?"

"Alexander likes to leave his mark," Jenny said.

"He left it on us," Seth said. "Now it's time to erase it."

They drove down to the front gates. Seth parked just inside the gate and wolfed down some of the Power Bars. They got out of the car again. Seth took Heather's hands and held them tight. Heather closed her eyes and smiled in pleasure as her wounds closed.

"Not too much," Heather said, pulling her hands back. "I need a little evidence on me." She gazed at Seth, then wrapped him in a tight hug, pressing herself against him. "Thanks for everything," she whispered. Her eyes lingered on Seth as she pulled, and Jenny got the sense that Heather wanted to kiss him. Jenny couldn't really blame her. Nothing in the world felt as good as Seth's healing touch.

Heather turned to Jenny. "I'm sorry if I made your life hell."

"Don't worry," Jenny said. "My life was hell long before you got involved."

Heather reached her hands toward Jenny, then hesitated. "Is it safe to hug you, or...?"

"Just stay away from my head." Jenny held up her gloved hands. "Everything else is covered. Believe me, I've had plenty of practice."

Heather hugged Jenny. Jenny hugged her back, awkwardly.

Seth took one of the toy remote controls from his cargo pants. A strip of masking tape had two words in Jenny's dad's handwriting: *Front Yard.* "We'd better do the yard," he said. "Don't want it blowing up in anyone's face. Are we ready?"

"Ready," Jenny said.

Seth pushed both levers on the remote. A huge cloud of sod and decorative landscaping erupted in front of the house, followed by an earth-shuddering boom.

"No zombies were harmed in that explosion," Seth said. He took out the other remote. "Now, let's say good-bye to Barrett House. May there be nothing left but ashes and bad memories. God, my dad's going to be happy when he sees it's finally destroyed."

"Bye, Barrett House," Jenny said.

Seth shoved both levers forward. This remote was labeled *Gas Main*.

The house seemed to shudder, and the first-floor windows blew out. Billowing flames erupted from the empty window sockets.

The fire moved quickly upstairs, helped along by some minor accelerants they'd applied to the house—sawdust in the carpets, streaks of flammable varnish along the walls, hopefully nothing that would be too obvious to investigators. A column of fire ripped out through one of the second-story windows as the remaining Molotov cocktails exploded.

Within minutes, flames and smoke poured from every door and window they could see.

Seth tucked the remotes back into his pockets, and he smiled at Heather. "So, what happened tonight?"

"You two kidnapped me from my house because you wanted to explain your side of the story, without Jenny getting taken into custody," Heather said. "Then, everything I just saw—Alexander and the zombies, just like on the video from the Charleston morgue. All of that happened. Except...you and Jenny were both in the house when it went up in flames. I barely escaped, and only because you paranormals were too busy fighting to pay attention to me."

"And what advice will you give your bosses?" Jenny asked.

"My professional medical opinion is that all human remains in this house should be incinerated immediately to avoid any contamination. There's no time for forensics or identifying individual remains. We don't want another outbreak of Fallen Oak Syndrome."

"We sure don't," Jenny agreed.

"They'll probably cover everything up," Heather said. "The White House won't want any questions about where the remains of Fallen Oak's loved ones have been for the last four months."

"I hope you're right," Seth said.

Heather took a deep breath and brought out her cell phone. "I think that's everything."

"I think it is," Jenny said.

"Just give us twenty minutes," Seth said.

"You got it." Heather winked at him, and Jenny rolled her eyes.

They left Heather standing just inside the gate. As Seth drove them away, Jenny opened up Esmeralda's purse and unwrapped a few Power Bars, which he wolfed down in a single stack. Under the Power Bars, she found a cheap Flip video camera and a rainbow of credit cards, all of them with different names, probably stolen by Ashleigh and Tommy from different people. One of the cards caught Jenny's eye, and she frowned.

"Seth," Jenny said. "We have to make one extra stop."

"We can't, Jenny. We need to get to the airfield right now. Hale is waiting for us." Seth's dad had paid a premium for Hale's help in smuggling Seth and Jenny out of the country, a huge fee that included Barrett Capital contracting with Hale Risk Management to evaluate a number of potential investments in India.

"It'll only take a minute," Jenny said. "I promise."

CHAPTER FORTY

"Hi, welcome to Taco Bell," Darcy Metcalf said, and then a look of wide-eyed shock appeared on her face. "Oh, holy cow."

"Hi, Darcy," Seth said. "Can we talk with you a sec?"

Darcy's eyes were huge as she stared at Jenny. Jenny gave her the best smile she could manage.

"Jeepers," Darcy said. "Um, okay. Did you want anything to eat?"

"Six chili cheese burritos for me," Seth said.

"Just take a booth. I'll wheel 'em right out for you. Well, not wheel 'em, I mean I'll just carry 'em," Darcy said.

"Thanks." Seth paid her, and then he and Jenny took a booth at the back corner of the Taco Bell.

At the counter, Darcy stacked paper-wrapped burritos onto a tray. "Hey, Ramon," she said. "Can you cover the register? I'm going on break."

A young Mexican man walked to the counter from the kitchen. "You going to eat all that yourself?" he asked.

"It's for my friends," Darcy said. "Thanks for covering."

"You know I got you covered," he said. He spanked Darcy's rear as she walked off with the tray, and Darcy giggled and blushed. She sat

down across from Seth and Jenny, and Seth immediately tore into the
burritos.

"Did that guy just smack your ass?" Jenny asked.

"Oh, yeah, Ramon." Darcy sighed, looking back at him. "Isn't he
the foxiest? He's so good with Neveah, too."

"Neveah?" Jenny asked.

"My little girl," Darcy said. "I named her that 'cause it's Heaven
spelled backwards."

"Oh! Congratulations," Jenny said.

"She's the best. Even my dad is nice to her. He's still being a turd
about Maybelle, though."

"Ashleigh's dog?" Seth asked.

"Yeah, she lives in my room now," Darcy said. "Daddy hates it, but
too bad, you know? He can't boss me around forever. Me and Ramon
are gonna get our own place soon, anyway."

"That's really great, Darcy." Jenny couldn't help smiling. Darcy
seemed genuinely happy. "Well, we won't take too much of your time. I
just wanted to give you something."

Jenny took out a PayPal debit card, which had a small pink Post-It
note affixed to the back side, and slid it across the table. The name on
the card was FALLEN OAK GIRLS' OUTREACH. Darcy's brow
furrowed as she studied it.

"The password's on the back," Jenny said. "That's all the money
Ashleigh raised for the pregnant girls in town. I'm not sure how much is
in there, but it might be a lot. She made the story into national news."

"Oh, wow," Darcy said.

"Darcy, you're in charge of this money now," Jenny said. "Share it
out with all the girls who need help."

"Really?" Darcy gaped at her. "Why me?"

"Because I know we can trust you to do the right thing," Jenny
said.

"I don't know," Darcy said. "That's a lot of responsibility."

"You can handle it, Darcy. I have confidence in you."

"Okay..." Darcy slipped the card into her pocket. "Wow. This is
big."

"One thing," Jenny said, "Don't tell anybody we were here. Just
tell them you found it on Ashleigh's desk or something when you taking
care of Maybelle."

"Why?" Darcy whispered. "Are y'all in trouble or something?"

"Don't worry about us, Darcy," Jenny said. "Just take care of the girls."

"I will," Darcy said solemnly. "I promise."

***

Representative Eddie Brazer felt a little uncomfortable as he was escorted into the senator's office. Junius Mayfield belonged to the opposition, the president's party. Still, based on the polling, it looked like Eddie might be joining the august body soon, and there was no reason to snub one of his future colleagues in the Senate. Mayfield's people had been very insistent that Eddie meet with the senator ASAP. Eddie had no idea what the man wanted with him.

"Eddie Brazer," Senator Mayfield said, standing up to greet him. The man looked like what he was, an old backslapping politician from the Deep South, jowly and gray, the nose and cheeks of a heavy drinker. "Whiskey for you?"

"No, thanks."

"One for me, then." Mayfield sank into his chair and poured himself a glass. "Looks like you'll be taking over Buddy Cobden's old seat."

"So far, so good," Eddie said.

"Old Cobden won't last for shit in retirement," Mayfield said. "I give him two weeks on the golf course before he's dead of boredom. Or maybe he'll have a heart attack in the arms of his favorite hooker, the way he always wanted to go. What do you think?"

"I couldn't guess, Senator."

Mayfield cleared his throat several times, as if a thick wad of phlegm were wedged inside.

"What can I do for you, Senator?" Eddie asked.

"Hell, call me Junius, we're practically co-workers," Mayfield said. "There's just a little mess I need your help mopping up. This damn Fallen Oak thing. I know you folks in the House aren't really planning to hold public hearings, are you?"

"We are," Eddie said. "We have substantial evidence that the President conspired to hide information of great importance to public health and national security—"

"The President is dumber than a paper bag full of donkey shit," Mayfield said. "Couldn't pee without Nelson Artleby holding his pecker."

Eddie was amused to hear that from a member of the President's party. He nodded.

"Nobody really cares what the President knew or didn't know," Mayfield said. "Hell, nobody cares much about anything, except who's diddling who. There's no good reason to raise a big stinking mess here, Brazer. You're just pulling a rabid dog's tail. You're gonna get bit."

"Is that a threat?" Eddie asked.

"Hell, yes, it's a threat. Look, those people down in that little place in South Carolina have been through enough. Nobody needs you upsetting them."

"I don't see how a thorough investigation would upset anyone." Brazer grinned.

"I think you're missing the big picture here, Brazer. Our basic job is to keep the public feeling safe and secure, so they go to work, pay their taxes, and leave us the hell alone. You don't want to get a reputation as a boat-rocker."

"That's pretty cynical."

"Hell, yes, it is," Mayfield said. "You don't think I survived this long in the game by believing a bunch of airy-fairy nonsense, do you? Now, look here. You're a freshman. You don't want to come in here making enemies, when you could be making friends. Why make your life harder than it has to be?"

Brazer waited to see if Mayfield was really finished. Then he said, "Okay. I'll consider your advice."

"Oh, will you 'consider' it, you little snot? You might want to consider this." Mayfield turned his flat-screen computer monitor to face Eddie, and then he pawed and clicked at his mouse.

Eddie watched as the monitor shifted from a PowerPoint presentation, to a couple of news websites, to an online poker game.

"Damn, I hate computers," Mayfield muttered. Eddie couldn't suppress an amused smile at the man's bumbling.

Mayfield pressed a button on his speaker phone. "Jordan, get in here and play that video of the congressman diddling his assistant."

The smile vanished from Eddie's face, and a jittery feeling formed in his stomach.

A stunning girl in a long, tight black skirt entered the office, smiling.

"Hey, Senator," she said in a Southern accent. She leaned across his lap and took the mouse from his hand. While she focused on the computer, Mayfield leered at her rear end, which was just in front of his face. He waggled his eyebrows at Eddie, as though expecting him to join in the leering, but Eddie wasn't exactly in the mood.

"Here you are, Senator," the girl said. On the monitor, a video window popped up. It showed Eddie taking Esmeralda from behind on the hotel bed, his face very clear as he grunted in pleasure.

"Oh, Daddy, oh, Daddy, oh, Daddy..." Esmeralda cried.

"'Oh, Daddy,' my word," Mayfield said. "It's like she was trying hard to sink you. Don't you have a daughter about her age?"

Eddie buried his face in one hand, shaking his head.

"Ever seen one this small?" Mayfield held up a narrow, palm-sized video camera. "My first telephone was bigger than that. I tell you, the things they make these days."

Eddie sank in his chair. Esmeralda had disappeared several days ago, and now he understood why. She really had been too good to be true—she was a spy for Senator Mayfield, or his cronies.

"That's it for now, honey," Mayfield said to the girl, and she left the room. "Now, Eddie. This is gonna get real ugly. The kids on my staff tell me it's no trouble to put a video like this all over the Internet. They say it would take about two minutes. Can you believe that? Two damn minutes, and you're dead in the water. What would your constituents think? Your backers? How about that wife of yours?"

Eddie didn't say anything.

"Now, again, I want this little investigation of yours sealed, shredded and forgotten. Is that clear?"

Eddie nodded.

"Say it," Mayfield said.

"The investigation's over. It never happened."

"Good man," Mayfield said. "That's it for today. If you do make it to Senate, you bear in mind I've got your balls in my back pocket. Don't you think about making any trouble for me and my friends. Now don't be a stranger, hear?"

"I won't," Eddie managed to say. He stood up and made his way to the door.

CHAPTER FORTY-ONE

Jenny stood in the crowded Cour Puget at the Louvre, a palatial gallery that felt like it was outdoors because of the glass ceiling soaring above her. She was fascinated by the huge bronze sculpture of Hercules, gripping a giant snake called Achelous by the throat. It reminded Jenny of the time when she was a toddler, and she'd almost been bitten by a rattlesnake, but the pox had killed it first. Her dad had freaked out.

"What do you think?" Seth asked, strolling up behind her.

"I think Hercules is going to win," Jenny said.

"Man, don't they have a pretzel cart or something? I'm hungry."

"We're in Paris, and the only food you want is a pretzel?"

"Or a hot dog."

"I like this sculpture a lot," Jenny said.

"Maybe you can make something like that one day."

"Seth, I work in clay, not metal."

"You can always branch out." Seth put an arm around her waist and hugged her close. "I think it would be badass, watching you make stuff with a welding mask and blowtorch."

"We'll see." Jenny smiled and leaned her head against him.

They'd been in Paris a little more than a week. Seth had rented an apartment overlooking the Seine, since Jenny wanted to be near the arts scene on the Left Bank. Jenny had spent a few past lives in France, so she was already fluent in the language, something that would have been handy to remember in her high school French classes.

Their arrangements had been made with care. The names on their passports were fake, but the passports themselves were real, manufactured secretly by somebody at the State Department who apparently did things under the table for Hale. Seth and Jenny also had green cards that enabled them to work, though Seth had enough money in an account in Lichtenstein to live on for the rest of their lives, in case they were never able to go back home.

"I love Paris," Seth said, and he kissed her. "And I love you, Jenny. More than anything."

"I love you, too," Jenny said, and she meant it.

She looked into his eyes. It was a long, endless road that stretched behind them, and ahead of them, too. Lifetime after lifetime. While others of their kind, the love-charmer and the dead-raiser, spent eternity in endless, hopeless struggles for power, Seth and Jenny had found their way to the very heart of what it was to be human. There was no reason to cling to what they might have been in the ancient past.

Love was all that mattered in the universe, Jenny understood now. Without it, existence was just a game of empty shells.

"We'd better get moving," Seth said. "The museum closes in an hour, and we've barely seen any of it."

"There's no hurry, Seth," Jenny said. "We have forever."

Jenny took his hand.

THE END

ABOUT THE AUTHOR

J.L. Bryan studied English literature at the University of Georgia and at Oxford, with a focus on the English Renaissance and the Romantic period. He also studied screenwriting at UCLA. He enjoys remixing elements of paranormal, supernatural, fantasy, horror and science fiction into new kinds of stories. He is the author of The Paranormals trilogy (*Jenny Pox*, *Tommy Nightmare*, and *Alexander Death*), the biopunk sf novel *Helix*, and other works. *Fairy Metal Thunder*, the first book in his new Songs of Magic series, will be available by October 2011. He lives in Atlanta with his wife Christina, his son John, two dogs, two cats, and hopefully some fish pretty soon. His website is http://jlbryanbooks.com. Follow him on Twitter or Facebook.

Watch for:

Fairy Metal Thunder
(Songs of Magic, Book 1)
October 2011

Made in the USA
San Bernardino, CA
09 December 2012